Bite Me!

(YOU KNOW I *LIKE* IT)

BOOK ONE
Spooky BOYS

FAE QUIN

(YOU KNOW I *LIKE* IT)

SPOOKY BOYS #1

Cover Art and Interior Artwork by Fae Loves Art

WWW.FAELOVESART.COM

Typography and Interior Formatting by We Got You Covered Book Design

WWW.WEGOTYOUCOVEREDBOOKDESIGN.COM

Dedicated to my husband

without whom my dreams would've remained dreams.

Chapter One

Blair

"FUCK YOU, MOTHERFUCKER," I grunted in peppermint flavored fury. *Tap, tap, tap.* My fingers danced an angry staccato on the worn-down pleather of my steering wheel as I watched my check engine light glare at me from the dashboard while I lamented my life.

The black polish adorning my nails had just the wrong amount of glitter. It danced in the flickering moonlight that slipped between the overlapping branches of the trees I raced past, unsure if I needed to stop yet.

I'd bought the polish over a year ago, blasting into the Sally Beauty store by my work in an explosion of black leather and rebellion. I'd made the glitter discovery later, under cover of darkness, when I began to slather the paint across my bitten-down nails. I'd tried to be neat. I really had. Despite the shit job, I'd still beamed with pride down at my first outward rebellion. That was, until I realized the name "Black Midnight" on the label did not, in fact, mean "Midnight Black."

What it did mean, however, was *glitter*.

The unassuming kind, sure.

But glitter is still glitter, no matter what form it takes.

I'd grown to love my almost-sparkly-rebellion-fingers just as I'd grown to love the piece of shit blue Yaris I'd gotten as a hand-me-down from Jeffrey.

The fact I'd been allowed to get a license at all was a miracle considering how tight a hold *she* had always kept on my leash.

Now, here I was, the pine trees climbing towards the indigo sky like little (big) parasites. It probably would've been beautiful if my eyes weren't dry as a forest fire and my blood hadn't been replaced with burnt coffee about four gas stations ago. Right now, my body composition was almost eighty percent righteous indignation.

Except the person I was pissed at was myself, so maybe it was more self-loathing.

I had almost reached my destination, but I had no plan of action, only trees, my own determination, and now my check engine light for company.

I'd never driven before.

Well, I *had*. But not beyond the city limits in my small hometown in Oregon.

Now that I was in Maine, there were thousands of miles of asphalt between me and the apartment—and the brother—I'd abandoned.

Zooming down the road, I realized I was nothing but a speck passing by on the distant highway. The houses I passed were lit up, the families inside sharing lives I would never know about.

They were people I'd never meet.

People who had dreams, hopes, ambitions just like I did.

Every glimpse I got of their silhouettes was nothing but a phantom of the lives I knew they shared, and I was just a voyeur.

A shadow.

A ghost.

With the rain-slicked road stretching out in front of me and the lights of houses glimmering behind me, the loneliness I'd felt for all my life came to mind. It had always been claustrophobic.

It had seeped inside my body like an ocean breeze. Slipping inside my cracks and crevices until I was made of nothing but isolation and the will to survive.

I felt loneliness now, but instead of claustrophobia, I felt power in it.

I'd been numb for so long, I welcomed each new feeling with open arms—good or bad.

It felt like I'd been asleep so long the world had moved on without me.

As I passed by driveways, mailboxes, and power lines, my heart stuttered to life for what felt like the first time in my chest. I was almost to my destination.

There was potential to my anonymity that made the parts of me that had long been dead begin to wake up.

This was the path *I* had chosen.

Not the one that had been given to me.

I wasn't being denied anything, because I had set myself on this course. I was following my own trajectory into the unknown. Maybe I should've been frightened of what I would become. *Maybe I was.*

Fear and I had always kept close company.

Frightened or not, I was an arrow traveling through space with no tether. And though the unknown was full of terrifying new things, thinking about falling face-first into it also made me feel…real, for probably the first time since I'd been nine years old and my world had been torn apart.

I was tangible.

This was just another step in a long line of rebellions.

First, after first, after first.

I'd been stuck, trapped like a bird in a cage built just big enough for me to squeeze inside. I'd had no room to flap my wings, no room to do anything but wilt.

After a while, it had almost been like I had forgotten how to fly at all. My mind *became* the trap, and I knew one day when the cage opened and I stretched my wings for the first time in over a decade, it would take me a long time to figure out how to fly again.

I was free now though.

My wings were spread wide, my puppet strings cut, and even though I was scared, at least I wasn't numb.

I passed the sign that led into Elmwood, my gaze catching on the text below the town name that was scrawled in nearly illegible white letters: *Come for a day, stay for a lifetime.*

I wasn't sure if this was an omen or not, but I figured I already knew what hell looked like. I could handle a few creepy locals and a dead-end job for a while if it meant finding my freedom on a larger scale.

For the first few years of my life, I'd lived in Elmwood, basking in the sun of my mother's smiles, until those smiles turned to storm clouds and I watched as the woman who raised me disappeared from my life.

I tried not to think about her much—either of my parents, really. I'd let the memories fade like old photographs in the hopes that if they were gone, somehow the hell I lived in would be easier to bear.

Forgetting had always been my coping mechanism of choice. But the happy memories seemed to cling despite the fact I'd lived sixteen long years with only my parents' ghosts for company.

I could still feel the places *she'd* last hurt me, the woman who haunted me like a specter in the night, her touch cruel, her smile even crueler.

My demon wore Gucci slides and acrylic nails. She smelled like cinnamon-flavored gum and open chapels, and when I looked in the mirror on days I was feeling particularly vulnerable I saw her eyes staring back at me.

She wasn't my mother, but her face was close enough that I had tried to forget my mother's likeness so it wouldn't hurt quite so much to look at *her*.

"Fuck," I swore under my breath, a sharp snapping noise echoing through the air as something deep inside my car broke, and every warning light known to man lit up my dash.

At least I crossed the town limits, I thought distantly as I was forced to pull onto the side of the road barely ten feet in front of the sign.

The exhaustion that had plagued me for the past five days—my whole life really—caught up to me as I saw my chance to sleep somewhere other than the back of my car slip between my fingers.

It was midnight on a weeknight. There was no way in hell any sort of mechanic was going to be open this late. The town I'd grown up in had been at least four times the size of Elmwood, and everything closed by nine most nights.

Which meant more than likely I was shit outta luck.

Frustrated tears burned behind my lids and I closed my eyes for a moment, my forehead pressed to the sticky pleather of the steering wheel as I tried to get my breathing under control.

Though the air was chilly where it crept through my open window, the night felt stifling. Anxiety squeezed its fingers around my throat as I opened my eyes and stared blearily at the trees on either side of me.

They were both familiar and unfamiliar; a glimpse of a past I didn't remember. Their spindly branches reached towards the stars, like they thought if they just tried hard enough, long enough, *desperately* enough— they could cross the distance and finally touch.

I could relate.

Wanting my car to be fixed wouldn't fix it though, so I did the only thing I knew how to do.

Smack, smack, smack.

No dice. Predictably, hitting my dashboard did not in fact fix my problem.

I hit it again just to be sure.

I glared at the dashboard where the engine lights remained on and I remained…just as lost, just as drained, just as frustrated as before. Except now I had a stinging hand on top of my morose thoughts.

"Fuck my liiiiife." My head thunked back against the headrest as I stared up at the gray ceiling only a foot above my head. It was discolored from years of use, the fabric worn but solid, still stained from that time I'd accidentally erupted orange Fanta all over the interior. I breathed a frustrated huff through my nose before I wilted and the wind left my sails.

I'd sleep another night in the back seat of my car. This was *fine*. This was *all* fine. It wasn't that big of a deal. It didn't matter that I had a roof waiting for me only a few miles up this very road. Just like always, I was going to have to do what I had to do.

This was fine.

Good, even.

It meant I would have daylight to light my way as I broke into my parents' abandoned house.

Everything would be *just* fine.

Maybe if I told myself that often enough I'd start to believe it.

The spring chill that crept through the cracked window felt a lot like the one I'd left behind in Oregon. I tipped my head towards it to inhale greedily, rolling it down further when the small trickle of air wasn't enough to make my lungs expand. The lingering breeze caressed my cheeks, blowing my bangs away from my eyes, and I taught myself to breathe again.

I had money. If I needed it. I refused to use it for anything other than a roof over my head or food to fill the ache in my belly. I'd need to add 'paying for a mechanic' to my list of approved expenses. My car was a major part of my get-out-of-Dodge plan and there was no way I could survive without it.

The sweet crooning of *Taylor Swift* singing about teardrops on her guitar echoed through the empty interior until I flipped the ignition off and the car became silent as the grave.

The CD had gotten stuck when I was sixteen, riding around in the passenger seat as Jeffrey sang—bellowed—with reckless abandon at the top of his lungs. He'd always been like that. The sun to my moon. The big brother that was mine in everything but blood.

That was part of why I'd had to run in the first place. One of us had to leave so the other could follow. And for the first time in my life, I'd decided that I wasn't content to sit on the sidelines. I'd let too much shit happen to me for too long. When I'd discovered papers hidden deep within my uncle's desk, my fate had been sealed.

I owned a house.

It was my parents' house, the one I'd spent the first half of my childhood in. It was halfway across the country, but it was mine. We'd hatched up a plan, and though I'd left earlier than expected, I knew where I needed to be if I was going to escape once and for all.

I, Blair the coward, would be brave for once in my goddamn life.

Even if it killed me.

I listened to crickets chirp outside my window as the cold crept into my bones and my hands began to sweat in the anxious way they did when I was about to sleep out in the open. I'd learned from a young age that being vulnerable only meant pain. I'd built walls, and forts, and fortresses to protect the parts of me I still had left.

So much of who I was, who I was *supposed* to be, had been broken apart to fit inside the mold my aunt had created for me.

Now I was Pinocchio, desperately trying to become a real boy, Frankensteined together from spare parts.

I moved to the back seat, noting not for the first time that my nails were due for a fresh coat of paint. When I looked at them I could still feel the original spark of the rebellion that had led me to where I was now, exhausted and dissociating, as I slumped across the cushions with a bruised knee and a chip on my shoulder.

Before the polish, my rebellion had started with even littler things.

Things so small even I didn't notice. Years of my soul fighting back before my conscious mind made the decision to do so. I'd always controlled what went into my body with a vengeance because it had been the only thing in my life *she* had allowed me to choose. With each food I crossed off, I felt a piece of myself slot back into place. After that, I'd expanded in specks of rebellion, scattered here and there. Anything I could get away with. The type of music I listened to when I was alone. The movies I downloaded on Jeffrey's laptop. Stolen eyeliner. Explicit Google searches when I was away from home.

Then came the lies.

One by one they grew larger until the sick feeling that roiled inside my gut every time I spoke faded to a numb sort of nothingness. Bits and pieces of who I was that had been buried long ago broke through the soil of my self-imposed prison with each battle I won.

And yet, despite the foundation of my escape, still—I had taken the nail polish off every time I went to *her* house for Sunday dinner. My cuticles bled from my nervous chewing, the sting of acetone nothing compared to the burning sensation that accompanied shutting myself back into my coffin once again. I became a corpse whenever I was in her presence. And even though I turned to clay for her—moldable, malleable—it was never enough to get her to love me.

I'd learned that too late.

I bunched up my sleeping bag, shifting it around into a makeshift bed as I leaned between the two front seats to turn the keys in the ignition enough I could roll up the windows until there was only a crack left open. The breeze was nice now, calming, but I knew the moment my eyes shut it would remind me of open spaces, of choices I now had but didn't know what to do with.

That much possibility was as stifling as it was liberating.

When the windows were rolled up and my ass was wedged between the seats I let myself breathe. The sound of crickets and other wildlife rustling outside was stifled by glass and I relaxed incrementally with each breath I took as I settled back into the back seat to wait for sleep to overcome me.

Suddenly, it occurred to me that someone might find me here.

Even though it was late, I was currently parked just off the main road into town, the *only* road into town. Elmwood was tiny, so an unfamiliar car would be more notable here than it would've been back home. Anxiety buzzed bright in my chest, but I forced it aside.

There was no hiding when I was stranded like this. I'd be lucky enough to have someone come to help me. Even though my brain screamed about serial killers, psychopaths, and that one scene in *Silence of the Lambs* that had made me swear to never help someone stranded on the side of the road.

I was a five-foot-nothing ball of rage. I ran on plant fuel and sarcasm— even dragging a thousand-pound chain of trauma behind me, I still only weighed about five pounds soaking wet. I knew I was about as intimidating as a bug-eyed chihuahua. Even with the vitriol I consumed like coffee I was still self-aware enough to realize I'd spent more of my life under fists than I had raising my own.

And *now* I was paranoid.

Great.

I tried to settle down but my pulse wouldn't stop hammering and my palms were slick. *Fuck.* Sometimes I was my own worst enemy. Thoughts of my own physical ineptitude were bound to keep me up as I imagined every scenario that could possibly ruin my night. The trees swayed outside my window and I startled when an owl hooted in the distance.

Get yourself together, Blair. You're fine. It's just a bird.

Likely story.

Just a bird, my ass.

God. What had that story been about? The one with the parked car and the guy with the hook and the—

Yep. I'd take angry villager over a murderous psychopath any day.

Headlights blinded me momentarily as a truck approached from down the road. I had only a moment to pull myself together before the truck was flipping a U-turn behind me and pulling up behind my car.

Fuck.

Did I have some sort of weapon? A flashlight? Pepper spray? I scrambled around under the seat and was greeted with a half empty bag of potato chips and a barren burrito wrapper.

My pulse tripped as I flailed the rest of my way out of my makeshift sleeping bag cocoon. I wasn't sure if it was too paranoid of me or not to wait inside the car to be approached. The feeling of fear that settled like lead in my gut was as familiar as slipping on an old pair of skinny jeans. Bile rose up the column of my throat and a voice in the back of my mind whispered *run, Blair.*

Run before they can hurt you.

Footsteps crunched on gravel and then a man's hairy face filled the window to my left. His eyes were kind, and even though my grip on my sleeping bag was deathly tight, his expression remained friendly. There was nothing noteworthy about him aside from his smile and his furry beard. He rapped on the window twice before pulling back and giving me room to move.

It took me an embarrassing amount of time to exit the car, and when I did I could feel sweat lining my temples, slick and colder than the rain that drizzled on my head the moment I stepped into the brisk night air.

"You need help?" the man asked. He was probably in his forties, his face weathered—but in a way that screamed kindness and a life full of laughter. He had sunspots and freckles, and I found myself relaxing despite my earlier paranoia. I curled my arms around my torso to keep in my body heat as I self-consciously hid my painted nails inside the folds of fabric in my hoodie, scared as I always was of standing out in a bad way, especially with no witnesses around.

There was nothing I could do about my bruising or the fact that I hadn't showered since passing through a Flying J in Indiana. I'd grown up practically glowing neon from an invisible sign over my head that said 'this one's gay.' I had little hope of hiding, even though I tried. I would probably always be wary of strangers, concerned how I was about to be received, not because I was ashamed, but because I knew how it felt for hatred to be turned like a knife toward me and I wanted to minimize the possibility of more abuse.

I'd been touched by unfriendly hands so often it was always my first thought. Maybe some day that would change. But not today. Not stranded on the side of the road with a possibly murderous stranger.

"Yeah." I flushed awkwardly, nails digging into my arms through the fabric of my hoodie. The rain was mist-like and it soaked inside the cotton, through my undershirt and my skin until it settled inside my very bones. "My car made this…snapping noise, or whatever? And it just—" I made a helpless gesture with my hand, remembering too late that I was trying to hide my polish.

Most people could 'handle' a gay boy.

Add in the goth part and they started to have a problem. Not that I was really much of a goth anyway, other than my obsession with all things fanged and furry and my tendency to wear weirdly erotic *Dracula* themed items of clothing. They were campy. I liked it.

Not everyone else did.

"Snapped?" He ran a hand over his beard thoughtfully, his headlights glaring from behind us as he hummed for just a moment and then shifted to move around to the front of my little hatchback. I'd always thought the car was cute. I'd nicknamed it the bat-mobile about the same time Jeffrey and I had watched the original *Dracula* for the hundredth time. He'd let me scribble doodles of it all over his arms in Sharpie as I gesticulated my plan for adding vinyl bat wings to the doors and fangs on the little grate between the two front headlights. The car was short and round enough it vaguely resembled a rodent and I'd thought I was brilliant at the time.

I hadn't gotten around to doing it yet, but I still had the vision inside my head, burned in the back of my mind along with my plans to get more tattoos and my nose and nipples pierced. There were a lot of things on my to-do list. But I knew the opportunity to do them wouldn't come until I was at least safe enough to breathe again.

After all, even though I was thousands of miles away from the condo I'd left behind, Elmwood was still my hometown. It would be easy enough for *her* to find me here. I didn't dare utter *her* name. She was my own personal Boogeyman and I'd avoided acknowledging *her* or what had happened to me as much as possible. Most of the time the memories faded quickly anyway. That was my brain's coping mechanism of choice. Forget, forget, forget.

It's what I'd done with my parents' deaths.

Self-preservation at its finest.

I watched the friendly villager pop my hood and 'hmm' and 'haa' for a minute before he turned back to me with a thoughtful look. "I can't be sure, but it looks like your timing belt broke."

"Okay." I nodded, not really sure what the hell that was but I wasn't about to admit that. I squeezed myself tighter, holding together the shattered pieces that threatened to fall off. I had no idea how serious this was going to be and the money I had been saving was barely enough to get me by. I needed a place to stay after all. Staying inside the abandoned house was a temporary measure, and the first thing I hoped to rectify.

Aside from the food thing.

Because *fuck*, I was so hungry I could feel the hollow ache all the way up my throat. I'd never understood the phrase 'hungry enough to eat an elephant' until now. Except, I was vegan. So maybe I was hungry enough to eat a prize-winning pumpkin?

"What did you say your name was?" the man asked me as he fiddled with his phone. It looked like he was texting someone and distantly I wondered if he had a mechanic on speed dial. Somehow I found it unlikely anyone would be willing to drive out here, especially considering the hour. Actually, if I thought about it, it was really strange that the man before me was out at all.

Paranoia struck again.

I watched his large shoulders absorb the rain as I inspected him for clues. My eyes caught on the extra body hair, the almost yellow glint to his eyes, and the way his nostrils flared every time a bird chirped in the distance. Or maybe he was just smelling me? In the end, my observations were inconclusive.

I took an awkward step back in embarrassment, suddenly worried he could smell the bean burrito I'd tried to clean off my jeans with determination, spit, and two unfortunate napkins just that morning.

"Blair." I realized belatedly it might actually benefit me to tell him my full name. After all, I was about to become a semi-permanent fixture in the town as I figured out a way to make some quick cash and sell my inheritance. "Evans," I added, as an afterthought.

If I hadn't been watching him so closely I might not have noticed the way his entire body tensed up the moment my name settled in the space between us. He went still before his fingers were blurring across his phone screen with purpose and his gaze snapped up to mine. I watched the blue light from his phone flicker in the whites of his eyes as he seemed to do a double take, as he clearly realized the startling resemblance I bore to my mother.

Despite having few memories of her, I knew that I was her spitting image. But where she'd been elegance and summer, I was rain and rocky shores. I could see her face hidden like a shadow beneath mine, and I was sure that those that had known her would be startled to see how closely I'd grown to resemble her.

In high school they'd called me Blair Bitch. For many reasons, though the primary one seemed to be because from the right angles I was just on the wrong side of feminine. My eyes were too large, my hands too small, my jaw pointed where other mens' were square. I'd long since come to terms with my differences however, and I pushed aside the self-loathing as best as I could as I waited for him to speak.

It took a long time.

Too long really.

He tapped at his phone for far longer than I would've expected. My skin flushed with humiliation as a raindrop caught in the groove between my nose and cheek and slid down to tickle my upper lip. It tasted like spring and memories long forgotten, and I swallowed bile as I waited.

"I've gotta get home," the man said, not acknowledging my introduction or offering one of his own. Even though he said it apologetically, I saw it for what it was. A rejection.

Though why, I didn't know.

Now I was fucked though. He was the only good Samaritan I was bound to run into. Maybe I shouldn't have told him my name at all? I had no idea why he would've reacted so strongly to it but…it wasn't like I knew my parents well either. For all I knew, they'd owed him money before they died or something.

I chewed on my nails, nodding along because what the fuck else was I supposed to do? There was nothing I could do but accept what he was saying, even though my pulse was sluggish with anxiety and I could feel a tension headache throbbing in the back of my head.

"Do you know of a mechanic in town?" I asked quickly as he turned from me. It was clear he was keeping his distance now, his eyes wary as he began the short trek back towards the pickup truck.

"Joe's usually open this late," the man said and I nodded, confused but grateful. "Good luck."

I thanked him for his help, even though all he'd done was make me stand in the rain and feel self-conscious, and watched him leave. There was a weird feeling in my gut that I couldn't shake. Like somehow I'd monumentally fucked up somewhere but no matter how many times I thought through our interaction I couldn't see how. I missed the quiet solitude of the road, the isolation, the peace.

My head was anything but peaceful. It was splashes of color and weather changes. Sometimes blistering with the heat of determination and others the cold chill of nothingness that reminded me of being nine years old with my back to the wall and only shadows for company.

No matter how far I traveled, it was clear I couldn't outrun the fact that I dragged bad luck behind me. I shook my head and climbed back into the car, shivering from the chill as I curled up on the damp seat and pushed my palms hard enough against my eyes I saw black spots. I wanted to erase the parts of me that made me feel like this was my fault.

It was always my fault.

Chapter Two

Richard

GROWING UP IN a small town meant that everyone knew everyone. Growing up rich in a small town made that impossibly worse. Add in the fact that I'd signed up to be an unofficial 'errand boy' for The Council, and I knew everyone's business before they did most of the time. People never hesitated to pull me off the street to tell me the newest piece of gossip or call me when they discovered something they deemed important.

Nothing was usually important enough for me to retain it. I wasn't great with people. I never had been. That was part of the reason I'd become the Youth Liaison in the first place. I'd hoped it would bridge the distance that had wedged between me and the townspeople when I'd been pulled out of school as a kid and my family had done the one thing they'd pledged to never do.

Take the change.

There were a lot of things that were different now. Some good, some bad. I was learning to cope with the pitying looks, the grimaces, the commiserating pats on the back. In some ways I'd gotten the shit end of the stick—that's what most people said anyway. Behind my back and to my face. *What was the point of turning if you had little to none of the benefits?* they whispered. *What a pity poor Richard took the change at all.*

I'd gotten what I wanted though.

Eternal life and the ability to spend time in the daylight with Collin. Everything else was of little consequence. I didn't want the 'perks' if having them meant I would become what my parents had become, what my brothers had become.

My phone buzzed and I sighed, shifting back where I'd been studiously going over a crossword I'd been saving from the Sunday paper. I was stuck on a four-letter word that meant desire. At this point it was either love or lust but I had no way of knowing which.

"Hello?" I answered the call, glancing over at the clock above my stove. It was still early, the moon had barely risen. Most people wouldn't be out and about until one.

"Hey, Richard." Ian Mattheson's quiet rumble filled my ear and I paused, surprised to hear from him of all people. He was off duty today. I only knew that because his secretary down at the station had been kind enough to inform me via text that his deputy would be filling in. Most people had my number nowadays out of necessity, not necessarily because I was much of a talker, or even wanted to be.

It came with the job.

Please the public, be aware, be alert, all of that. Deal with the nuisances.

"Hey, Ian," I hummed, waiting for him to tell me why he was calling. He was silent for a long moment, like he was expecting me to ask how he was doing or something equally unimportant. I didn't. I didn't actually care. Not that I didn't care about Ian, because I did. I wasn't a sociopath. I just didn't have time or energy to spend on people I hardly interacted with. Everything I had went into my job and my little brother.

He finally spoke and I huffed a sigh of relief as I listened.

"I was just heading out of town to pick up my brother for full moon night," Ian said, rambling onward while he shared more information than I cared about. I waited patiently, grunting in all the parts I'd learned I was supposed to react in. "Anyways," he grunted. "There's a kid stranded out by the town limits sign. I stopped to help him."

Okay...

My brow furrowed in confusion and I shifted forward, zoning out of the conversation again as I stared at the crossword in front of me. I filled in the next word, skipping love-lust, so I could deduce which one it was. Eight letter word that meant 'often done out of repetition.' *Hmm.* Repetition. I frowned.

"Cute kid. He's all beat up, bruises all over, these horrible black eyes— and so since I'm curious— I ask him his name," Ian droned onward.

I tapped the page with my pen thoughtfully, mulling over my reply. Sometimes people called like this just to have a chat, like they thought every single visitor in town was worthy of The Council's attention (that's probably why they had a Youth Liaison in the first place). They weren't. Otherwise, I'd be run more ragged than I already was. It was almost like they all got into a habit of calling me and couldn't seem to stop—

Oh.

Habitual.

I penned it down, pleased with myself before I registered what Ian was saying.

"Get this. He's an *Evans.*"

My whole body grew rigid, flashes of childhood memory blurring through the back of my mind.

"What?"

"Blair Evans." Ian perked up, clearly happy to have my attention. "Amanda and Victor's kid."

I didn't need him to explain to me who the Evanses were, but I held my tongue, not reacting to his words other than to feel my world tilt on its axis.

Blair Evans.

An Evans back in town—

Shit.

"Thanks for bringing this to my attention," I said, back in business mode, my crossword only half filled out as I pushed away from the table and immediately moved to grab my keys from where they hung on the key ring. "Did you get his car fixed?"

It had been broken right? Now I regretted not paying attention.

"Nah. I think it's the timing belt. He'll need it replaced before he can drive again."

"So he's just…?"

"Looked like he was camping out in his car. Sleeping bags and all."

"Huh," I grunted, grabbing my jacket and slipping it on, the buttery leather familiar and comforting as I donned it like armor before stepping out into the cool night air.

My head swam as I drove down Main and watched the town slowly begin to wake up. Moonies, the only gas station and favorite hotspot for wayward teens, was packed to the brim like it always was. Cars filled the tiny parking lot as aqua colored neon lights flickered along the surrounding tree trunks that framed the building. The bulb on the giant sign out front would need replaced soon. It blinked at me as I whipped by, the engine thrumming with pent-up energy that mirrored my own.

I couldn't remember the last time I'd felt this much emotion.

It was exciting and terrifying. Both.

I exhaled through my nose, releasing tension. Curiosity and anticipation burned inside my chest in a way it never had before as I sped down rain-slicked streets and towards the long stretch of road that led out of town.

I spotted Evans the moment my car crested a hill barely a minute from the city limits. The car he was hiding inside was tiny, the paint a soft well-worn blue. It was an older model though I had no words to describe it other than...cute.

It was cute.

I wondered if he'd look the same as he did in my memories.

I'd only seen him once— when I'd been young enough he'd become little more than a fantasy in my mind. He'd been smaller than me, even then. His big green eyes had blinked up at me from where he stood swallowed by wildflowers at the bottom of our treehouse. The glass between us had caught with the waning sunlight and I'd been stricken as I stared down at him. His hair was a nest of wayward curls, and he flinched when he realized I could see him. After what looked like an internal battle he'd waved shyly up at me, an awkward flash of his tiny dirt-smudged fingers that shouldn't have cut me down the way it had. My heart had been racing as I raised my shaking hand to mirror the movement.

He hadn't stayed long.

Like a forest creature himself he'd skittered off, and I'd watched him go—stricken by the feeling of warmth that fluttered and squeezed tight around my heart.

I knew now that what I'd been feeling was the beginnings of a crush, my first and only crush.

I'd never seen him again.

I pulled to the side of the road across from him and exited my car, my body buzzing with adrenaline as I crossed the abandoned road. Pine needles stuck to the wet soles of my shoes and I waited, nerves tingling up my fingertips.

I expected Evans to exit his car.

I wasn't sure what I expected when he did it.

Would he be as unhinged as his mother? Would I be able to see the sickness behind his eyes? See the depravity bled through his bloodline like poison? Would looking at him remind me of what I'd lost? Or would it wake up the parts of me that had been killed by years of pain and responsibility, just as it had that first time I'd seen the way his nose scrunched up and his eyes glittered with mischief?

I shook my head to clear it, staring at his foggy back window for a moment before I squinted to see past the fog. Evans didn't exit.

He didn't exit because he was asleep.

This was obvious even to me. I stepped closer to see better as I listened to his heartbeat. That should've been the thing that alerted me first, the sluggish *thud thud* of it as he exhaled and his narrow shoulders rose and fell with each breath. I watched him move for a moment, fascinated by the lithe man in front of me before my gaze snapped to his face for the first time in sixteen years.

Looking at Blair Evans was like staring into the sun. Too long, and I was sure he would blind me.

He was as beautiful as I remembered, his dark hair spilling like ravens' feathers against the worn back seat. He had a sleeping bag zipped up to his middle, exposing his upper torso. I watched him with fascination, surprised by the way my body reacted to his petal-pink lower lip and the flutter of his lashes like spiderwebs against his cheeks. His fingernails were painted black, his hands covered in the most beautiful set of blue veins I had ever seen as he clutched at his sleeping bag.

He looked exhausted.

Even I could see that, as unobservant as I usually was when it came to other people. Ian hadn't been lying when he mentioned the bruises. They marred his delicate complexion, the broken skin flared through with splashes of olive and grape, spiraling outwards in a cruel caress beneath both his eyes like watercolor painted by the brush of misfortune. Somehow the presence of bruises only managed to add to his already devastating sort of beauty.

Something in my chest shook loose and a feeling overcame me that I had never in my twenty-five years experienced.

Blair was a hurricane, a storm, a natural disaster. Beautiful and world-shattering, with the power to rewrite the future and repaint the past. He looked fragile like that, the paper-thin veins on the insides of his wrists spreading out like cobwebs as he shifted to get comfortable.

He didn't notice me, even though I was a predator. I stared, and stared, and stared—

And then, he shattered me.

Something glittered on Blair's cheeks, pearl-like and infinitely pretty. It took me an embarrassing amount of time to figure out that what I was staring at were his tears. I broke down in that moment, my legs unsteady for the first time in my life, as I watched this beautiful boy—no, man— leak his sorrows privately onto polyester.

He was cataclysmic. He was beguiling. He was…vulnerable.

This boy wasn't the little boy I'd seen in the woods all those years ago. He wasn't the man I knew the town would fear either—that much was clear.

I hadn't earned his tears so after one last lingering glance I stepped away from the window to inspect the rest of the car. He hadn't properly shut the hood. I was going to fix it, but froze in my tracks as my fingers met chilled metal. I could see Blair from the front of the car again, curled up and shivering. My hands flexed and I balled them into fists, confused by my own emotion.

I wanted to take him home with me.

That was madness, wasn't it?

Yes.

I shook my head and headed back to my own car, leaving the man undisturbed as I tried to stop the shaking in my fingers. Tiny and vulnerable. Sweet and sharp. Blair was…

He just.

He…was real. Real in a way nothing in this small town had ever felt before. I didn't know how to describe the way I was feeling other than completely unsettled as I headed back into town and towards the local mechanic shop with a weird anticipation in my chest.

Chapter Three

Blair

WHEN I WOKE up, the sun peeked over the treetops and dew speckled the windows in a way that refracted the light. Mini rainbows decorated the normally plain interior of my car, and I took a moment to admire them even though my lids were still heavy and my eyes dry with the vestiges of sleep. I was exhausted and hungry, but at least my sleeping bag had held up against the cold and luckily, aside from a few nightmares, I'd managed to sleep through the night.

I decided to try my luck at starting my car one last time before I spent more money than I had paying for a tow into town. My limbs were still tingling with the pins and needles of leftover sleep as I wiggled my way into the front seat and flipped my keys in the ignition.

When the car spluttered to life I nearly cried. All the engine lights were off, the engine purring happily as I sank with relief into my seat and felt my eyes burn with unshed tears. *Maybe I'd imagined the whole thing?* It wouldn't be the worst trick my brain had ever played on me.

Last night had been bizarre to say the least. It was possible that I'd fallen asleep and the man I'd met had been nothing more than another nightmare.

I pulled onto the road, feeling rejuvenated as I headed into town towards the nearest grocery store. Thank god for GPS, or there was no way in hell I would've made it out of my hometown at all. I gorged myself on a cup of pineapple and a loaf of French bread after I checked the label twice for eggs, then headed to the gym just across the parking lot to find a place to shower.

I couldn't find a potential roommate, or roommates, if I smelled like gas station burritos and stale sweat. Now that my stomach was full and my car was working, I was feeling rather optimistic about the whole thing.

Everyone stared at me. It was unsettling. Their eyes followed me wherever I went, the feeling heavy and cloying as their attention tickled the back of my neck and made my pulse throb as I fought my fight-or-flight instincts.

I tried to convince myself that they weren't looking at me. That I was paranoid.

But the emptiness of the businesses haunted me long after I left them, the solitary sets of eyes stark in my memory as there had been so few people I passed by, and all of them had delivered the same suspicious gaze. Maybe I'd accidentally stumbled upon one of those hive-towns. Hive people? I wasn't sure what to call them.

The towns where the people were brainwashed—their minds empty of their own opinions—violence at their fingertips.

Despite my trepidation, showering was a religious experience. Normally I did it as quickly as possible, too self-conscious to be naked too long, too frightened of the scrutiny that would come when our water bill was due. After the first time I'd been blamed for that mess I'd started timing myself. Two minutes under the spray was all I allowed when I knew there were cameras watching.

This was different though.

I was a free man now.

So I let myself bask in the hot spray and I thought about nothing and everything all at once just because I could. My tense muscles melted as days of uncertainty sloughed off me and swirled down the drain. It felt like a stain that had been on my soul was slowly separating from my body. With each step I took towards independence the stain lifted, until one day all that would be left was a discoloration so unnoticeable maybe even I would forget.

I hoped anyway.

When I was finished I slipped into an oversized hoodie with a cross-eyed Dracula on it. He had his tongue out and a cross was laid atop it, his eyes winking in a cartoony style that was both erotic and just a little sacrilegious.

Jeffrey had gotten it for me for my birthday in secret. With the allowance our aunt had given him he'd saved up for my presents, always conscious that the moment he spent the money in too big a chunk she'd ask him for proof of where it went. So he scavenged away dollars here and there and pieced together enough that she would never know what he did for me. He was sweet like that.

Part of me always thought he felt guilty for those first few years living with *her* as kids. I felt guilty too. It had taken me a long time to realize that throwing Jeffrey under the bus never saved me from punishment. And it had taken him even longer to realize that his failures were met with me becoming an example why failure was never an option. He was the golden boy, but not by choice. We were two children thrown into a life we never asked for, forced to figure out how to survive when every step we took only made us sink deeper into quicksand.

Despite everything, Jeffrey was a good brother.

Even when he wasn't.

Google Maps led me down a long winding road called Spruce, which bisected the town from east to west. The name struck me as funny, considering the fact that the town was called Elmwood. Which in my head could be broken down into tree-tree. So technically, I was driving down Tree Road in the town of Tree-Tree. Which felt hilariously comical.

When I arrived, the house itself towered over the skyline. It was taller than it was wide, with the front angled down and the back shaped in a massive triangle overlooking the forest behind it. The exterior was made of what looked like dark wood. It was worn from the weather, but well maintained considering the fact the house had been abandoned for more than half my lifetime. Vines of ivy clung to the siding, as it reached ever upward, digging its greedy finger like shoots into every crevice and crack.

The rickety front porch had seen better days. It looked much less stable than the house did, the wood warped and brittle, steps lopsided and sagging slightly to the left.

Tree trunk shadows gave the house the illusion of being glossy black. It was Gothic in a way that would've been fantastic if I'd picked it myself but, because I was nothing but a voyeur, just looking at the pointed silhouette of the house caused an unsettling flip inside my gut.

The prospect of resting my head somewhere with a roof that wasn't made of metal was too good to pass up, so despite my reservations and the fact that I'd felt eyes on me all day long, I exited my car.

The sun would set soon, the day swallowed up by my wanderings through town in search of bulletin boards and roommate-wanted ads. I'd come up empty, so with a heavy heart I navigated my plants from the trunk of my car and took my first unsteady step onto the battered wood of the staircase.

The steps beneath my feet creaked as I stumbled, my arms too full to see past, up to the front door. I'd have to get the keys remade. My uncle, unsurprisingly, hadn't had a set lying around with the paperwork I'd nabbed. I tried the door only to discover that it was, also unsurprisingly, locked.

I'd have to break in.

I prepared myself for violence, though it hadn't ended up being necessary.

After setting my leafed companions down, I wandered the edge of the property in search of entry. There was a half open window on the side of the building. I cheered when I saw it, tripped over an overgrown tree root, and face planted in the weeds. Extra bruised but triumphant, I pushed the window further upward and slung my leg over the ledge. I was grateful there was no one around to hear my grunting as my belt buckle caught on the sill only moments before I plummeted to the hardwood floor inside the house with a quiet *oof.*

It was cold, but I'd prepared for this, so I wasn't alarmed as I wound my way through the empty living room to the front door and unlocked it. I was sweaty and wheezing by the time I finished dragging everything inside. My plants lined the wall beside my sleeping bag and as I collapsed onto my makeshift nest with a painful wince, I marveled at the lack of dust underneath the window. It wasn't like I was a dust expert, but it seemed to me for a house that had been abandoned this long there was a suspicious lack of it.

I could've spent the next few hours obsessively stalking Jeffrey on Facebook but I somehow managed to refrain. Instead, I searched the house for something more comfortable to sleep on. I hadn't anticipated the hardwood floor being quite so unforgiving. I discovered an entire room in the back of the house that was stuffed full of furniture covered in white sheets. It looked like a graveyard for Ikea and I grunted, wiping away sweat and dust from my brow as I whipped off yet another sheet and realized I'd hit the jackpot. *A mattress.*

It took me a while, and a lot of coughing, to tug the thing into the room where I'd decided to set up camp. I could've grabbed one of the bedrooms I discovered, there were six of them after all, but the idea of sleeping somewhere I'd existed a lifetime ago seemed…too much for me. Besides. This was a temporary measure.

I'd spent very little time in the front room as a child, so it was the safer bet emotionally. Harder to reconnect with the ghosts of my past when they existed hidden in corners and I banished myself to open spaces.

When the mattress was finally set up I lay my sleeping bag on top of it and piled up the blankets I'd pilfered from our apartment before I'd left. I almost laughed when I realized that there was probably footage of me stealing them sitting on my aunt's laptop just waiting for her to discover it. If she hadn't already.

I'd changed my number before I'd run. Cut all ties I possibly could aside from the most important one. Jeffrey didn't have my new number though, and I didn't plan on calling him until I at least found somewhere more permanent to live. I owed him an explanation and some peace of mind, and I couldn't give him that yet, so I stayed silent.

I stared at the artful rafters decorating the twelve foot tall ceiling above, cringing as I coughed on a wayward plume of dust that exploded from the mattress when I shifted. The lack of dust under the window looked even more suspicious now. The exposed beams that stretched along the ceiling looked like the love child of a Gothic cathedral and an old time-y cottage. It was both unholy and cute in its ugliness.

I tried to force myself to relax.

But the thing with forcing yourself to relax is that you quite literally can't do it. So I just continued to stare blankly at the ceiling and tried not to freak the fuck out. I didn't know what to do with all the open spaces. For someone with claustrophobia, I sure seemed to be complaining a lot. I should be grateful. I should be a lot of things.

"It's just a house," I reminded myself, shifting uncomfortably as that prickling sensation along my skin that had followed me all day returned. I thought back on the faces I'd seen throughout town, all suspicious, their eyes heavy—accusatory. Was it because I looked like Edward Scissorhands? Or was there just something about me that screamed *look at me, judge me, hate me*?

My aunt had certainly thought so.

Stop! Stop.

Fuck.

I rolled over, digging my fingers into my scalp and pulling at my hair so hard it began to sting. *Stop it.* That line of thought only led to madness. I'd run to get away from her influence over me, it did me no good to allow her words to corrupt me even when she was thousands of miles away.

So why couldn't I get her out of my head?

Pathetic.

Fucking *pathetic.*

I shook as I reached for the back of my own neck, my face smooshed into the slick fabric of my sleeping bag as I squeezed tight with both hands. It was a soothing gesture, one that Jeffrey had used on me over and over when we were kids. If I could just—*if I could just pretend*—maybe I could get my skin to fit my body again.

I trembled, nails biting into my flesh until the pain grounded me in the present and I was finally able to breathe. It could've been minutes or hours that passed while I was in limbo but I had no way of telling. Not when my world had turned to darkness and my head to nightmares.

It was nearly three a.m. by the time I managed to get situated in my little pile of blankets. The noose of anxiety that had tightened around my neck finally loosened enough for me to relax. Though my mind had finally gotten on board, my body didn't seem to get the picture. Every time I thought I was about ready to drop off into sleep, there would be a creak from upstairs or a rustle outside that would cause me to jump and tense inside my sleeping bag all over again.

At least tonight I was warm.

I lay in the dark, sighing inky bangs out of my face and stared blankly up at the wood beams that climbed the ceiling. Man, the architect of this place was either a creative genius or a Tim Burton-obsessed asshole. Even inspecting the house as closely as I was, I could hardly remember this place. Realistically I knew I'd lived here until I was eight. Wading through my memories felt like pushing through a wall of molasses, thick and cloying and impossible to pass through.

The numbers on my phone climbed higher and higher, three o'clock, three-thirty, three forty-five. My eyes burned, my body numb with fatigue. By the time four rolled around it seemed my body had taken over for me, the sluggish feeling in my veins making me leaden as my eyes drooped and I finally, blissfully, let the exhaustion overtake me.

I jolted awake ten minutes later when I heard a scraping sound at the window.

I'd closed it right?

Right?

I tried to soothe myself thinking maybe it was just a branch. *Yes. Just a branch. Nothing more.* It wasn't like one of the creepy townies had followed me back to my house just to murder me unaware. Right?

The scraping noise happened again and I flinched, cuddled up like a black caterpillar in the dark as I tried to force myself not to look. *You're not going to see a face in the window*, I told myself over and over. *You're being stupid. This isn't a horror movie. Nobody followed you here.*

Despite how many reassurances I gave myself, there was no way I could force myself to keep looking away. Not when I heard the window begin to shudder and whine as it was shoved up. It was clear now I wasn't imagining things. My pulse beat its fists against my breastbone as the window climbed up inch by inch, until finally it settled presumably just the way I'd found it.

My head turned slowly, carefully, a dark tendril of hair slipping across my brow as I forced myself to look.

The wind whistled in my ears, slinking through the now open window with an almost howling desperation as a quiet little noise echoed from just outside. It sounded like a grunt.

I froze.

My blood turned to ice in my veins as I dragged my eyes over the window frame, peering through the foggy glass to see the exact thing I had promised myself wouldn't be there.

A face.

I stared, my fingers slick with nervous sweat where I gripped the fabric of my sleeping bag like a lifeline. Thank fuck I hadn't actually fallen asleep. *Holy shit.* Maybe there *was* a god.

Upon closer inspection, I realized the face was not in fact a ghost. It was, however, a boy. He was pale, his eyes large and dark, with a wounded quality that eviscerated me. He scrambled to climb through the window. He was probably close to fifteen, his face just on the side of puberty where his jawline had begun to square but he still retained the hint of baby fat along his cherub-like cheeks. His red hair was a flame in the night, his eyes nearly black as he forced the window open wide enough he could sling one knobby knee over the windowsill. In that moment he looked so much like a young Jeffrey that I was filled with a homesickness so visceral I thought I might throw up.

"What the fuck dude?" I said, unable to help myself as I jerked to a sitting position the moment his small frame hit the floor. He jumped, slamming back into the wall in alarm and holding his hand out like he could somehow air-bend me into submission. Against my better judgment

I found him…adorable. Intruder and all.

"What—" he spluttered, confusion flaring across his face as his head snapped around the room in an attempt to locate me. When he finally spotted me, wrapped in my cocoon in the back corner of the room, he deflated. "Oh my god! you can't squat here," he pointed out, obviously alarmed.

"I'm not squatting," I told him pointedly. "Besides. Why are *you* here?" I asked, attempting to get the power back in the situation even though it was hard when I looked like a shiny caterpillar and my eyes felt like they'd sunken nearly a foot into my skull. I probably looked terrifying to him. Gaunt. The bruises around my eyes giving the illusion that I was just a skeleton of a person, my black hair windswept and wild.

I looked more like a ghost than he did. Which was…depressing, but I was weirdly okay with it.

"It's none of your business," he huffed, obviously freaked out as he continued to hold his hands out like a little ninja ready to attack.

"Pretty sure it is my business when you're breaking into my fucking house at four in the morning," I pointed out. He frowned.

"This is your house?"

"Yes." I gritted my teeth as I reached for the zipper on my sleeping bag, the noise far too loud in the quiet room.

"Prove it," he said, obviously a stubborn little shit.

"Look. I'm not going to fucking prove to you that this is my house. It just is. Also, why do you care? Why are you here? *Who are you?*" Questions burst from my tongue as I glared at the little dude across from me. The smudge of dirt on his nose revealed itself to be freckles when he drew closer, his eyes wide and dark as he seemed to assess me. He was quiet

36

for a while, too long really. Long enough I thought at first maybe I'd imagined him in a fit of exhaustion fueled hallucinations. But then he spoke again, plopping down only a few feet away from me, a cloud of dust billowing up in his wake.

"I'm Collin," he said softly, holding out his frankly massive hand to me. It was so at odds with his skinny body it made me want to laugh. I bet he had big feet too—like a little red-haired hobbit.

"Blair." I accepted his handshake, treating it very seriously because he was. The tension left Collin's shoulders immediately and he beamed at me, releasing my hand before he wiggled in place in excitement.

"I remember you!" he said eagerly, even though I was pretty sure he hadn't even been born the last time I was in Elmwood. "Well, I mean. I remember *hearing* about you," he clarified.

I nodded because that made a lot more sense, even though I thought it was wild that people still talked about my family. "So why are you here then? Breaking into my parents' house on a school night?"

"I'm homeschooled." His expression called me an idiot without him ever having to utter the words. Despite the fact that he was the one breaking and entering, accosting strangers with his sass at four in the morning.

"And…?" I waited.

"And what?"

"And why does the fact you're homeschooled mean you can break into other people's houses?"

"I didn't *break* anything," he said in a confused little huff, his brow scrunched up. "Did I?" He looked concerned.

I honestly wasn't sure why he was asking *me* that, considering the fact that *he* was the one that would know if he'd broken shit. But, oh well.

"That's not what I meant and you know it," I pointed out.

Collin wilted, losing his steam as he fidgeted and began picking at the hem of his shorts. "I just…sometimes I come here to think, you know? It's never been a problem before." He grimaced, his fluffy little head bobbing. "It's so loud at home and no one is like me—and I just…I don't know." He trailed off with a frown, shrinking as I observed him. And for some reason, watching this brave little boy grow small made my heart hurt.

"Hey man, don't let me stop you," I grunted, arranging my sleeping bag around my waist. "I'm not gonna tell you that you can still break in since I don't want to get sued when you like…impale yourself on a nail or something. But I don't mind if you use the front door."

He perked up immediately, his eyes full of light as he bounced to his knees. "Holy shit, *really?*" his eyes narrowed like he expected me to retract the offer. When I didn't, I got to see the way the tension in his shoulders bled away.

"Yeah, sure, bud," I replied. God…I was going to regret this.

We exchanged numbers and Collin left an hour or so later. By the time he was gone my head was gloriously blank. His sunny presence had scared away the shadows in my mind and I was finally able to fall asleep peacefully, for the first time in what felt like years.

Chapter Four

Blair

NIGHTMARES CAME AS they always did—fragments of my memories choking through me like shards of broken bone as I recalled the night that had spurred me into leaving a month ahead of schedule.

It had been another stage in my rebellion; LEGOs made of courage I had spent years constructing.

I'd found myself at a gay bar. The only one in town really. As out of place as I felt, I still was more at home in the crowd of strangers than I had been at the home where I'd spent more than half my life, or the condo that was supposed to mean freedom but only meant more lies.

I'd had sex before sure, but only in secret, choking on cock in dark closets with gritty fingers in my hair and a lack of reciprocation that I didn't mind at the time, but later realized made me feel nothing but empty. That night I was looking for something different.

Something…more.

Connection.

I'd been feeling disconnected for so long the sensation was beginning to settle under my skin. Covering my skeleton in a cloak of dissociation that was so familiar it terrified me. I wanted to feel something different.

I wanted the numbness that welled up inside me to fade for just a moment.

I ended the night dissatisfied with another bathroom blowjob added to my list of sexual encounters. My lips were chapped and numb, my head foggy as I made my way home. Somehow, despite the physical connection, I'd felt emptier after sucking the cock of the nameless man than I had before I'd entered the bar.

Every mile closer to home I donned another layer of deceit like armor.

There was something about hiding who I was that made me feel like a fraction of a person. There were many things that made me feel that way, that had always made me feel that way, but at twenty-three with cum in my empty stomach and acid in my throat, I felt like nothing but a puppet of my own design. Forced to rebel because without rebellion I was nothing but a shadow.

I'd crept into our shared apartment. I was well aware of the blinking red light from the camera placed at the end of the hallway that separated our rooms. It winked at me and I had half a mind to flip it off.

Somehow I refrained, even though my soul ached with the repression.

I'd thought I was alone.

Jeffrey's new car was missing from the parking lot so as I stumbled into the kitchen to fix myself a snack I hadn't expected to see a figure waiting for me.

She was everything I feared, larger than life, despite being just as small as I was.

Her silhouette was severe, her eyes hooded in the dark as *she* sat at our dinky little dining table and waited like a messenger ready to bring me down to hell.

Except hell was *here*.

And *she* was my devil.

"I got an interesting text," she'd said without greeting me first, her voice cool and detached in the way it always was.

And that was how it started. I was eight years old again, my body shifting and morphing until I was nothing but a scared little boy in her presence. As always I froze, invisible arms wrapping around me, restraining me, choking me, holding me still. *She* rose from her seat with a commanding air about her, her fist closing around the cross she wore around her neck, green eyes flashing. She crossed the small distance between us with the click of heels on tile.

She was speaking, but the words didn't register, her small figure merging with the demons in my mind as *she* grew ten feet tall and the wings of her destruction spread out behind her. Her words were weapons, sharp with the force of their damage, and I crumpled beneath them long before her fists met my body.

It was like a weight was holding me down, pinning me to the floor as I was sliced to ribbons both in flesh and spirit.

I watched the bone-white of the cross she always wore around her neck flicker back and forth, back and forth.

Invisible hands squeezed my wrists as pain erupted from every aching blow.

You're an embarrassment.

You're disgusting.

How dare you do something so revolting.

You're lucky I'm so merciful.

I can't believe I raised such a repellant little boy.

Repulsive.

Wrong.

Wrong. Wrong. **Wrong.**

By the time she finished I lay in pieces at her feet. My blood stained the tile, my vision blurry, as I stared at her designer heels and tried to reconcile the woman whose fingernails were full of my flesh with the woman who had taken me in as a child and raised me.

She was supposed to be my mother. My protector. My caregiver.

And for the first time in my life, I realized if I didn't leave right then, I never would. Her curse would follow me for the rest of my days, poisoning my thoughts, my heart, my mind. With her words *she* wove a spell around me, casting me into darkness, taking away the pieces of me that brought me light.

I had to go.

I *had* to go.

So I licked my wounds in private. I watched her leave without a backward glance through swollen eyelids. And as I stared at the swish of her blonde ponytail, the hate that blossomed inside me evolved into a determination so fierce, so fiery, it burned me. When *she* was nothing but a painful memory, I packed my bags. With each item of clothing, with each plant I carefully packaged into the back of my car, a part of me that had festered from her callous words broke off and crumbled away.

By the time I hit the road, there was a feeling bubbling up inside me that felt like a cousin to hysteria. But instead of laughter, tears escaped. As the open highway spread out in front of me and the lights twinkled by on either side of me in a blur, I realized just how easy it had been to leave. Escape had seemed so impossible for so long—but it wasn't.

Because here I was.

And leaving had been the easiest thing in the world.

I spared one last thought for Jeffrey, wherever he may be. He'd be cleaning up my blood from our kitchen floor no doubt wondering if this was the time *she* finally killed me. And the funny thing was that maybe… maybe in an alternate dimension it was.

Maybe somewhere, far, far away, another me had died.

But I hadn't.

And I was going to fucking live, no matter what it took. I was going to teach myself to be the boy I should've been had I not been raised by a demon.

The next morning the sun woke me. I'd made a point since graduating not to rise till long after the sun had reached its peak, in defiance of the years I'd spent half drunk on nightmares, trudging aimlessly before sunup through the halls of my high school. Apparently the fact I hadn't set an alarm wasn't a demand for the universe to let me sleep in like I'd hoped it would be.

The sun's rays that had crept their way methodically across the floorboards to reach me turned my eyelids red as I groaned and tried to force myself back to sleep. The birds outside my window sang cheerily. It was adorable and absolutely fucking infuriating. After the fifteenth little *chirp chirp* I wanted nothing more than to slam my head against the floor until the noise melted blissfully away.

When hiding in my sleeping bag became too muggy and largely unsuccessful, I finally admitted defeat and headed off into the woods to pee. My eyes were still blurry with leftover sleep as I stumbled out the front door and down the creaky steps. I sneezed through the dust that wafted in my wake and tripped over twists of wayward tree roots hidden in the overgrown grass intent on sending me into an early grave. I'd already fallen once and I wasn't eager for a repeat.

Trees are assholes, I decided, *beautiful assholes, but assholes all the same.*

It was less creepy out in the woods with the sun acting as a peeping tom through the tree branches, but I was still so foggy from sleep that every time a squirrel so much as chirped in my direction I jumped about a foot in the air and squawked like an overgrown chicken. Which was… *inconvenient* considering the fact that I was trying to pee.

Thankfully I somehow avoided a major disaster, and I headed back to my car with renewed vigor crackling through me in search of food to fill the hollow ache in my belly. I had about a gallon of hand sanitizer in my car that I showered over my hands. I scrubbed the foul-smelling liquid liberally across my skin, ignoring the way the little cuts along my palms stung as I did an unhappy little ow-what-the-fuck-when-did-those-get-there kinda jig.

My breakfast of champions for the day was the remainder of the bag of stale chips from my back seat and a half empty bottle of water I'd found rolling around. I probably should've bought more at the grocery store the previous day but planning ahead was not one of my strengths. Because I was a lucky motherfucker, I choked on a piece of chip halfway through my meal and ended up hacking up about six lungs trying to get it out.

Tears burned my eyes as I struggled to breathe, cursing the potato gods with renewed vigor as I slapped my hand on my steering wheel so hard it stung. *Again.*

On *that* positive note, I headed off into the woods for the second time that day. I avoided the spot I knew I'd peed in, grimacing at myself as I headed down the familiar path I'd traveled countless times as a child. The woods were more familiar than the house had been. My mother and I had spent hours out here when I was little, hunting for flowers and climbing trees.

She'd taught me what it meant to be a free spirit, the sun caught in her dark hair, so like my own but so different. She'd always reached for me with kindness and a spirit so mischievous she might as well have been a faerie.

I didn't have many memories of her, but the memories I did have were lit with sunbeams and painted in understanding.

She'd been not much older than I was now when she had me.

I took my time, inhaling the scent of early spring air, rainstorms on the horizon as the trees rustled above me. I followed the broken branches, curiosity buzzing inside my chest as I walked the path that my legs remembered even though my mind did not.

Part of me was curious if this was the way Collin had come. It had been drizzling the night before, and he hadn't been soaked, which might be an indicator that he'd spent most of his walk through the trees with their branches' protection.

Did he come into the woods to think?

To take a break from his family and their cruel attention?

I couldn't get his words out of my head; they played like a song on repeat as leaves brushed my skin and I followed my feet further into the woods. The deeper I got, the quieter the outside world became. The forest was greens and blues, painted in timeless evolution, with the sounds of life fluttering in every bird's wing and every rustle of a squirrel climbing the massive trees.

It's so loud at home, and no one is like me and I just—

I paused, Collin's words echoing through my head as I leaned my palm against the rough bark of an oak tree, its branches drooping down towards me, the wind whispering through my hair and caressing the tree trunk as I processed why what Collin had said had affected me so strongly. I barely knew him but I saw myself in him. I saw Jeffrey. A little boy desperate for affection, terrified of rejection, just trying to figure out who he wanted to be.

All my life I'd searched for love from a woman who was not capable of loving me.

I'd thought it was my fault, and it took me far too long to realize the fault lay with her.

I begged for scraps of her attention. I gave her everything I could. I let her make me believe that there was something fundamentally unlovable about me. I let her teach me that who I was wasn't worth accepting.

I'd let her break me.

I'd let her mold me.

But here I was, finally. Free. This was different. This wasn't a little rebellion. This wasn't painting my nails, or getting a job without permission. This was escape. This was freedom. These were baby steps for a man that had never learned to walk on his own.

I'd moved here to be brave, hadn't I? So I was going to be. And the first thing I was going to do as a free man was take care of someone who wasn't myself. I was going to be the person I always wished I had growing up. A man to look up to. Someone to trust. I would take care of Collin, in whatever way I could. I couldn't control what happened with his parents, but I sure as hell wouldn't let him be alone the way that I'd always been.

I continued walking with renewed vigor as I worked my way towards a break in the tree line. Sunlight danced through the branches like a long-forgotten friend and I tripped a little as I stepped through the last line of trees and out into open air.

Sunbeams painted my skin in their gentle caress. The air was crisp and cool, dense with the moisture of a rainstorm yet to come. I let my eyes shut and my eyelids absorb the sunlight, red and orange, my lashes fluttering as I inhaled the scent of freedom. I could feel my choices in the air around me, lifting the hair on my arms and legs, caressing my soul until I could finally breathe through the blackness that had corrupted my heart for so very long. I inhaled, my lungs filling with promise, my soul alight as magic tingled my fingertips along with the caress of tall grass.

When I finally opened my eyes I took in the sight in front of me. Overgrown grass and wildflowers of every color kissed my fingertips as wind danced through the air. The grass rippled like a colorful painting come to life, golden and green. My eyes widened in wonder as I took in the new growth around me.

I'd been here before. Though it was long enough ago it felt like a lifetime had passed.

A feeling of déjà vu filled my soul as I stared out at the field, sunlight painting it gold. The trees surrounding the clearing were dark and greedy, reaching their fingers towards the sky, their branches quaking with the vibrations only nature can see.

In the midst of the clearing, there was a tree.

It was gnarled and old, its bark rough and black, branches twisted and broken like bits and pieces had been consumed and eroded away. It was a husk of the tree in my memories. A hollow shell with the soul gone, and in its place a fairy tale that spoke only of tragedy.

I remembered there being a treehouse there when I was little. But the memory was shallow enough I wasn't sure if it was a memory at all, or just a wishful thought.

It was clear something had happened here and a feeling of deep sadness choked its way up my throat. I stumbled back, stricken, and escaped into the forest as quickly as I could to get away from the heat in my eyes and the shaking in my limbs.

The sadness followed me all the way home.

Something bad had happened there.

I could feel it in my very bones.

Chapter Five

Richard

CHASTITY STARED AT me from across the counter at Benji's. I'd worked there during high school despite not needing the cash. I'd wanted to get out of the house, to be as far away from my parents as possible. We had that in common, only when I'd quit she'd stayed on to become manager. The laminate counters glistened from her attention, the overhead lights just as over-bright as they'd always been. Checkered floors streaked with age only added to the atmosphere, and the scent of grease was so thick in the air and so familiar it always gave me a feeling of déjà vu. Like stepping into the past.

"So…" Chastity frowned. "Let me get this straight." Her hair was pink that day, tossed up into twin buns that looked weirdly like mouse ears. I had never understood her penchant for color as I was fond of dark colors myself, primarily black, and rarely deviated.

She was a rainbow kind of person. Always shifting. A chameleon of pastels.

"You want me to hire Blair Evans? The kid with a psycho mom? Because The Council is concerned that he's going to be just as psycho as she was… and you want to spy on him?"

"That's correct." I nodded, folding my hands over each other as I stared at her.

"And you're going to, what? Pretend to work here too?"

"Correct."

Chastity shook her head, clearly disbelieving. I didn't understand why she thought my plan was so far-fetched. It made sense. From what Ian had said, the kid looked like he needed some sort of stability. I had no doubt the first thing he would do was look for somewhere to earn some quick cash, and since I still remembered—for the most part—what I needed to do at Benji's, it made sense. It would be easy enough to pretend I'd never left.

Besides, connecting to somewhere I'd frequented as a human couldn't be a bad thing. Some people lost their humanity if they focused too much on the change, and I refused to be one of them.

I'd known Chastity for as long as I'd known my own brothers. She was one of the only people in town I trusted to be impartial. I'd stayed up the rest of the previous night with green eyes and bruises haunting the back of my mind. After speaking with The Council, it was clear if I didn't fight for the truth, no one would. It would be easy enough to sweep under the rug, to "solve a problem before it arose"—as one of The Council members had callously put it. But I was nothing if not fair. It was one of my faults and virtues. Blair didn't have a lot going for him right now, especially with The Council already thirsting for blood, and he deserved, if nothing else, a fair trial run.

It had taken all the persuasion I had to convince them to give him a chance to prove the apple fell far from the tree. The only reason they'd even accepted my proposal was because, out of everyone in town, I had the most reason to hold a grudge against his family. What occurred had been a town-wide tragedy, but it had been *my* life that was ruined, forever impacted by one woman's rash decision.

God, I probably *should* hold a grudge. I should hate Blair on principle for what his mother did to my family. I should loathe him.

But instead, I thought about his eyelashes, and the way they fluttered like spider kisses on his bruised cheeks. I kept thinking about the sweet parting of his chapped pink lips and the way he'd clutched his own shoulders tight like even in sleep he was trying desperately to keep the pieces of himself together.

And I couldn't hate him.

I couldn't.

I was wary, sure…a pretty face didn't mean much but…

Blair was…

He just—

I shook my head, back on task, as I stared at Chastity with a stubborn twist to my lips. My jaw ached from the tension as I waited. Talking to people was like playing chess. You always had to plan out your next move. "I can ask someone else if you aren't willing to do it," I told her, even though that was a big fat lie. There was no one else I could ask, and she knew that.

Chastity stared at me, a patron brushed up behind my chair, and Ty flipped a burger on the grill. Her arms were folded over her ample chest as she pursed her lips in thought.

"He'll probably need a place to stay," she commented. "I've been looking for someone to clean my place and we've got a spare bedroom. I could offer him that, too."

Relief flooded through me as tension I hadn't even known was there bled from my body into the checkered linoleum beneath my boots. I nodded. "Yes, that would be acceptable."

She raised an eyebrow at me, clearly seeing through my 'cool' act. "And you want me to…spy on him?" she asked again to clarify. I liked that she was thorough.

I shook my head. "Not in so many words. More…" I tried to scrounge through my mental rolodex of social situations for a way to describe what I wanted without sounding like a total psychopath. It didn't escape me that we were accusing Blair of being a psycho but The Council—and me by default—were the ones concocting wild plans to spy on him.

Hypocrisy at its finest.

"I want you to keep an eye out for him," I said, clearing my throat. "Not necessarily to…spy…but to—"

"To make sure he's not being falsely accused," she nodded, reaching for the rag she'd been using to wipe down the counter, clearly done with the conversation. "Fine. I don't mind. But you better be ready for me to call you at ass-o'clock in the morning if I think something's up."

I nodded, keeping my expression neutral even though I wanted to leap for joy.

Mission accomplished.

Excellent.

"Call me at any 'o'clock' you need, and I'll be there."

Chastity shook her head at me, smiling a little as she flicked her rag. Dirty water scattered along the counter and I grimaced, distracted, before I looked at her again. "You're a big softie, you know that?"

I winced. "I'm not," I denied quickly, glancing around to make sure no one had overheard. I had a reputation to uphold, after all. There were no werewolves present, thank god, and the only other patrons were human, so I knew I was safe. Elmwood had a variety of residents, but werewolves tended to cause the most trouble. I knew them all by name.

My attention caught on a couple that sat in the corner of the room, senses whirring as I listened to the scrape of forks on ceramic and quiet laughter. The wives giggled with their twins sitting beside them, their faces tipped together with a private smile, then a kiss, as they shared a plate full of eggs between the four of them. The taller of the two caught me looking and she nudged her partner. They waved at me, and I gave a little wave back, watching the two little girls' eyes fill with mirrored glee as they whispered to their mothers. Something about…ladybugs and spots—I didn't catch all of it, turning back to Chastity to see her eyeing me thoughtfully.

My stomach hurt. My throat was dry.

"Still getting used to it?" she commiserated and I nodded. I was sure that was where this aching feeling came from, and not from the loneliness that crept along the cobwebs in the back of my mind when I lay in bed as sunlight trickled through the cracks in my blinds and I wondered *what if.*

"Hard to turn it off." The new senses, though dull in comparison to others, still ended up being endlessly distracting sometimes. They were stronger than my human senses, though not by much. Thank god I hadn't ended up like my brother Christopher. He could barely leave his room those first few months, and even an ounce of sunlight caused him to break out in a horrid rash. His powers, however, were the strongest our town had ever seen. My parents had been overjoyed, until we realized that power meant responsibility.

He was rarely home now, often out doing work for The Council in sanctuaries like our own. Sometimes I thought about what might have happened if I'd presented the way he did. God forbid, it would've meant an end to my time with Collin.

I shuddered at the thought, picturing the look on my little brother's face when I'd announced on a quiet Sunday that I was ready to take the change after my twenty-fifth birthday.

He hadn't spoken to me for weeks, his eyes haunted every time he looked at me, like he was mourning my loss before it had even happened. *No.*

I was glad things had happened as they did. The sun was an inconvenience sure, the new noises overwhelming, but at least I got to be a part of Collin's life despite everything else.

My phone chimed with a new text just as I was pulling into the parking lot at my apartment. I'd been planning on sleeping through the remaining daylight in the hopes the headache I could feel coming on would go away. I scrubbed at my temple, frowning as I pulled out my phone. I sighed when I saw who it was.

I called him back instead of replying, and he picked up on the first ring.

"Ugh, you're such an old man. Don't you know how to text?" Collin sighed in that put upon way he always did when I did something he considered 'old.' His words, not mine.

"What do you need?" I asked, instead of dignifying his remark with a response.

"I need a ride."

"Ride your bike," I replied, though I turned my car back on and began reversing out of the parking lot immediately.

"Richard. It's supposed to rain," Collin whined. "It's gonna get all slippery and I'm gonna slip right off into the road and then some car is gonna be going too fast to see me and they're going to hit me and I'm gonna die and you're gonna be like 'Oh man, too bad I was a dick to Collin and abandoned him in his time of need.'"

Jesus Christ.

"Where are you?"

His response came quickly. "Home."

I rolled my eyes heavenward and peeled back onto Main towards Spruce. "Where am I taking you?" I asked as houses rolled by my window in a blur of familiar shapes and colors. I'd lived here my whole life. I knew the town like I knew the back of my own hand. It was comforting and depressing to realize I'd never driven farther than an hour away from Elmwood. I didn't know when it had happened, but at some point I'd forgotten how to do things for myself— to be something other than Richard Prince, responsible big brother, responsible member of society, responsible public servant.

I was stuck going through the motions, moving from day to day doing what I should be doing but never what I wanted to do.

The problem was that I didn't really know what I wanted.

I was a ship stuck at sea waiting for a lighthouse to show me the way.

"I wanna go to the diner," Collin replied. Except he said a bunch of words before answering my question that I didn't pay attention to because I knew he just wanted to chat. He got like this sometimes, especially after an argument with one or both of our parents. It was like there were so many words inside him they boiled outwards in a cloud of steam.

"I was just at the diner." I sighed and shook my head, pulling past the church, the police station, and Town Hall as I sped down Spruce toward my childhood home. The memories I had there were bittersweet. It was why I'd moved out the second I turned eighteen. I could feel Markus's ghost hidden in the walls, his spirit caught in limbo, dragging the house into the past where it could never move on.

It was a time capsule of nothing but the worst time in all of our lives.

It was no wonder Collin did everything he could to spend as much time away from it as possible. He hadn't been there for the devastation, but he still felt its mark. The sickness spreading like black mold in the foundation of the home, poisoning the air with its sadness.

Collin was waiting for me at the end of the long driveway like he always was. I pulled over and he climbed inside my car, rattling away about the newest episode of *The Flash* he'd watched before I'd come to pick him up. He'd been distracting himself with TV lately while he waited for my parents to go on vacation again so he could come stay with me. I waited for him to buckle up, eyeing him pointedly as he rolled his eyes and clicked the belt into place.

Good.

I smiled at him, adjusting my sunglasses as I headed back into town for the second time that day.

"What's wrong with your face?" he asked, face scrunching up adorably in disgust.

"What?" I reached up, confused, worried I had a piece of food or sauce on my cheek, only to realize that I hadn't eaten food for over six months. It was a habit that would probably stick with me for a good decade. I removed my hand, embarrassed.

"You're smiling."

I blinked.

"You never smile." His big brown eyes were full of accusation, so similar in color and shape to how mine used to be that it freaked me out sometimes. Like looking into a mirror that showed the past. And then his words registered.

"I smile," I defended.

"Yeah sure, like. Only when you're doing a crossword or staring at a cute puppy or something." He blinked. "It's just. Weird."

I smiled more fiercely at him just to make him uncomfortable.

"Creepy." He shuddered and shoved at my shoulder even though I was driving. "Stooooop."

"Why did you want to go to the diner?" I asked, instead of acknowledging his sass.

He just shrugged. "Chastity's hot and gives me fries."

Wow.

"And you thought this was important enough to interrupt my beauty sleep for?" I joked. We both knew I had never prioritized sleep and I never would. Especially now that I didn't need it the same way I had before.

"What? I'm a teenager. Let me be gross." Collin scrounged around in my glove box for the candy I kept there for him, crowing his triumph when he found a handful of Hi-Chews and began unwrapping them one by one and popping them all into his mouth at the same time. I'd never told him I kept them there for him, but I knew he appreciated it all the same.

I watched him stick most of his wrappers down into the crack between the car door and his seat but didn't comment. When he kicked his feet up on the dash only I shoved them off with a quiet growl.

"Ugh. You're no fun." Collin shook his head at me, flicking a wrapper my way before he settled down with a pout.

Chapter Six

Blair

COLLIN TEXTED ME not long after I'd caught my breath, my head sinking against the warm metal of the shell of my car. I'd stopped outside it, searching for familiarity in a world that had twisted itself upside down.

Collin: I have a friend that has a room for rent

Collin: And a job

I blinked down at my phone, then blinked again, and again. I reread the text, trying to figure out if I was seeing things. After my moment in the woods, it seemed almost surreal that Collin would come like an angel from above to deliver to me the two things I needed the most. Especially after I'd decided I was going to be the one to save *him*.

Was this…was this the universe's way of apologizing?

Fuck.

I texted back.

Blair:?

Collin:????

Blair: Where?

Blair: Who?

Blair: Explain.

Collin: So I secretly work for the diner in town. Under the table. DON'T TELL ANYONE. And I was talking to my manager and she was telling me that she has a room available at her place and she needs like, someone to clean it? Not the room. The whole apartment. So of course I was like!!!!! I gotta put in a good word for my good ol' buddy ol' pal, Blair Witch.

Collin: *Bitch

Collin: Sorry, that was cuter in my head. You're not a bitch. Only if you want to be. Because like, power to you and all that.

I snorted down at my phone as warmth filled my chest and my cheeks flushed. It was weirdly…poetic that Collin would use the same name I'd been tormented with for years as a term of endearment. Maybe it was a sign. I moved to text back, but he beat me to it again and I watched in fascination as his texts rolled in. I'd never met someone who texted this much. I was having a conversation without ever having to provide any input.

Collin: Anyway. Then she was telling me that she's hiring. And you can guess the rest. So when can you come down?

Collin: Oh sorry. Google Benji's. I'm already there. She says she'll give you the keys and you can move in right away if you're willing to clean like immediately

Collin: Her and her sister throw these raging parties. Which is just unfair because only adults are allowed. So like. I hear about them but I've never been invited. Fuck my life.

Collin: Anyway. It's a big mess. Like HORRIBLE so she needs help like ASAP. Are you down? Please say yes because I already told her you were.

I laughed again and quickly swiped to text back, shaking my head as I chewed on my thumbnail, the polish chipping off between my teeth.

Blair: I can be down in an hour. Does that work?

Collin: Yes! But like I said. This is on the down low! So don't tell anyone I work there. Or you're on my shit-list. Especially my brother.

Blair: Alright, dude. I get it. Secret-secret.

Collin: Sweet :D See you soon

Man. Things were looking up. The warmth that had echoed in my chest earlier filled me again as I quickly slid into my car and stared at my duffel bag. I'd need to come back to pick up my plants and sleeping bag but for now what I really needed was to fucking shower. Jesus Christ, I couldn't show up to meet my new landlord/boss/lady smelling like last night's nightmares.

I shuddered and pulled out onto the street.

Trees blurred past and I hummed to myself, so chipper I turned up the volume on my stereo and head banged to Taylor Swift finding love and losing it once again. It reminded me of Jeffrey and how many days we'd hidden away in this very car, his hair like flames in the wind with me curled up on the passenger seat, my feet on the dash and the danger blissfully behind us.

Even though the foundation of my childhood was built with uncertainty and fear, it hadn't been all bad. We'd found our rhythm after a while. Jeffrey and I had stolen moments together, becoming a family of our own, us against the world. He'd been the big brother I never had, and I'd been his problematic little brother with a chip on my shoulder, grasping desperately for him.

Soon things would look up for the both of us.

I'd sell the house. I'd settle down somewhere far enough away no one could find me, and I'd call for him. We'd be a family again, like we were always meant to be, and no one would hurt us ever again.

We'd stop being the scared little boys bonding through trauma. We'd stop being the kids that snuck into each other's rooms at night, stealing minutes of childhood everywhere they could because in the daylight world all we knew was survival.

Benji's was a small little business, old fashioned in a way most things in town were. The parking lot was empty aside from a beat-up pickup truck. I wasn't surprised. Everywhere in town seemed abandoned during daylight. Even on my first day here when I'd been absorbing judgmental attention the amount of people that were out and about was shockingly small, even for a small town.

The roof of the diner was sloped, the front made entirely of glass. Large white letters spelled out "Benji's" across the red exterior. It was light enough out the windows became nothing but mirrors as I pulled into a parking spot out front and slipped from my seat and onto the hot asphalt. I could still smell rain in the air though it had yet to fall.

When I looked up there were storm clouds on the horizon, steadily creeping in where they caressed the mountain tops, a problem for the future and not for the present.

I caught my reflection in the windows as I crossed the sidewalk on my way to the front door. The bruising under my eyes had faded some, turned the color of green daylily and lilac. I swallowed bile, forcing myself to be brave as I watched my expression shudder, and awkwardly shoved the rat's nest of black hair atop my head behind my ears.

My eyes were just as green as I remembered, bright with promise I had never felt before despite the gaunt twist to my lips as I pushed open the front doors and listened to the bell chime overhead.

The scent of fried food hit me immediately and my stomach growled the same moment I heard cheering to my left.

"Blaiiiiirrrrr," Collin yelled, and I turned to face him, distracted as he waved a mop at me, splattering the checkered floor by his feet with soap suds. "Bestie." He grinned, doing a weird dance with the mop's handle that was both obscene and honestly fucking cute.

What a weirdo.

"Hi, Collin." I smiled at him, the expression foreign enough my cheeks began to burn immediately. He smiled back and my heart hurt. I'd never had effortless interactions with people like this. It was…nice. To be something other than Blair, the problem child. Blair, the problem in general.

"Oh my god, you have to meet Chastity." Collin bounced, waving me over. I followed obediently, avoiding the wet spots on the floor as I took in my surroundings. The diner was well maintained and old fashioned, the countertops a blue laminate that was clean but chipped at the edges. The overhead lights were bright and I felt my heart swell as I caught sight of the register and fifties-style stools that lined the long L-shaped counter that swung through the entire diner.

A part of this place was going to be mine now.

I'd work here and leave a mark with each interaction. It would change me, just like everything else had from the moment I'd tossed my bags into the back of my Yaris and never looked back. I swallowed and my eyes caught on the girl standing behind the counter with her hands on her hips.

"Collin. You're a pest." The girl–who I assumed was Chastity–accused, before giving me a wave with a dainty little hand. She was smaller than I was—an amazing feat—and curvy all over. Her cheeks were cherubic, her hair pulled up into adorable pink space buns that were lined with hair clips that looked like little baby hearts.

Aesthetic AF.

"Hi." My voice scratched on its way out, I was trying not to be as awkward as I felt but I was clearly failing. Chastity just laughed and waved a hand at me in greeting. Thank god she seemed alternative herself, because I'd forgotten to hide my nails. She didn't seem to care however, and I relaxed a little.

"Hi!" Chastity patted the counter and Collin shoved me towards her. I took a seat on one of the bar stools, eyeing her warily even though she didn't strike up the same anxiety inside me most women usually did. I had a distrust of them for obvious reasons, even though I knew it was unfair to judge an entire group of people based on one person's faults.

I couldn't help it though.

I'd been conditioned to be scared since I was small enough to develop a personality.

"I'm Blair." I held my hand out to her. That was what I was supposed to do right? Shake her hand? That was the normal thing to do?

"Hi sweetie." She grinned, shaking my hand even though I could tell it amused her. Fuck. Okay. No hand shakes. Only with Collin, I guess. "Collin said you can help me?"

I shifted awkwardly, cheeks flushing when the chair made a horrible squeak that sounded suspiciously like a— Collin laughed, because of course he did. I wanted to promise her that I hadn't made the noise, but I didn't want to come across as a weirdo. Even though I was pretty sure

65

that ship had sailed about the time a fifteen-year-old had championed for me to be her new live-in house lady—man. Houseman? *Houseman*. No. House*keeper*. Housekeeper.

"Um. Yeah." I blinked. "You…" Fuck, I was messing this all up. *Why weren't the words coming?* "You…" *Fuck fuck fuck.* "Needed someone to clean? And someone for the diner, right? Both?"

"Yes, sir." Chastity saluted, grinning. There was a rag tucked into the front of her apron that had a ketchup stain on it and I stared at it because making eye contact with her made me feel stripped bare in a way I didn't have strength for in that moment. "Can you start today? I've got a pretty massive mess back home and no time to take care of it myself."

"I can start right now." I perked up, forcing myself to look at her face when I realized it might look like I was staring at her boobs. My cheeks burned. "That would be great."

"Do you want further compensation? Aside from the room." She blinked. "Obviously I'd pay you for your time at the diner separately. But I want to make sure that you feel you're being compensated fairly for the work you do at the apartment."

"Wait." I blinked. "The cleaning is like…in exchange for the room?" I blinked again, relief flooding through me. I had about seven hundred dollars to my name, and I'd been so sure I'd have to spend every last cent on my first month's rent. I swallowed, waiting for her answer with my heart in my throat.

"Oh yes. Definitely." Before she could speak again I quickly interrupted her.

"I don't need anything else. The room's fine."

"Really?" She cocked her head at me, an assessing look on her face, a little wariness there that I only noticed because everyone in town had been looking at me that way from the moment I'd driven across the border.

"That's plenty. I promise."

"Sweet!" She perked up, pulling the rag from her apron and chucking it at Collin. "Man the fort with Ty. I'm gonna go show Blair the place." I glanced behind her at the only other man in the room. He had a handkerchief on his head and headphones, though I caught him peeking at me—just once— before he turned back to the grill.

Collin rolled his eyes but nodded, clearly unfazed as he quickly finished with the mop and hopped around the counter. "Okay, but you *know* I gotta be off and out of uniform by six—cuz otherwise *you know who* is gonna figure out I work here—and the jig will be up." He made a cutting motion across his own neck and Chastity rolled her eyes at him.

"I know." She snorted, making an amused expression at me that clearly read *look at this guy* before she pulled her apron off and shoved it into his hands. "Listen to Ty. We'll be back in like half an hour."

"Aye, aye captain." Collin saluted, and then we were off.

Chastity's apartment was not at all what I expected.

It was massive for one thing, and located at the top of the largest— fanciest— apartment complex I had seen in Elmwood. I hadn't known a town with a population of five could house such a luxurious building. Incredible.

There was a man in a fancy little uniform that opened the door for Chastity while giving her a posh little wave. His eyes lingered on me as I passed, heavy as a lead weight, that same suspicious gaze that was becoming more than familiar creeping along my skin like ants. As we strode past him I shuddered, the hair on the back of my neck rising. I scurried towards the elevators to escape the accusation in his eyes.

Chastity hadn't been exaggerating when she'd said the place was a mess.

Even if I hadn't already been warned, the fact there had been a party here was made clear by the sheer amount of red solo cups that littered the floor like an alcoholic's autumn fantasy. The beige couches had been pushed back against the walls, presumably to make room for a dance floor, and there were empty alcohol bottles and the butts of joints dispersed like confetti on every available surface.

Aside from that, the apartment itself was nice. It was all creams and whites and there were crosses on the walls, though I doubted either sister was as religious as the memorabilia would have passersby believe.

"You can see why I needed help ASAP," Chastity joked, though it was clear she was a bit uncomfortable. Understandable. I was a stranger after all. "You sure it's not too much?"

I blinked and shook my head. "No. It's-it's *great*." *I could do this.* I'd kept our apartment back home meticulously clean. It had been one of the rules both Jeffrey and I had to follow when we'd begged to leave the main house. We'd wanted privacy.

What a joke that had become.

I jumped back when I noticed Chastity was walking on the cream carpet with her dirty shoes still on. A sick feeling of déjà vu caused me to remember words uttered what felt like a lifetime ago.

Get your dirty feet off my rug.

What is wrong with you?

Don't you know how to use your eyes?

It's no wonder with a mother like yours you don't have manners.

I swallowed bile, quickly shucking my tennis shoes off and shoving them in a back corner by the door. Chastity showed me around, completely unaware of my inner turmoil as she beckoned me first into the kitchen, then the two bathrooms, then what she dubbed my bedroom with a flourish.

The room was simple. There was already a bed inside—thank god—and a nightstand made of beech wood. The white walls were decorated with stock photos that depicted the New York City skyline. Though it was generic, it looked like *home*. The bed was made, black comforter tucked in tight. A feeling of relief washed through me as I realized the bed being made meant it was likely that no one had fucked in it at the party the night before—not that I was in any position to complain. A bed was a bed. Cum-stained—or not. I shuddered at the thought, despite it being my own fault my brain had gone there.

"This is your room." Chastity gestured around. "There's an attached bathroom, and a walk-in closet."

Despite looking like it'd stepped straight off the pages of 'how to tell your friends you're rich with your guest bedroom,' it was the nicest place I'd ever been.

Because it was mine.

Mine *alone*.

I'd never had something that was just mine before.

"There's a lock on the door for when you have guests over and—"

I must've made a noise because Chastity stopped talking, turning to look at me with a confused expression on her angelic face. I could feel that my eyes were wet but the feeling was just a distant sensation. The hurricane of emotion in my chest drowned me and I rapidly blinked the wetness away, embarrassed by myself. "Sorry. Just." I shook my head, throat tight. "I've never had a lock before." God. I sounded like such a fucking weirdo. *Shut up, shut up! Don't ruin this before you even have it.* The thought of her retracting her offer was enough to make me sick.

Chastity cocked her head at me, brow furrowed in confusion as she seemed to inspect me for a long, quiet moment and her expression smoothed over. She shrugged. "Lock the door as much as you want, baby. It's your room."

It's your room. It's your room. It's your room.

Warmth filled my chest and I nodded as she took a step back, clearly sensing my need to bask in the silence of the space for just a moment.

My room.

My home.

No cameras.

No one to tell me what to do.

A lock on the door.

Privacy.

The idea of privacy was so novel it felt fictional. Maybe it wouldn't have felt that way before, but it was something I'd never had. A locked door for me was a palace, a fairytale, a fantasy. A spell of safety woven to cocoon the fractured pieces of my shattered soul.

"I've gotta get the keys copied and head back to the diner," Chastity said after a long pause. She squeezed my elbow and I was so surprised by the touch that I automatically flinched back.

Shit.

Mortification flooded my cheeks and as they burned I held still, hoping to god that she hadn't noticed how much of a freak I was—flinching back from friendly contact, like I'd never been touched kindly before. Old habits died hard. Being myself was absolutely exhausting sometimes.

I wished I could take a vacation from it. She continued speaking, not acknowledging my mistake. "Come pick them up in an hour or two? I'll be there late. Then when you get to the apartment if you don't mind—"

"I'll get this all cleaned up tonight," I interrupted quickly, swallowing the lump in my throat, voice solemn. "I promise." Maybe I was being too serious about the whole thing, but it felt important in that moment she knew how grateful I was, even if I wasn't ready to say the words out loud yet.

"Oookay." Chastity laughed and moved to pat my back, this time her touch was gentler. "I'll get you on the schedule for the diner tomorrow. We'll start off slow. You can pick up a night shift. They run from seven to two."

"Sounds great," I told her honestly, still staring at the bedspread slung carefully across my bed.

My bed.

"Cool."

On our way out the door I noticed all the picture frames hanging on the walls, making a mental note to take a better look at them later. I was curious about the illusive sister that kept getting mentioned. And from where I was standing it was clear most of the pictures housed not just two girls but a boy as well. He was older than the two of them by a sizable gap and I wondered if he was their brother. A cousin perhaps? Something about him was familiar.

Just as we were stepping out of the apartment and into the hallway a figure approached us. She was tall, taller than either of us, her legs long, her silhouette made of lean angles that belonged on a runway and not in a small town like Elmwood. Even from a distance I could tell she was gorgeous, magazine gorgeous, Hollywood gorgeous.

She paused when she drew close enough to see us clearly, an expression crossing her face not unlike the ones I'd seen on everyone else I came across in town. Though hers for just a moment looked more akin to horror than anything else. Her eyes were dark, assessing. Calculating. Cold.

"Vanity," Chastity greeted. And I knew with certainty that with a name as horrible as *that* they had to be sisters.

"Chas." Vanity twiddled her fingers in a lack luster wave, arching an eyebrow at both of us as she raked her eyes down my figure. I wanted to slap a hand over the fat bat pattern strewn across my chest to protect them from scrutiny but I refrained. It wasn't my fault I looked like a goth toddler. Okay, so *maybe* it was. But it was better than looking like a regular toddler. At least my clothing screamed adult, even though my face didn't.

"Who's this?" Vanity waved a hand at me, her pointed acrylic fingernails glinting red. I flinched on principle, then coughed to cover up the movement, embarrassed by myself once again. Sometimes it was like my body had a mind of its own. I was unable to help the way my gaze gravitated to Vanity's nails. Looking at them, I could still feel the phantom of my aunt's touch, her own nails nearly a mirror image as they had sunk into my flesh. I still bore the scars.

Freak, she'd whispered, her nails biting deep enough the words punctured through skin, through muscle and marrow, burrowing deep inside my soul.

"This is Blair." Chastity waved a hand at me. "He's going to be living with us and cleaning up our...messes." She laughed, obviously trying to lighten the mood. It was like she could sense the flashback that was flickering behind my eyelids.

"Oh, great." Vanity smiled, though the expression seemed artificial. There was a gaunt twist to her painted lips, a haunted light to her eyes I only recognized because when I gazed into the mirror, I saw the same look in my own. "I don't want anyone in my room though," she made a point to say, and I melted in relief, the tension leaving me.

Of course.

She wanted privacy. That's why she was looking at me like that. She was worried I was going to go through her shit. *That* I could relate to. "I swear I'll just stick to the common areas," I spoke up quickly, embarrassed by how young my voice sounded.

"Then we'll get along just fine." Vanity grinned, her expression warmer than before as she held out a hand for me to grasp. "I'm Vanity. The other member of the not so itty-bitty-tity committee." She blinked clearly cottoning onto the fact I had no idea what she was talking about. "Because we're Van-ity, and Chas-tity."

Oh.

Her grip was cool and just slightly sweaty. Or maybe that was mine? I flushed and pulled back, trying not to show how much the scrape of her nails affected me. My skin was crawling and I tried to force myself to remain present, pinching my thigh in retaliation to quell the dark thoughts creeping in.

Vanity was everything I avoided. Poised. Controlled. Manicured. She reminded me so much of my aunt, bile threatened to rise up my throat the moment I had the thought.

Stop it.

"Will you be home tonight?" Chastity asked as Vanity stepped past us and pulled her keys from around a bracelet she had on her wrist. She paused, arching an eyebrow and flipping her blond ponytail behind her shoulder to look at her sister. It was tipped with red, so artfully executed it was obvious it had been done professionally. The sisters were so different, if it wasn't for their names and the fact they seemed too close to be friends, I never would've assumed they were related to each other. One was all sharp angles and one all soft curves. Yin and yang.

"Not tonight." Vanity opened the door, stepping into the apartment though she peeked her head out with a little pleased grin before we departed. "I'm planning another party though."

"Again?!" Chastity laughed, but didn't complain, just shook her head in exasperation, and caught my gaze before grabbing my elbow. She tugged me down the hallway and to the elevator. It was clear to me already that the two sisters were going to be nothing but trouble.

And I was so fucking grateful I couldn't breathe.

Chapter Seven

Blair

BY THE TIME I reached my house to retrieve my plant babies and my sleeping bag, the clouds had opened and poured their despair down upon us. The sun had sunk below the horizon, the rumble of thunder vibrating the ground beneath my feet as I made trip after trip out to my car to deposit all my children safely in the trunk. They'd lost a bit of dirt here and there, but overall they were doing fairly well all things considered.

I'd never had a green thumb, though I'd always fancied myself a gardener. Back home, I'd had the entire patio covered with plants of different shapes and sizes, terra-cotta pots familiar and striking even from a distance. Sometimes I'd stared at them from the parking lot and admired the way the sun played like magic across their waxy leaves.

As rain tickled down my neck and across the bridge of my nose, I shoved my hand through my damp hair to get it out of my face and gingerly lined each pot up in a careful row between blankets to keep them upright.

It took me three trips before everything was packed.

Every time I stepped on the rickety porch steps I feared they would break, the wood quaking and groaning beneath my weight. It was clear the north side of the porch had already collapsed. There were wood beams that had shattered, overgrown with ivy, where they disappeared into the soil and the mirage of overgrown grass.

On my last trip I paused at the top of the porch, listening to the rain fall, watching the droplets slip down the hood of my car and trickle into the darkened earth beneath it. I breathed in the scent of spring soil and shut my eyes, allowing myself to experience the rain for the first time in my life with nowhere to be but here.

There was no one behind me to tell me to hurry, and no one in front of me beckoning me to run.

So I stayed still. Because I wanted to.

It was healing, it was home, it was peace.

I breathed in the scent of moss and trees and new growth and something deep inside me settled as the crack of lightning that lit up the skyline painted my eyelids red. When I opened my eyes it was to gaze at the stars breaking through gaps in storm clouds, so familiar and so different, thousands of miles away from the last time I'd stared up at them.

I missed the ocean back home fiercely for a moment. Our balcony had overlooked the bluffs below and sometimes when I'd felt lonely I'd sat on the cold cement and listened to the water wave hello. Ice had crept into my limbs, numbing my ass and thighs but still I'd stayed statuesque, listening to the world move around me, existing without me, my insignificance a comfort.

I shook my head to clear it, pausing on the top step as a quiet noise caught my attention.

What…what was that?

It was almost a squeak, a quiet little sound I had no name for but spoke to the deepest depths of my soul. I hurried down to the car, depositing my last load and turning back to the porch with purpose.

I paused.

I listened.

Nothing.

For several long minutes there was only rain and silence.

And then I heard it again.

A cry.

I startled into motion, my body buzzing with pent-up energy as I made my way around the bottom of the porch and to the side that had collapsed. I had the feeling that something was trapped there. What? I didn't know. But I could hear its desperate little voice, the soft noise aching in all the empty parts of me, resonating in my body in a way nothing else had before.

I stumbled through the gnarled tree roots and pushed aside rubble, carving my way through branches and broken bits of porch planking until I had finally made a hole large enough I could see underneath the porch.

What I saw in the darkness broke something deep inside me.

There was a cat. Well. A kitten.

It was tiny, its little body caught under a fallen beam that was too heavy for it to lift. Big green eyes, nearly yellow in the dark, blinked up at me with desperation as its tiny little paws scrabbled weakly at the wood for purchase. It was clear from the scratch marks etched deep into the board that it'd been trying to get free for some time. But as I watched, I could see its desperation waning as it lost the energy to fight. It was giving up. Its little voice raw, its body weak.

I couldn't leave it. I couldn't let it die in the dark like that. I just couldn't. Which meant that I had to do the thing I was most scared of in order to make it not happen. I had to go in there. I had to. There wasn't a choice.

I'd avoided small spaces for as long as I could remember. They reminded me of darker times. Of isolation, of being trapped, humiliation.

Walls built of my own terror would close in on me, my body crushed as I struggled to breathe. Claustrophobia. The fear of small spaces. I'd Googled it once and ever since the word had been carved into my mind like a brand.

I swallowed bile, struggling to breathe as I stared at the kitten, so far underneath the porch that I knew I'd have to crawl to get to it.

I had to do it.

I had to do it.

I had to do it.

I had to do it.

Oh fuck. Blair. Fuck. I forced myself to breathe, grabbing the back of my neck and squeezing it tight to self-soothe, my nails biting into flesh. *Blair. You have to.* I tried to hype myself up, but I couldn't get my legs to work. I was shaking so hard I wasn't sure if the wetness I felt building on my skin was rain or sweat.

The kitten cried again, a soft broken little noise, desperate and giving up, like it looked at me and smelled my fear and it knew I couldn't do it.

But I could.

I could do it.

I could do this.

I wouldn't let him die.

Fuck that shit.

I moved.

Inch by inch I crept through the hole I'd made, wet dirt clinging to the knees of my jeans, my head full of the fog of fear. Thoughts spiraled outward, a hurricane of paranoia. *It's going to fall on your head. You'll be crushed. No one is going to find your body. It'll only get smaller, smaller, smaller. Tighter, tighter, tighter.*

Every breath that wheezed from my chest grew harder to expel, the darkness closing in on me as I moved incrementally deeper and deeper inside of it. Cobwebs brushed my cheeks. Splinters caught in my fingers as I scrabbled through the rubble, stubborn and quaking. It felt like a thousand years had passed by the time I reached the piece of wood trapping the little body beneath it. I was hyperventilating, I could recognize this—but that wasn't enough to stop it from happening, my body frozen as I shook and *stared* into those beautiful green eyes and tried to force myself to move.

Just one more time.

Move the wood.

You have to move the wood.

My body took a while to respond but eventually it did and my hands shifted. They shook so much it was hard to get a grip on anything but I managed, forcing the piece of wood up and over, praying to god it wasn't one of the ones supporting the weight of the porch.

When it was gone my thoughts of impending doom melted away, and instead a small furry body leapt on top of me. Claws dug into my chest, hooking my flesh through my hoodie, a tiny soft head tucking under my chin. I could feel his heartbeat, quick as a hummingbird's wings. I swallowed.

I did it. I saved him.

Relief made my eyes burn, a broken sob leaving my chest as I held the kitten tight, cradling him close. I didn't know if he was a boy or girl—but in that moment he was my salvation. His fur was damp and covered in dirt, though his body was thankfully warm still as I forced myself to begin slowly, carefully, moving backwards. This had been the hardest thing I'd ever done—and now I just had to do it all again. Except—backwards, *holding a kitten.*

Inch by inch. Centimeter by centimeter I shifted back towards the promise of fresh air and spring rain.

After what felt like a century, but could've only been a few minutes, I felt tall grass tickling the small of my back where my hoodie had bunched up and I knew that I'd made it.

I made it out.

I made it out.

My chest expanded with what felt like my first breath of air. My rebirth lay behind me, lost in the darkness. A feeling of pride overwhelmed me, so visceral it made me shake all over again. With dirt covering my entire body and cobwebs in my hair, I laughed with the thunder, rain blurring my vision as I collapsed back on the dirt and let the sky open up above me. I looked like a mess. *I felt like a mess.* But it didn't fucking matter because the kitten was purring against my chest and I had saved him, the sound of his thanks vibrating my heart until it started again, buzzing me from the inside out.

I sobbed out a sigh of relief, scrubbing my hand gently over the kitten's delicate little spine, feeling his tail flicker out to curl around my wrist. It felt like a promise—

And I was gone.

I was in love.

I lay on my back, letting the rain hit my cheeks as I taught myself to breathe again with my heart three sizes too large to fit. The cat's body quaked against mine and I laughed—a bright broken sound—as I felt the thunder vibrate the earth beneath me.

I was reborn.

Blair the coward was now Blair the cat rescuer. Fuck. My cheeks hurt from smiling and my tongue tasted like spring rain and soil and I didn't fucking care as the wet earth seeped into my clothes and the sky poured its triumph upon me.

I'd done it.

I'd saved someone.

Chapter Eight

Richard

A STORM RAGED outside the window and I sighed, watching the few couples that were outside at this hour laugh and run to shelter, their faces rain-kissed and happy. Collin sat beside me, chowing down on a burger and fries, his cheeks puffed up like a chipmunk as he glared out at the storm. He'd been here all day working and I had no idea how he could honestly handle socializing for that long.

"See? Aren't you glad you dropped me off?"

"Don't talk with your mouth full," I responded, not acknowledging his sass as I turned back to where Chastity was sneakily giving Ty's ass a playful smack. I wondered if she really thought no one had noticed she had a thing for him. He was as quiet as she was loud, his hair tied back with a colorful handkerchief and headphones on his ears. I'd never actually spoken verbally with him, only communicated via hand gesture and head nods. Objectively speaking Ty was nice looking, but looking at him didn't make me feel…anything.

Over the last day, I'd spent a lot of my free time ogling people, trying to figure out if the feelings that had woken up inside me were real or not.

Maybe what I'd felt when looking at Blair had been a fluke? After all, I'd only seen him twice. Three times technically if you counted me coming back with Joe the mechanic. It had only taken half an hour to fix the problem with the car and I'd stood there and watched the little figure in the back seat the entire time, expecting him to wake and me to have to explain myself.

But the universe conspired in my favor.

Because he'd stayed passed out.

Which was a good thing because I genuinely had no idea what had overcome me. I wasn't the kind of person to just…look at someone, and *want* them. What I felt wasn't love at first sight or anything silly like that. But it was a desperate sort of curiosity I couldn't quell. No matter how hard I tried.

I wanted to see him again.

I knew I *had* to see him, regardless of what I wanted, but it wasn't… It wasn't the same feeling I usually had when I had a mission to accomplish. Learning about Blair would give me pleasure beyond a job well done. It was something else entirely. New. Foreign. Terrifying in its implications.

Chastity pulled her phone out of her back pocket and I watched her face flicker with a myriad of emotions, anxiety welling up inside me as I leaned forward automatically in response.

"What?" I asked, more than a little nervous.

"Blair." She waved a hand at me as if to signify to give her a moment. I didn't want to but I somehow managed to anyway.

"What's wrong?"

"Nothing's...wrong."

Jesus woman. "What's wrong?" I repeated, with more steel this time.

"Jeez, Dick. Don't be a *dick*." Collin smacked my arm and I glared at him. "Let the woman reply, and then I'm sure she'll tell you."

Collin didn't know the full extent of what was going on with Blair. I'd enlisted his help befriending him after he'd admitted to running into him earlier that day, but I didn't have high hopes that anything would come from it. He didn't need to know what would happen if I couldn't prove that Blair was harmless. He didn't need to know that I couldn't get Blair out of my head. I'd mentioned to Collin that The Council was having me keep an eye on Blair, but other than that I'd kept my feelings silent.

Because that's what they were, weren't they?

Feelings.

I shuddered.

God. The suspense was killing me. My hands bunched into fists, my knuckles white as I watched for what felt like an eternity as Chastity texted out a response. Then she deleted it and I lamented my life. Finally, she broke her silence and set her phone down with a frustrated sigh.

"I don't know what to tell him."

"About what?" I jumped in quickly.

She just waved a hand again and slid her phone across the counter towards me. I grabbed it greedily, flipping into the texts, my gaze zeroing in on first Blair's text to her, and then the fact that Chastity clearly hadn't replied yet. That was fine. Maybe I could fix this—whatever *this* was.

Blair: Hey, it's Blair. I found a kitten and I can't leave him. I understand if that means I can't take on your cleaning position anymore. I'll still come by to clean up tonight as a thank you for your consideration. I'm sorry.

Okay.

Okay.

A cat.

I could work with that.

"I'll buy it," I blurted out, my hands still gripping the phone, probably too tight because it began to make a creaking noise and I had to force myself to relax my grip.

"The cat?" Chastity raised an eyebrow.

"No." I shook my head, because it was clear that Blair wanted the cat. "Whatever it needs. Vaccinations. Medical care. Food. Litter." That was all an animal needed right? "I'll make sure it's not a problem."

"Well…" Chastity shifted, eyeing me warily again, cocking her head to the side like she was studying me. I didn't like it. "That's not really the problem."

"Then what is?"

Collin was staring at me too, his eyes bugging out of his head and I glared at him, daring him to say something.

"I'm not sure I'm like…prepared to have an animal in the house, Richard." Chastity told me gently, "I love them sure, but…I mean. I've never had pets."

"If you hate having it around then I'll adopt it," I told her immediately. Problem solved.

"Wow." She blinked, eyes widening. "You…really want him to have this cat, don't you?"

"Yes." It wasn't the cat. If Blair didn't move in with Chastity I had no idea where he'd end up. Chastity was the only person in town I trusted to be impartial when it came to Blair's judgment. And I needed that impartialness if I was going to get an accurate read on him. I still didn't know if he was what everyone had already decided he was.

Crazy. Murderous. Unstable.

But he didn't come across as anything other than a scared kid. A man who was desperate for a leg up.

"You don't even like animals," Collin told me, even though I clearly already knew that. I glared at him.

"I like them," I defended, even though he was right.

"Riiiiight." He shared a look with Chastity and they both stared at me for a moment. My skin crawled from the attention but I forced myself not to react. Instead I just glared back, glowering them into submission.

"Fine. Tell him he can bring it home." Chastity sighed, shaking her head in disbelief as she left her phone with me and headed over to the register to check out the customers that had walked up.

Success.

I typed in the text, added a few unnecessary exclamation points so that I could believably be Chastity, and a rainbow emoji to be safe.

Blair's response was immediate. A giddy feeling bubbled up inside me as the phone buzzed and I opened the text.

Blair: Thank you so much!! I'll come by the diner for the keys. I can pick up all his stuff before I head back to your place. I

promise I'll still clean tonight.

Again with the cleaning promises. Why was he so set on this? Surely it didn't matter whether he cleaned today or tomorrow. I typed out another response.

Chastity: Don't worry about cleaning tonight.

And then I put the phone away because clearly I was going to get myself into trouble with it.

The idea that Blair would be coming by soon set my teeth on edge. I wasn't sure if I was ready to meet him yet. What if he didn't like me? I needed him to like me. He wouldn't open up to me if he didn't.

We'd need to be friends at least so he would answer all my questions.

But how did I build a friendship with someone I knew next to nothing about? I wasn't even friends with Chastity and I'd known her all my life. Fuck.

It didn't matter.

I'd figure it out.

I had to.

His life was on the line.

When the diner door dinged I had to force myself not to look. The smell of rain and blood filled my nose, making my senses tingle as I stared resolutely forward, unblinking. *Was he hurt? I'd have to check.* Collin perked up beside me like the eager puppy he was, his whole body waving as he lifted his hand to beckon someone over.

"Blair!" he called. Loudly. Right next to my ear. I glared at him, then turned back to the chip on the backsplash behind the sink that I'd been staring down for the past thirty seconds. *Breathe. One, two, three.* Never mind the fact I didn't need to breathe anymore. *Play it cool. Cool guy. Everyone loves a cool guy.* I turned, slow and measured, exuding as much *coolness* as I could muster, my chest shuddering as I caught the sight of a floppy black mop of hair and my frozen heart began to race.

It was excitement, adrenaline, desire. Everything inside me zapped to attention, like being shocked into motion by a cattle prod. I swallowed, and swallowed, and swallowed. I stared at him.

Blair was everything I remembered and more. Because this time he was awake. His eyes were moss, spring apples, and the bright green of plant buds when they pushed through soil for the first time, reaching for the light. They were large and ringed by thick dark lashes, his bruises smudged across the bridge of his nose and in the hollows beneath his eyes.

He was beautiful.

And he looked like he'd been through hell.

His dark hair hung limply around his face, soaked through from the storm, his jeans ripped and muddy, his knees bloody. I could scent the blood before I saw it, my dick throbbing as I ran my tongue along my fangs, forcing them to retreat back to the hell they'd come from. I'd never responded to someone like this before. In fact, even before I'd been turned, I'd always thought there was something fundamentally broken about me.

Blair was also tiny.

Absolutely fucking tiny.

I hadn't realized I liked that. *Really* fucking liked it.

"Hey." Blair's voice was a quiet rasp, deeper than I would've expected, sweet as honey with a scratch to it like he'd chain-smoked a pack of cigarettes. I couldn't smell any on him though, so I figured that must just be how he sounded. His lips were thin and blue with cold as he stayed inside the doorway, refusing to come inside. "Sorry." He flinched a little, his whole face scrunching up. "I'm really wet so I don't wanna cause a mess."

"C'mon in!" Chastity waved at him, clearly unfazed. "I'll have to mop at the end of my shift anyway."

That seemed to only make him more self-conscious, and he shook his head, staring down at his muddy shoes with a grimace. "I just thought I could grab the keys and then maybe head out."

"Why don't you eat something?" I blinked, realizing that the question had come out of my mouth and no one else's. My cheeks burned a little, that same sensation they'd had when I was human, though I knew that little blood would rise to the occasion. It was just sensation now. Fleeting. A parody of humanity.

Blair stared at me, his attention catching on my face for a long pregnant pause. I held very still, suddenly irrationally afraid that one look at me would send him running for the hills.

My hands were sweaty. My hands were never fucking sweaty. What was happening right now?

He kept staring at me.

I stared back.

Collin cleared his throat. "Richard will buy you dinner."

Shithead.

"I'll buy you dinner," I tagged on quickly, not wanting Blair to think I wasn't on board with the idea. "A burger. Fries. Whatever you want."

Blair stared at me for a moment longer, his eyes narrowing as a kaleidoscope of emotion crossed his features. "You're Collin's brother?"

he asked, instead of answering my request.

I nodded. "One of them."

"Then no."

What?

What?

My eyes widened in helpless surprise as I turned to Collin immediately to see if he knew what was going on. He had a guilty look on his face that I knew I'd need to investigate, and a weird feeling bubbled up in my chest. Was this what it felt like to be rejected?

But why?

I didn't like it.

"Are you sure—I really don't—" I turned back to Blair, watching him drip onto the floor. He was wearing a hoodie about five sizes too big for him and it had an obscene illustration of Dracula embracing a werewolf on the front. It was also dry–where the rest of him was soaking wet. The loose drape of the fabric only made him appear smaller, though where it slipped off his shoulder made it clear that he had the muscle definition of a man, despite being tiny.

"Not interested." He smiled.

He *smiled.*

But it wasn't a nice smile. It said 'fuck off' and I was so confused I could feel my head spin.

"Some other time then."

Confused.

Confused, confused, confused.

Collin finished his last fry and shoved his plate back towards Chastity with a wiggle of his eyebrows. He thought I didn't know he'd been picking up shifts under the table here for spare cash. I assumed free food was part of the deal. Part of me figured he liked the secrecy so I didn't say anything, even though I could've. He then turned to me and cocked his head towards the door. That same guilty look was thinning his lips and a feeling of anxiety twisted like barbed wire around my heart. What if he'd told Blair I was watching him? Somehow. I don't know when he would've had the opportunity. What if he'd told him what was going on?

I'd been asleep for hours. *Hours.* Anything could've happened.

Oh fuck.

Oh fuck, oh fuck.

"It was nice to meet you," I said quickly, trying to be polite even though panic unlike anything I'd ever felt was welling up in a reservoir in my chest. Collin grinned and Blair moved out of the way as we pushed through the door. I was taller than him by a fair bit, and as I passed I inhaled his scent greedily, my dick throbbing against my zipper.

Down boy.

What the fuck.

I could see the top of his tangled mess of hair clearly and it haunted me as I stepped out into the rain and clicked my key fob so my headlights would turn on. I was so blindsided by my own desire I forgot to ask Collin about the faces he'd been making earlier as we pulled out onto Main Street and headed towards the pet store, which shared a parking lot with the grocery store.

Collin helped me pick out a cat bed and I spent a good five minutes staring at all the cat food options and feeling completely lost. One of the employees flagged me down and before they could accost me with a problem they wanted me to bring to The Council I quickly asked him to point me in the direction of the best cat food.

It took entirely too long for them to decide which one was the best, but eventually they did and I piled the cart high with food and approved treats. When Collin came towards me dragging a cardboard box with a picture detailing something called a 'cat tree' I just rolled my eyes heavenward and gestured for him to put it inside.

"Fuck yes!" he cheered, and I glared at him.

"Language."

"Freak yes!" he cheered again, clearly unfazed. I knew my chiding would do absolutely nothing, so I just shook my head and turned down the toy aisle. Big mistake. There were too many choices.

I had no idea where to start.

But I'd learned my lesson not to ask for help. It just wasted time, so I did a quick Google search and snagged the first five toys I saw on a 'Best toys of 2022 for your cat' list on Buzzfeed. And then I saw it.

Clearance.

I wasn't normally the kind of person that cared about price tags. Things had a purpose, and that purpose came at a price. However…

I wheeled the nearly full cart closer, staring at the variety of Halloween toys that were clearly on display. I remembered Blair's shirt, and a laugh bubbled up unbidden in my throat. I figured if anyone would appreciate these, it would be him. So I grabbed a bunch of Halloween themed toys and sweets and a pumpkin outfit that looked like it was vaguely the size of a cat.

And then we were off.

It was…kind of exciting honestly.

Despite Blair's rejection, I was convinced I would make him like me. I had to. I just did.

Collin was snacking his way through my candy stash and I shoved his feet off the dash again as we pulled into Chastity's parking lot. He complained about the rain but I ignored his whining as we headed into the building, our arms full of cat supplies.

We were like Santa's elves. Except larger, and in his case—louder.

Jackson, the front desk manager, waved at me with a friendly smile, though his eyes widened when he saw what I was carrying. We'd gone to high school together for the last and only year I'd attended. I acknowledged him with a bob of my head, though I kept it businesslike. There was no time for making friends when I had a cat tree to set up.

Vanity opened the door to their shared apartment and stared at us, a look of shock on her face that I couldn't help but relate to.

I hadn't expected to be here either.

"Special delivery," I said, pushing through the door. I kicked my shoes off politely, glaring at Collin till he did the same, and then turned back to her. "Show me Blair's room?"

She did.

There was this feeling of excitement buzzing through the air as I pulled up to the stop light outside the diner. It was red and I allowed myself a moment to inspect the parking lot, telling myself I wasn't looking for Blair's car when I clearly was.

Lying to myself was harder than lying to everyone else.

It didn't take long to find him. Blair was only ten feet away, curled up in the back seat of his tiny little vehicle with the door open. If I strained I could hear him talking over the sound of the rain and something inside my chest fluttered to life. Collin's chatter faded into the distance as I caught on every word uttered out of the stranger's lips.

"You're gonna be just fine, alright?" Blair threatened the kitten, his voice soft. "You're a fucking badass. Even though you look a bit like a wet rat right now and people say black cats are kinda unlucky. That's okay. I'm kinda unlucky too." He was gently stroking between the kitten's ears, his painted fingernails chipped and bloody. He didn't seem to care. Blair's head was down, dark hair spilling in a swath of inky strands across his forehead. I couldn't see his face, but I didn't need to, to feel the emotion aching in his words.

"You're like *Batman*. This is just your redemption arc." My heart throbbed. "And besides, people may underestimate you, looking at how tiny you are, but you're...you're a *fighter*. So you're gonna be fine, okay? You'll be fine."

"Rich." Collin jabbed at me with his pointy elbow. "The light's green."

I swallowed, shaking my head to clear it.

I put my foot to the pedal and peeled off into the darkness towards the roll of thunder and the flicker of lightning on the horizon. I drove off because I was supposed to, even though my heart got left behind, stuck on wet pavement, listening to a lost boy's quiet reassurances.

Chapter Nine

Blair

IT SHOULDN'T HAVE surprised me that Chastity had had cat stuff delivered to the apartment. It was clear she had a bleeding heart—she'd invited me home with her, after all—and after I'd explained what happened with the kitten she'd been quick to stop me from going out to buy the stuff myself.

I was grateful, though confused.

Her generosity was…puzzling, to say the least.

After I'd fed the cat and petted him (he was in fact a boy) until he fell asleep, I let myself breathe for what felt like the first time since saving him.

I could still remember the look on Collin's brother's face when I'd rejected him. A sense of perverse pleasure had filled me, but only after I remembered Collin's broken words, the way he'd spoken of lack of support, of hate from his own family. I'd asked Chastity what his name was later, wanting to put a name to the face of the man that tormented a sweet little boy.

Richard was one of the homophobic brothers.

But that didn't mean he wasn't drop dead gorgeous.

I'd never looked at another man and felt my entire body realign before. He was tall, and broad—big in every sense of the word—though he retained the grace and power of a jungle cat instead of the clumsiness of most men his size. His eyes were a dark almost mahogany color, so close to red I was sure it had to have been a trick of the light. Everything about him had screamed intimidation, his thick dark brows at odds with the pale almost white shade of his buzzed hair. It was trimmed and styled with military precision, his body groomed to perfection, his nails closely cropped, his flannel shirt unwrinkled.

And he'd been wearing a leather jacket.

Leather.

And boots. *Wait. That was a good cat name!*

Oh god, *the boots!*

They were designer, I could tell just by looking. With custom laces that made my poor soul scream. He probably didn't even know the boots were custom—god. They were wasted on him. I shook my head, trying to clear it as I stepped under the hot spray of the shower. It was a novel feeling having a shower of my own and I basked in it, melting under the heat of the spray as I let Richard's eyes haunt me.

God.

The way he'd pressed his lips together, this stern, perplexed expression on his face, like he couldn't quite figure me out. It was the first time someone in town had looked at me with anything other than suspicion, and I welcomed the change, even though I knew he was just a homophobic prick.

At least that sort of hate was familiar.

Stop thinking about him.

I scrubbed my skin raw in punishment, distracting myself as I stepped out of the shower and changed into an outfit from my duffel bag. It was the same variation of jeans and hoodie that I usually wore, but this time it felt different. Because for a moment I stared at myself in the mirror in the bathroom and instead of a scared little boy looking back at me I was beginning to see the man behind my eyes.

I pressed my fingers to the glass, leaving smudges just because I could. My stomach growled and I ignored it, spending a moment too long hunting for my mother's face in my reflection.

Chastity came home halfway through my deep clean of the kitchen. The living room hadn't taken long because the majority of the cleaning came from disposing of trash in bags and moving the furniture back into place. My muscles burned from use, but it was a welcome feeling. My legs were still a bit stiff from days on the road.

"Man. You could've waited till tomorrow." She laughed, leaning up against the doorframe. I was proud of myself because I didn't jump this time when she reached out to give my elbow a squeeze.

"Couldn't sleep," I told her half-honestly. Truthfully, there was no way I could fall asleep knowing that I was living there without having completed my side of the agreement.

"Me neither." She shrugged. "I'm a night owl." She moved into the kitchen, hip checking me as she scrounged around in the freezer before procuring a bag of frozen fries. "Don't think I haven't noticed that you haven't eaten today."

My stomach growled in response and she laughed as I flushed in mortification.

"I'm vegan," I tried to explain. "It's hard to—"

"Find options," she finished for me. "Fries okay?"

I just nodded because what else was I supposed to say? I'd already turned down free food once today on principle, I wasn't strong enough to do it again.

She helped me clean while the fries cooked in the air fryer even though I told her to stop. I was quickly learning that I had no control over what Chastity did. She was a whirlwind, kind, charitable, with steel for a backbone.

I envied that.

By the time the house was clean and we'd both been fed, I was feeling blissfully sleepy. Chastity sprawled on the couch beside me, her head tipped towards the ceiling as my eyes wandered the apartment, taking it in now that it was clean.

For the second time that day my eyes caught on the pictures hanging on the walls. There were so many of them it was hard to pick one to focus on. I settled on a large frame to my left. It depicted what I assumed to be a young Chastity and Vanity at the beach with the boy I'd noticed earlier. He looked quite a bit older than them, in his teens, his blue eyes ice white, his dark hair at odds with his sister's bright colored heads.

"Who's that?" I asked curiously, that same feeling of déjà vu overcoming me as I stared hard at the boy's face. He really did look familiar. My mind could've been playing tricks on me, but I was fairly certain I'd known him. *Before.* Before my life turned upside down. Before I moved in with demons. Before I was a shattered stained glass window.

"Prudence," Chastity hummed, shifting a little so she was sitting up. "My brother."

"Oh." I should've guessed that. I flushed in embarrassment, my gaze slipping to another photo hung up beside the one I'd been looking at. There was an older couple standing in front of a frankly terrifyingly large mansion. They looked severe. Everything about them screamed old money, old ideals, old mentality.

Three children stood in front of them, dressed to perfection, their postures stiff and unyielding. It took me a second to recognize Chastity, so young and without her bright hair and wardrobe. Their parents, I realized. Their family. Their childhood home.

"He died," Chastity said after a moment and I startled, turning to look at her, bewildered.

"I'm sorry." God, what a stupid thing to say. Saying 'I'm sorry' wouldn't bring him back. But what else was I supposed to do? I couldn't imagine losing a brother. A life without Jeffrey would be...

Would be...

Unfathomable.

"It was a long time ago." Chastity rose from her spot on the couch, clearly done with the conversation. "You better get to bed if you're gonna be rested enough for your first shift with Richard."

I blinked in surprise, shooting up from the couch, sufficiently distracted. "My first shift with *who*?!"

That night I dreamed of small places.

It was dark.

It was dark.

It was dark.

I was back home. Nine years old and hunting for some sort of god in the dark closet I was locked inside. I didn't know how long I'd been in there. Only that I was hungry, and the hollow feeling had become all-encompassing.

It was a ravenous ache inside my belly, consuming, merciless, cruel. I could feel the ice in my fingers, my lips chapped and raw. The water bottle I'd stashed in here from the last time I'd been locked inside had long since been emptied.

When my mouth moved my lips split and I tasted blood.

The coats above me were my only company and I knew better than to pull them down to make a nest for myself, all that would get me was more time in the closet. More punishment. More isolation.

There were footsteps outside the door and I startled, fear and elation bright on my tongue as I listened to a key slide into the lock and I realized it was time. *I was finally getting out.*

Except instead of my aunt's face through the crack it was Jeffrey's.

His dark eyes were wide with fear, his lips drawn tight. He was barely a year older than me but that had never stopped us from connecting like two sides of an orchestral duet, at least not since we'd figured out the only way to survive this was together. "Blair," he said quietly, his voice nothing but a broken whisper. "I can't let you out."

A noise left me, broken and raw. It hurt on its way out because I'd forgotten I could even speak.

"I'm sorry." His eyes were wet, his long fingers shaking as he shifted the closet door just slightly more open. Far enough he could reach inside to squeeze my knee where I had it bunched against my chest. I'd curled into a ball to stave off the worst of the hunger, but that had stopped working hours ago. "I brought you food."

Relief flooded through me and I grabbed onto his wrist, suddenly terrified he was about to leave.

"You have to be quiet though," he whispered softly, his voice music to my isolated ears. "And you can't make a mess."

I nodded, desperate for something, *anything*.

He relaxed a little, his auburn hair painted blue in the night. It was clear it was late enough the adults were in bed. A burst of gratitude shook through my body like an earthquake as I realized what Jeffrey had risked to bring me something to eat.

He turned away from me, and then turned back, shoving a plate into the closet that had three dinner rolls on it as well as a bunch of carrot sticks. I began eating immediately, my instincts kicking in as my hands trembled and I shoved the food in my face. I remained careful, as careful as I could be anyway, shaking as I felt Jeffrey's eyes on me.

His gaze was heavy, as it always was.

"I'm sorry," he said softly after a moment, for the second time that night. "I would've brought more but I had to sneak it into my pockets from my plate."

I nodded again, because honestly this was more than enough. When I finished eating I shoved the plate back to him and he smiled, shifting it into the hallway beside him out of sight. There was an ache in my chest that burned brighter and brighter as I stared at the streak of moonlight creeping through the cracked closet door. I'd been in the dark so long, counting the shadows of footsteps as they passed, that the idea of being shut inside it again made me want to die.

I wanted to die.

Jeffrey reached for me, somehow sensing my mood, his little fingers, so much larger than my own already, bunching up around the back of my neck as he pulled me against his fragile chest. He was bigger than me, even though when I'd first arrived we'd been the same size. I fell against his bony body and I cried. I cried for the parents I'd lost. I cried for him. But most of all I cried for myself, because I knew I was trapped and there was no way out of the mess I'd fallen into.

Eventually he had to release me but he didn't go far. I cried when he shut the door again, silent and shaking, my palms shoved into my eyes as I listened to the sound of the lock click back into place. I heard him sit down outside the door and we just sat there like that, sharing a wall in a house that was really more a prison than anything else.

There was nothing else to do so I fell asleep, and every time I woke I could still see his silhouette under the crack in the door. Until the sun rose and the crack turned golden with its first rays. And Jeffrey was gone, and I was alone again.

It was dark.

It was dark.

It was dark.

Chapter Ten

Richard

THE CAT WAS staring at me. Judging me.

I glared at it, frowning as I continued to rifle through Blair's duffel bag. It smelled like him, like laundry detergent and sweat. I wanted to inhale it into my every pore and roll around on the mattress with it. But I wasn't a teenage boy anymore so I refrained. Not that I'd ever had those kinds of urges when I'd been a teen, but still.

This was new for me.

I was still coming to terms with it.

"Stop looking at me like that," I huffed after a few moments, carefully folding up Blair's clothes and placing them back in his bag. After a quick inspection of the room it was clear he had nothing to hide. Not that I'd really expected to learn much, but still.

The cat meowed in accusation and I growled under my breath, zipping up the bag and rising to my full height so I could properly glare down at him where he clung to the cat tree that I had bought.

"Look. I'm doing my best here," I tried to explain, not sure why I was talking to a cat at all. "I get that you're loyal, but can't you see that I'm trying to help?"

He stared at me.

I stared back.

"Do you want attention? Is that the problem?" Blair was at the diner working the first part of his shift with Chastity. And it had worked out perfectly with my schedule because it meant I had just enough time to spy on him before joining the rest of the shift for even *more* spying.

God, what had my life turned into?

The cat meowed and I sighed, reaching out towards him with an exasperated sigh. "Fine. Come here."

To my surprise he launched himself at me, scurrying up my pant leg, then climbing my torso until he rested like a parrot atop my shoulder. He rubbed up under my chin and I reached up with a startled hand to stroke over the soft fur on his back. He smelled good. Which meant Blair had bathed him. He began to purr softly and I scratched up behind his ears.

Well.

Maybe he wasn't so bad after all.

"You're very lucky you know," I told him softly, listening to him purr, feeling the buzz in my throat as his long tail flickered along the back of my neck. "Your owner is a very kind man."

He mewed his agreement and I melted a little, stroking my finger along the bridge of his velveteen nose.

"Neither of you are unlucky, are you?" I hummed thoughtfully, staring at the blank white wall, finding it odd that there was no indication that Blair had been there aside from the cat. Everything was meticulously clean. So clean, it almost looked like *I'd* been the one living there. Normally I would've appreciated the cleanliness but...

It didn't make sense.

It didn't match my idea of Blair at all.

He should be messy. Young. Colorful. He made a mark wherever he went. This... blankness was just wrong.

When I walked into the diner after lint rolling the cat hair from my shirt, I wasn't sure what to expect. Maybe Blair would take one look at me and realize that I'd been spying on him. Or maybe I'd be met with that same cold gaze I'd received the day before.

Or...maybe, *just maybe,* I'd see that flicker of heat in his eyes again, his initial reaction, the one before the ice had closed up around his heart.

Maybe he'd look at me and he'd want me just as desperately as I wanted him.

I couldn't do anything about it but it was a nice fantasy.

"Oh good." Chastity smiled at me when the bell chimed over the door as I stepped inside, waving me over. "It's your turn. I've got Blair trained up and he's real good on the register already but he's still getting the hang of where everything's at."

"I can help with that," I said stupidly, because my brain to mouth filter was apparently broken the second I caught sight of his dark mop of hair.

Blair.

It was like I was magnetized to him, my fingers fluttering nervously at my sides till I forced them to stop. He didn't acknowledge me, but I didn't mind because it gave me ample time to ogle the long line of his throat and the knob at the top of his spine that I wanted nothing more than to bite. There was a hint of black ink peeking out of his oversized hoodie and just looking at it made my gums throb and my dick twitch.

Jesus fuck, it was like going through a second puberty. Except I was twenty-five and a vampire, and Jesus god I had no idea how to deal with the feelings that were bubbling like Vesuvius inside me.

"Alriiight." Chastity laughed, clearly amused by my struggle as she slapped my arm and pulled her apron off. I watched her hang it up and then leave, caught in limbo because for the first time in my life I had no plan, no mission, only…desire.

I stepped into Blair's space, nostrils flaring as I inhaled the scent of apples and spring air from the back of his neck. He must've been outside before this. Obviously. I shook my head at my own ridiculousness. Of course he'd been outside—he'd had to walk in from the parking lot.

"Hi," I said, because apparently I was both stupid and socially inept.

He turned around, gaze meeting mine for the first time that day. "Hi."

Okay. I'd said hi successfully. Now what?

I swallowed.

"Why are you here?" I asked, and then had a mini panic attack because I'd sounded incredibly accusatory and I hadn't meant that at all. *Baby steps, Richard. C'mon.*

"I'm working." Blair was staring at me, and I couldn't even blame him because for some reason my brain had broken the second I saw his skin and thought about sinking my teeth into it.

"Yes." I cleared my throat, looking around, grasping for something—anything—to make this better. "I mean in town. Elmwood isn't exactly the most…well-traveled or popular place."

He eyed me warily for a moment but then he relaxed a little, seeming to accept the reasoning behind my questions, thank god.

He was so fucking pretty I wanted to crush him like a petal between my fingers.

What the fuck.

What the fuck, Richard?

"Oh." He blinked. "My family is from here," he answered, going the honest route. Good. *Good.* That was good.

"Evans right?" I asked, feeling bad for manipulating him even though it was for his own good.

"Yeah." His lips twitched a little, some of the ice in his expression melting. There was another long awkward silence.

It stretched on for an eternity and I scrambled for something I could say.

Blair took pity on me and just cocked his head, eyeing me with narrowed gaze, his expression thoughtful, assessing. "You're bad with people," he pointed out, an observation, nothing more.

Some of the tension bled from my shoulders and I nodded, a short jerk of my head. "It's not my strength."

"I can see that." He warmed up to me a little more, his lips twitching as he stared at me. "So…" He waved around. "You gonna show me around, or what?"

Right.

Right. I was supposed to be working here.

I could do this.

By the end of the shift I had gotten no closer to any answers. Blair didn't seem crazy though, and I was absolutely glad I'd taken a chance on him, especially after how kindly he'd accepted my social ineptitude earlier.

Despite not getting answers, the shift wasn't a total bust. Every time Blair bent over his shirt would shift up and an inch of porcelain skin would flicker just above the hem of his too-tight jeans. I'd spotted the base of his tattoo and dimples at the top of his ass. *Twice.* And god... It was a glorious ass. The fabric would pull taut over the generous curve of it and my brain would short circuit as I stared at the round, muscular globes. I imagined what it would feel like to bury my cock inside his tight little hole and watch his cheeks bounce as our hips slapped.

So, no. It hadn't been a waste of a day, even though I'd ended it just as frustrated as I had started.

Blair clearly didn't like me, but I was determined to change his mind.

How?

I didn't know.

But I would do it. I had to.

When I got home, Collin was passed out on my couch. I had no idea why he didn't sleep in the bed that I had there for him. I'd even let him decorate the room. Part of me suspected it had something to do with the fact the TV was in the living room, though he was always quick to turn it off before I could catch him watching it too late at night.

"You're home!" He woke right up, popping up eagerly when he saw me, scrubbing the sleep from his eyes as I puttered into the kitchen to warm up a cup of blood. I only drank it from opaque mugs or glasses, too self-conscious still for anyone to watch me, especially because of the euphoria that filled my body after each sip.

It was…different than eating. In a way I couldn't describe.

Intimate.

Like scratching an itch you'd been aching to scratch all day but couldn't reach.

As I sipped at my mug I listened to Collin chatter and gesticulate, his fingers spread wide.

"Chastity said Blair's a vegan," he said, and that caught my attention. I blinked, bringing my mug down from my lips as he stared at me.

"Ha! Got your attention," Collin crowed in triumph. But instead of being cruel he just continued. "She says he struggles to find things to eat. So she bought a whole bunch of frozen fries. Dude's like…way too small. Not in a body-shame-y way. It's just obvious no one fed him much before."

I nodded, my mind already whirring. I had my own suspicions about Blair's upbringing, but they were nothing more than a paranoid feeling based on instinct.

My fridge thus far had been full of junk food for the past six months because it was the only thing Collin grabbed when we were at the store. I'd tried to convince him to eat healthier, but he was resistant down to the core.

I made a mental note to stock the fridge with some more vegan friendly options should Blair ever come over in the future.

And then my cheeks tingled with embarrassment as I realized how stupid that was. The man couldn't even stand to be in the same room as me. Why would he want to come to my apartment?

This was just a job.

Just a job.

Right?

When I awoke the next evening Collin was still home. Except somehow, magically, he'd procured the cat.

I blinked down at where he was sitting in the middle of my living room, his back to the couch, the little black menace on its back and kicking its feet at a feather he dangled above it. It writhed and screeched, and I couldn't help but be moved, even though I was confused more than anything.

"Collin," I grunted, all my questions rolled into that one single name.

Collin burst to life, stilling the movement of his hand for just a moment before he continued, somehow simultaneously launching into his tale while playing with the cat in an impressive feat of dexterity that, knowing him, probably came from playing video games.

"Vanity's having another party. And she invited Blair. And it's like this *huge*-big deal, but Blair was worried that Boots wouldn't like all the loud noise and I was texting him and offered to babysit him till tomorrow!"

I blinked.

I blinked again, cocking my head. "You offered to babysit the cat at my house? Without asking me?"

"It's really more our house than anything." Collin batted his lashes at me and I caved. I cleared my throat.

"Fine." I plopped down onto the carpet beside him and reached for the cat. Boots. He had a name now.

"Wait—Rich—don't—" Collin tried to stop me but I ignored him, gently scratching along Boots's belly with my pointer finger. He looked so tiny beneath my hand it made something protective well up inside me. Until recently I'd only ever felt that for my little brother.

"Oh."

"What?" I asked, turning my attention back to Collin. His orange hair was flickering in the overhead light, his expression thoughtful.

"I just…I was playing with him so he was being all bite-y. So I thought he was gonna scratch you."

I stared down at the cat where he purred beneath my hand. "He's not biting me."

"Yeah. I can see that." Collin cocked his head curiously, inspecting me for a long moment before he shrugged and muttered something under his breath that sounded suspiciously like 'cat whisperer.'

I smiled down at Boots, staring into his big green eyes, unable to help but compare him to his master. "You look like Blair," I told him quietly, ignoring the choked noise that Collin made from beside me.

"Yeah," Collin hummed thoughtfully. "He kinda does." He blinked. "Tiny, wiry, wild—"

"Beautiful," I said at the same time, and then flushed.

"Wait. Hold up. Who are you and what did you do with my brother?" Collin slapped a hand over his chest in mock offense and I glared at him.

"Shut up."

"Seriously. I've never heard you use the word beautiful in my entire fu—*freaking* life."

"Shut. Up. Collin." I rose from my seat, glaring at him as I headed into the bathroom to get changed. There was no way in hell I was going to leave Blair to fend for himself at that party. There could be a whole bunch of creeps there. Besides, it was a good opportunity to learn more about him.

"You're a closet sap and I didn't even know!" Collin called after me and I flipped him off before disappearing inside the bathroom to shower.

Chapter Eleven

Blair

VANITY WAS APPARENTLY notorious for her parties. Both sisters were involved in the process but while Chastity was more of a participant, Vanity planned and instigated each and every celebration.

Collin had told me this earlier that day, chattering at me as he followed me around like a loyal dog with a mop in his hands and a smile on his face. He was pretty good about quieting down when I was actually working, and I couldn't say I minded the company. It was nice to be chased after for reasons as simple as 'I look up to you.' I'd never had that before. Collin waited until Chastity was in the bathroom before his ramblings launched into a rant about their complicated family history.

"Our families have had beef for like forever," he informed me as he followed me to where the dishes had begun to pile up. I was grateful that

I didn't have to see Richard again—he only worked the night shift—though it meant little sleep between shifts for me. It was a small price to pay. "The Rains and the Princes that is."

"Why?" I asked, my curiosity getting the better of me. In a town as small as Elmwood it felt like major family feuds should be less common. What would they even fight over? Who won the blue ribbon at the fair? Who got the best parking spot at the one and only gas station?

Collin's entire face squashed, his jaw dropping as he suddenly grew shifty as a kid getting caught with his hand in a cookie jar.

"Doesn't matter," Collin moved on quickly, waving me off as he obviously realized too late that he was sharing private information. His round cheeks were bright red as he grabbed each dish I handed him so he could dry it. "Also—my parents are out of town for the next couple weeks and I've decided I'm crashing at Richard's for like—infinity."

"Why?" I asked, brow furrowed. A bad feeling was churning in my gut as I turned to look at Collin again. Except instead of just a glance this time I actually *looked* at him. It was clear to me that he was exhausted, dark circles ringing his eyes, his lips chapped and drawn thin. Despite his sunny disposition, this thing with his family was really wearing on him. It made protective instincts inside me well up with a fire I had no way of quelling.

"I was arguing with my brothers again," he admitted quietly, his usual smile gone, a haunted expression crossing his face. "Without my parents at home, there's no buffer so…"

It's so loud at home and no one is like me—and I just…

His earlier words had rattled around in my skull, siphoning in through the cracks in my anxiety and filling me with a sense of purpose unlike

114

anything I'd ever felt before.

No one is like me, no one is like me, no one is like me.

I didn't want to assume I knew what he was talking about, but why else would he come to me, a complete stranger? It was like people only had to take one look at me and somehow they just *knew* that I was different.

I'd known about my sexuality since I was ten years old, but the first years of personal discovery had been shoved on the back burner in favor of my own self-righteous expedition. With my aunt's words leaking from my lips I'd shoved aside the pieces of myself I didn't deem suitable for public eyes. They'd been the loneliest years of my life.

And siding with her, fighting for her, had never mattered.

I'd still ended up here, the way I was always going to. Bruised, battered, and broken. Her words a companion to whisper self-doubt in my ear when I was alone in the dark.

At least I didn't try to hide behind a facade of straightness anymore, and I certainly never stopped myself from checking out a nice pair of biceps or a gifted pair of thighs. But that didn't mean I didn't know what it felt like to have to hide from the people that were supposed to support you, to love you, to accept you.

It felt like giving a piece of yourself away every time you talked to someone.

"Sorry." Collin waved me off, startling me from my reverie, clearly embarrassed by himself.

"Hey, man." I shook my head. "It's cool. You can talk to me." My heart was in my throat, my palms clammy with sweat. I didn't know how to be the person someone could count on or look up to. But I wanted to find out.

Collin paused. For a really long time.

And then he just kinda wilted, his head sinking down until all I could see was the whorl of hair at the top. A long, broken sigh escaped from his lips and I felt his weariness in my very bones.

"They just don't get it, you know?" he said softly. "They think I'm going to change my mind."

Change his mind?

What the fuck.

What the *actual* fuck. So they *knew*? But they were trying to, what... convert him? Righteous indignation burned inside my chest and a steel I didn't know I possessed melded along my spine as I straightened and looked him dead in the eyes.

"That isn't how that works." I pointed out, my words sure, my expression steady despite the anxiety that still warred inside me.

"I know!" he agreed adamantly, turning towards me with a spray of soap water. "Sorry," he said and then moved on. "They say I'm too young to know—"

"Fuck that."

"Fuck that!" he exclaimed, clearly happy I was agreeing with him.

"I knew by the time I was ten," I told him. That didn't mean that I'd been open about it. Or that I'd accepted it. But I'd known. Because every time other little boys talked about how pretty the girls in class were, I couldn't help but stare at them in an attempt to figure out how they all could be so blind. It had seemed obvious that boys were better.

They liked getting dirty. They liked playing the same games I did. When I was little it had started so simple, something so instinctual inside me I couldn't give it a name. But just as surely as I knew I liked them, I knew it wasn't something I was supposed to feel. To be open about. To accept.

I knew in that moment that I would rather die than let Collin continue feeling just as unsupported as I had for most of my life.

I'd be leaving as soon as I sold my house—if I could ever get around to that—but that didn't mean that I couldn't be here for him now. Maybe when I was gone, thinking back on this would give him strength. Maybe when his heart was dark, his head foggy, he'd remember the unapologetic way I'd lived my life. That it was okay to be him just as he was.

"Right," he agreed, even though he looked a bit confused.

"You're allowed to be whoever you are, just as you are," I told him, maybe not as eloquent as I'd meant to be. "And that's enough."

And that was how we'd ended the conversation. With me ready to fucking fight to the death for the kid, and him staring at me like I was a puzzle he was trying to solve. He looked a lot like his brother, actually. Jeffrey too. Like an even mix between the two of them, orange and gold, kaleidoscope freckles.

Sometimes just looking at him made me so homesick it hurt.

I felt that homesickness even now, hours later, my conversation with Collin nothing but a memory as I stared down at the black screen on my phone and I held an internal battle over what to do next.

I knew I should probably text Jeffrey, at least to let him know I was alright.

Collin talking about his trouble at home had only managed to remind me of my brother—and the way I'd left him stranded without a word. I felt like shit about it, honestly. He deserved better. Maybe he'd been right all along. Maybe I *was* a coward. This should be simple—easy even. It shouldn't make my skin shrivel up, or my breath come in short.

I stared down at my phone, sitting on my bed as I listened to the party rage outside my closed door. I knew Jeffrey's number.

I could text him.

He'd want me to.

He was probably worried.

I chewed on my thumbnail, biting into the flesh until it stung as I debated with myself, trying to figure out what to do. This shouldn't be such a big deal. I could send a simple text. I'd changed my number for this exact reason, so that I could get into contact with him again without fear of my aunt finding out.

I could text him.

So why was it so hard?

Maybe I felt like I hadn't earned it yet.

There came a knock at the door a few minutes later and I startled into action, shoving my phone into my back pocket before I rose to my feet to unlock the door. Hopefully it wasn't a random drunk person looking for the bathroom. I had my limits, and cleaning up a stranger's puke from inside my private bathroom sink crossed about six of them. I flopped back down onto the bed immediately, prepared for disaster, my knees shaking with jittery nerves.

My prayers were answered as the door opened to reveal Vanity in all her six-foot-something glory. The woman was a god. Six-inch heels adorned her dainty feet where she stood gracefully wrapped in a tiny black clubbing dress with shoulder pads reminiscent of the eighties. Despite the fact that Chastity had informed me she'd been drunk since one that afternoon in preparation for the party, she still managed to look elegant and entirely sober. I'd been informed that Vanity called the early drinking 'pre-gaming.' But everyone knew it was really just an excuse to day drink.

I relaxed a little, watching Vanity warily as she slipped into my room, her hip cocked. She inspected the place, hands on her hips before she turned her attention back to me after what felt like a century. She'd stared just a little too long at Bartholomew, one of my succulents that I was pretty sure was hanging onto his last limb of life. I wanted to jump up to protect his dignity from scrutiny but forced myself to hold still. I already looked like a freak to these people—the last thing I needed was to give them another reason to stare at me.

Not that Vanity stared. After that first encounter she'd actually been really…nice to me. It was a bit unsettling, though that wasn't her fault. Sometimes when she moved too quickly all I saw was a blur of my aunt in my peripheral vision. I'd flinch back, but thankfully she hadn't noticed yet. I didn't want her to. It wasn't her fault I was…odd.

"You look like shit," Vanity commented, and I relaxed. Sinking into the insults felt like coming home. It was banter that was so reminiscent of my relationship with Jeffrey, something that had ached in my chest since leaving without a word settled.

"Thanks," I replied dryly and she grinned. The ice that had been between us since my move in melted away and I realized for the first time that Vanity was not just gorgeous, but pretty too. Like a sunflower, or a field of wheat. She beckoned me closer.

"C'mon. Wallflower time is over. You need to do something fun." I take it back. She was a heinous, heinous creature.

"No." I shrugged helplessly. "I'm not a party person." Vanity opened her mouth to respond but a voice in the hallway interrupted before she could.

"Just means you haven't been to the right party!" Chastity was apparently right behind Vanity because her voice echoed loud enough to be heard over the music and if I squinted I could see the tips of her space buns in the gap in the door. Her hair was aqua today.

I laughed. Because they were both ridiculous. Vanity was still grinning, and I couldn't help but smile back as she reached for my arm and pulled me to my feet. "C'mon loser," she hummed, and I tried not to shudder when her nails dug into the sensitive skin on the inside of my wrist.

Act normal.

Don't be such a freak, I reminded myself as she tugged me out into the hallway and Chastity cheered.

I hadn't been to a party in ages. The last and only one I'd ever been to, my entire shirt was doused in a cocktail of misery and cheap beer. I'd been young and stupid then, dressed in high collars and armed with a cross and a misplaced moral high ground.

I'd looked down on the other teenagers, scoffed at their wet tongues, rolled my eyes at the way they gyrated, shifting like serpents trying to become one. The air smelled of sweat and desperation and I'd thought I was too good for their company, even though like the rest of them I was too blind to notice the way my eyes caught on the sway of the other boys' hips.

I wasn't that boy anymore though.

Maybe the new Blair would love parties?

"Yay!!! And the hermit emerges." Chastity latched onto my other side and the sisters corralled me through the party raging in the living room and into the mostly empty kitchen. I could hear the echo of music and smell the scent of sweat and booze in the air. Chastity poured my first drink and I sipped at it tentatively, grimacing at the flavor.

Ew.

I'd never really drank before. The most I'd ever done was steal a sip of Jeffrey's beer when we'd been sandwiched in the bed of his new pickup truck a month before I'd left. Showing up inebriated to our apartment was just asking for trouble when my aunt was only a ten-minute drive away. Even golden boy Jeffrey kept his drinking to parties and outdoor escapades. There was never evidence of our 'sins' for the cameras to pick up.

When we'd lived at the main house, the surveillance had been even worse.

So, yeah. I'd never partied.

I winced as I swallowed my first sip of whatever concoction had been shoved into my hands. It wasn't so bad—though the taste wasn't necessarily what I'd call pleasant. It made my tongue feel thick, and my brain buzz-y.

Chastity abandoned me when Ty, the cook from work, showed up, and Vanity disappeared not long after. It didn't take long for the alcohol to begin to get into my system. It hit almost hard enough I could ignore the eyes that followed me as I wandered my way into the throng of bodies that occupied the living room. My skin crawled from the attention, the heavy bass throbbing in the back of my skull as I found a spot against the far wall next to Prudence's portrait and stopped to people watch.

I glanced back at Prudence's portrait after a few minutes, curious.

Pale blue eyes glared at me from the canvas and I shuddered, looking away from the cold twist of his lips. He was attractive, in a cruel sort of way. Power exuded from the pull of his muscular chest, his arms folded tight, the beginnings of a tattoo hidden beneath the cuff of a long white button-down. Somehow I doubted he'd be caught dead in an outfit that formal any other time. He didn't seem like the type. It was clear he hadn't gotten Vanity's height, though staring at the swell of muscles in his biceps, I figured he'd been blessed in other ways.

Lucky bastard.

It was a shame that he'd died so young. Death always was. Looking at the photo, I couldn't help but feel like I was intruding as he stared out over the crowd, judging this small town with a twist to his thin lips, his dark brow furrowed. Maybe he was watching over his sisters from beyond the grave. Maybe—I blinked at him, frowning.

He still looked familiar—but the alcohol began to turn my blood to syrup and I looked away, trying not to think about the fact that Prudence must've died not long after the photograph had been taken.

I stared out at the crowd, ignoring the creepy-crawling sensation of eyes on me.

People ground against each other to the throbbing echo of a singer I recognized but couldn't put a name to. There were so many people in the group that for the most part the party itself was just a blur of bodies. The scent of sweat trailed through the air, weirdly comforting in its humanity. A guy fucking *howled* and I had to hide my laugh behind my red solo cup.

Maybe I fit in here better than I'd thought.

Elmwood was full of a whole bunch of weirdos—

Hairy people who sniffed their food before eating it, people who ordered food but didn't eat it at all, people who licked blood off their plates and had apparently never learned how to properly use forks. I giggled a little, shaking away the memories of my first few shifts at the diner as I felt my fingers grow sweaty and fat with blood flow.

Had they always felt this big? This…clumsy?

The room was just a little swimmy around the edges a few minutes later and I blinked it into focus, staring down into my empty cup before squinting to figure out where Vanity and Chastity had gone. When I finally spotted one of them I relaxed. Vanity was manning what looked like a makeshift bar in the back of the room. She was just as poised as ever and had a long line of suitors waiting for refills that she was ignoring.

I liked that about her though. She had a no-nonsense kind of personality and it was refreshing. I never had to guess at what she was thinking. She was honest to the core.

After I watched six guys slip over the same abandoned leather jacket on the floor, and realized by Vanity's laughter that she'd placed it there, I officially decided parties were not as bad as I'd originally thought.

In fact, they were kinda fun.

Maybe it was just my empty cup talking, but watching people hit on each other while drunk was endlessly amusing.

No one hit on me. Which was fine. I didn't want to be hit on. Even though the weird looks still stung. Was I really that hard to look at?

Yes. Obviously.

I still had two black eyes and I'd come rolling into town with two metaphorical middle fingers up and a chip on my shoulder. It's not like there was an option in town to pick a Blair model out of a line-up at Goth-Boys-R-Us. Fuck. Even if there *was*, I wouldn't even pick me.

So...why did it hurt?

Feelings fucking suck.

Everyone in the crowd was too busy being freaked out every time they caught me looking in their direction to think about anything like 'let's have sex.'

It was unsettling. But also the part of me that still craved reciprocation, connection, *affection*—wasn't ready to give up on the idea of having sex for the first time with someone I actually liked. I didn't count all the fumbled blow jobs in the dark with strangers. It didn't feel like sex when I left untouched, feeling emptier than I had before I'd sought connection in the first place.

I'd noticed another goth-looking guy on the other side of the room and no one was giving him weird looks. He flipped me off and grinned, just a little meanly, so I flipped him off back. My original thought that it had something to do with my eyeliner, or painted nails, or vampire themed party shorts was immediately thrown out the window. Nope. He turned from me and snagged the guy next to him into a match of tonsil hockey.

Apparently the honor of being stared at was reserved for me, and me only.

Yay.

I tried to ignore the way my skin crawled as I wandered my way to Vanity's makeshift bar. The lonely ache in my chest dissipated somewhat as I grinned at her in greeting and she offered me an awkward half wave. "Ready to top off?" she hummed, reaching for my empty cup. I nodded and handed it over, noting the fact I'd forgotten to paint my nails again.

"Do the neighbors not complain?" I asked, my words falling flat in the space between us. She arched an eyebrow at me, clearly deciding whether or not I was worthy of response.

"We own the apartments both below and above."

"Oh."

I watched her perfectly manicured nails flicker in the light as she reached for several colorful hangovers in a bottle, and the flashing lights rigged to the ceiling with duct tape and determination caught the slash of her cheekbones.

There was the glimmer of sweat across her brow and a tremble to her lip that I wondered about. Maybe it had something to do with why she'd thrown two parties in one week. Bad break up? Despite this, she looked beautiful as always. Perfectly put together, her hair done in an artful Hollywood wave—the blend of blonde to red immaculate. I wondered how much she paid her hairdresser to get it just right.

It had to be a lot.

"Oh hey," Vanity said after a moment, a weird twist to her expression as she glanced around behind me for a moment. "Look! Richard's here."

Oh.

Oh fuck.

Immediately my pulse began to race.

My head whipped around as the memory from the last time I'd seen him flitted to the forefront of my mind. He'd been wearing a confused puppy dog face as I'd blown him off at the end of our shift and hurried away from the diner. Richard had clearly been confused, even though he was the confusing one.

At least he's hot, my traitorous mind supplied. *Also homophobic. Don't forget that part. And your boss, kind of.*

God, my brain was an asshole.

"Shit," I swore, turning back to Vanity in alarm. She'd finished filling up my drink, her expression pensive as she handed it over. "Do I look okay?" I wasn't sure why that had been my first concern. But hey— apparently drunk Blair was also horny self-conscious Blair.

She cocked her head to the side curiously, inspecting me. "Passable.

Better now that you're not sober."

"Good." I sighed, relaxing a little and trying not to look too obviously drunk as I took a fortifying sip of my now full cup and then set it down on the table. She snatched it off the edge so it wouldn't spill and I smiled gratefully, smoothing my hand over my long sheer button-down covered in little black bats. I didn't want to talk to Richard, but I couldn't help but make sure if on the off chance he *did* see me, that I didn't look like a snotty, red-faced, bat-covered gremlin.

I had about a minute to escape to my bedroom before Richard discovered I was available for ogling again.

Now or never.

I spotted Richard's blond head first. It was tricky seeing around everyone when I typically was one of the shorter people in the room but Richard was easy to spot. He had a presence unlike anyone I'd ever met before. And I needed to get the fuck out of here before he noticed me. If he caught me off guard like this I was bound to do something stupid. Like yell at him—or ask politely to sit on his dick, which would lead to some rather awkward shifts at the diner.

I don't know why I cared so much, but *man*. The guy did things to my insides I didn't want to admit even to myself. He was…*something*. That was for sure.

I edged along the crowd, my head spinning a little as I made my way towards the hallway. If I could just get close enough then I could slip unnoticed into my room and lock the door.

It should be simple.

It *was* simple.

So why was it taking me so long?

I hugged the wall, fumbling against the dips and grooves in the plaster, my head spinning as I tried to cross the distance more quickly. That only managed to make me even slower somehow. Something was…something was weird.

Weird.

The alcohol maybe? My head was spinning more than before, my lips tingly and a little numb as I watched bodies press against each other, and each blink only made the room foggier. And then the euphoria hit.

It zinged up my spine, a sense of excitement flickering in my chest though the sluggish movement of my body didn't seem to get the memo.

Why was I stressed out again? Where was I even going? I stopped. Blinking out at the blur of bodies with my lashes fluttering. God. I felt…I felt *good*.

This was good. This was all good. The people—the atmosphere—the fact that for the first time in my life I had *actual* friends to hang out with. *Man*. And my body—*wow*.

Just, wow.

I could feel my heartbeat in my fingertips and it was fascinating.

Was this what being drunk was like? I stared down at my hands, trying to figure out if they looked different now that I was inebriated. *No wonder people liked it.*

It was a good thing I hadn't finished the full drink that Vanity had poured for me or there would've been no way I could escape into my room without being noticed. If *this* was how affected I was by a cup and a sip of alcohol then I didn't want to know what happened when I drank as much as Chastity was clearly capable of.

I started moving again, a feeling of paranoia slipping over me as I realized that people could see me like this, unguarded, vulnerable. I didn't like the idea of being touched right now—of being ogled—not that I wasn't *already* being ogled.

What had started as a need to get away from embarrassing myself in front of Richard turned into a desperate need for privacy. I had to get away from the crowd. I could feel the walls closing in on me—

My head was spinning, my knees weak, as I slid along the wall towards the hallway again. Two steps? Ten steps? God, I couldn't tell how close I was anymore. I couldn't feel my toes and it was freaking me out. My heartbeat was too loud. My breathing too. I held my breath, convinced everyone could hear it.

What was happening?

Fuck.

Just as I'd almost reached the entrance to the hallway a voice called my name. It was hard to hear over the echo of laughter and the thump of music but I heard him anyway. *Richard.* I lifted up my head, my breath whooshing in again. *There was no way he'd found me so soon, right?*

Wrong.

Motherfucker.

I could see the top of his blond head approaching and I hurried into the hallway to escape. Though my mad dash was really more of an awkward flop than anything else; I seemed incapable of using my limbs. I didn't want him to see me like this. My earlier euphoria was quickly fading as I realized what little control I had over my body. Like I was the operator behind one of the crane machines and my body's physical functions were the toys.

Move faster, fucker. C'mon, C'mon, I urged my legs, glaring down at my knobby knees where they peeked out of the hem of my red shorts.

They didn't move quickly enough, *assholes*—and Richard finally reached me. I could sense his presence before I saw him. The scent of pine and cocoa filled my nose and I held very, very still, facing the end of the hallway as I felt him reach tentatively to brush a hand along the swell of my shoulder to get my attention. If you asked me how I knew it was him I would have no way of answering. I just…did. I had no choice but to turn to face him, grimacing immediately when I looked up and realized just how stupidly handsome he still was.

God played favorites, and Richard was clearly loved.

His nostrils flared and I tracked the movement, licking my lips to wet them as they'd suddenly gotten very, very dry. Richard looked like sex on legs. He was dressed as I was coming to realize he always was. The same variation of black jeans, dark flannel, and leather jacket. I glanced down to see if he'd taken his shoes off, and nope. Designer boots were tied in perfect symmetry on his frankly massive feet.

It must be genetic, because it was clear that Collin had the same affliction. Big feet. Big hands. Big everything else.

Oh fuck. I really shouldn't be thinking about Richard and his 'everything else's' right now. Serious time. *C'mon, Blair.*

I didn't like alcohol. I changed my mind.

Weren't beer goggles supposed to make people *less* attractive? Or was it the opposite? Fuck. I couldn't remember.

"Hey," Richard said, brow furrowed in concern, his lips thinned in a way that made me want to bite them. "You look a little—"

"Drunk?" I supplied, arching my eyebrows sardonically at him. He blinked, and then cocked his head, inspecting me carefully like he was trying to figure out if I was telling a lie or not. What the fuck. Why would I lie about being drunk? Wasn't that clear by how much I was struggling to stand upright?

And besides, shouldn't it be the other way around? Shouldn't I be convincing him I *wasn't* drunk? That's what people did in movies. Like being a lightweight was a bad thing. Which…I could relate to now.

I felt vulnerable, laid bare before him, my walls unable to rise as I struggled to remain standing. I reached for him without meaning to, my fingers bunching up in the fabric of his shirt to steady myself. It was soft, almost velveteen. I clung to him as I breathed out a shaky sound that might have been a whine because *holy fuck* he was ripped. I could feel his abs tensing beneath my touch, even through the fabric, and I was suddenly struck with the naughty urge to slip my hand under the hem of his shirt and lay my palm flat against them so I could *really* feel them tremble.

I bet they tensed like that when he was fucking. *Oh god.*

And then Richard did something that made my toes curl and my head spin.

He leaned in, all six-foot-four of him, the scent of pine and cocoa overwhelming my senses. My heart was throbbing in my chest, a nervous prickle of sweat at my brow as my cock twitched and I felt his nose bump up against my ear. *Was he going to kiss me? Oh fuck. Yes. Yes please. Holy shit.* His nose brushed along the sensitive skin and I trembled, waiting in anticipation as he shuffled closer and—*sniffed me?*

He fucking *sniffed* me.

"Did you just smell me?" I asked incredulously as he pulled back, a thoughtful expression on his face.

"You're inebriated," he decided, even though I'd *literally* just told him that.

"Ugh. Fuck off," I huffed unhappily, shoving at his chest even though it didn't fucking budge no matter how hard I pushed at it. *Why was that so hot?* That shouldn't be so hot?

My fingers traced over the soft fabric for a second time and I wanted to groan, pushing up against his torso so I could feel his abs jump again. Every time I did it he fucking twitched. Oh fuck. Why was he so—

So—

Ugh.

"Let me get you to bed," Richard offered, sweet as sugar even though I knew underneath that facade was a hateful, horrible bastard.

"No, thank you." I was almost fooled by him. Almost.

"Blair." The way he said my name made my cock twitch with want. It was exasperation and care. It said, 'listen to me,' it said, 'let me help you,' it said, 'I'm here.'

I probably would've said no again if that single sweet uttering of my name hadn't made me too weak in the knees to walk. "Okay," I agreed softly, my gaze dropping to where my hands were still bunched up in his shirt. The fabric was a dark ruby red today, though it was the same cut and style as the one I'd seen him in the day before.

"Good boy," Richard hummed, his voice almost playful. His words however shocked my system. I was frozen. Paralyzed by how casually he'd manage to hit all my buttons at once. When it was clear I wasn't going to move he gently reached down to untangle my hands from his shirt and I was embarrassed by the whine that left me the moment he was free.

I wanted him *back.*

"I got you." Richard didn't go far, he just reached for me, casual as all fuck as he wrapped his thick arms around my torso and hefted me up with an effortless swing into his arms. He arranged my legs around his waist like I was a rag doll and I was too shocked to do anything other than squeak as we made our way down the hallway to my bedroom.

I probably should've asked how he knew which one was mine, but I didn't. I was far too distracted by the fact that his abs were now directly in line with my dick. Maybe if I hadn't been so drunk I wouldn't have embarrassed myself so much, but every time he shifted, a bolt of pleasure burned down my spine and I couldn't help the way I pressed toward the friction every fucking time.

It just…felt so *good* to be touched.

By the time Richard gently laid me on my mattress, I was mortified.

"You good?" he asked softly, sitting on the edge of my bed as I stared up at him, embarrassed and turned on and far too drunk to deal with any of this.

It felt like I'd been drugged.

"I'm good," I said softly, surprised by the truth in my words. He was watching me, his gaze steady and heated. His eyes…god. They looked red in this light, glowing softly as I counted the freckles faded nearly to nothing across the bridge of his nose. "Why are you helping me?" I asked, surprised when I realized that I'd reached for his wrist without meaning to. My fingers wrapped around it and he stared down at them, his brows lowered in concentration.

He was quiet for a long time. Or what felt like a long time anyway.

"Because you deserve to be helped," he finally told me. He weighed every word before he spoke it. So at odds with me and my garbage-disposal-mouth that it was almost jarring. I liked it though. Richard seemed to do everything carefully. Even though I'd known him for such a short period, that had already become apparent.

He was confusing.

And just a bit wonderful.

And I was completely totally fucked, and *not* in the fun way.

When I glanced around, everything in the room was wobbly and it was both hilarious and a little terrifying. I was lucky Richard had been there to help me to bed because I was starting to realize just how dangerous this could've gotten on my own.

My bed at least was a comfort beneath me. It didn't smell like me yet, but it did have cat hair on it, and that made me more than a little glad.

God.

Richard was so fucking cute. All perplexed like that. *I should tell him.*

No. Just no. Don't go there.

It was better this way.

He was too cute, and I was too...I was too *me.*

It was a bad idea.

I fell asleep soon enough, my face smooshed to the pillows until Richard forced me up onto my side. He tucked me in, stoic as ever, and I inhaled his scent from the fragile skin at the inside of his wrist as he pulled the blankets around my chest. The last thought I had as the world spun into darkness was the fact that I was never fucking drinking, ever again.

Fuck parties.

And Fuck Richard. *Yes please.*

God, my subconscious was a dick. As I slept, every so often my lashes would flutter just enough that I could check the room for threats. What I found instead was a figure that looked suspiciously like Richard sitting vigil at my bedside with a paper on his knee and a pen in his hand. At one point he disappeared and I heard angry voices in the hallway, but he was back quickly enough, writing away—and I dozed off again to the sound of him muttering, "Lust! Ha."

And if the next day I wondered if I'd made the entire thing up, that was my own business.

Chapter Twelve

Blair

I WOKE UP with the worst hangover in the history of hangovers. Or what I presumed to be, considering the fact I'd never had one before. My head was pounding, my mouth uncomfortably dry as I stumbled into the bathroom and forced myself to shower and brush my teeth. I guzzled water straight from the tap, letting it slip down my chest, cold and refreshing. The light above was overwhelming and frankly rude as fuck, so I squeezed my eyes shut until I'd managed to adjust enough I didn't feel like I was going to keel over and die with a loofah in my hand and soap on my ass.

Richard was gone.

I wasn't even really sure he'd been there in the first place.

The previous night was nothing but a blur of color in my mind and I grimaced, rubbing at my temples to dissuade the migraine that threatened like a storm on the horizon from settling behind my eyes.

When I was clean I stumbled damp but apple-fresh into the living room and stared at the mess from the party the night before with a detached sort of apathy.

Right.

Cleaning.

My job.

It was slow going, but I managed it, fumbling all the empty cups and bottles into plastic bags as my stomach growled at me and my eyes refused to fully open. They were half stuck shut with my bad decisions. I was pretty sure at one point a woodland creature must've crawled into my mouth and made a home behind my molars, my breath was that rank. And that was after brushing my teeth. *Twice.*

Fuck my life.

I tried to be quiet but despite my efforts after wrestling the couch back into place with a lot of extra swearing and maybe a few well placed, well-meaning kicks—Chastity woke up.

She looked about as horrible as I felt. Though somehow she managed to still look both cuddly and adorable in her exhaustion, her makeup smudged all over her face, her space buns uneven and skewed, the blue hair chalk rubbed mostly down the back of her neck and not on her hair anymore. There was a pillow crease on her cheek and I couldn't help but stare at where it peeked out from beneath her sunglasses as she flopped down onto the couch close enough she could reach where I was still cleaning. Her toes dug into the meat of my bare thigh. I forced myself to remain still, as I was still getting used to Chastity's particular brand of casual touch. She plucked at the hem of my shorts, pinching one of the half-cutoff werewolves with her toes and tugging at him till his little animated face stretched out and I frowned down at her in confusion.

"Motherfucker." Her voice startled me as she flopped back down, splayed out in her matching fleece pajama set like an adorable panda-covered starfish.

"My sentiments exactly." I actually felt a little better watching her struggle. Maybe that made me a bad person? But it made the hangover seem not quite as bad. At least I was functioning enough to dress myself. Small mercies and all that.

"When did Richard leave?" Chastity asked me curiously, shoving her sunglasses up to stare at me blearily. Her dark eyes were ringed with smudged makeup, and a feeling of affection welled up inside me so strong I was floored by it for just a moment.

And then her words hit me.

I stopped moving, empty beer can pausing halfway to the trash bag in my grip as my brain short-circuited.

"What?" My voice was choked, my body stiff as I stared at her.

"Richard?" She blinked, cocking her head. "You don't remember?"

"No."

"Oh." She laughed, clearly coming back to life as she perked right up. "He was here like all night watching over you."

"Why?" There were so many feelings welling up inside me I didn't know what to do with them. Confusion. Anger. Gratitude.

"You got shit-faced, buddy," Chastity told me with a sympathetic frown. "He was worried you were gonna choke on your own vomit." Wow. What a horrible picture.

New fear unlocked.

"He…he stayed the whole night?"

"Oh definitely. Not sure when he ended up leaving, but it was sometime after I went to bed. So, late since I was up with Vanity till like…five?" She pursed her lips in thought. "No. *Four*," she corrected herself. "Four." She nodded, clearly feeling very confident with this answer.

Four in the fucking morning.

Richard had sat beside my bed and made sure I didn't… That I didn't… Fuck. *Fuck.*

Maybe Richard wasn't as bad of a guy as I'd thought he was?

No. One charitable thing didn't change the fact that he made his little brother feel alienated, unsupported, unloved enough to vent to a stranger about it. Chastity continued to talk and my gaze snapped back to her as I shoved the can I'd been holding deep into the plastic bag. I launched into action, anxious energy buzzing just under my skin like I was an electric fence just ready to zap.

"He was all concerned someone had drugged you." Chastity laughed. "But I told him the only people that had touched your drinks were me and Vanity, so." She shrugged. "Was this like…?"

"My first time drinking alcohol?" I said awkwardly, cheeks red. I turned back to my task, shoving the can I had in my hand into the trash bag as Chastity nodded. "Yeah." I swallowed, mortified. "It was."

"Oh." She blinked. "Shit. Probably shouldn't have left you alone then."

My skin prickled with heat and I shoved another can into the bag, clearing off the side table with an agitated flourish. "I'm not a little kid."

"I know, sweetie." Chastity was quick to soothe, and I hated it. I hated that it worked. I hated that I needed it. I hated that no one had been this gentle with me before. It fucking sucked. All of it. "But we're friends. And I care about you. I would've wanted to be with you more if I'd known."

Oh.

Well.

That was nice then.

Chastity climbed off the couch and squeezed my shoulder on her way past me. I flinched a little but she didn't comment, probably sensing that I was brittle as burnt sugar, liable to crack if she pushed. "I'll help you clean," she said instead, and I moved to protest but she just glared at me until I conceded and she returned with a trash bag of her own.

It was silly, but it was nice to not be alone for once.

After nearly an hour of trash collecting, Chastity broke the silence between us. "So, what's your next step?" she asked, eyeing me as we waddled our way to the front door to deposit the trash bags in a pile for later.

"What do you mean?" I asked, even though I knew exactly what she meant. I just needed a moment to figure out how to reply. I wasn't sure why it was so hard for me to open up, to talk to someone else. Maybe it was because I'd spent so much time just me against the world it seemed… unthinkable that I could have a friend that was genuinely interested in helping me, in asking how I was doing, what I was doing.

I kept expecting manipulation. Betrayal.

Old habits die hard.

"You have a job now. Somewhere to stay," Chastity hedged, obviously struggling to figure out how to explain. I felt bad for being the one to make her struggle, so I piped up, cheeks pink. She'd been nothing but nice to me, it wasn't fair of me to treat her like she was anything like my aunt. Chastity didn't have a manipulative bone in her body.

"I'm going to figure out how to sell my house," I told her honestly, surprised by how easily the words left my lips despite it feeling like I was pulling teeth. "I need quick cash."

"Why?"

Shit.

Why hadn't I anticipated that question?

I swallowed the tightness in my throat. I wanted to tell her, I really did, but then I'd have to explain everything. *Why* I wanted to run. *Why* I wanted to take Jeffrey with me. *What* I was running from. And I just… couldn't. I couldn't even admit it to myself. Maybe that made me a coward, but at least I was working on changing that. Baby steps, and all that. Maybe one day I'd be able to openly talk about my past, but today was not that day.

You're a coward, Blair. Jeffrey's voice echoed in my head and I swallowed bile. *It's fine. This was fine. This was all fine.* Chastity was staring at me and I wanted to disappear, become one with the beige carpet and slip into nothingness so I wouldn't have to feel the ache of my heart anymore, or the way my chest squeezed too tight to breathe.

You're acting like a fucking weirdo. Answer her question.

"Just need it. That's all," I said softly, embarrassed by myself for what felt like the hundredth time.

"Well," Chastity hedged, a soft expression on her face as she studied me. I watched her purse her lips, head cocking to the side as she latched onto my arm and tugged me towards the kitchen. "My aunt is the only real estate agent in town. She could probably help you out if that's what you're really wanting to do. Have you got into contact with the insurance agency that's in charge of your house?"

"I don't…know how to do that," I admitted.

"If you don't mind my asking…" Chastity eyed me warily as she pulled a bag of frozen fries out of the freezer and began piling them onto a baking tray. It hadn't escaped my notice that the entire freezer was now full of frozen fries. "Why would you sell it? Why not stay here? You could probably get it fixed up pretty easily." She chewed on her lip, clearly debating what to say. "Isn't it the last thing you have from your parents?"

My heart throbbed.

I was silent for long enough that the oven finished preheating during the time I tried to figure out what to say.

"It is," I said softly after I gathered the strength to speak. "But they're gone now. I loved them but…" I shook my head. "I have to think about my future. And I can't…"

"Keep living in the past," she filled in for me, even though what I was really going to say was 'be caught.'

I couldn't be caught by *her*. Not again. My time in the spider's web was over. I never wanted to see *her* face again. I never wanted to hear *her* voice. I never wanted to think *her* name. I never wanted to feel the bite of *her* fingernails or listen to the sound *her* heels made when *she* clacked towards me. I wanted *her* to fade into my memories like a nightmare that I had woken up from. Maybe that made me a coward. But—

You're a coward, Blair.

I couldn't do it.

You're a coward.

I just couldn't.

You're a coward.

Not again.

"You've reached Sandra Murphy, I'm not available right now so please leave a detailed message after the beep with your name and number and I'll get back to you shortly." A soft voice echoed through the empty room from my phone's tinny speakers and I grimaced, a sudden wave of panic hitting me as I was forced to make a split second decision over whether or not I was going to leave a message.

I decided not to.

I regretted it the moment my finger hit the end call button.

I called again. Rinse and repeat. Except this time after the beep sounded I froze, the words drying up in my mouth as I hastily jabbed the end button once more the moment I realized with sickening clarity that I had no idea what I was going to say.

Desperate. Crazy. Irresponsible.

Fuck. Fuckfuckfuckfuckfuck.

I wished fiercely for a moment that there was someone there that could tell me what to do. But there wasn't. I was unfortunately the only adult here. So I just called Sandra again, my fingernails whittled down to stubs as I waited for her message to repeat and I inhaled raggedly in preparation for my response.

"Hi. Sorry. Um." Jesus fuck. *Get it together.* "This is Blair Evans? I'm Amanda and Victor Evans's kid. I don't know what I'm doing but I seem to have like…inherited their house? And I guess I just have some questions. So…*yeah.*" *So yeah*? Fuck. I sounded like a thirteen-year-old who had stolen my mother's phone to order pizza.

I left my phone number, fumbling through the numbers in a panicked jumble as shame enveloped me and I stared at the closed door of my bedroom and willed the voices in my head to shut up. Even with the window open it was uncomfortably warm in the room.

It was an annoying time of year apparently, like spring had an unreliable twin. Some times of day were almost achingly hot while others made my balls feel like they were about to shrivel up inside my body and hibernate.

I waited.

And waited.

Boots mewed to my left and I was pulled out of my reverie as I reached down to scratch his little head. After a week of being fed and pampered he'd really filled out. He wasn't the mangy little thing I'd found stuck beneath the porch. Instead his coat was glossy, the little white spot on his forehead that looked almost like a cross flickering as he stretched out his long back and stared at me.

We both knew I'd been putting off this phone call.

"Look. I know I look crazy, okay?" I told him softly, his fur tickling the pads of my fingers as I sighed. I forced myself to put my phone down, patting my lap until Boots launched himself into it and began rubbing up and along my belly and sides. "But I don't know how to do any of this shit."

Talking out loud helped, even though it also made me feel even weirder at the same time. I was talking to a cat for god's sake. Except Boots wasn't a cat. He was a friend.

This was proven when he made a cute little *harrumph* sort of noise and plopped his ass right down on my phone so I wouldn't have to look at it anymore while I waited.

A really solid guy, that one.

"Thanks, man." I flopped down, relaxing a little now that I couldn't see it anymore. This was fine. She'd call back. I'd sell the house. I'd talk to whatever insurance dude Chastity said I had to talk to, collect my check and get the fuck outta Dodge before anyone was the wiser.

Easy peasy.

Chapter Thirteen

Blair

NOT EASY PEASY.

Not fucking easy peasy. Not one bit.

I managed to schedule a meeting with Sandra before my next night shift despite having a panic attack over not having enough time to mentally prepare or Google the questions I should be asking. I really only had an hour to get ready and get rid of the worst of my hangover before heading to the office for my appointment. I had nothing nice to wear so I settled for something as plain as I could manage.

Back home, my closet had been full of clothes my aunt had deemed appropriate. I hadn't taken any with me when I'd left. I had enough ghosts in the back of my mind, the last thing I wanted was a physical reminder of the person she had wanted me to be.

When I stepped out of my room and Chastity saw me, she laughed.

And then she corralled me into her bedroom in all its rainbow clutter and forced me to borrow something both generic and hideous from her closet that she claimed her mother had gotten for her for her birthday that year.

If that didn't say everything about their relationship, I didn't know what would.

In what universe would Chastity ever be caught dead in something so…plain and…disgustingly sensible?

I suppose I shouldn't be surprised though, not after I'd discovered earlier that day that Chastity's mom had been the one to decorate their apartment. She sure was a fan of anything beige, depressing, and vaguely religious.

The shirt was a button-up in a cream sort of color, and I wasn't sure if I should be concerned that it fit me like a glove or relieved. Either way, it was uncomfortable, and despite being made out of fabric that probably cost a small fortune, I still couldn't help the way I was sweating up a storm and plucking at the starched collar as I waited inside Sandra's waiting room.

My ass was positioned on a black velvet couch that made entirely too much noise whenever I moved. I hoped I didn't leave a butt print when I stood up. I bit at my thumb nail, nibbling at it nervously as I inspected the office around me, too distracted to notice the blood, or the fact that I was bound to get nail polish in my teeth.

I felt like an impostor sitting there pretending like I was an adult and I knew what the fuck I was doing when clearly I was just a joke wrapped in his roommate's silken throwaways. I still hadn't figured out the name of the business. It hadn't been displayed out front and since I'd gotten the number from Chastity I had little hope of discovering it that way. Though after a quick glance around I figured I could probably peek at the business cards proudly on display at the front desk to figure it out.

The whole room was decorated in white and black, the stark contrast managing somehow to be both minimalist and inviting. There were several hanging plants in the corners and armchairs that mirrored the long black velvet chaise that I was perched atop. The only other piece of furniture in the room was a tall wooden desk covered in black and white sketches of what I assumed must be houses Sandra had sold. It was tasteful and artistic—and just looking at it made me clench my jaw so hard my teeth began to ache.

Someone like me didn't belong here. The whole place was too…nice.

I felt six years old, chewing at my fingers till copper burst on my tongue and I was forced to stop for fear of accidentally staining my borrowed shirt.

A tall woman sat in a high-backed chair behind the desk, her long fingers click-clacking on the keyboard as she finished typing something on her computer before glancing across the room to look at me. The desk's surface glistened like it had been freshly stained. I stared at my reflection in the glossy wood, trying to decide whether or not I should push my hair behind my ears. It tended to make me look younger, but I was worried the rats' nest currently residing at the top of my head, despite being clean, didn't scream 'sell my house, please and thank you.'

The receptionist didn't acknowledge me as she smacked her gum and enjoyed the use of her AirPods. I fidgeted, and then stopped, self-conscious of my fidgeting. The fact she was ignoring me was almost soothing. I probably could've calmed the racing of my heart if there hadn't been windows behind me. Everyone and their dog that passed by on Main Street had a clear shot to ogle.

And they did.

Ogle, I mean.

Like I was a groundhog in spring and I'd emerged from my hidey-hole for the first time since winter.

It was still strange to me how empty Elmwood was before sundown. Day shifts were barren of customers aside from the random hairy-man or Collin and his gaggle of awkward teenage buddies. He was usually alone when he visited though, opting to work rather than sit in the back and abuse the old-school jukeboxes that sat in some of the booths.

During night shifts, Benji's looked like an entirely different restaurant—full of laughter, life, and increasingly weird food orders. There was always a rush after midnight till nearly two in the morning. Everyone seemed to pop out of the woodwork the moment the sun dipped low on the horizon, parents and kids alike. And every business I'd stumbled upon in town seemed to stay open either twenty-four hours or until the ungodly hour of three in the morning.

The town I'd lived in growing up hadn't been large by any means, but it had certainly been larger than Elmwood. And even back home everything closed by nine most weeknights. I added the fact that Elmwood's only gas station practically had a rave after midnight every day to the list of peculiarities I was noticing about my temporary home.

I caught a little kid staring at me through the window ten minutes into my wait and I waved, not sure what else to do. It wasn't like I could flip off a little kid, even though I kinda wanted to. His eyes bugged out of his head and his jaw dropped, his hair twitching in a weird way that looked…almost like *dog ears*? I shook my head to clear it, sure that I was making things up. It was just the hangover talking. I scrubbed at my eyes and when I looked again the ears were gone. Weird. Weird, weird, weird.

Maybe I was still drunk?

Fuck alcohol. Seriously.

I figured I must've imagined it.

He just had spiky hair.

That was all. Spiky hair. Yep. No dog ears here. Because that would be absolutely bizarre and impossible of course.

Fuck you, Blair. You need to get your eyes checked.

The kid was still staring though, and I couldn't help the way I fidgeted uncomfortably beneath the weight of his gaze. Eventually someone I could only assume was his father grabbed onto him and steered him away down the sunny street. Even from behind he was a big man—burly, hairy, intimidating. And when he looked back at me and bared his teeth over his shoulder, I almost pissed myself.

Holy shit.

Wasn't my fault the kid had never seen a gothy teen before. Except I wasn't a teen. And wasn't particularly goth right now considering the fact I was wearing a silk blouse and my only pair of blue jeans.

"Mr. Evans?" a voice called and I turned away from the street. "I'm ready to see you now."

Oh goody.

Sandra's office looked pretty much the same as the reception area. It was clear who had decorated—or hired someone to decorate—both. The only difference was the fact that the entire back wall was made of glass, the forest cascading in evergreen glory behind a severe looking woman sitting at her desk watching me with hooded dark eyes.

"Mr. Evans," Sandra said, her voice cool, expression unreadable. She looked more like Vanity than Chastity did, but the light that flickered in both sisters' eyes was missing in hers as Sandra eyed me up and down, her gaze snapping to my borrowed shirt like she somehow immediately knew it wasn't mine. I swallowed.

"Ah. Yes. That's me."

"Take a seat."

I sat.

Now that I was looking more closely I could see that there were crow's feet around the corners of Sandra's eyes. They made her look less severe than I'd originally thought, the hint of years of smiling evident despite the cold way she continued to look at me. I felt small. Smaller than I normally did, carefully keeping my expression neutral as I squirmed on the black velvet armchair.

Because I had no forethought I'd grabbed the chair on the right, the one that was coated in sunbeams from the massive window before it. It was so bright I had to squint against the light so that I could properly see, but I refused to make the walk of shame to the other armchair, despite how uncomfortable staring into the literal sun was. There was a black screen folded at the top of the window, clearly to keep the sun out, but it was tied up. I wondered briefly why she had it in the first place if she wasn't going to use it.

In fact, most of the people in town seemed to have some variation of the same blinds. It made it impossible to peek inside their windows during the day. Not that I was trying to but…I couldn't help but be curious.

"Why are you here?" Sandra asked, cool as a cucumber.

"Oh. Um. I had a meeting with you because Chastity said that you might—"

"No," Sandra cut me off, folding her long taloned fingers together atop the desk as she watched me. I couldn't help but stare at her nails, a curl of irrational fear bubbling up inside me, like a bear waking up from hibernation. She was looking at me like I was a bug that she wanted to squash beneath the toe of one of her pointy designer shoes. I swallowed, clammy sweat breaking across my temple. "Why are you *here*, Mr. Evans? In Elmwood."

Suddenly the fear that had overwhelmed me earlier made a violent resurgence and I shook my head, fumbling with my feelings as I tried to force myself to remain unaffected by her cold tone. I wished I wasn't so intimidated by women, but fuck. I could see my aunt in every flicker of her face, in the way she held her shoulders, in the way her lip curled with disdain. She watched me struggle with the question, the weight of her eyes growing heavier as I squirmed. I felt about an inch tall, my hands so sweaty that when I rubbed them off on my thighs I was terrified they'd leave a mark on my pants.

Don't be a coward for once.

Find your backbone.

It's none of her business.

Don't give in.

"I don't really think that's any of your business," I answered just as coolly somehow, even though I kinda wanted to throw myself off a cliff. *Why was she being so cagey? Why did she care? What the fuck was wrong with this town?* The only people who had been even remotely friendly were a teenage boy with a penchant for breaking and entering, and a frankly terrifyingly friendly set of sisters who apparently wanted to adopt me. Oh! And my cat. Couldn't forget him.

Sandra didn't respond, the brown of her eyes nearly black as her lips thinned in a barely perceptible grimace. If I hadn't been so terrified of her she probably would've been beautiful. The dark of her hair cut a stunning contrast with her caramel skin, her cheekbones high and her nose hooked in a graceful swoop.

"I like to make this sort of thing my business," she finally answered, after a minute-long staring contest, her expression neutral as she flicked a wrist in my direction. "At least when I'm taking on a new customer." She cocked her head at me and I squirmed, the cold sweat at the back of my neck growing hot with a humiliated flush that rose to the surface of my skin without permission. "If you're not willing to cooperate, then I don't think there's much else we can discuss, is there?"

God. She spoke so flippantly. Turning me away like I was worth less than nothing. *Why had I even come here?* A fury so bright it enveloped me blazed through my body like wildfire. I spoke before I even had a chance to worry about my words.

"Are you trying to blackmail me into telling you gossip?" I asked, hands shaking. The polish on them was nearly gone and I regretted its absence keenly. I wanted to hide behind my punk exterior for once, call upon the alternative gods for strength. Without my bats, my vampires, my coffins—I felt naked beneath her gaze.

"I suppose that's one way you could put it," she answered with that same infuriatingly chilly tone of voice. My jaw clenched and I rose from my seat, surprised by the hot ball of anger that festered inside my chest. I'd never been a confrontational person but…there was just something about this town that brought the core of my emotions to the surface.

"I just want to sell my parents' fucking house, okay?" I spat, angry as a hissing cat. "Jesus. You'd think you'd want to make some money, right? I mean. Isn't that how this works?" *I had no idea how this worked.* "You sell my house and you get paid, right?"

Sandra cocked her head again, though this time her expression had softened a little around the edges like a well-worn book. The silence in the room was deafening, my own pulse ricocheting through my body like a sledgehammer demolishing slabs of drywall. "You want to sell your parents' home?" she confirmed after what felt like an eternity.

"Yes. *Jesus.* Yes! That's all I fucking want. I want to sell it and get the fuck out of here. *Why* is that so hard to understand?" It wasn't even her I was upset with. It was the helplessness of the situation. All my life I'd felt like everyone else called the shots. They took and they took and they took and *they took* until the only pieces left of my self-worth were broken and splintered. All I fucking wanted was to make decisions for myself, to get the opportunity to discover who I was, to survive the shitshow that was my very existence.

"I see." She watched me, probably judging the sweat at my temple and the way I was shaking all over, like I'd run a marathon and not simply stood up for myself —for what felt like the first time in my life. "Well, selling in this situation is going to be very difficult."

Finally we were getting somewhere. "Why?" I asked, brow furrowed. "I own the place. I have the papers."

Papers that I'd left inside my car like an idiot. Maybe that's why she was so reluctant? Maybe she hadn't realized the house was mine? *Or maybe…A traitorous voice whispered. Maybe the house was never yours to begin with. Maybe this is just another game you were forced to play for* her *amusement.*

"If the town of Elmwood wasn't as small as it is, selling would be easier," Sandra explained. "But unfortunately, because the community is so tightly knit, we're all incredibly aware of the history of the Evans's property."

"The…history?" I asked, confused. My head was buzzing as I sat down in my seat, thighs trembling despite the fact that I hadn't done anything other than swear and sweat up a fucking storm. Maybe I needed to get a handle on my language? No. I'd read an article once that stated people who swore all the time tended to be more honest. In my life I'd often found that to be true. Neither my aunt or uncle had ever sworn in front of me; if that wasn't an indicator of their dishonesty I didn't know what else was.

"Yes, the history." Sandra looked at me for a moment, something softening in her gaze as she spoke in a far gentler tone. "Are you not aware?"

Am I not aware of what?

"I'm confused," I said, brow furrowed. She grimaced in response, a dark curl escaping her loose bun to trickle along the side of her neck as she seemed to debate the best way to proceed.

"Your father was murdered in that house, Mr. Evans." Sandra said this with cutthroat honesty, her expression sympathetic but cold, like a surgeon declaring their patient hadn't made it.

Detached.

God, how I wished I could be detached.

"My father…*what*?" Black spots swam across my vision and I shook my head, trying to clear it as my temples began to throb and the white walls surrounding me began to close in tight. "He was…"

"Murdered, yes," Sandra clarified. "In the kitchen." She continued to speak but the buzzing in my ears only got louder the longer she talked. Of course, I'd known something had happened to my mom and dad—I could recall the day it happened with clarity despite the fact I'd only been eight. I remembered blue-and-red lights, I remembered rain, strangers. The smell of copper in the air as I sat down in the front room and a tall man in a navy suit put big hands on my shoulders. I remembered being taken away, the roaring in my ears, the way the water that welled up inside me had drowned out the world until I was nothing but a blank canvas, ready to be painted in the shades of misery.

But…*murdered?*

What about my mother?

The memory came back to me bit by bit, like pieces of a puzzle. I knew there was more to that fateful night, but I didn't push myself to recall it, the ringing in my ears far too loud for me to push past the wall of cotton my mind had constructed to protect itself. That was—and always would be—my most reliable coping mechanism.

Forget, forget, forget.

"Mr. Evans?" Sandra said, her impatience clear. It was obvious she'd been speaking for a while, maybe even calling my name. I just shook my head at her. A strand of dark hair fell across my cheek and I blinked it away from poking my eye, still at a loss for words. "So, as you can see, as much as I'm sympathetic to you and your…situation, there's simply no guarantee that someone would be interested in the home. I'm not turning you away. I just think you need to be aware that what you're asking of me may take much longer for us to accomplish than you'd originally planned."

But the thing was I didn't *have* much time. Soon enough Jeffrey would spill the beans out of self-preservation, or my aunt and uncle would put the pieces together and find me. It wasn't like it would take that long for them to figure out where I'd gone. They were both smart people, they'd find out eventually. A little part of me hoped that now that I was gone they wouldn't care.

But I knew my aunt better than I knew myself, and if there was one thing she hated, it was feeling like she didn't have the upper hand.

My chest was tight as I nodded, a sinking feeling of dread sitting in the pit of my stomach as I realized I had nowhere to go but back to my borrowed bedroom to stare at the ceiling and try not to think about floorboards stained red with my parents' blood.

How had I not remembered how they died?

This was fucked up, even by my standards.

Or maybe I had...maybe I *knew*, and I'd just wanted so badly for it not to be true I'd let the truth bury itself in a grave of other memories. It didn't escape my notice that Sandra hadn't mentioned my mother's death, but the part of me that still had some semblance of self-preservation realized suddenly that I didn't really want to know.

"Thank you," I finally managed to say, though I was sure it was evident just how shell-shocked I was. "Will you let me know if anything changes?" *What a stupid thing to ask. It wasn't like Sandra could change the fact I apparently inherited a murder house.*

"Of course."

I was in a daze that day at work. Richard noticed, because of course he did. Despite being a hateful prick, he was surprisingly attentive. He kept asking me if I was okay in that same stilted way he had, all gravelly voice, and stern, kissable lips. He didn't mention the party. I didn't either.

I wanted to scream but I didn't.

Instead, I just ignored him. I knew I was being rude, especially after finding out what he'd done for me the night before. But, fuck…

Hangovers and murder were probably the worst combination ever. A cocktail of misery. The diner was busier than normal, too, so there was hardly any time between ringing up customers for Richard to ply me with his usual brand of well-meaning but invasive questions.

It was clear he was concerned, because by the end of my shift he'd stopped bothering me. Instead, he'd taken to silently passing me refilled glasses of orange soda. The first time he'd done it I'd just blinked at him in confusion, and he'd remarked something about getting my blood sugar up. I didn't know how he knew orange soda was my favorite. Maybe he'd noticed it was the only drink I consistently filled up on during my shift? My two brain cells couldn't piece it together, so I stopped trying.

I loved soda so I didn't complain, even though Ty was eyeing us with quiet curiosity from where he manned the grill in the back. I had no appetite, despite the smell of sunflower oil and french fries in the air, so the soda was a god send. It settled the pit in my belly and I sipped at it till the glass was empty, only to disappear to help a customer, and return to find it filled to the brim once more—Richard's broad shoulders retreating back to his corner of the room as quickly as he'd appeared.

I glanced at him curiously, trying not to be too entranced by the way his shirt bunched up between his shoulder blades. He was thick all over, which should've been intimidating, especially given what I knew about him. But instead, looking at him just made me feel…safe. Like I was observing a blond domesticated bear, all dark red flannel and burgundy eyes.

We clocked out at two-thirty and I drove home in silence, Taylor Swift off for once. I observed with apathy the usual amount of foot traffic bursting along Main Street as people wandered through the urban areas in the dark, their pale faces flickering in the moonlight.

Sometimes driving through Elmwood felt like driving through an alternate dimension.

I was numb. It was a weird sort of detachment. I didn't want to speak, or think, or do anything but curl up in bed with Boots on my chest and my plants' silhouettes sitting sentinel in my window.

Despite my relief when I came home to discover Chastity and Vanity absent, the silence was stifling. As I lay in bed and stared at the fan whirring on the ceiling, I tried not to think about the fact that my parents had died only ten feet from where I'd slept my first night back in town. Sixteen years had passed, and yet now that I knew what had happened, I couldn't get the scent of blood out of my nose. I needed to get out of here. Out of my head. Out of town. Out of the hellish trap that was my memories as they tried to burst to the surface no matter how hard I tried to shove them down. I needed escape more than I'd needed anything else in my life. Well…that wasn't particularly true but in the moment it felt that way.

Boots purred from where he was tucked under my chin and I inhaled the scent of spring showers from his coat. I'd left the window open that day, wanting to give him a chance to explore the fire escape and absorb sunlight. He'd returned just as I had, with a leaf on his head and rain in his fur.

I didn't mind the dampness. It made him seem real. Solid.

Right now, I was feeling anything but that. I was glass—transparent, breakable, brittle. Pinocchio once again reminded of why he'd had to stop being a real boy in the first place. It made me wonder if all along I'd done this to myself. Maybe I'd broken off my pieces and shoved them into dark corners, because looking at myself only made me sick to my stomach.

"Stop it," I hissed to myself, just because I could. My cheeks were cold from the fan above, my neck damp and warm as Boots's purr rumbled my throat, nearly choking me. I knew the nightmares would come, just as I knew the sun would rise in the morning.

It was inevitable.

I avoided it as long as I could, but eventually Boots's purring lulled me to sleep along with the *pit-pat* of rain on the window. Just as I'd feared, my memories rushed to the surface to drown me.

My dreams were filled with the scratch of acrylic on skin and the soft sound of hymns echoing through chapels. I woke up halfway through the night when the rain outside my window began to come down in earnest, lightning flickering through the clouds, thunder rumbling my bed frame.

Behind my head, I could hear the screech of the fire escape trembling in the wind and the haunted feeling that had followed me all the way home settled like sediment inside my bones. Weighed down by memories, I fell back asleep—only my ghosts, my cat, and the rain outside my window to keep me company.

There was a man's hand on my knee. His knuckles were thickened with age, his skin weathered by the sun. He was speaking, but the words he spoke bounced around inside my head like a game of ping pong. I felt like I was floating underwater and I had bubbles inside my head instead of thoughts.

I stared at the red-and-blue lights that flickered in the reflection on his badge. Slashes of shadow from the windowpane created a mosaic of color on his uniform, ever shifting, as they painted the swell of my skinny knees. They were scraped from a fall I'd taken on my way home, but I couldn't feel their sting. I couldn't feel much of anything. I tried not to inhale the scent of blood, but it burrowed inside my nose, clogging my senses with its toxicity.

"I'm going to need to ask you a few questions, Blair," the man spoke and his expression was kind, his dark brows furrowed as he crouched in front of me to catch my attention. The ticking of the clock on the wall behind me was the only other sound in the room. Time moved through molasses as I slid my gaze over the man's shoulder.

Ticktock.

My birthday cake sat on the table behind his head just in my peripheral vision. It was green and purple with little stars painted lopsided all over it. I'd helped Mom frost it myself just that morning. We'd laughed together, and she'd squirted frosting at me in revenge after I smeared the back of her blouse with it.

Eight years old. Eight. I turned eight today.

It all felt so very far away now.

I nodded my head, but no words came out. They were stuck inside me, swirling around my chest and snagging on the shards of ice that resided there, a direct result of the words I'd overheard the moment I'd crossed the police tape and into my home.

Ticktock.

"Did you see or hear anything unusual when you came home today?" the man asked, because he had to, not because it made sense. I shook my head. I'd only just gotten home. I'd been off in the woods as I often was, traipsing through the leaves, ducking under branches, painting my knees with dirt and memories as I bewitched the woods with spells from my imagination and spied on the boys living in the treehouse.

My pockets were full of river stones and pine cones—heavy with regret.

I picked at the dried paint on my pants, fingernails filled with dirt, my fingers raw.

I swallowed bile.

"I just got home," I managed quietly, feeling the water inside me begin to dip between my toes. It was cold. I was cold.

Everything was cold, cold, cold.

"I know, son. I mean earlier, when you arrived back with your parents, before you went off to play."

I shook my head again.

"Did your mother say or do anything unusual the last time you saw her?"

The water met my shins as I shook. I could smell copper. Pennies. It smelled like pennies. "Mom said she'd make dinner," I said softly, staring at the officer as he watched me with an expression that made my skin crawl. It was an adult expression. Something I'd seen before but didn't have a name for yet. "Did she make it?" Behind the scent of copper I could taste steak in the air.

161

Maybe I was smelling the meat? "She said she would. She always makes steak on our birthdays. She says it's fancy."

The officer nodded along, his eyes creased at the corners. He had frown lines. Not like Mom.

Mom was made of smiles. So was Dad, even though he was hardly ever home.

The way the man looked at me was all wrong. My thighs grew cold as the water inside me reached them, chilling me to the bone as it sucked away the feeling in my toes.

Ticktock.

"It smells like she cooked," *I told him, aware that I was getting stuck on the wrong thing. Always stuck. Forever and ever.* "It smells like meat—"

I woke with a start, my pulse racing as the rain fanned its fingers across my windowpane and I struggled to catch my breath. I could still feel the water and its cool touch, receding inch by inch as I struggled not to drown.

I wasn't sure if my dream had been my imagination filling in the gaps in my subconscious or memories I'd long since forgotten. In the end, it didn't matter. So I did my best to shake it off, rolling away from the sweat spot I'd left on my sheets. I watched the rain patter, matching my breathing to its steady fall as sweat dried on my forehead, sticking my bangs to my skin.

Pit-pat, pit-pat.

It slid along the window, blocking the rising sun and painting the day in its dreary light.

"Fuck," I swore softly as I felt a furry body slip along my feet, warming them where I'd kicked off the covers. I looked down at Boots's little head, his big green eyes blinking up at me as he dug his claws into the comforter and did that weird kneading thing I'd only ever seen in movies.

"You're probably hungry, huh?" I said softly, my own stomach growling. Boots mewed.

So I gave up on sleep and forced my wobbly limbs to cooperate as I filled up his bowl and sat at the window. A few of my plants were struggling, but that wasn't new. I'd always loved them but I'd never had a green thumb. In fact, most of the plants I currently had were recommendations from the guy at Home Depot who'd assured me they were of the hard-to-kill variety.

Yeah, right.

Apparently, I was particularly gifted at one thing at least. Inadvertent plant murderer. I should get that tattooed on my back, right along with a sign that reads 'handle with caution.'

I hated a lot of things. But I hated myself most of all as I stroked Bartholomew's leaves and cooed my apologies into his soil.

"Sorry buddy."

I'm sorry I'm such a fuck up.

I'm sorry.

Chapter Fourteen

Richard

THINGS WERE NOT progressing.

At all.

Blair was resistant to all my lines of questioning, and honestly I couldn't blame him. I was shit at this. Worse than I'd even expected. I wasn't sure what I'd done to piss him off, but it was clear he didn't like me.

I wasn't sure what was worse, knowing that he didn't like me, or wanting to be near him even though I knew he didn't like me. It wasn't even about my job anymore. I genuinely enjoyed him. Over the past week I'd gotten to know him through anecdotes from Collin and Chastity, begging for scraps of his attention at work despite knowing I didn't really deserve it.

Was it deceiving him when all I really wanted was to give him a chance?

Yes.

Deceit is deceit.

Collin rustled in the passenger seat and I sighed, leaning my head on the steering wheel as I listened to him munch his way through his third box of Pop-Tarts that week. I needed to be better about policing his use of my credit card but—fuck.

My mental bank was overdrawn.

"Working with Blair again tonight?" he asked curiously, his mouth clearly full.

"Chew your food," I said, more lackluster than normal. Usually I liked pushing him, and he liked pushing back, but I didn't have the energy. The Council was growing impatient, and thus far I had zip. Nada. Nothing to prove that Blair wasn't a problem that needed solved ASAP.

Apparently the fact that he was trying to sell his house didn't mean anything. I still felt dirty getting that information from Chastity and not Blair himself. I doubted he was lying, but fear ran deep as tectonic plates in this town.

Despite the whole towns' and my parents' suspicion, I knew deep down that he was innocent. I'd *seen* him the past few weeks—and while he was a little jumpy and overall fairly prickly, he was soft deep down. A gooey caramel-y center with not a flicker of crazy in sight.

It felt like a disgrace to Markus's memory to frame Blair with the ghost of his death when he'd had nothing to do with it.

It didn't help that Blair was, for lack of a better word, pretty. I was biased. But I couldn't help it.

"So," Collin started again after he'd finished chewing. "Blair."

"What about him?"

"You figured out why he's here yet?" Collin probably knew more about my mission than he should, considering the fact that he was a horribly skilled eavesdropper and I apparently had little self-control when it came to talking to him.

He was my best friend.

All six-foot-one, hundred and forty pounds of sass. Maybe I should be depressed that my best and only friend was my little brother. But fuck, Collin was cool. Fifteen years old and he already had everything all figured out.

I could remember being that age.

Isolated.

Depressed.

Lonely.

Collin was none of those things.

"I have yet to figure out *why* he's in town. I need a stronger motive for his return. They think he's lying about the house. I have nothing to back him up—other than the belief he's telling the truth, and well…" I shrugged, settling back in my seat, my sunglasses propped on my nose as I observed the front of the diner from where I'd parked down the street, just waiting for Blair to show up.

He'd stumble over the front step like he always did, then check to make sure no one had seen, and disappear from sight behind the reflective glass. You'd think he would've figured out where the edge was by now—but he hadn't. There was a little giddy flip in my belly when I started fantasizing about what sort of graphic tee he'd have on that day.

Would it be Dracula this time? And if it was, would it be the orgasm face Dracula or the cartoon one with the cheesy quote above his head? 'I vant to drink your bluuud.'

"Helloooo, Earth to Richard?" Collin waved a hand in front of my face and I turned back toward him.

"Sorry," I grunted, because I hadn't meant to be rude. I just…had a lot going on.

Things he didn't need to know about.

"I think he's running from the mob," Collin told me, his face entirely too serious. "He's always checking over his shoulder, or like, flinching whenever someone touches him. I bet he was like, raised in it. He probably could kill a guy with his bare hands."

"I don't think you really know what a mobster is." I raised an eyebrow.

"Yeah, sure, whatever. I don't know. Maybe he's a spy? But like…one of the good guys."

"I have my own theories," I interrupted him before he could tell me Blair was an alien. "And none of them involve the mob, the CIA, or extraterrestrials."

"Ugh. You didn't even let me get to my alien theory."

"I've heard it, Collin." I tried not to laugh. "Intimately. And in great detail."

"Why don't you just ask him?" Collin asked, clearly not phased.

"Because." My jaw clenched.

"Because, why?"

"Because, Collin." I glared at him, my sunglasses shifting down enough I could use the full force of my don't-ask-me-any-more-shit-or-else face. He opened his mouth, brown eyes flickering with mischief and drama.

"Don't."

He cocked his head at me, that same light flashing in his gaze as his lips turned up. "He told me the other day he's got a brother, maybe he's running from him," Collin said, knowing the only way to calm my ire was to give me information.

God. I sickened myself sometimes.

I perked up against my will.

"A brother?"

"Yeah." Collin nodded. "Jeffrey."

"Jeffrey." I blinked at him. "Blair was—*is*, an only child."

"Not what he says." Collin shrugged, flashing me a cheeky grin because he knew he'd got me. Little shithead.

"So…adoptive brother."

"Cousin probably." Collin shifted around in his seat, making the leather squeak as he moved to prop his feet on the dash and I shoved them off for the millionth time. "I have more information," he told me, a shit-eating grin spreading across his freckled cheeks. "But it'll cost you."

I glared at him, debating with myself, though we both knew he'd already won.

"What are your terms?"

"Number one." He held up a hand. "I require you to go to the mall with me. And the movies."

"Both?" I grimaced, trying to mentally plot out my schedule for the next few weeks to figure out when that would even be plausible. I didn't have time for frivolities right now.

I was on a mission.

"Also—" Oh god, there was more. "Also I want you to promise me if you and Blair become…a thing…I'll be the first person who finds out."

"We're not going to—"

"Rich. The deal isn't whether or not you're going to. You just have to tell me if it happens," he interrupted me, glaring at me in a frankly adorable but terrifying way. It was like staring into the eyes of a demonic chipmunk. Except taller. A *lot* taller.

Not as tall as me though.

"Fine," I agreed, holding my palm out and spitting into it with an arched eyebrow.

"Ugh. You're so gross," Collin said, though his grin was pleased as he spit into his own palm and we shook on it. A pact was a pact.

I wiped my hand off on my jeans and turned towards him, waiting expectantly. "So…" I waited for him to speak, waving my hand at him to continue.

"First, before I tell you what I learned I have to say something. And I'd like to start by saying that I'm sorry in advance—" Collin grimaced, his smile falling after a moment as he fidgeted awkwardly in the seat. It only took him five minutes to explain how he'd accidentally fucked up my chances with Blair from the get-go. Jesus fuck. What was I going to do about that?

He thought I was…what? An asshole?

What did he think Collin was talking about, if not the change?

Did he even remember the change? Or that Elmwood was a sanctuary?

"Do you want me to tell him that when I say 'my brothers,' I don't mean *you?*"

"No." I shook my head, still trying to process what this new information would mean for my investigation. "No. Just…let me figure it out."

Collin moved on quickly, trying to lighten my dour mood with more Blair information.

God, something was wrong with me because I knew it would work.

"So. Three things! Chastity told me Blair said he'd never drank before that night at the party. Which, laaaaame. He lost like ten cool points. But then gained them back because she also told me he's like—super fucking good at like…anything artistic. She caught him doodling on napkins at work and she pinned them to her bedroom wall because they were *that* good."

Artsy.

Okay. That made sense considering who his mother was.

The drinking though…even if that had been his first time drinking alcohol his reaction to it had been…off. Something hadn't been right, and I could feel it in my gut no matter how much everyone tried to explain it away.

"You said there were three things."

"Yeah, yeah. I'm getting there. Jeez." Collin smacked my arm, a shark-like grin crossing his features as he leaned in, all conspiratorial. His breath smelled like Mentos and I shoved him away, my nose tingling in the way it always did when I smelled something too strong for my enhanced senses. "Get this—"

"I'm trying to—" I huffed.

"Blair…" Collin paused for dramatic effect. "Is a…*virgin.*"

I blinked.

I blinked again.

And again.

I wasn't sure what I'd expected his big news to be, but it hadn't been *that.* My cheeks tingled and I glared at him. "How could you possibly know that?"

"I just do." Collin shrugged, popping another Mentos into his mouth as I wrestled his empty box of Pop-Tarts away from him.

"When I asked you to learn about him, it wasn't because I wanted to know his sexual history."

"Uh-huh. Sure, Rich." He nodded, clearly not believing me. I huffed, all my annoyance expelling in that one harsh breath.

"Unhelpful. You're unhelpful." I flipped the keys in the ignition until the car spluttered to life and pulled out onto the road, turning into the parking lot behind Benji's. My movements were jerky as I tugged my keys free and shoved them into my pocket. I was dazed by the new information, my imagination running wild as I tried to shake off the mental picture of Blair with his legs spread wide, knees by his ears, his cock leaking against his abs—and oh, god.

A virgin.

Motherfucker.

"You're still taking me to the mall right?" Collin called after me, rolling down the window as I slammed my way out into the parking lot and stomped toward the employee entrance. I flipped him off for good measure, listening to him cackle as the whirring of the window going back up filled the silence in my head. I knew he'd use my spare keys to get his bike from the trunk when he was finally done tormenting me. Maybe he'd work his evil-chipmunk magic and convince Ty to give him fries for free like he always did. I wasn't worried.

I was, however, worried about how I was going to survive my next shift with Blair knowing what I knew now—

Fuck. Me.

There was something about knowing that Blair was a virgin that made me even more determined to get answers out of him. He made me curious. Everything about him was made of poetry just waiting to be read.

He glared at me over his shoulder, his arms crossed tight over his yellow-and-green apron. I swallowed and tried not to get hard every time he turned away and I got to watch his tight little ass flex.

I was coming to terms with this new change in my apparent sexuality. It was like something that had always been asleep inside me was finally waking up. Not for everyone though. Just Blair.

He was special.

There was something about his grungy, smudged eyeliner, chipped nails, and scraggly black hair that just really did it for me. I wanted him to like me.

I wanted him to *look* at me.

"I still owe you that veggie burger," I told him when he was scrubbing down the counter halfway through our shift. Collin had come and gone, and it didn't escape my notice that he was not treated with the icy gaze Blair always gave me.

Demon-chipmunk.

"Yeah. I'm good." His shoulders drew up tight and I tried not to be affected by how uncomfortable I was making him but I couldn't help it, especially after my chat with Collin in the car. My chest throbbed and I clenched my fists tight to keep myself from reaching out and touching him.

I didn't know how to deal with social situations at the best of times. This was…complicated. I cared too much.

God, what had I gotten myself into? Maybe I should've let Collin explain after all. But… I swallowed, scrambling for something to say to get him to understand that I wasn't the monster he thought I was.

"You haven't eaten," I blurted, following after him as he moved. Ty gave me a funny look like he always did, his colorful bandanna pulled tighter than normal today to keep his curls from falling forward.

"How astute of you to notice."

He wasn't impressed. That was fine. This was all fine. I soldiered onwards.

"You eat when you work with Chastity." Shit. I probably shouldn't know that. Except she'd told me.

This was already going way off the rails. I kept plowing forward anyway. Blair walked away from me and I followed, hell-bent on getting what I wanted for once. "Why is it any different?"

"It's different."

Thank god he didn't question how I knew that.

"But why?"

"Richard." Blair spun around, his hands on his hips, his big green eyes flickering with anger as he glared up at me. Except, he wasn't half as impressive as he seemed to think he was because I couldn't help but notice the slope of his collarbone where it crept from the stretched collar of his black hoodie, or the fact that his lashes were big and spiky like he'd been crying.

He deflated, shuffling uncomfortably before he brought his hand up to his lips in a subconscious motion, biting at his fingernails in a way I was sure was more habit than conscious thought.

"You're hungry. I can make you food." I offered again and then added, "I want to get to know you."

Blair made an annoyed little noise, uncaring that he'd completely floored me just by looking up at my face. He was so small, but so masculine. Everything about him screamed *man*, just in a pint-sized package. His surprisingly broad shoulders. The veins that danced across the tops of his hands. The bob of his Adam's apple, the way his jeans slung low across his hipbones highlighting the shape of his cock between his legs.

Blair continued to chew on his nails as he looked at me, and the scent of blood spiked through the air. My gums began to throb as I forced my fangs back, tongue suddenly dry, my dick twitching as my gaze immediately snapped to where his little white teeth had whittled a cut into the meat of his thumb.

Jesus god, give me strength.

I reached for Blair's arm without thinking, my fingers wrapping around the delicate bones in his wrist as I tugged his hand out of his mouth and gently stroked over the delicate skin between the pads of his fingers. "I'll ask again later," I promised, surprised by how deep my voice had become. It rumbled out, embarrassingly low in a way I was sure must betray just how hard my dick was pressing against the zipper in my jeans.

He was still bleeding; the scent was a siren call to my senses.

So I bent down, my tongue flicking over the meat of his thumb, stroking over the salty-sweet flavor until my saliva healed the cut into nothing but smooth, unblemished skin. There was no way he'd notice what I'd done, the cut had been so small and god, I couldn't help myself, swallowing the bright burst of citrus on my tongue as I felt my hips twitch incrementally in response, looking for friction.

I stepped away, embarrassed and confused as I hurried over to the cash register to take over for the evening rush.

What the fuck was wrong with me?

I couldn't stop thinking about Blair's face. The dark circles under his eyes, his chewed raw lips, the way his tongue looked bright pink when it flickered out to wet them.

Everyone had always been intimidated by me because of my family status, our money, our dark past. Even my size caused unease— but Blair didn't care about any of that. He had defiance etched into his body in a way that screamed 'I'm not scared of you.'

I wanted him.

I wanted him so fucking bad.

Chapter Fifteen

Blair

RICHARD WAS STARING at me again.

I ignored him, though the hair at the back of my neck prickled. I finished ringing up the last customer for the night, grinning as she slipped me a sizable tip. Everyone that came in still spent half the time staring at me, but I was learning to use it to my benefit.

That didn't stop it from being creepy as fuck though; I was starting to realize that most things in this town were. Creepy as fuck, that was.

Though, honestly, the longer I moonlighted here, the more used to Elmwood's particular brand of abnormal I became. It only took a week before the town no longer seemed as strange to me. The constant staring felt almost creepy-friendly, and the weird symbolism in a lot of residents' names was almost quirky.

When I'd asked a few days earlier, Vanity's explanation about the town's odd business hours had lacked something, but I was learning how to ignore the little voice in the back of my head that screamed that something wasn't right. She'd said that everyone 'worked from home.' It seemed like total bullshit, but hey. Maybe they really did.

Besides, observing the late-night customers was the most fun I'd had in ages. The weirdest couples came in at that time. Most of them had wild age gaps, but all had this unnatural, pale glow to them. Man. Botox did wonders, honestly. They often ordered food only to stare at it for a good hour over conversation and then leave. Wasteful but fascinating. Part of me wondered if it was a new fad diet to go with the Botox.

One time I even saw Ian again, the man I'd met on the outskirts of town. He'd introduced himself, then proceeded to stare at me while chowing down on three plates of red steak. Three. Entire. Plates. He was a mess. Blood everywhere. Catching in his beard, his chest hair, slipping down his cheeks. He made these happy little growly noises too and I struggled not to stare as he abandoned his fork halfway through the meal and began pawing the steak bare handed. I brought him some extra napkins, received a grunt in response, and then headed back to my safe spot behind the counter to watch. The only thing I'd been missing was popcorn.

Just looking at him was like watching one of those Japanese game shows.

Entertaining as fuck with a side of maybe disgust?

I hadn't seen him in a while, though he wasn't the first or last to abandon their forks for the pleasure of digging their nails into red meat. My current customer was a perfect example; except unlike Ian, she'd known how to use a napkin—and apparently appreciated my attentiveness.

"Have a nice night!" I called to her as she left, pocketing my fresh new twenty with a pleased little grin. She waved back, looking wary, though her smile warmed the longer I smiled back.

It took everyone a while to warm up to me. I was like NyQuil. Maybe my flavor wasn't the best but man, when you needed it, I was surprisingly palatable. Though in this case the 'it' was nearly raw meat, soda refills, and extra napkins as opposed to a decent night's sleep.

I wasn't sure what made everyone so wary of me. Maybe it was the gay thing, the goth thing, or the newcomer thing. Or maybe a hybrid of all three?

Eventually they all seemed to understand that I was a good enough guy. Not astounding, but passable. Average. Acceptable. A phantom passing through.

Soon enough I'd hopefully be gone from here and the memory of my brief adventure would slip from everyone's minds like spider-silk.

"I still owe you that burger," Richard said from behind me for the second time that day. I was still getting over the whole thumb sucking incident, honestly. But because I was so used to his creeping up on me bullshit I only jumped half as high as I normally would. I whipped around, heart pounding overtime, my hands clutching the front of my apron right over the 'B' for *Benji's*.

"Thanks man, but I'm good." I smiled at him faux pleasantly while I rejected his offer because I knew it would drive him crazy. He was one stubborn little (*big*) fucker.

I was right.

His nostrils flared and he cocked his head at me. "You haven't eaten all night."

"Ah. How cute of you to remind me. *Again*," I cooed with just enough sarcasm I got to watch him try to figure out if I was playing him or not. "You know, considering the fact that I'm working right now and you haven't taken a dinner break either."

It took him a second, but he eventually figured out I'd been making fun of him. His dark brows lowered, the muscle in his jaw flickering as he clenched his teeth. He looked cute when he was all disconcerted like that. It made me want to piss him off more and see what happened. Like poking a snake with a stick. Not that I'd ever do that. Because *rude*.

Richard wasn't a snake though. He was…Richard. I liked perplexing him. It made me wonder how perplexed he'd be if I divested him of his black jeans and sank my ass down on his lovely cock. There was no way with hands and feet like his that riding his dick would be anything other than a religious experience. Praise be, Richard and his monster cock.

Bad.

Down, Blair!

We don't think homophobes are cute!

"You don't complain when Chastity offers."

"True." I shrugged, smiling pleasantly again as I enjoyed the little flip in my belly when I watched his nostrils flare. His face was always so stoic, but it was easy enough to figure out how he was feeling if I watched his nose. Sometimes he reminded me of a wolf, a downright primal sort of shift to his expression every time I defied him.

I did not envy Collin one bit. Richard was as bossy as they came.

"So why won't you let me buy you a burger?" Man. I had to give him points for tenacity.

"Two reasons," I explained, holding up a finger. His eyes flickered to my hand immediately, his brow lowered in concentration as he waited for me to speak. "One. I don't like you." I held up another finger. "And even more importantly; Two, I don't like you." I turned my back on him and headed to the sink. I could feel him right behind me, the puff of his breath on the back of my neck sending a flicker of want, like a secret, twitching between my thighs.

Richard made an annoyed little huffing noise that did things to my dick I refused to explain even to myself. "Why not?"

I rolled my eyes heavenward and ignored him. Almost.

He stalked behind me as I passed the sink and grabbed a rag. Like a loyal mutt he remained right on my heels, wiping up behind me as I finished scrubbing down the counters until they gleamed. His stalkery ways didn't end there, however.

He was at my elbow refilling napkin dispensers.

He bumped up against me when I wiped the grill down.

When I washed the dishes he dried them, continuing to watch me with a gaze so heavy it felt like fingers trailing down the sensitive skin at the top of my spine.

By the time Ty had flicked the 'open' sign to 'closed' and we'd turned off all the lights, I was about ready to jump out of my skin. Over-sensitized and horny.

I was a second away from breaking, my nerves shot. Each brush of Richard's breath against the shell of my ear sent shockwaves down my spine—and the worst part of it all was the fact I genuinely didn't think he realized what he was doing to me.

The dude probably thought he was being nice. Befriending the weird goth kid who his little brother had latched onto like a gay mother hen and her equally gay duckling.

Richard was right behind me as we pushed out the back door, garbage bags in hand. His car was parked next to mine, and I glared at them both. I still hadn't figured out how to get up the nerve to go through the back door into Benji's on my own, like I belonged. Richard didn't have that problem. I could feel his breath puffing along the back of my neck and I shuddered the entire way to the dumpsters. Even his shoes made sexy noises when he moved, heavy and rubber-coated, like I wished his dick would be.

By the time we'd thrown every bag away, I'd had enough. The scent of old bread, ketchup, and sour meat stuck in the recesses of my nose as I swiftly turned around and clocked him with what I hoped was a sufficiently frightening glare.

Richard stood his ground.

His hair glowed in the single streetlight behind the restaurant like a blond beacon. He was perplexed again, that little flicker between his brows his only tell as I stomped both my feet just to feel the vibrations from the earth shoot up my skinny legs.

Maybe I could use his stubbornness to my advantage. It was clear that Richard wasn't going to back down anytime soon. And I'd had Collin's sad face haunting me every time I closed my eyes—So. *Fine.* Mutually beneficial. I could make this work.

"Okay. Fuck. *Fine.*" I threw my hands up in frustration. "You can buy me a fucking burger, okay?"

He perked right up, a surprised expression crossing his face as the crinkle between his brows relaxed and he nodded with enthusiasm. "Really?"

"Yes." I rolled my eyes heavenward and held my pointer fingers out in a cross-like shape in front of myself to ward him off. "But you have to promise me something in return."

Richard's eyes narrowed suspiciously, gaze flickering to my fingers before they slid back to my face. A whiff of his pinewood cologne tickled my nose as the cool night wind rustled the fabric of his flannel shirt. Jesus, the boy wore a variation of the same outfit every single day. He looked delicious but, man. Maybe he needed a subscription to a fashion magazine that was more creative than 'lumber-jack-vogue.'

"What do you want?" Richard cocked his head, dark eyes flickering red in the lamplight.

"I want you to lay off Collin. Support him. Leave him alone. Whatever."

He blinked. He blinked again. His head cocked to the other side and he seemed to think for a long minute before he eventually, reluctantly, nodded his head with a confused expression on his face like he was trying to suss me out. To figure out how to reply. Maybe he hadn't realized what he'd been doing? Maybe he wasn't such a bad guy after all? "Why do you care?" he asked.

Why do I care? *Why do I care?* Was the man blind?! Jesus.

"Because. It's not right." I pointed at him, my newly painted nails flickering with subtle glitter when they caught the light. "He's your brother. You're super fucking lucky to have him, and he deserves better than to feel uncomfortable in his own home. Kids need allies."

Richard continued to watch me, his eyes narrowed in concentration before his expression softened and the stern set of his lips grew fractionally sweeter. "Fine," he said.

"Wow." Now it was my turn to be surprised. "Really?"

I hadn't expected it to be that easy.

"Sure." He shrugged, his nostrils flaring again as a burst of cool wind whispered its way along my exposed collarbone. "You're right. He needs an ally. I don't see why I can't be that for him since I can't change his mind."

Change his mind? Jesus fucking Christ. I wanted to strangle him. I barely refrained, but only because I could see his brain was hurting. One step at a time. Maybe there was hope for him yet.

"So. Where in town serves a veggie burger at this hour?" I asked as I turned and inspected our cars.

"Benji's does."

"No shit, Sherlock." I snorted and shook his head. "Did you forget the part where we work there? And we just closed shop?"

Richard paused, glancing at the back door of the diner with serious contemplation. "Who says we can't close again?"

I stared at him. I could feel how wide my eyes were as I watched him seriously pitch the idea of turning the diner into our own personal restaurant. "Who are you and what did you do with Richard?"

He snorted, an amused little twist to his lips as he glanced down at me through the corner of his eyes. "You don't know me as well as you think you do."

"Yeah. I'm getting that."

Richard was surprisingly fun to be around when he wasn't riding my ass. Fuck. I hadn't meant to give myself that mental image but now there was no way I could think about anything else. I could so easily picture the face he'd make when he sunk his thick cock inside me. He'd probably look pissed off—like he normally did, sweat dripping between the swell of his pecs, his muscular thighs tensing. I wanted him sex-drunk. I wanted him to feel so good his eyes crossed and he plowed me like an animal.

I shook my head to clear it, shifting where I sat on a stool by the counter as I stared at his broad shoulders where they pulled the fabric of his black flannel shirt taut. He was prepping the grill with oil, and while he reached for one of the veggie patties that were normally kept in the freezer, I wondered how long he'd worked here.

I watched him quietly for a few minutes, enjoying his rebellious side probably a little too much. It wasn't like I was normally one to break rules myself, aside from my little rebellions, so this was novel for me too, even though I'd never admit that to him.

His ass in the jeans he was wearing was absolutely godlike. I sent up a prayer of thanks to the heavens as I watched his hamstrings flex and imagined biting into all that thick, supple flesh. Would he spank me into compliance? Oh god, please let him be just as bossy in bed as he was outside of it.

Ew. Now *I* was the one sounding like a creep.

"Why do you hate me?" Richard asked, breaking the silence between us. The grill sizzled as he slapped a burger onto it and I was momentarily blinded by how bite-able his forearms were. I wanted to follow the vein dancing up the underside with my tongue. His words hit me like a slap to the face a moment later and the heat of lust that had been flickering inside me snuffed itself out.

"I don't hate you," I told him, realizing it was true even as I said the words. I didn't hate him. Did I think he was ignorant? Yes. Did I think he could be a better brother? Yes. Did I think he was wasting an opportunity to bond with his sibling? Yes. I'd never had what he had. A big family.

Brothers. Camaraderie.

I had Jeffrey, but half our childhood we'd been throwing each other under the bus just to escape the worst of the punishment. We were different now—but the trauma remained. I didn't blame him. Not anymore.

"But you don't like me."

How astute of him to notice.

"I didn't know you knew how to cook," I changed the subject quickly, wanting to avoid the topic at hand for as long as possible. Richard gracefully followed my cue. For that I was grateful. For an asshole, he was surprisingly accommodating.

The best part about him, however, was his shoes. *God.* I wanted to lick his boots, marry them, and run off into the sunset.

I'd read an article once on Apple News that talked about a lady who'd married a roller coaster. Maybe I could marry a pair of boots? Boots would make a better husband than a roller coaster.

I realized I was being rude a second too late when Richard stopped talking and peeked over his ridiculously round shoulder at me. "You weren't listening," he observed. He spoke differently than anyone I'd ever known. Richard's words were more a statement than an accusation. They said 'I can repeat if you need me to, I know how to be patient.'

No one had ever been patient with me before.

"Sorry." I flushed a little and realized it was true. For probably the first time in my life I truly felt bad for spacing out. I refocused my attention on him, watching his expression soften before he turned back to the grill. "Didn't mean to."

"S'okay. I'm used to it." He shrugged. "I'm the third youngest of six brothers, so…comes with middle child territory."

Man. That was a weird way to phrase that but—

Wow. Six brothers. *Double-wow.*

"So…" I trailed off, watching his back muscles twitch. *I could salvage this.* At least I still remembered my question. "Is that why you know how to cook?"

He nodded, his blond head bobbing in the overhead light. It suddenly occurred to me that people could easily be watching us from the street. At night like this, the lights would make the view inside clear as day. I forced the crawling sensation on my skin to go away as I waited for Richard to respond, this time ready to give him my full attention.

"I grew up taking care of Collin," Richard explained after a few seconds of slapping my burger with his spatula. I figured it must be a nervous tic since there was no meat juice to squeeze out. "There's a gap between me and Charlie, so it fell to me to make sure he was fed."

I didn't want to pry even though that made no sense to me. "Your parents aren't around?"

"Oh. They're around." He shrugged, a wry twist to his voice. He didn't look at me and I hated him just a little bit for making me sympathize with him. Though I had to hand it to him, it was hard to hate him when I knew what he sounded like when he was uncomfortable. "They're just really…*busy.*"

I could picture what his life was like with sudden clarity. Except… something wasn't adding up.

"What about your other brother? The one between you and Collin."

Richard froze, a tenseness creeping over him that I'd never seen before. It was so at odds with the almost loose way he'd been moving only seconds before that it gave me emotional whiplash. I froze along with him.

186

It was quiet.

The grill sizzled and he held very still for a moment too long before he released a ragged sigh. For a moment there it had almost been like he didn't need to breathe.

"He died."

Oh.

Oh fuck.

"Oh fuck." My fingers stopped their drumming on the counter and began to chew on my nails as I stared at the swell of Richard's back and regretted every decision that had led me up to this moment. I felt like a complete tool. "I'm so sorry."

Richard shrugged but he was quiet again. His silence felt worse than his earlier stalking. I wanted my grumpy little Labrador back, not this stiff board of a man. I wasn't cruel enough to interrupt his mourning, however. Instead I did what any decent human would do, I offered him a piece of myself to pay for the part of him that I'd stolen with my careless words.

"You asked me, back when I first arrived, why I came here." My heart beat a wild staccato in my chest as I spoke. I swallowed the bile in my throat. "The real reason I came here wasn't because I inherited my parents house, or even because running was my only option."

Richard was very still as he listened. My heart creaked open as pieces of me fell out on the counter between us. "The truth is I'm here because I'm scared."

There was a curl of blond hair along Richard's nape that I wanted to twist around my fingers. It was slightly longer than the rest, like he'd missed it when buzzing the back of his head. I focused on that one imperfection with the desperation of a drowning man. "I'm scared I'll die the same sad man I see every time I look in the mirror."

It wasn't everything, but it was enough.

Richard's posture softened and he grabbed a bun from under the counter. He prepared my burger and slid it across the counter to me with a quiet clatter and I stared at it, trying to find meaning in the lettuce that I couldn't find in my own life.

"I've always been a coward," I told him quietly, picking at the edges of the bun before I began plucking sesame seeds off, not because I didn't like them, but because—just like when I was a kid—sometimes there were wiggles inside me I had to let loose.

You're a coward, Blair. The memory of Jeffrey's voice echoed in the back of my mind as seeds scattered on my plate and anxiety burned like acid in my veins.

My feet tapped along the legs of the stool I was sitting on as I tensed beneath the heavy weight of Richard's gaze.

"Somehow I don't think that's true," Richard finally said. He leaned onto the counter across from me, for the first time respecting my unspoken need for space. He looked especially bite-able like that, his thick neck twitching as he swallowed, pupils dilated, his lips wet from the flicker of his pink tongue. "I think you're brave."

I laughed, because that was the stupidest thing I'd ever heard.

"No, really," he protested, shifting a little, a whiff of pine tickling my nose. My stomach growled. "I mean, you came here all on your own. Traveled across the whole country even though you didn't know anyone here." I rolled my eyes. "You saved a kitten and chose its welfare over your own, even though it ended up working out, but still. You always speak your mind, no matter who you're talking to. You're independent. You're brave—" My cheeks began to heat up and I nibbled nervously on my nails again, watching him burn with a passion I only wished I could feel. "And…" Richard added, a pleased little twitch to his lips. "You stood up to me. *No one* does that."

I looked up at him at that, my eyes wide with surprise, as I watched his expression twist into something almost warm.

"*No one.*" He blinked.

"Besides Collin," I corrected him immediately. Richard was startled into laughter, as surprised by it as I was. He shook his head in disbelief.

I decided I liked his laugh. He kinda sounded like one of those geese you hear when it flies overhead. He had just the right amount of wheeze to it, like he felt the amusement all the way down to his toes. Somehow I doubted that Richard laughed all that much.

He looked like he was barely older than me and he already had a frown line forming between his eyebrows. It added to his whole me-against-the-world-grumpy-puppy-dog-chic thing he had going on.

"Besides Collin," he agreed, eyes flickering with heat. I watched him for a minute longer, burger forgotten. Eventually he nudged it towards me, his thick fingers making the plate appear small.

"What do you remember about Elmwood?" Richard asked me after I'd taken my first bite. Flavor exploded across my tongue and I practically moaned as I inhaled another bite of burger before answering him. There was nothing like warm food to take the edge off an awkward conversation. Richard was a good cook.

Way better than I could ever be.

"Like…from when I was a kid?" I questioned around my mouthful and Richard nodded—that same serious expression on his face I'd come to associate with him. "Not much. I remember my parents, kinda, and that's about it."

I remembered the night of their death. Pieces of it anyway.

The way it had rained and rained.

The way my knees had stung for days afterward.

The way I'd picked at the paint on my clothing until it disappeared.

The way I'd been taken away before I'd had a chance to collect more memories.

The scent of pennies.

Drowning.

"So you don't remember anything about the town itself?"

Richard was getting weirdly specific and I frowned as I shook my head. A black curl tickled my nose and I blew it out of the way, watching him with a pensive expression. "I was eight, Richard. My parents were murdered. I'm pretty sure I blocked any and all memories out of self-preservation."

He nodded, though something seemed to loosen the tense way he held his ridiculously broad shoulders.

"There's nothing else you remember?" This question seemed different somehow, less interrogation and more…gentle. "From before. When you lived here with your parents."

I grunted, lapping at a stray bit of ketchup that decorated the pad of my thumb. Richard looked fascinated for a moment, his eyes dark as he watched my tongue move.

Okay, weirdo.

"Oh. Um. Not much, really." I shrugged, picking at my bun again until more little bread bits joined the seeds in a golden pile on my plate. I kicked the stool again, just for something to do as I stared at my blurred reflection in the napkin dispenser to my left. "My whole childhood is kinda a blur." I had a hard time making eye contact with people on the best of days, and Richard was…intense. When I looked into his eyes it was like falling through time.

"Do you have a bad memory?"

"More like—bad memor*ies*." I shrugged again. "The parts I do remember about being here are just stupid shit, you know? Like…my mom's spaghetti having weirdly huge meatballs, or how she shed worse than a dog and my dad was always picking her hair off things and brandishing it like a weapon." I could remember flashes of his smile, his teeth overly white and just slightly too large for his mouth. "Or the way she was always painting. Fucking always. There was paint on everything, me included. Half the time I looked like one of her art projects."

Richard snorted, crossing his arms and leaning against the counter like he was settling down to wait for me to continue. His chest was wide and full, and I was once again drawn to it like a moth to a flame. I felt pressured to talk to him, though it was a nice kind of pressure. He wasn't asking me about my trauma or my parents' death—which was what I thought he'd been going after. Instead, Richard seemed genuinely interested in my broken memories. When I chanced a glance at his eyes they sparked with interest, ringed by the black kiss of ebony lashes, nearly wine-red in the single overhead light above us.

"My childhood wasn't the best either," Richard said softly. He seemed to debate with himself before he continued. "When we lost my brother it was like everyone in my family forgot how to move forward. We were stuck in this endless loop of 'what ifs' and I grew up with my parents' grief as a companion instead of my brother."

I nodded, a tightness in my chest as I watched his gaze flick over to the window and a lost expression cross his features. The emotion was hidden away quickly enough I doubted he even felt the shift. But I did. I felt it in my very bones.

"I honestly forgot about what happened to my parents until the lady at the real estate office made me feel like shit about it. There's a lot of memories I think I've blocked out of self-preservation," I told him honestly, taking another bite and talking through my full mouth. "Pretty much everyone here has been a dick to me," I backpedaled when I realized that wasn't strictly true. "Well. Not everyone, but a good amount of people."

Richard laughed, then grimaced, clearly not impressed with my chewing skills. My aunt had drilled table manners into me from a young age and it was one of the first things I'd dropped the moment she was out of sight. Somehow I didn't mind Richard's scrutiny though. It wasn't the same. So instead of dwelling on the negative memories, I found the strength to push them aside. I stuck my tongue out at him, food and all, just to watch him make a disgusted expression.

I laughed and swallowed the rest of my food. "It's kinda weird actually. Like—I get the whole *small-town* thing. You'd think what with the whole 'Evans family murder debacle' everyone would've been more pitying. Not that I *want* pity—because I really fucking don't—but instead it's like…" I trailed off, not sure what I was even trying to say, or why I was talking to Richard about it.

"It's like what?" he pressed, lips drawn in their familiar flat line.

"It's like they think I'm up to something." I blinked. "Which is just… ridiculous, right?"

Not too ridiculous, a little voice whispered in my head.

You're trouble, just like your mother.

All they have to do is look at you to know you're a freak.

"Are you?" Richard asked, cocking his head to the side and watching me with an expression I didn't know how to describe.

"Am I what?"

"Up to something."

"Not unless you count sneaking back into my place of work and eating apology veggie burgers without permission." I shrugged, trying to lighten the mood. It had gotten dark rather quick, and for some reason I was having a hard time tracing back to when the heaviness of the conversation had started.

"I gave you permission," he reminded me.

"You're not the one who hired me," I sing-songed back.

"Touché." He was grinning, a dimple flickering in his cheek that I'd never had the pleasure of meeting until that moment. Richard was gorgeous when he was grumpy—but happy Richard was...*god*...looking at him was like staring into the sun.

Well, hello there handsome.

Stop creeping on the straight guy. He's not into you. You just had to bribe him into supporting his brother, remember?

I forced the thoughts from my mind for once and moved my attention back to Richard's smile and his cute little dimple. Angsting could wait until there were no cute boys to ogle.

I finished my burger and chatted with Richard about stupid things we both loved. Apparently he was a big fan of Bela Lugosi—the original Dracula—and when I discovered this I ranted to him for nearly five minutes about that movie having caused my sexual awakening.

Half the stuff that came out of my mouth made Richard's eyes bug out of his head. But then he'd laugh, that same squawking sort of noise that made me want to both smother him with a pillow and smile for a million years.

The smiling part won. Obviously. But only on the inside.

By the time we parted ways in the parking lot, one thing was absolutely certain.

I maybe, possibly—*probably*—might not, in fact, hate Richard.

Chapter Sixteen

Blair

OVER THE NEXT few weeks, I spent a lot more time with Richard. I was warming up to him despite my best efforts, unable to help how charmed I was by his awkwardly serious demeanor, and the way he was always toting Collin around like a redheaded duckling.

When he'd admitted he didn't like classic slasher movies but enjoyed a good story, I'd spent half our next shift reading him the episode synopsis to every *Friday the Thirteenth* movie in the history of ever.

He always acted appropriately scandalized–and amused–when it got to the gory bits.

I liked that about him.

I liked a lot of things about him actually.

I liked how he was always first to hunt down a solution. Like that time

Ty had found a spider on the toe of his shoe and screamed bloody murder while banging on the counter vehemently. Without even blinking Richard had hurried forward with a plastic cup and a plan. At the time I'd been shell-shocked because I'd never heard Ty speak. It had only taken Richard seconds to slip the piece of paper he was holding under the spider and place the cup on top. And with no casualties to the workplace—or spider population—he'd dashed outside to a chorus of applause from the entire diner. When he'd returned he'd smelled like spring rain, his chest puffed up triumphantly, empty cup in hand, and his short hair windswept. I'd stared at his lopsided smile and realized I wanted to kiss his stupid face more than I'd wanted anything in my life.

And that was the problem.

Because the more I interacted with Richard, the more I liked him.

And that was dangerous for a multitude of reasons.

The number one reason being the fact that I was starting to be grateful it was taking Sandra a long time to find a buyer for my house. Because the longer it took her, the more time I got to spend with Richard and everyone else I was starting to fall in love with in this strange little town.

It was nearly three in the morning by the time I pulled onto the main stretch of road that ran from one end of Elmwood to the other. I could see Moonies sitting atop the hill at the end of the street. It had this spooky aqua glow that lit up the trees behind it like a cheap haunted house. My car made a sad rattling little noise as I rolled over a dip in the road that was unfortunately deep enough my bumper scraped up against the asphalt.

Unsurprisingly, the parking lot at Moonies was empty.

Wait.

Except…this was *Elmwood*. So it was actually more strange that it was barren than if it had been packed at this hour. The diner had been especially busy that night until the end of my shift when they'd all shuffled out the door so quickly they might as well have been doing a conga line. Every time I'd passed by the gas station during my time living here, no matter what time it had been, there had always been a full parking lot. Munchies abided by no man's schedule.

Maybe three a.m. was too late even for the night owls?

No. Well... *Maybe.*

I frowned to myself, pulling left off Main Street and out towards Spruce, the road my parents' house was at the end of.

There were two roads that intersected the town like a giant X. Most of the main businesses, the new ones anyway, were located down Main. Moonies was at the south end, with the 24/7 Mart and the gym near the north end where most of the residential buildings were.

My parents had lived off Spruce which was the road that bisected Main from west to east. It had been the original Main Street back when the town was founded, but in recent years they'd built the new Main Street and renamed the other one to make room for new businesses. The only reason I knew any of this was because Chastity had spent a good hour during one of our shifts together explaining all of it with straws and napkins during a lull in customers.

I didn't know what compelled me to turn down Spruce instead of head home, but I did. Maybe I was chasing moonbeams. Or maybe it was because my skin was still buzzing from my last conversation with Richard.

I wasn't ready to sleep so I decided to take a detour.

All of the old buildings were still located on Spruce. They dated as far back as the late 1800s. As I drove east I rolled my windows down, letting the crisp night air bite at my cheeks. My knuckles were white in the moonlight, bleached by its creeping fingers across my dash as I watched buildings blur by on both sides, shapeless and full of histories I didn't have a part in.

Some buildings were so old they'd been practically abandoned, maintained only by the city as museums. They were relics of a past no one was ready to let go of. The rest of the old buildings were still used on a daily basis. They'd been remodeled inside with future-proof skeletons, though their shells still spoke of generations gone by to anyone that looked. One of the more notable buildings was a church with stones crumbling from its steeple. I admired it as I passed, slowing down fractionally as the wind curled around the shell of my ears and over the bridge of my nose. I stared at it for a few seconds, just so I could watch the moon paint its spires and bleed through its shingles like silver ink.

I knew from all the times I'd driven down Spruce that after the church came the police station, and then city hall. There were other buildings between them, but none of them had the names so clearly displayed out front so I was still figuring out what they were. I continued at the same crawling pace down the road, the night encasing the buildings in darkened silence.

Jeffrey would've loved this town. He would've found the people and their quirks charming. He would've made me visit the graveyard at night just so he could sit beside the tombstones and light up a joint.

I shoved thoughts of him aside as I stared blankly at my surroundings. It was three in the morning so I suspected all the buildings would be empty, like Moonies had been. It made sense that even in a town like Elmwood there was such a thing as being out too late.

I was wrong. Again.

I blinked in surprise as I began to notice the black silhouettes of cars lining the street. They filled in every available gap from the back of the church all the way past city hall. When I got close enough, my eyes widened in surprise, realizing belatedly that the building was lit up inside. At first I thought I was imagining things. It was 3 a.m. why would the building be open? I checked the clock, confirming what time it was before I blinked up at the building again only to find it just as brightly lit and packed with cars as it had been the first time I'd looked.

What the fuck?

There were figures silhouetted in the windows, gold fragments of light spilling from the window panes onto the lawn. It was so bizarre to see the building lit up like that, knowing the time, that I couldn't help but stop to get a closer look. Instead of being comforted by the light, it haunted me, the shadowy figures moving around inside the windows as they interacted with each other like faceless specters.

Something inside me screamed that I should turn back, that I needed to move on, to do anything to avoid the creepy-hive-meeting that was obviously taking place. But…I'd been getting to know these people as they'd come into the diner, and despite what I'd said to Richard about them being dickish to me, they didn't seem nearly as frightening now as they had when I'd first arrived. Sure, they still stared at me, but to be fair I was new here, and I had come rolling into town with black eyes and two metaphorical middle fingers up.

I'd be nervous around me too.

From an outside perspective, I probably looked like a little shit. In fact, I *knew* I looked like a little shit. I owned a mirror, after all. I didn't blame the townies for their nerves around me. The nails they could brush off, the eyeliner too, but the bruises were harder to explain. It's not like you could take one look at me and know that I hadn't deserved to be hit. Hell, maybe I *had*. In my aunt's twisted logic I'd deserved every injury, every foul word, every punishment she'd bestowed upon me. Half the time I believed her, and the other half I was so upset with myself for believing her just thinking about it made me sick to my stomach.

Fuck.

Behind that train of thought lay madness. I couldn't help but spiral, falling back into the abyss that had swallowed my sense of self for more than half my life. Anxiety clawed at my chest and I struggled to breathe, searching for escape as bile rose in my throat and my aunt's voice threatened to claw its way to the surface once again.

Worthless.

Freak.

Just like your mother.

I had no choice but to search for a parking spot. As much as I hated myself for being affected, I was shaking too hard to continue the trek down the street without a breather. The only bonus of my predicament was the fact that now that I was parking, I'd have a front row seat to view the city hall in all its freakish glory. I ended up parking down the street from the building itself and the space was tight enough it really shouldn't have been considered a parking spot at all. *Small cars for the win! Fuck yeah.*

My hands shook, sweaty and cold. I exhaled raggedly, allowing myself a moment to calm down as I turned the engine off, leaving the keys in the ignition. My chest expanded and the breath I'd been holding since thoughts of my aunt had surfaced stuttered out as I finally managed to force the shakiness out of my fingers. Sometimes it was so mentally exhausting being around myself I wished I could turn in my two weeks.

You're safe. You're safe. You're safe. I repeated this mantra over and over again as I taught myself to breathe again and stared blankly out the open window at the car parked in front of me. *No one can find you here. You're safe for now. She isn't going to hurt you ever again.*

No distance was great enough to make me forget what it felt like to be pinned between her taloned fingertips. I reached a hand up to grip the back of my neck and began counting the cars in front of me to distract myself. I cataloged their shapes and colors, tracing the fragments of light cast from the street lamps above on their glimmering rain-spattered hoods. When that didn't help, I let my gaze skip along the cracks in the road, focusing on anything that wasn't the turmoil inside my head. I squeezed tight and let myself breathe, exhaling the poison, letting myself cope in the only way I knew how.

God. *What the fuck was I doing here?*

It was three in the fucking morning. I was alone and scared and so out of my depth it was almost laughable. Why did I think this was a good idea? Any of it? Why did I think that moving here would magically make me a different person? A braver man? I moved to grab my keys, ready to twist them in the ignition and start the car again so I could leave.

Something stopped me.

Maybe it was something instinctual. Maybe it was the memory of Jeffrey's voice in my head again. *You're a coward, Blair.* Or maybe it was just sheer dumb luck—but for the first time in my life instead of running when I was scared, I paused.

My ears strained through the darkness, searching for *something* even though I didn't know what it was yet.

And then I heard it.

The scratch of feet on the pavement.

The sound filtered through my anxiety and I realized with sudden clarity that I could hear people approaching my vehicle.

I hid.

Maybe I'd used up all the courage I had by staying. I don't know. It could've been instinctual, something animal and older than time itself. *Hide*, it whispered as I slipped down as low as I could, sliding my legs into the well beneath the steering wheel. For once in my life I was grateful for my short stature as I was easily able to fit deep enough in the crevice that I couldn't be seen above the dashboard. It was cramped down there but I only spared the physical discomfort a brief thought as I held my breath and waited.

The footsteps grew closer and closer.

With each shift of shoes on the pavement my pulse beat faster.

Thud, thud, thud.

I felt a sickening lurching sort of feeling, it tugged at my insides like my blood had been replaced with icing. Luckily—*or unluckily*—for me the discomfort was so familiar it felt like slipping on a pair of well-worn shoes. It was clear to me now as I listened that there were two people approaching, two sets of footsteps, two voices. Men more than likely, judging by the heavy thud of their feet.

"You think Jason is going to choose the change?" one of the voices said as they passed my car. I blinked, brow furrowed in confusion as I strained my ears to listen closer. Maybe I was being nosy but there was no one there to judge me but myself. And listening to them distracted me from my own approaching panic attack. My knees looked knobby where they stuck out in front of me. To soothe the part of me that refused to hold still I smoothed a thumb over one of the holes in the knees of my jeans as I listened. A hangnail I hadn't realized I had caught on the fabric and I aborted the movement with a wince.

"Shit, I dunno. I think he and Beth are still planning on having a few more kids."

"Well, yeah. But he could still turn and she could wait till after they have the rest of them."

"Dude." Man number two huffed, clearly exasperated. It sounded like this wasn't the first time they'd had this conversation. "It's no one's business but Beth and Jason's whether or not they take the change."

What the actual fuck. What 'change?' What were they talking about? I covered my mouth with a hand to stifle the sound of my breathing, irrationally afraid they'd be able to hear me as I listened to the two men pause as soon as they passed the bumper of my car. The curious, self-sacrificing part of me wanted to peek over the dash so I could see who was talking. Maybe I'd recognize one of them from the diner? Maybe knowing who was talking would help me understand what they were talking about? Despite my curiosity, luckily I still had *some* sense of self-preservation left so instead of peeking I forced myself to remain still. My legs began to cramp where I was folded over like a human-size pretzel but I ignored the pain and instead held my breath and listened.

"Look, I'm just concerned. I mean, won't they regret it?"

"I guess that's a possibility. Not like it's uncommon though."

"I feel like I should at least talk to Jason about it. What if Beth says it's fine now but then later she's all 'Ah, but Jason, it's not fair that you're younger than me.' And then it becomes this whole *thing*." The man's voice took on a different pitch as he mimicked who I assumed was Beth.

Second dude laughed, and then made a scoffing noise. "Like I said, man. None of your business."

"I guess you're right."

They moved on, thank god, and I was left alone with my thoughts. My brow furrowed as I stayed huddled in my painful crouch for a few extra seconds before I awkwardly—gracelessly—pushed my way back up into my seat. The fabric creaked as I settled back down, kicking my legs out as quietly as I could to get the cramping to stop. Dread settled into the pit of my stomach. Something about the conversation had seemed…private, like I hadn't been supposed to hear.

I'd joked about the town being full of hive people more times than I could count, but this…this was… something I didn't even have an explanation for. Not a logical one anyway.

I mean, fuck. I'd been watching vampire movies since I was thirteen and figured out I could download them illegally on Jeffrey's laptop. I'd spent most of my prepubescent years with a hard-on for anything fanged and furry. I'd spent years of my life pilfering his computer just so I could get my spook on, for more reasons than one.

So, of course, the first place my brain jumped was the supernatural.

I frowned at my dashboard, for once in my life completely still as I tried to think through the cotton that filled my head. Time froze as I realized the two figures up ahead had stopped to argue again. There was no way I could hide again without alerting them of my presence, so I just held very, very still. Eventually one of them clicked their keys and the headlights of a car about six down flared to life.

I let my emotions grow blank as I tried to get my thoughts in order.

I missed Richard's laugh desperately for a moment as I warred against myself. Then because I was in the privacy of my own head, I gathered strength from recalling the flicker of Richard's dimple and the scent of cocoa that clung to his skin like he'd spent all day brewing hot chocolate.

My thoughts derailed again.

Could it even be possible that I'd stumbled upon a town with supernatural creatures? Were supernatural creatures even real? Jesus. That was a sobering thought. I'd always had this feeling of open-ended disbelief when it came to things like that. Part of me wanted them to be real, and the other part of me was terrified at the prospect. Anytime anyone had asked me whether or not I believed in werewolves, vampires, or ghosts I'd always responded by saying, "Why not?"

Why not, indeed.

I could hardly take care of myself in a world run by humans, to add beings that were natural predators and much more physically capable than me seemed like a cruel joke. It also seemed *impossible*. But maybe that was my own ignorance talking? I'd grown up sheltered, terrified of anything new before I had a chance to get used to it. If those…*things* were real, what did that say about me? I'd always known I was ignorant, but this was just an entirely new fucked-up level of naivety.

An entire species of beings existing, and no one knowing about it?

Not likely.

Except…maybe it was? Maybe the movies, the books, and the comics all hinted at something right on the surface of reality. Maybe they weren't fantasy after all, but a compendium of creatures that only survived because of the shields they'd put up to protect themselves. Hiding in plain sight.

Stupidly genius.

I was probably crazy to even think of this as a real possibility. Suspended in my own disbelief. This was just… It was too much for even me to make that leap, my obsession with the fanged-and-freaky notwithstanding.

I couldn't help but recall the blinds in town though, the way people only came out at night, the abandoned plates full of food that hadn't even been touched. Maybe the people here were just weird…or maybe they were vampires.

I didn't want to hear more or see anything else I wasn't supposed to, so I did the only thing I could to preserve my sanity, and I pulled out of my parking spot as soon as the two figures had driven off. I drove blankly down the road in silence, only my thoughts for company. The woods had never felt quite so lonely as I realized with a start that I'd subconsciously driven towards my parents' house and not the apartment.

I hadn't been back since I'd learned what happened here.

I should've turned back, but the same feeling that had compelled me to stop outside city hall inspired me to turn my car off and stare at the husk of my childhood home.

The house loomed in the dark, its silhouette stark against the starry sky as I stumbled out of the car, suddenly exhausted. I could drive back to the apartment, but that would mean having to go down Spruce again and I didn't have the energy to drive through the crowd of people that were probably leaving city hall at that very moment.

So instead, I pulled out the spare blankets from the back of my car and my duffel bag, suddenly grateful I'd had the forethought to toss it in the back of my car on the way to work. I hadn't had a chance to wash the clothes at work like I'd hoped–but they'd serve their purpose tonight, dirty or not. I spared a thought for Boots, suddenly concerned that he'd miss me as I stumbled up the broken wooden steps and pushed my way through the front door into my childhood home.

Chastity would be awake at this hour. Maybe Vanity too? But of the two sisters I was more comfortable with the former. Vanity intimidated me. She was...cool. High school-mean-girl-convince-her-boyfriend-to-throw-you-into-your-locker kinda cool. The kinda cool I'd always admired but didn't know how to approach.

Blair: Can you check on Boots for me? Sleeping at the hose.

Blair: *House

I flopped down onto the dusty mattress, coughing a little as I looked toward the rafters hidden in darkness. It was just as creepy in here as it had been before. Worse, actually, because now I knew what had happened only ten feet away from where I lay.

Chastity: Sure thing, bugaboo. Why are you at your parents' and not here?

I didn't bother answering, feeling guilty about it, but I had about two ounces of mental energy left and I was about to use them pulling on as many hoodies as possible so I wouldn't freeze to death in the middle of the night. Without my sleeping bag, the house was bound to get frigid. The blankets would only do so much. They were thin and worn, covered in plant dirt and dust. I eyed the permanently cracked window with a wince. I could already feel where the night crept its cold fingers through the opening. After I'd donned my third and last hoodie, I shoved my phone and car keys into the front pocket.

Three pairs of socks later, I flopped back down in my boxers with sleep on the horizon. As much as I didn't want to be bare to the elements, my jeans were far too uncomfortable to possibly be able to sleep in. They did, however, make a decent enough pillow, though scratchy. I shoved my duffel bag under my head as well, shuffling around uncomfortably till I managed to get its remaining contents flat enough I could relax. I glared down at my shoes where I'd tossed them at the bottom of the mattress, eyeing the hole in the bottom of the right one as my eyes began to grow heavy. *Come, sleep,* I commanded. *C'mon you fucker.*

Sleep.

Yes.

That would be good.

No more thoughts of monsters.

No more creepy villagers.

Just…sleep.

Chapter Seventeen

Richard

"THERE'S A WHAT?" My voice echoed as I clutched the phone to my ear, my fingers fumbling as I sat my spatula haphazardly down on the counter.

"A fire." Ian's voice was clear on the other end of the line, but my head was spinning too much for me to make sense of his words. "I just arrived on scene. Neighbors saw smoke—"

The closest neighbors to the Evans property were the Princes, and I was having a hard time wrapping my head around the fact that someone in my family had just called 911 about Blair's house catching on fire. It was like two worlds were colliding and I had no idea how to stop it, or even if I wanted to.

"We suspected arson at first," Ian spoke again and I zoned back in, "but there's no evidence that points to the house being lit up from the outside."

What the fuck.

"Did you call Blair?" I asked, surprised and embarrassed when Ian paused. Clearly he hadn't expected me to feel as strongly about this as I did. Hell, I was surprised too. Ian was silent for what felt like an eternity and I held perfectly still, my phone clutched in one hand, the other shifting the tofu scramble I'd been cooking off the heat. I'd made it with the hope of inviting Blair over for breakfast some time.

I didn't know how to cook tofu.

Even when I'd been human, my diet had consisted of anything plain and made of protein. Plant alternatives of any kind never made it to the menu, despite being healthy enough they probably should've.

"Evans was here," Ian told me.

Wrong. Wrong, wrong, wrong. That couldn't be right. It was five in the morning. Blair was safe at home in bed—I'd watched him drive off myself.

"He came to check out the fire?" I rationalized.

"No," Ian said, impossibly patient, gentler now that he sensed my panic. "He was inside the building. At first, we suspected he'd started it."

"He was *what?*"

My ears were ringing.

I blinked and I was out the door, my hands shaking as I stumbled down the three flights of steps and skidded my way towards my car. I'd never wished to be stronger or faster, until that moment.

"We think it might've been a suicide attempt," Ian hedged, clearly hearing the fear in my voice and misinterpreting it. "Looked an awful lot like the gasoline setup his mother—"

"Where is he?"

"I dunno, bud," Ian grunted, making a few rustling sounds like he was calling someone over. I felt young again. A lost little boy, looking for reassurance. Except unlike then, I hoped my nightmares wouldn't become reality for a second time. *God, let him be okay. Please.* There was some muttering I couldn't understand before Ian came back. "Paramedics were looking at him, but he's run off now."

He's run off.

He's run off.

Fuck. Shit. Fucking shit. Mother fuck.

"Was he okay?" I asked, trying to keep my cool even though I was failing.

"Bit spooked far as I could tell." I could practically hear Ian shrugging over the line. "Lil' banged up from hopping out the window. Had the paramedics with him for a minute before he skedaddled."

I swallowed bile, shoving my car door open and climbing inside. I needed to be ready to go to...wherever he was. It was a feeling unlike anything I'd ever felt before—The desire to be close to him, to comfort him, to check that he was safe with my own eyes.

It was overwhelming and terrifying and glorious all at once.

I realized with sickening clarity that I *cared* about Blair.

Not just because I wanted to fuck him, or because learning about him was a part of my job, or because he was different than anyone else I'd met in my entire life but...

I cared about him. I cared about the state of his cuticles because of how often he chewed his nails. I cared about the way his nose scrunched up unevenly when he was angry, or the little flicker of tension in his jaw that appeared every time he thought of something unsavory. He fought for everything, all the time, but even he couldn't disguise the way he flinched away from being touched. I cared about the way he'd leaned into me that night that I'd carried him to bed. He'd clung, his green eyes wide and lost. Staring into them had broken something inside me because he'd let me *hold* him. Vulnerable and sweet, he'd picked *me*.

I couldn't imagine what he was going through.

And now a *fire*.

What the fuck.

Was it just a coincidence? Or was there something at work here? First the party and now this? I couldn't help but connect the two instances. I had no proof, nothing but gut instinct, but something inside me said there was something more nefarious at play.

"We're ruling it an accident officially till we know more about what's going on," Ian continued and I gripped the steering wheel tight, staring unseeing out at my apartment building. I wasn't even sure I'd shut the front door, but it didn't matter.

"Just thought you should know."

"Thanks, Ian," I said, swallowing bile as I forced myself to breathe. I didn't need to. Not anymore. But the motion was soothing as my mind whirred into motion. "Let me know if you find him."

"Will do, boss." Ian hung up on me and I burst into action, pulling my phone from my ear so I could fumble to Blair's contact. I'd only recently gotten his number and had yet to find the guts to call him.

No time like the present.

Chapter Eighteen

Blair

MY LUNGS BURNED as I stepped inside the tree line. The paramedic was yelling after me but I ignored him, my heart in my throat as I fumbled my way over tree roots and ducked under branches, searching the darkness for answers I knew I'd never find. Pine tree silhouettes reached high into the sky above, blocking out the stars and the moon so all I had to guide me was my own panic and years of long-forgotten memories.

I wasn't even sure why I was running, only that after sitting for fifteen minutes in the back of the ambulance with a respirator on, watching my life go up in smoke, I couldn't...*I couldn't* do it anymore.

You're a coward, Blair.

I could hear voices calling after me but I ignored them, the battery on my phone dwindling as I turned on the flashlight with shaking hands and fell deeper and deeper into the twisting wood. It was hard to get the screen to work with bandages on my fingers but I managed. Branches whipped the tender skin on my thighs and shins, lacing my body with paper-thin cuts that stung as I moved.

I was grateful then for my clothing layers as I wobbled around in three smoke-stained hoodies, my legs chilly and soot smudged. I didn't have shoes, and each step I took ached. Branches snapped beneath my socked feet and plants clung to the fabric, poking up inside the wool hard enough to make me wince.

Moving through this part of the forest was familiar in a way nothing else in town had been. I'd spent so much time here as a kid—exploring the woods and discovering all its adventures—falling inside its depths almost seemed like coming home.

My mother's memory lived here, a ghost caught between branches.

I spared a thought for the abandoned tree that I'd rediscovered my first day back in town. It wasn't far from where I was headed so I looped back the other direction, not wanting to deal with the way just looking at its burnt husk made me feel.

Unsettled. Haunted. *Wrong, wrong, wrong.*

When I was too exhausted to move anymore, I shoved my phone in my pocket and sat down heavily on a boulder. I stared at a particularly knobby tree in front of me. Ten minutes could've passed, twenty, thirty. I didn't know. All I knew was that the twin bumps on the base on the tree in front of me reminded me of my knees. I snorted, covering my face in one hand as my laughter turned almost hysterical. A bird startled in the trees above me, probably feeling just as unsettled by my laughter as I did.

Crickets chirped. The stars continued to shine. But I was blind to everything but the tension in my chest and the whirlwind of thoughts in my head.

Was someone trying to kill me?

What was going on?

Jesus, god, my house.

Every plan I'd had for my future fell away as I realized with sickening clarity that with no house there would be no paycheck to get me out of here. I was stuck, well and truly. A sitting duck just waiting for whoever had set my house on fire to find me again, or my aunt to show up and finish what she'd started that last night I'd been in Oregon.

Freak, her voice whispered.

Disgusting.

Fuck. Fuck. Fuck. I reached up to squeeze the back of my neck tight enough my nails bit into skin. Stop it. Stop it, stop it, *stop it.*

I was too emotionally raw to deal with the aftermath of any of this. I just wanted to go back. *I wanted to go back.* I wanted to go home to Boots and my plants. I wanted to curl up with my duffel bag full of Jeffrey's gifts and forget about this whole thing.

But I couldn't do that.

Because now I had to figure out what lay in store for me. At least I still had a place to live, and a job, and…a few people that maybe could be considered friends. I wasn't really sure because I hadn't had friends before. It was hard to make them when you were hiding your bruises beneath long sleeves and parroting back your guardian's hateful opinions. Other kids had never understood me. Hell, adults didn't either.

Maybe I really was the freak she'd said I was.

Leaving Oregon had been something I'd wanted since I was old enough to know I shouldn't mention to the other kids what happened at home if I wanted them to invite me to their sleepovers.

I'd sit quietly in the darkest corners of the room, rolled up in my sleeping bag with my black hair a nest of curls on my pillow, and I'd listen to the other children breathing, quiet and content because they knew the monsters wouldn't get them while they were safely cocooned in their beds.

Sometimes it was nice just to lay there, pretending I was like them, pretending like my demons didn't wear Gucci sunglasses and acrylic nails formed in the shape of claws. Pretending like my demons weren't also my angels. Like I didn't crave the scratch of fingers through my hair or the quiet burst of love that only ever accompanied a particularly harsh blow moments before.

I'd felt so alienated as a kid, my insides twisting with snakes as the neanderthal inside me taught itself whether or not we were a fighter or a runner.

I was twenty-three now and I was only just figuring out maybe I was a bit of both. That realization didn't make me feel any better about the years I'd spent in limbo, stuck like a fly in a trap as I watched the world move on without me, my chances at escape slipping through my fingers one after another in a single file line.

Maybe I *was* a freak.

I'd stayed after all.

I'd stayed even though there were cameras watching me. I'd stayed even though I had to hide behind a facade every waking moment of my life. I'd stayed even though just looking at the four walls of my bedroom made them feel like they were closing in on me, crushing me tight with their oppression.

But worst of all I'd stayed because despite the beatings, despite the hateful words, despite the cruelty, somehow deep down I'd still been waiting for *her* to love me.

How fucked up was that?

God, it was like my life was one huge cosmic joke.

I was a fucking joke.

A clown pieced together with fragments of my broken sense of self. Desperate for love. Desperate for acknowledgment. Desperate for kindness.

An owl hooted behind me and I jumped about a foot in the air in response. My pulse throbbed as I panicked for a moment, gripping the boulder I was sitting on tightly to steady myself. The rock was cold to the touch. Rough. My fingers hurt, despite the cooling cream that was currently soothing them beneath the bandages the EMT had wrapped them with, but I couldn't help but squeeze the boulder tighter, looking for stability from it that I didn't feel inside.

I felt like a little kid again, fucking running away from the people who were trying to help me. A giant fucking toddler. Ridiculous. Stupid. Stupid. *Stupid.*

Running had been a terrible idea, I realized that now. What had I been running from anyway? My house was already smoke on the horizon.

Hindsight, and all that.

Soon the sun would begin peeping over the tree line. I could sense it in the flutter in my pulse and the way the creatures in the woods were beginning to settle. Branches hung low, twisting in the breeze as dew clung to the bottoms of my abused socks and my panic began to slowly subside.

The fear fled like the tide as I coughed some of the leftover smoke from my lungs and that same sense of loneliness I'd felt earlier began to creep back inside me. Like a ship at sea I was stuck unanchored, dreaming of the day I'd find land again while knowing that that day may never come.

My phone buzzed against my belly, breaking me from my reverie. I fumbled with bandaged fingers to get it free before I stared at the caller ID for a moment too long.

Richard.

What the fuck? I swiped left to reject the call.

It rang again.

I declined it again.

It rang a third time and before I could reject it a third time a text pinged at the top of my screen.

Richard: Blair, I swear to god if you hang up on me one more time I will hunt you down and make you answer.

Before I even knew what I was doing I swiped left again and opened the chat box.

Blair: Kinky

Richard: Blair. Answer the phone.

Blair: No :P

I watched the three little dots appear that meant he was typing for nearly a minute before another text pinged at the top of my screen. My battery bar was getting low, despite the fact I'd charged it at work earlier that day. Figured. First the weird dudes outside my car talking about some sort of *change* like they were a version of fucked-up Pokémon, then the fire—and now my fucking phone was going to die while I was in the middle of the fucking woods.

Richard: Why won't you answer the phone?

Stubborn motherfucker. My first response was to ignore him. But then I remembered how lonely I'd been just seconds before. My lonely ship had seen a lighthouse lit by growly-grouches and their geese-laughs. My cheeks started to hurt and, surprised, I reached up, brushing the pads of my fingers along them only to discover that I was *smiling*. Soot-stained, burned, and stupid, there I sat, smiling down at a cute—*homophobic*—boy texting me at ass-o-clock in the morning.

What kind of alternate dimension was this?

I responded, even though normally I probably would've ignored him, except instead of texting back I hit the return call button and listened to his phone ring, and ring, and ring…And…*Nothing*.

He didn't pick up.

Mother*fucker*.

"Did you seriously just demand for me to answer my phone just so you could ignore my call?" I said into his voicemail box, for once not overthinking my message as I spoke. "Dude, I thought *I* was a little shit. This is like, a new level of shittery. I'm impressed."

I hung up.

Richard called me back a few seconds later.

"Sorry," Richard said breathlessly as soon as I picked up the phone. Except *I* wasn't sorry, because I couldn't stop smiling, even though my nose smelled like a campfire and I could feel the remnants of tears I hadn't approved burning lines down my cheeks. "I was cooking breakfast, forgot I left the stove on."

That was suspiciously human of him.

"Dude, it's like five in the morning. Who the hell eats breakfast at five in the morning?"

"Me, apparently." Richard's voice was wry as he spoke, familiar in a way nothing else in this fucking town was.

You better not be falling for the village homophobe, I threatened myself. *I will cut you.*

"Are you okay?" Richard asked, his voice gentle. "You sound…weird."

"Well, I mean, it's five in the morning, Richard. You're calling me at *five in the morning.*"

The noise he made was apologetic as I listened to clattering along the other line. It really did sound like he was cooking. Or at least turning the stove off like he'd said he was. I could hear the sizzle of something probably greasy he was about to devour. My stomach rumbled.

"Sorry. I forget sometimes not everyone runs on our schedule." He seemed to realize he'd fucked up a second before I realized he had, because he fumbled quickly to correct himself. "Collin and I, I mean. We get up early."

Likely story.

"He's not here though. Right now, I mean. He's at my parents' place," Richard awkwardly rumbled.

For some reason my earlier suspicions began to rise. If Richard was something supernatural, did that mean Collin was too? As growly as Richard was, I had a hard time picturing him as anything supernatural. Maybe he was a vampire? It would explain why he never fucking ate— this weird breakfast shenanigan he was embarking on notwithstanding.

"When the fuck does Collin sleep?" I replied, head spinning as my earlier theories resurrected themselves. If Richard was a vampire, wouldn't it make sense that he slept through the day? So why was he up? Maybe staying up till sunrise was the vampire equivalent of being a night owl.

Jesus.

This was confusing.

Was I really entertaining the idea that *Richard* could actually be a supernatural creature?

"He sleeps like any normal kid," Richard bristled.

"Sure," I agreed, because I wasn't in the mood to fight about it and I desperately wanted sheepish, perplexed Richard back, not disgruntled Richard. Even though I knew he was probably equally as adorable.

Blair, stop it. We don't find homophobes cute. Even the cute ones.

"I got a call…" Richard spoke again, his words a little stilted and awkward. "That your house…"

"Burned down?"

"Yes." It was clear he was trying to be careful of my feelings. That alone was enough to make the natural wariness I felt ebb away. I doubted he could lie that efficiently. And besides, if he had been the person that had tried to kill me I seriously doubted he'd call me about it afterwards. Unless…that was his secret plan all along?

"Man. The town gossips sure are quick," I mused after a quiet minute, my head whirring.

"Unfortunately so," he replied. Except anxiety was still bubbling up inside me and the part of me that was still a little kid couldn't let my suspicions rest until I spoke them aloud.

"Did you do it?" I asked, before I could stop myself. My voice wobbled, the words coming out all funky and technicolored, like children's building blocks.

"Did I...burn your house down?" Richard confirmed, his voice quiet and even. I heard the thud of footsteps on his end of the line and then something scrape like he'd moved to sit in a chair.

I waited.

A bird chirped to my left.

The wind rustled the treetops and blew my bangs into my eyes.

The inky night sky began to melt into the beginnings of gold.

And then Richard finally spoke. "No, *baby*. I didn't burn your house down." His voice was made of patience, of kindness, of comfort. But most of all, there was understanding laced like spun silk in every word.

It weaved around me, squeezing me tight in its blanket of warmth and concern. When Richard said the word 'baby' somehow it didn't seem condescending. It was gentle, kind.

Baby from Richard meant, 'It's okay not to be in charge right now, it's okay to feel small.'

It meant, 'It's okay because I've got you.'

It meant, 'I'm sorry for your loss.'

It meant, 'It's going to be okay.'

I hadn't realized how badly I'd needed that soft-spoken affection until it tore its way through me, breaking apart the cage I had built over my heart. Carefully cultivated despair leaked from my every pore to slip into the soil of the forest, making its home among the roots and dark things, never to be seen again.

I needed Richard to say it again so badly, the desire made my veins fill with poison.

A dry sob threatened to escape my throat so I turned it into a laugh instead, brittle and broken, like me.

"Did you just call me *baby*?"

He paused, seeming to weigh his words carefully before responding. "I suppose I did."

His voice was honey over toast on a rainy day. Comforting. Warm. Safe.

I didn't know what to say because I'd never felt those things before. "Cool."

Richard snorted, a sound of relief. I wanted to comment on how calling me baby wasn't very 'toxically masculine' of him but somehow I refrained. "Are you okay, Blair?" Richard asked after another tense silence.

A breeze pushed a dark curl across my forehead and I realized I was still laughing. Like a goddamn crazy person. *God, I couldn't go a single day without sounding like a nutcase.* My laughter cut off abruptly and I was left staring at the tree in front of me, skin covered in cold sweat, the night air stinging my heated cheeks. "I'm okay," I said, even though we both knew I was lying. "Why did you call?"

"Because I got a—"

"You got a call about my house burning down?" I finished for him, exhaling raggedly. "I know *that*. But…*why*, Richard? Why are *you* the one that called me? You hardly know me. We've talked a total of like, three times, unless you count all the 'where's the ketchup refill' conversations we've had at work."

That wasn't true, but still. It wasn't like he cared. How could he? We were practically strangers. Even my own family hadn't cared about me. It was unfathomable to think that someone I'd known for a few short weeks would care enough about me to call to check on me.

How could he care about you? A voice that sounded suspiciously like my aunt whispered in the back of my mind.

You're not worth it.

Shut up, shut up, shut up, shut up.

Richard was quiet for a moment before the soft rumble of his voice filled my ear again. "I called you because I was concerned."

Blood rushed to my head and my hands began to shake as I processed his words.

For some reason they made me bristle. All my life I'd been told how incapable of taking care of myself I was. I'd searched for independence like a drowning man in search of air. To be so casually informed that he was *concerned* about me made me feel like I was a fucking burden.

I only do this because I care about you, Blair.

I was concerned, Blair.

You know I love you, Blair.

Lies, lies, *lies.*

"You don't need to be *concerned* about me." My voice came out brittle and sharp, shards of my anger bursting citrus-bright across my tongue as I spoke my truths for the first time aloud into the frigid night air. "I can take care of myself. *I do.* I can. I'm fucking—" I shivered, my bare legs trembling from the cold as the boulder beneath me scratched my tender flesh. "I'm fucking brave, okay? So, *fuck you.*"

"You know, if you keep saying that I might start thinking it's an invitation," Richard responded with a wry laugh. "But no. I wasn't concerned *about* you. I was concerned *for* you." He sighed. "Just like I'd be concerned for any friend if I found out their house had burnt down."

I could practically picture him pinching the bridge of his nose as he spoke. He did that sometimes, when he was particularly vexed by a customer's horrible handwriting, or when Ty told him we'd run out of tomatoes before the late-night rush had left.

Then his words finally hit me, and I was on cloud nine again.

"We're...*friends?*" I asked tentatively, my words delicate as butterfly wings. At that moment, I was so fragile I knew all it would take was one unkind word and I'd be crushed.

I'd never really had friends before. I'd never felt honest enough to be open. Plus, I was shit at making them in the first place, and even worse at *keeping* them around after they'd figured out how not worth it I was.

"Yes, Blair." He chuckled, pausing for a long moment as he seemed to think. Everything Richard said was with purpose. Each word handpicked to accomplish a mission he'd already planned every outcome for.

We were polar opposites in that way. Words shot out of my mouth like bullets so quickly I couldn't even load the gun before it went off again.

"Do you think I go out of my way to manipulate everyone I meet into eating dinner with me?" Richard finally spoke.

"Well...*no*, but—"

"No," he continued onwards, ignoring me and my waffling. "I called you because I have a spare bedroom, a shower, a massive amount of tofu scramble, and Collin would *literally* murder me if he found out I let you go home without making sure you were safe." He paused for a moment.

"Text me your location and I'll come pick you up."

I wanted to argue with him, especially because he was being so bossy, but I refrained. He didn't mention my lack of a vehicle, which I was grateful for. I didn't want to think about the fact that I'd abandoned it at the end of my driveway. When things calmed down I'd go back for it, but right now I wasn't ready to deal with the aftermath.

The exhaustion hit me as I realized that Richard was…surprisingly gentle. It's like he could see the 'handle with care' tape wrapped around me without me having to warn him first. "Okay, Bossy McBosspants," I grumped, even though the noose that had been squeezing around my heart finally began to loosen.

A bed. A shower. Food.

Sure, I had those things at Chastity's apartment. But…*Richard* wasn't there. And suddenly–I needed him, my heart aching, my eyes burning.

I blinked away the wetness that threatened to spill down my cheeks. Crying wasn't a luxury I afforded myself. It cost too much.

"Only problem is that I'm kinda in the middle of fucking nowhere."

Richard sighed, a low huffing sort of noise that did things to my knees, and my thighs, and the space between my thighs. *Jesus.* "We'll figure it out," he finally said.

We figured it out.

Chapter Nineteen

Blair

BY THE TIME Richard found me, I was a Blair shaped popsicle. My sweat had refused to dry and instead had frozen along my skin, making my many hoodies stick uncomfortably to my back as I shivered and shuddered and did my best not to jump every time the wind rustled too loudly through the trees.

The world was painted a pale shade of lavender as the rising sun cast its orange glow across the slash of indigo that remained of the night sky. I would've probably appreciated the beauty of it more if I wasn't trembling so fucking hard and my bony body wasn't burning calories so quickly to keep warm that my stomach had become a cavern.

I knew I looked like shit. I didn't need a mirror to know that. Honestly, it was pretty amazing that I could look *worse* than I had when I first arrived in town, drunk on caffeine with my eyes punched out. Go me, I guess. Record setter.

Shit-face extraordinaire.

Literally.

I heard Richard before I saw him. His footsteps were careful and steady, just like him. He didn't trip around like I did as he weaved through the tree trunks. He didn't swear when the branches whipped his skin—maybe they didn't, maybe they just moved to the side like the Red Sea moved for Moses. He was graceful as a jungle cat. Just as big. Just as intimidating. Except jungle cats didn't often wear leather jackets or sport sunglasses in the early hours of the morning. In a way, his resting bitch face was starting to become comforting to me. Like playing an album I'd listened to a hundred thousand times. Familiar.

When he broke through the last line of trees that separated us I stared at him. Richard shoved his sunglasses atop his head so he could look at me. His face was shrouded in shadow, pale hair lit in pastels as he took another hesitant step forward. His nostrils flared, his eyes brightening for just a moment as they flicked to the cuts on my shins before he seemed to steady himself and continue his determined journey towards me.

When he arrived, he paused in front of me, a leather-shrouded enigma. The toes of his designer boots bumped up against my socked feet, and I shivered. Whether it was from the cold or the heavy blanket of his gaze, I didn't know. His eyes were painted scarlet by sunbeams, ringed by ebony lashes, as they flickered in the light from the rising sun. Their weight trailing over my shins, my knees, inspecting the cuts that served as a reminder of where the tree branches had whipped my flesh. It almost looked as though Richard was fascinated with the blood that had dried on my cold-reddened skin and into the hems of my knee-high bat-themed socks.

Vampire? Maybe.

"That's a lot of socks," Richard observed after a moment. I stared at him, slack jawed. Because that had to be the stupidest observation I'd ever heard. A snort-laugh burst from my chest and I just nodded, grateful he'd broken the silence. Richard's eyes slid like syrup from the top of my head, down my throat, my collar, to the hem of my over-large hoodie, and down, down, *down* my scrawny legs. There was an almost hungry look to him, his fingers twitching at his sides as a muscle in his jaw clenched.

It felt like a stalemate.

I trembled from the cold and Richard reacted immediately. He slipped his jacket from his shoulders, the material catching around his ridiculous biceps as it slid from his body and into his hands. Once liberated, he reached over to gently lay the fabric across my shoulders. The jacket was made of butter-soft leather, cool to the touch, like he hadn't even been wearing it at all.

Vampire? Probably.

No. *Not now. Jesus, Blair. One crisis at a time.*

I pulled the fabric tighter around myself, staring at him in silence. He stared back. I didn't have the heart to tell him the jacket was probably not going to help unless I was able to take off my sweat-frozen clothing. But I got distracted by how hot he was. Again. With his jacket off, his thick chest swelled beneath it, pushing the limits of its buttons, the way it gripped his pecs honestly obscene. I wanted to lick him.

Richard's lashes looked even more ridiculous in the morning light, spiky and dark, leaving spiderwebs of shadows across the bruised hollows of his eyes. He reached out tentatively, his movements smooth and slow, careful, as he reached for one of my shaking wrists. His thick fingers looped around bone, his grip firm as he gently directed my hand, and then my arm, into the arm hole on the jacket.

The silk on the inside was slick to the touch. When my arm finally popped the rest of the way through the sleeve, Richard's lips twisted into an almost pleased little smile and he reached for my other wrist in that same bossy, but caring, way I was growing accustomed to.

"I can do it," I complained, though I made no move to stop him as he gently threaded my other arm through the sleeve and began arranging my hands inside the pockets.

"I know," he responded simply, reaching for the zipper at the bottom of the jacket. It flickered in the light as he gently dragged it upwards, the soft *ziiip* noise filling the silence. From an outside perspective we probably looked ridiculous together. This golden god with his crew cut and cultivated muscles and me—a prickly little punk with too much hair and pointy knees.

"I'm fine."

"I know," Richard said again as he smoothed a hand down the front of the leather jacket and pulled back. "I know you're fine."

"Well… *Good*," I huffed, glaring at him. Somehow I didn't think he actually believed me. Maybe he was too smart to see through my bullshit. I don't know.

"You don't have shoes or pants on," Richard observed.

"Wow." I looked down, mock surprise on my face. "No kidding?"

He laughed, his brow scrunched up in that same amused-confused expression he always seemed to wear around me. Like I was a puzzle he couldn't figure out how to solve. The laughter died quickly however, and there was a grim twist to his lips as he held a hand out for me to take. I stared at it.

His palm was wide and devoid of calluses, his fingers thick and just slightly too long. Piano fingers. That's what I'd always thought they were called. Jeffrey had them too.

Even though it felt fundamentally wrong to accept help I did it anyway, because I figured it would be a lot more embarrassing to end up falling on my frozen ass if I had refused his assistance beforehand. At least if I ended up on the ground I could blame him. Not that I *would*. Probably, anyway.

When my palm slipped into his, something settled inside my chest. It was a tentative feeling, *newborn*, so tiny it was barely more than a flutter. But still… It was there. And it didn't go away, even when we finished traipsing through the woods and reached his car. Richard headed to my side first, clearly expecting to open the door for me. I elbowed him in the ribs. Hard.

He didn't react.

"I swear to god if you open my door for me I am going to bite you," I warned, because being coddled through the woods was bad enough but I drew the line at chivalry. My nerves were too raw today to take anymore kindness. "I'm not your girlfriend, Rich." I wanted to call him something creative like 'gargantuan,' or 'dick-chard,' but somehow I managed to refrain. He wasn't being *so* awful right now. I'd save the name calling for later.

If he was surprised by the nickname he didn't say anything. He just shook his head and held his hands up placatingly. "Believe me, I have never once looked at you and thought you were my girlfriend."

"Well. Good." *Fuck, what was I supposed to say to that?* I couldn't tell if I was offended or relieved.

Richard shook his head at me, his lips thin in a way that made him look like he was trying not to smile. Amused by my inner turmoil again, the bastard.

"Which, I don't have. By the way. A girlfriend, I mean. I don't have a girlfriend," Richard clarified.

"I'm...sorry?" I climbed into the car, my legs stiff and uncoordinated as the leather squeaked beneath me. Richard shut the door after me and began the short trek around the front of the car. Its headlights lit him up, though they looked dim in the rising sun as he made his way to his side and slid into the driver's seat.

Richard's seats were way too far back but I didn't bother adjusting mine. I figured the last person to ride in here with him had probably been Collin. They both had ridiculously long legs. I wouldn't even know what to do with that much leg. Ugh, and now I was thinking about Richard's legs.

There was a half-full Pepsi in the cup holder and a whole bunch of Hi-Chew wrappers stuffed secretly in between the door and the seat. I was no Nancy Drew, but it didn't take a genius to confirm that Collin had been the last person to ride in the car. I honestly had a hard time picturing Richard chauffeuring around anyone else. He was too serious to fraternize. Too...frowny.

Except fuck anyone who wouldn't want to spend time with Richard, anyway. Richard was the shit. Kinda. Though to be fair, if you had told me earlier that day I'd be riding home with Richard fucking Prince I would've probably had a mental breakdown, so... There was *that* to consider also.

I liked Richard.

Which was why I needed to stay as far away from him as possible.

I'd go back to avoiding him tomorrow. Right now I was too weak to deny the magnetic pull I felt towards him. It felt...monumental in a way most things never had.

Being with Richard was like learning how to ride a bike. It was a lesson that would follow me for the rest of my life no matter how old I became, or what distance I traveled. There would always be Richard, underneath my skin, the memory of his Roman nose and plush lower lip, a covenant I had no choice but to keep.

"So..." I said as I settled down. Richard arched an eyebrow at me, looked at the seatbelt, and then back at me. It took me a second to figure out he was commanding me to put my seatbelt on. Nerd. I did, but I glared the whole time out of necessity for my own sanity. My hands were still shaking but the heat that had incubated inside my borrowed jacket was beginning to help despite my earlier misgivings. Something was bothering me though, and the words left my lips before I'd given them permission to. "Why don't you have a girlfriend?"

Oh god, I must be a masochist.

Why was I asking about this? I didn't want to know.

Truly I didn't.

Richard paused, his fingers trailing over the flicker of silver that was his keys in the ignition. He was frowning, a deep furrow in his brow as he sat back with a perplexed look on his face. I noticed that he hadn't buckled *himself* in, which seemed...weird to me. That perfectly pressed-big-brother-Richard would be so insistent that *I* buckle up and then leave himself totally vulnerable.

It was hypocrisy at its finest, and just another piece behind the puzzle that was Richard Prince.

"I don't..." Richard paused, seeming to weigh his words before he turned his attention back to me. "I don't...*people* well."

"You don't...people well?" My eyebrows rose. *What an interesting way to put it.*

"Well. That's the first reason." He shrugged. "There's a lot of reasons but...yes. Aside from work, I don't...socialize all that much. I *try* but, I've always been more mission-oriented and less...small talk." For the first time Richard looked almost nervous, his dark brow furrowed. "Talking to *people,* getting to *know* them, getting them to like me? I'm not...very good at that sort of thing."

Suddenly it made sense why he'd been so upset when I'd said I didn't like him.

Shit.

"You do well with me," I told him honestly. "Even though I'm a bit..."

"Prickly?" He offered. *Jerk.*

"Sure. Yeah. Prickly." I glared at him, but the expression smoothed out as something warm fluttered in my chest. Somehow coming from him it didn't seem like an insult. It was almost said fondly.

"Thank you." He looked so sincere I couldn't help but flush. My throat hurt, and my leg hair was singed, but hey—at least I had *this*, right? Whatever *this* was.

Instead of snarking back at him I just nodded, a smile blossoming across my lips for the second time that day as I reached up to nervously tuck my hair behind my ears. A single lock flopped forward and I blew it away, done with sincerity for now as I ducked my head and looked out the car window at the forest and its golden sunrise.

Richard's apartment was located on the residential side of town, conveniently close to the grocery store but far enough from the main road he had privacy. He pulled into parking spot number three with the sun over our shoulders, a tenseness to his frame that only faded away when we were safely in the shadowy stairwell leading up to his third-floor apartment. I couldn't help the way my mind wandered.

If Richard was a vampire…how was it possible he was out during sunlight? Shouldn't he burn up? Turn to ash? Get a nasty rash? Something?

"You can shower while I warm up the food," Richard offered, his voice a quiet rumble against my ear. I startled, shifting away from him and out of the way so he could work the keys gracefully into the lock. The door swung open and I shuffled forward when it was clear he was waiting for me to go first.

Richard's apartment was…plain.

It lacked personality in a way that was frankly startling. But it wasn't like the vast emptiness of Chastity and Vanity's apartment. Clinical. Fashionable. Stale. Richard's apartment was plain because it had a lack of him. There were no throw pillows, no pictures on the wall, nothing memorable aside from a Scooby Doo throw blanket slung haphazardly over half the large, well-loved couch that faced a modest television set. I knew immediately the blanket must be Collin's, probably the TV too. For some reason I had a hard time picturing Richard sitting down to enjoy an episode of *Keeping up with the Kardashians* or *That 70's Show*. Actually, the thought was pretty laughable.

The most notable thing about the entire apartment, from what I could see, was the massive floor to ceiling windows that lined one wall of the living room. They had the same black filter across them that I'd seen decorating most homes around town. The filter looked like it was removable, but the top was so covered in dust it was clear it had been a long time since it had been opened. Hardly any sunlight crept through the cracks, the room bathed in artificial light instead of the sun.

That seemed very...vampire-esque? Maybe. I wouldn't be surprised if the blinds blocked out ninety percent or more of the sun's rays. Maybe Richard was one of those vampires that had some sort of immunity to the sun? *Fuck*. Depending on what TV show you watched there was all sorts of vampire lore that pointed in about a hundred different directions in that regard.

God, Richard better not sparkle like Edward fucking Cullen or I was going to have to do something drastic. Like burn the city down.

"Your place is nice," I said quietly, my feet aching as I curled my toes in my now dirty socks and stared at the beige carpet.

Don't put your dirty feet on my carpet, Blair.

Did you make this mess?

I shuddered, shaking my head to clear it as I awkwardly shuffled back onto the small square of tile that lined the front entryway. Richard was watching me, that little crease between his brows present again as he cocked his head.

His gaze made me feel bare.

"You okay?" he asked softly, reaching out towards me. For a second I thought he was going to brush my hair behind my ear but he didn't. I wasn't sure if I was disappointed or relieved. Instead, he just pulled his hand back and awkwardly shuffled away from me like he was worried he'd cross a boundary by touching me. *Weirdo.* God, Richard was such a mom-friend.

It occurred to me then that Richard had never looked at me the way everyone else in town did. He was wary, sure, but it was almost like he held a softness to him that I hadn't seen in maybe my whole life. The wariness was gone now though, instead it was replaced with heated promise and emotion I didn't have a name for.

"I'm fine." God. I kept pausing. My responses were so stilted I knew there was no way to pass it off as something normal. Richard was…again, surprisingly considerate though. He didn't comment, he just nodded at me and gestured down the hallway.

"Two doors down, on the left. There are spare towels in the cabinet across from the toilet. I'll bring you something to change into and we can wash what you have on."

"Okay." I nodded gratefully, ducking my head as I took a steadying breath and stepped onto the carpet, my shoulders drawn high with tension. I made my way towards the bathroom, stepping lightly in an attempt not to leave marks.

It should be an unspoken rule that all carpets be darker than dirt. Owning anything lighter than that was just masochistic.

Richard's bathroom was just as nice as his living room had been. It wasn't overly lavish or anything like that—but it *was* clean. Everything seemed to have a place. I snooped through his cupboards, noting the labels on everything and the fact his medicine cabinet was alphabetized.

Who did that? Who had the fucking time to alphabetize their medicine cabinet?

Richard, apparently.

I snorted to myself, feeling quite a bit cheerier as I gently peeled off my borrowed jacket and hung it on the hook above the door. I tossed my own clothes on the floor in a smoke-infused heap, frowning at the jagged scratch through Dracula's head on one of my hoodies. I'd probably scratched him when I'd been running through the woods—unavoidable but heartbreaking all the same.

This shirt, like all the others, had been a gift from Jeffrey.

I swallowed, staring down at the piece of fabric that meant far more to me than it should, before I crouched down on creaky limbs and carefully folded it up for the first time, smoothing my hand over *Dracula's* little cartoon face in apology. "Sorry, bud," I whispered softly, rising up and shuffling towards the frankly glorious shower in front of me.

As the hot water rushed over my body, I processed what had happened. In twenty-four short hours my whole life had been overturned. *Again.* Jesus. Maybe I really was unlucky.

I thought about my life back home, the constant fear, the politics. The fact that every day I had to put a mask on just to survive. Even good behavior didn't seem to have a lasting effect. I was always the bad one, the unstable one, the one that was too young to take care of himself but too old to rely on anyone else.

Jeffrey had taken care of me growing up. He'd protected me from our aunt, stepping in front of her wrath almost as many times as he turned a blind eye and let me take the brunt of her fury. We were like two orbiting planets waiting for our turn for the sun to burn us once again.

I didn't like to think about what had happened as it was. Thinking about it like that made it tangible in a way that made my head hurt and my lungs too tight for breath. Speaking the words aloud was unthinkable so I had stayed silent. A prisoner of my own cowardice, on the precipice of a canyon full of options I was too terrified to fall into. It was embarrassing, thinking back on it now with distance between me and my aunt's fists, especially when most of my life I hadn't even recognized what she was doing for what it was.

Abuse.

There was something about the give and take of my aunt's love that made it deceiving. For months on end it would almost seem like things were good. And when the dark came again, Jeffrey and I spent so much time remembering the light, searching for fractions of it, that the darkness almost seemed like a nightmare we both could wake up from.

Jeffrey was the golden child. The loved older brother, straight-laced and kind. He was patient where I was impatient, he was soft edges where mine were all hard. I had no idea how we could be related when we were so different. Different faces, different personalities, different planets. Jeffrey was Mars—copper and heat—blistering with potential. I was Pluto, small enough to be forgotten, only remembered when there was something to be angry about. Cold. Distant.

Desperate for acknowledgment.

I sighed as I cut the water off, dragging my hands down my face and wincing at the gumminess of the tape on my bandages. Luckily the burns weren't too severe, but I still probably shouldn't have gotten them wet. I picked at their edges with clumsy fingers, stepping out onto the chilled tile. The condensation was slippery beneath the pads of my feet as I wandered to the toilet seat to sit down.

Water droplets tickled their way down my back and I sighed again, continuing to pick at the tape, the reflection of my back in the mirror dancing in my peripheral vision. My tattoo looked haunting where it danced its way up my spine, long boughs tracing the knobs, its pine needles like fingers, reaching, reaching, *reaching* for something I didn't have a name for. It was a pine tree, tall and noble, its roots caressing the swell at the top of my ass while the tip of its black branches hit the knob at the top of my spine.

I'd gotten it on a whim a few months before I'd found the papers hidden in my uncle's desk. Another stepping stone in my rebellion. It had been my secret. My choice. I hadn't told anyone about it, or shown anyone, not even Jeffrey. Though he'd given me a knowing look when we'd sat across from each other at the dining room table and I'd winced as the bandage pulled when I moved. The bandages then had been just as stifling as the ones I wore now.

When I finally had the bandages completely off, my fingers felt both better and worse. They stung in the humid air though the sting was more forgiving now that they were given the opportunity to dry out. As I stared at their pruney, swollen tips I thought hard about my future.

I didn't know what I was going to do moving forward.

My house was nothing but a memory. A pipe dream I'd traveled across the country for. I had a paycheck coming in from Benji's, but that would only get me so far when I only worked part time and the pay was modest. Going home wasn't an option. For now, at least, I had a place to stay and the beginnings of friendships.

Without realizing it, I'd begun to lay roots here.

But was that even what I wanted? When I knew that staying here meant eventual discovery?

Richard had roots too, I realized, as I stared at his matching bottles of shampoo and conditioner and the way his towels were meticulously folded on the rack. The place was devoid of mess. Barren. But somehow, despite this, all the empty spaces were filled with echoes of Richard. His stupid alphabetized cupboard, his row of identical designer boots neatly stacked at the recently swept doorway, the fact that everything was clearly meticulously cleaned.

This was Richard's home, down to its barest bones. Despite the fact I still held a grudge for his treatment of Collin before we'd struck our deal, I still felt comforted being here. If Richard was really that bad I doubted I would've seen Collin with him as frequently as I had. Richard was as much a papa duck for Collin as I was. Except he was probably better.

He had more patience. I should know, because he'd exercised a lot of it with me today.

Fuck. Richard deserved more credit.

The dude was trying. That much was clear. Someone who truly looked to improve themselves and learn from their mistakes was a rare thing indeed. When I'd asked him to lay off Collin his response had been effortlessly in my favor. It made me think of him in a different light. Maybe he wasn't as much of an ass as I'd previously thought?

Plus, the man could cook a mean veggie burger, vampire or not.

And that was a whole other can of worms I needed to get into. Were vampires real? Werewolves? I couldn't think of any other creature that would need to be 'turned.' And if they were, was I really comfortable sticking around a town full of them?

Maybe if I hadn't grown up the way I had I would've taken my paycheck and my Yaris and high-tailed it out of Elmwood for the sake of my own sanity. But...

I knew what demons looked like, and Richard Prince wasn't one of them.

He was sweet, and as princely as his name suggested. A bit of a dick too, but I wasn't complaining. Sticks and stones and all that.

Did he want to suck my blood?

Probably.

Was I fine with that?

I pursed my lips, curling my toes and shivering before I stood and began toweling off. *Did I want to become a vampire's chew toy?* The answer came to me as I heard a quiet knock at the door.

"I brought you some clean clothes to change into. They're right outside the door. Breakfast is ready," Richard called, his voice both gentle and stern. Awkward. He was...awkward. I bit my lip to hold back my smile as I waited for his retreating footsteps before I opened the door and grabbed the pile of clothing.

When the door was safely shut I had my answer.

Did I want to be Richard's chew toy? *Fuck yes.* Was it going to happen? *Probably not, but a boy could dream.*

Actually, all things considered, this was kinda a god send. So much of my life had been full of nightmares that it seemed almost laughable that the one thing I'd always been obsessed with might actually be a part of reality.

I held Richard's clothing to my nose and inhaled the scent of pine and cocoa, melting a little as I rustled around until I was fully dressed. The fog on the mirror had cleared now and I stared at my reflection. My eyes still had that hunted quality to them they'd always possessed, like a deer during open season. Maybe that's why they called it hunter green? I snorted to myself at my own joke as I pulled on the too long hem of Richard's black sweatshirt and sighed.

It was surprising he had a set of sweats honestly. I'd never seen him in anything other than dark flannel and designer jeans. He was a regular old small-town-bad-boy type, except without a single bad bone in his entire *ginormous* body despite his impressive resting bitch face. The sweats were comfortable though as I hopped my way into the pants, frowning when I realized I practically drowned in them. I leaned down to loop them up my shins, even though it hurt my fingers, then straightened to inspect myself in the mirror.

Yikes.

I looked like a giant fucking toddler.

I laughed, shaking my head and moving to push my hair behind my ears, the water tickling my already sensitive skin. It was like the fire had never truly left me, my body still pink from its cruel caress. For a while I just watched myself blink, noting my dark circles and the fact my lips were chapped.

Normally that's something someone would've noticed from the sensation of lips tugging and cracking but not me. Apparently I was so far removed from reality that even putting on fucking lip balm deserved a gold star.

Luckily Richard had some filed under 'c' for 'chapstick' right next to a box in his cupboard full of bandages. It looked like he'd put them in their own container. Because god forbid he keep the original packaging like us normal folk.

Maybe there was something to be said for alphabetized medicine cupboards after all.

Chapter Twenty

Blair

MY STOMACH GROWLED as I made my way down the hallway to the kitchen. I could smell the tofu scramble before I saw it, my body tuned to its flavor like a hound on the hunt. I had no idea *why* Richard had fucking tofu scramble, but hey, I wasn't going to judge. Not when his forethought meant getting to eat.

Maybe vampires liked tofu? Who knew.

Vegan vampires. What an interesting thought.

I coughed as I took a seat at the little table tucked into the back left corner of the kitchen. It had another massive blacked-out window facing the front of the street. I could just barely make out the fuzzy shapes of the parking stalls and the cars inside as my chair creaked and I wiggled to get comfortable.

My feet bounced on the legs of the chair as I watched Richard's broad back flex as he scraped the reheated food onto plates and turned around to face me. Somehow he looked even better like this, his thick chest pulling at the fabric of his flannel, the veins in his forearms flickering as he made his way over to the table to set the plates down with a quiet *clink*.

"Was the shower okay?" Richard asked, because he was hospitable like that.

What an asshole.

"It was great, thanks man," I spoke softly, though the scratch to my voice surprised me. I blinked in confusion as Richard reached into a cupboard to his left and grabbed down a glass. He filled it with water from the fridge—because of course the man didn't drink tap water—and then passed it to me. It was like he was somehow fucking psychic as well as a vampire because the second the water was in front of me I began to cough.

It was a horrible coughing fit too. The kind that shakes you down to your very bones. The kind you hide during school because you don't want every single kid and teacher in the entire fucking universe to stare at you like you have leprosy. Red-faced, spittle flying, wishing you could disappear.

It seemed to go on forever—my lungs quaking, throat burning. By the time it ended I was fucking exhausted, my head swimming as I reached for the glass of water gratefully. Except, like always, I miscalculated the distance and ended up knocking the glass over. Luckily it didn't break but the water did spill everywhere, traveling the grain of wood on the table. I watched with a sort of stunned fascination, my reaction time lacking once again, as I gaped at the water like it had personally betrayed me.

I waited to be yelled at. Reprimanded. Something–anything.

Instead Richard's hand appeared in front of my gaze, his wrist surprisingly dainty and decorated in green-blue veins that shifted as he efficiently swiped the mess into a rag with a flick of his fingers. I watched the golden hair on his arms with a desperate sort of want, my mouth dry, my heart fluttering. He didn't yell. He didn't get angry. In fact, he didn't say anything at all, just grabbed my glass, left with it, and returned with it full again.

Soft.

He was so fucking *soft*.

All hard muscles on the outside but gooey caramel beneath, like his glare and his biceps were only there to scare off those that were unworthy. Those that would look at him and judge him based on appearance alone and not the content of his character.

My throat clogged up again, but this time it had nothing to do with the smoke that had scraped down my throat. It was emotion.

Foreign. Terrifying. Freeing.

My eyes burned with the beginnings of tears and I forced myself to look away, processing Richard's casual acceptance of my folly. If I'd done anything like this back home, I would've ended up humiliated for it at the very least, or at worst with a new set of scratches like track marks along my face.

The fact that Richard so casually accepted my faults and didn't... fucking *comment* on them made something heat lava hot inside my chest and threaten to explode.

"Thanks," I croaked again, reaching for the glass much more carefully this time. I brought it to my lips, sipping at it as I peeked through my lashes at the man in front of me.

"Do you like ketchup?" Richard asked, expression neutral as he moved to the fridge. I peeked over his shoulder inside it, surprised by the sheer amount of vegetables and fruit that overflowed. My stomach growled again and I nodded.

"Yes."

He returned once again, gently setting the bottle down with a quiet thunk. My stomach gurgled embarrassingly loud and I grabbed it, liberally dousing the plate in front of me as I inhaled the salty-sweet scent. Fuck! Bell peppers! There were *bell peppers*! I grinned a little, unable to help myself as I grabbed the first red bell pepper piece I saw inside the scramble and popped it into my mouth.

"Fuck yes." I wiggled happily, not really noticing I was doing it as I plucked up another piece of pepper and paused before it met my lips.

Richard made a weird snort sort of noise that I figured was supposed to be a bastardization of a laugh and I glared at him, slipping the food onto my tongue and sticking it out at him just to watch the way his face scrunched up in disgust.

Eating like this was liberating. Being *allowed* to eat like this was liberating. To be gross, to be uncultured, to be…young. Carefree.

I grinned at Richard again and toasted him with a fork full of scramble, the light above catching the ketchup and making it appear like blood from one of the '80s horror movies I loved so much.

Richard sat down on the other side of the table, watching me with hooded eyes as I shoveled the food down my throat with reckless abandon.

"This is fucking *good*," I told him as I scraped ketchup onto a large piece of tofu and popped it into my mouth with my fingers. When that stung I picked up my abandoned fork again, eating with a gusto I'd never let myself indulge in before. I enjoyed the way that Richard was observing

247

me. I could feel his gaze like fingers dancing over my pulse, almost like he was fascinated just by watching me do something as normal as eating.

I slowed down a little, self-conscious, as I realized just how messy I was being. He didn't seem to mind though, he only pushed the bottle of ketchup toward me again.

It felt amazing to get to make a mess, so I did. And Richard continued to observe in that weird silent way of his, his whole expression neutral even though I could see warmth flickering inside his scarlet gaze.

The overhead light painted Richard's pale hair in a soft yellow glow as he blinked at me, expression evolving as his eyes narrowed and his lips thinned in thought. He cocked his head to the side, the little furrow in his brow returning where it had been absent.

Hello, old friend.

"What's got your panties in a twist?" I questioned after I finished chewing a particularly awesome bite. I would've stuck my tongue out to disgust him again—but he was being really nice so I managed to refrain.

"I was just thinking about you," he said quietly, actually answering the question honestly to my surprise.

"Why?" I asked, tipping my head forward as I lapped at the ketchup on the pads of my fingers and grimaced immediately afterward. Richard's nostrils flared and he flinched a little in response. For a second I'd forgotten that my fingers were burnt and apparently the brush of my tongue was too hard for the fragile skin to handle despite the way they'd managed most of the meal just fine.

Maybe I'd just been distracted by dark eyes and the way Richard's Adam's apple bobbed when he swallowed.

"You're hurt." Richard rose from his seat and disappeared down the hallway. I was left staring at his vacated chair with a weird sense of both longing and loss for the conversation we'd been about to have.

Oh well. At least I had food.

I finished my plate.

Richard returned a few minutes later, his eyebrows twitching in what I assumed was amusement when he saw that I had finished in record time. He didn't comment though, instead he casually hooked the leg of my chair with his foot and dragged it towards him. I skidded across the floor, my belly swooping as he pulled me into place effortlessly before flopping into the chair across from me.

The fact he was strong enough to move me around like a Barbie Doll wasn't lost on me.

Or my dick.

Down boy.

Our knees brushed and Richard held a hand out expectantly for mine, brow lowered over hooded eyes. I responded obediently, somehow unable to refuse when he commanded me so effortlessly, wordlessly, carefully. It was like spell-less magic. All he had to do was look at me with those big dark eyes and I was fucking weak.

Stop it.

Stop it, stop it, stop it. He's not yours, Blair. He's straight. He's not yours.

No matter how much I whispered that to my treacherous heart, it still beat an unsteady staccato as Richard held my hands in his large palms, smoothing his cool fingers over the creases in my palm and up the slender bones of my fingers so he could inspect them. "What happened?" he asked softly, reaching for the first aid kit he'd brought in with him.

Because of course that's where he'd gone.

The idea that Richard fucking Prince wouldn't have an entire arsenal of first aid supplies was laughable. He was a man with a plan after all.

The plastic box opened with a click though he kept one of my hands hostage inside his own, refusing to release it as he gently picked apart the contents searching for what he wanted. I watched him, enamored with the way the square tips of his fingers moved dexterously with purpose. He was a dancer but his dance was precision, not grace.

"The fire?" I offered, voice still scratchy. A car passed by on the street with a quiet woosh as Richard remained silent. Clearly my answer had been unsatisfactory because his thick dark brows had sunk even lower. "Um. The window. When I was getting out of the house. It…burned me."

"What?" His head snapped up, somehow managing to look even more pissed off than before, that crease between his brows ever present and cemented with concern. "What do you mean?"

"My house was on fire, Richard…" I stared at him in confusion. "Remember?"

"No, I know." He shook his head, not appreciating my sass, nostrils flaring. "I mean, why would you have had to climb out of the window? Was the fire blocking the entrance?"

"Oh." I blinked. "Yeah. It was. I almost…I mean…I almost didn't get out."

His grip on my hand was bruisingly tight now, so tight it hurt, but I said nothing, instead watching the mosaic of emotion play across his face as he seemed to realize just how close to death I had come. I relived the experience through him, trembling as I remembered the pain, the confusion, the fear. "Fuck."

I was pretty sure that was the first time Richard had sworn in front of me. I didn't comment on it, I just nodded, my fingers slipping between his until our palms lay flat, skin to skin, and I could give him a painful squeeze in return. "I'm okay," I reassured him quietly, not sure why he cared but too grateful to do anything but hold him tight. My knees burned where they touched his, like every point of contact between us was electrified.

"The window—" Richard continued, almost like he hadn't heard me. "How did you get it open? That house has been sitting abandoned for years. I wouldn't be surprised if the windows were sealed shut."

"Collin," I answered, squeezing him tight enough my knuckles turned white. I watched his mouth twitch with barely concealed emotion. "Um. He's been getting into my house for who knows how long through the living room window. He…He saved my life."

"Fuck," Richard said again.

Fuck indeed.

Half an hour later my clothes were in Richard's washing machine and I was watching *SpongeBob* on his tiny TV. After being banished to the couch to rest, he'd bundled me up with blankets like he thought I had nearly frozen to death, not burned, turning me into a five-foot burrito full of angry goth.

I could hear him in the other room, cleaning up the dishes and the wrappers from the million and a half adhesive bandages he'd painstakingly placed on all my fingers. The scent of cocoa began filtering through the air and I peeped over the top of the couch, biting my lip to keep from laughing as I watched him dump far too many cocoa packets into a mug that sat steaming on the counter.

Richard hadn't dealt with the cuts on my legs and I hadn't asked. I figured maybe that was too much temptation even for him. I'd seen the way he eyed them though, hungry and hot, his pink mouth slightly parted. It only seemed to solidify my fang-themed suspicions about him, and by extension, this whole fucking town.

Richard was a cocoa wielding, flannel wearing, sex machine who may or may not be undead.

But my house was still burned down so instead of ogling his ass and contemplating whether or not I should beg him to bite me, I just stared blankly at the TV in front of me and watched *SpongeBob* while my brain stressed the fuck out.

"I was going to take Collin out today," Richard said from right behind me. I jumped, my hand slapping against my chest in an attempt to still my racing heart as I whipped around to face him. I hadn't noticed his approach. Maybe my lack of sleep was catching up to me? Or maybe it was just Richard. The way he got under my defenses like water through cracks in a dam.

It was wild actually. Apparently the walls I'd erected to protect myself had a door and Richard just so happened to have a key.

"Jesus fuck, Dick-chard. Warn a guy." I looked up at him, my hair spilling in inky black waves across the cushion behind me. Richard's expression was far from innocent as he shifted, leaning his hands against the back of the couch so he could stare down his nose at me with a perplexed twist to his expression that even I couldn't explain away.

"Dick-chard?" he asked.

"You know. Because…Richard. And Dick. Haven't you heard of Dick Grayson?" I blinked, weirdly embarrassed. I hadn't actually meant to call him that, out loud anyway. "*Batman*. You know. *Robin*? Dick is a nickname for—"

"Richard. I know." He continued to blink at me, but then amusement won the battle waging on his face and he laughed, his nose scrunching up into a million tiny wrinkles I wanted to personally thank for their service.

Richard smiling was—*god*—it was the most beautiful thing in the world.

I was soooo fucked.

"That's a new one," he commented, cocking his head curiously. "I've heard Dick plenty. Collin calls me Bitch-ard when he thinks I can't hear. But Dick-chard… That's…very—"

"Insulting?"

"Clever." He shook his head. "If you had meant it to hurt me I wouldn't like it but…I don't think you meant it as an insult."

Motherfucker. He was right. It was almost frightening how quickly he was discovering that my love language was actually insults. I flushed bright red, turning back to the TV completely mortified. How could he see through me so transparently? I glanced at him with suspicion before turning away again.

When I was with Richard it felt like I was made of glass.

"You said something about taking Collin out," I reminded him, pulling the blankets tighter against myself. "I can head out if you need me to." I was sure Chastity would come pick me up. And if she couldn't, Elmwood was small enough it would only take me an hour or so to get back to the apartment.

I didn't want to leave though. But I didn't know how to ask if it was okay if I stayed.

I stared hard at the TV, my knuckles white where I gripped the blankets as I waited to be kicked out. Instead, Richard did something much more surprising. He reached out, tentative at first, his fingers gentle as they began to comb through the back of my hair, scratching along the short fuzz at the nape of my neck before he stroked through the longer bits on top. It was pleasure unlike anything I'd ever felt before and I melted into the touch, practically purring as my head sank low and Richard's fingers moved to squeeze the back of my neck. "I was thinking you could come with us," he said softly. All the tension in my body seeped out as his grip grew firmer and I slumped forward like a rag doll.

Fuuuck.

It felt so fucking good I could hardly breathe.

Richard made a noise so quiet I was sure I'd imagined it. A little overwhelmed groan, like maybe watching me become putty inside his hands was doing it for him just as much as it was doing it for me.

But that was crazy. *Right?*

God, I was weak. My knees trembled, my cock twitching as his fingers began to move again and he rubbed up behind my ears. My lashes fluttered and he moved, his touch softening until he slipped back alongside the delicate slope of my spine to frame the center of my neck once again. He was massive. Fucking–deliciously big.

I shuddered and Richard made that same noise in the back of his throat. This time louder. *Hungrier.* It was carnal and deep with desire. Decadent. Desperate. Dominating. Fuck. Fuck. *Fuck.* I needed a dictionary to learn the meaning of all of Richard's noises. Because I wanted to, no, *needed* to, desperately.

"Blair?" he asked softly, his voice sweet as honey and thick with gravel. The way it curled around the shell of my ear made my dick twitch and my pulse flutter. Jesus fuck. He'd never spoken to me like that before. It took me a second too long to realize he'd been asking me a question.

Right. Collin. Shopping.

"Uh. Yeah. Sure. I'll come with." I didn't move, though I couldn't help the way I tipped my head down even further, welcoming the firm, cool grip of Richard's palm where he squeezed my nape. His hand was big enough that his fingers could dip into the sensitive skin at the front of my throat, his palm encasing the entire back of my neck as he gave me another gentle squeeze.

"Good." His breath tickled the back of my ear and I trembled, some of the anxiety that had lived rent free inside me trickling its way out the longer he squeezed. I was putty in his grasp and *god*…it was like his hand had a direct connection to my cock. With him holding me like that there was nothing I could do but obey him. "Get some rest. We'll leave tonight."

He released me and like a puppet, all my strings were cut. It was a weird sort of severance though, it spoke of 'laters' and 'maybe's' and not of abandonment. I curled up in a little ball and with Richard's command curled warm around my heart I fell asleep.

Chapter Twenty-One

Blair

"NO FU—REAKING WAY!" Collin cheered the moment he saw me. We'd picked him up from the Prince's family home and I was unsurprised to discover it was only half a mile down the road from the burnt husk of my parents' house. The driveway was so long I couldn't actually see the building through the trees but it didn't seem to matter because when we pulled closer I saw that Collin was waiting just outside the large wrought iron front gate.

I knew the Princes were rich. It didn't take a genius to figure that out. But getting lost between a pile of blankets in Richard's surprisingly normal apartment had not prepared me for the obviousness of his family's fortune.

What eccentric assholes. Who needed a ten-foot-tall gate to block the driveway?

What were they hiding from? Elmwood had a population of basically five.

Maybe it had something to do with the vampire thing?

Either way, it didn't matter. The Princes were rich. *Rich*-rich. Disgustingly rich.

I'd known this, of course, because who the fuck wears a $300 T-shirt? Correction. Who buys a $300 T-shirt for a teenager who is just going to grow out of it, unless they have extra money to throw around?

"Blair's coming with?" Collin hopped into the back seat with enthusiasm, slamming the door probably harder than necessary though it was clear in this aspect of his life Richard didn't mind a little over-exuberance. His lips just twitched into what I was coming to realize was his version of a smile, his dark sunglasses perched atop his nose as he tipped his chin back and arched one of his bossy-eyebrows in Collin's direction.

Ah. Right. *Seatbelt.*

"Ugh. Fine, *Mom.*" Collin rolled his eyes heavenward, clearly understanding the look without words because he reached for his seatbelt and clicked it home.

"They're showing *Lost Boys* at a theater out in Ridgefield," Richard said, segueing cleanly into driving the moment he deemed me and Collin both sufficiently buckled.

"*Lost Boys?*" Collin asked curiously, leaning forward as far as his seatbelt would allow as he gripped the back of both of our seats. His dark eyes glittered in the light and I was suddenly overwhelmed with a sense of loss as I looked at him. I'd seen that same expression on Jeffrey a hundred times growing up. Fuck. Collin reminded me of him so much that sometimes it hurt just to look at him. "What's that? Like…a retelling of *Peter Pan* or something?"

That was when his words finally caught up to me. "Dude." I blinked, snapping around to face him fully. "You're kidding right?"

"No?"

Richard shook his head from beside us but remained silent as he pulled off Spruce, casually swinging a right before the stretch of street that the city hall was on. I probably would've thought it was weird he didn't take the main road, the faster option, if I hadn't been so completely morally offended by the fact that Collin thought *Lost Boys* was a movie about fucking Peter Pan.

"*Lost Boys* is a cult classic," I educated him, shaking my head. "It's about vampires. It's only one of the *best* vampire films of all time."

"Oh." Collin gave me a weird look, his gaze sliding to Richard for a moment before he turned back to me, the apprehension melting away. Probably because Richard was a fucking vampire suggesting we go watch a movie about vampires.

Maybe I was crazy? But I didn't think so.

Not about this.

"It's fucking awesome and you're going to love it." I jabbed a finger threateningly at Collin, my eyes narrowed.

"It's also rated R," Richard added, sweetening the deal.

"But I'm fifteen—" Collin blinked. "Oh. *Oh*. Richard." His grin came back full force, eyebrows wiggling. "Are you smuggling me into an R-rated movie? Holy shit. Who are you and what have you done with my brother?"

Collin squawked for a while in the back and I was suddenly filled with a sense of belonging I'd never really felt before. The two brothers were ridiculous in an adorable way. They poked at each other, squabbling like squirrels over everything, the song on the radio, the radio station, the car temperature, what way was the quickest out of town.

"The movie theater is like an hour away," Collin warned me when we'd finally settled on an indie/folk station. It had been Richard's choice, which I found kind of hilarious but I kept to myself. "But it's at this sick mall, which has like the best pretzels known to humankind." His face fell. "Wait. You don't eat pretzels do you?"

God, he looked like an adorable little puppy. I laughed and shook my head at him. "If they have an option with no butter, then yes."

"Fu—reak yes!" He perked right back up again, slapping the back of my seat with enthusiasm until Richard grunted at him in his growly way, a clear 'cut it out' that didn't need words to be impressive.

"They have kettle corn at the theater too," he informed me with a look of importance on his face. "Is that vegan?" He blinked. "One sec." There was a rustling noise and then silence before Collin's head popped back up. "I Googled it and Google says that most kettle corn is 100 percent vegan. I bet we could just ask the dude up front if it is or not, right Richard?"

Richard grunted.

"Oh shit—sorry." Collin blinked, failing to stop the swear from escaping despite his best efforts. I wasn't sure why he was even trying. Maybe tall, dark, and growly had a thing against him doing it? Richard rolled his eyes. "Oh, shoot," Collin tried again, moving on quickly. "But then they might remember my face. How will we accomplish movie theater espionage if they remember us?"

Movie theater espionage. Jesus.

"I can get the popcorn," I offered, because I didn't like seeing Collin freak out. Except now that I knew I wasn't going to get any money from my house, thinking of spending the small amount I had set aside made me want to throw up.

Richard glanced at me and I shrank in my seat, my mood souring as I watched the trees whip by the window and I tried to think of a way out of the hole I'd dug myself into. It wasn't a big deal. I wanted to do this. It would be fine. *It would be fine.*

"I'm buying the popcorn," Richard dismissed us both. "I'm the least suspicious looking out of the three of us."

God, they were both ridiculous.

Relief flooded up inside my chest at the same time a laugh burst from my lips. "Says the six-foot-four sun god with a chest I could bounce a quarter off."

Richard's stare was hot on the side of my face but I couldn't look at him, too embarrassed by my own flirting because I hadn't really meant to flirt in the first place. The words were just too close to the surface. And true. Entirely too fucking true.

I never would've pegged Richard as the kind of person that was willing to sneak his fifteen-year-old brother into an R-rated movie, but hey. This was the same man that had convinced me to break into our place of work to make burgers. Richard was an enigma, and the more I learned about him the more I liked him.

"I'm also buying the tickets," he added, not looking at me though I knew that the words had been for my benefit. Politeness dictated I argue but I had no money to argue with, so I just nodded and flushed, shrinking into an embarrassed little ball.

"Heck yes!" Collin cheered from the back.

"Not for you," Richard corrected, glancing over the rim of his sunglasses into the rear-view mirror at Collin. "You still owe me fifty bucks from the last time I took you to the mall."

"What?" Collin gasped, though it was clear he was guilty by how pink he got. He flopped back into his seat. "Fiiiine."

Richard was smiling again, an amused look to his plump lips and I couldn't help but look at him gratefully, my eyes tracing the expression on his face with fascination. How could he be so gentle and firm at the same time?

Sorcery. That had to be it. I'd never met anyone like him before.

Everything went without a hitch when we arrived at the theater. We made a funny group. One giant, one half-giant, and one hobbit drowning in twenty pounds of black fabric. I had to grab the legs of my borrowed sweatpants like a medieval woman would her skirts, waddling around so they wouldn't slip off my ass and onto the ground.

Richard took pity on me halfway down the hallway after he'd procured tickets—for all of us—and snuck Collin in. He passed the popcorn to Collin and reached for me, falling to his knees on the dirty carpet, his expression tentative like he expected me to run. That hesitance is what made me hold still. Besides. I hadn't done anything to deserve punishment. So I doubted what he was doing would be bad. He relaxed when I did, reaching out for the hem of my hoodie. Thick fingers bunched in the fabric, dragging it upwards till his cool knuckles brushed up against the sensitive skin on my belly. I stared at the top of his head when he found the hem of my sweatpants and painstakingly rolled the fabric up until they sat snug on my hips.

"Better?" His voice was gravelly again, his dark lashes a smear on his cheeks as he peeked up at me through them, eyes nearly blood-red. I shuddered, my belly clenching against where his knuckles continued to brush my sensitive skin.

Richard's nostrils flared, a look crossing his face that made me weak-kneed as I bobbed my head.

"Sure, yeah." My voice cracked and he nodded, releasing me and smoothing the hem of my hoodie down before he rose to his feet and reached for the popcorn again. He led us down the hallway and I couldn't help but stare at the broad slope of his back, confused and horny and perplexed myself. Fuck.

Collin sat between us when we found our seats and I wasn't sure if I was disappointed or grateful. For a small theater the seats were surprisingly comfortable. I was able to tuck my knees up against my chest and sit comfortably without the armrests digging into my ribs. The lights dimmed as the commercials began to play and I heard crunching to my left as Collin dug into the food immediately.

He offered me a handful with an eyebrow waggle and a sly, slick little grin. I let him dump it into my lap and plucked at pieces eagerly, peeking over Collin's body to catch glimpses of Richard through my lashes, casually, so he hopefully wouldn't notice my staring.

Richard didn't eat any of the popcorn.

It hadn't escaped my notice that he hadn't partaken in the tofu scramble from this morning either, or the burgers from the night he'd cooked for me. When I'd inquired about it earlier he'd claimed that he'd already eaten.

But *when*?

And when did either of my companions ever fucking *sleep*?

That was answered quickly enough when halfway through the movie Collin conked out completely. His head lolled to the side, his nose nuzzling against my shoulder as he slid down in his seat, long legs bent awkwardly to fit in the small space.

I held very still and something warm inside my chest lurched as I glanced up from the movie screen and to my left. Richard was watching me again, a soft, confused expression on his face. He wasn't even trying to hide it either, he just…sat…and he observed. Careful as always, a man of few, but meaningful, words.

He was quiet now though so I was left wondering, watching him watch me with a flip in my belly no amount of swearing would squash.

It was honestly pretty laughable that I was in Maine at the movies just one seat away from the hottest guy I'd ever seen, only hours after my house burned to the ground. Like stepping into a parallel dimension where I was allowed to be normal and go on dates and just…exist without my past to haunt me.

It felt like being real for the first time in my life.

Pinocchio becoming a real boy.

When the movie ended Collin pretended like he hadn't slept through more than half of it. I wanted to get mock-angry at him, but I was too drunk on wine-red eyes to put up much of a fight. I figured we could always watch the movie again later. Maybe when my dick wasn't so hard and my head wasn't so spinny.

Collin walked between us out into the hallway, chattering away about the last five minutes of the movie because it had been the *only* part he'd actually been awake for.

"I'm hungry," Collin declared. He slung an arm around my shoulders, smooshing himself against me for a moment before he launched into a jaunty little tune he claimed had been stuck in his head all day.

And yet…still Richard watched me. Despite his brother's antics, his eyes never seemed to leave my face. I didn't want to get caught staring back again so I forced myself not to look even though my skin tingled all over from his attention.

God. What was his *deal?*

Did I have popcorn on my face or something? I reached up surreptitiously to check, casually wiping my face on the over-long sleeve of my hoodie just in case. Nothing. Nada. So…why? And why did it feel *so fucking good* to be the center of his attention?

It almost seemed laughable to think that I could be anyone's sun even for a moment, to alter a person's orbit in the same way my world was always rotating.

"Richaaaard," Collin complained from beside me, bumping his hip up against his brother's in a way I was sure he meant to be just as annoying as it was. Richard rolled his eyes heavenward, before he released a long drawn-out sigh and steered us towards the entrance.

"Do you have more money?" he said evenly. Without his gaze to heat me I felt ice cold, trembling in my borrowed shoes as my feet slipped into the open spaces. They were Collin's so they weren't too big, but they still made me feel like I was waddling around wearing clown shoes.

"No." Collin pouted, forcing us all to a stop as he blinked his big doe eyes in Richard's direction. A couple speed-walked around us, giving us the stink eye as they hurried towards the exit. It was lined with light-up posters of the movies showing down the hall we'd come from and moonlight crept through the windows and across the carpet, painting the entrance in the shade of blue night always seemed to be no matter where in the world you were. Familiar. *Comforting.*

Collin batted his lashes, and it was clear what he was trying to do. I watched in fascination as Richard's face performed Olympics while he debated how to respond. To feed the annoying brother and get him to stop being annoying? Or to let him go hungry because it was his own fault and clearly he thought that he could get whatever he wanted just because he was cute.

He *was* fucking cute though, and as he blinked and pouted I didn't envy Richard in the slightest. It did however make me wonder why the two brothers were so close. There was clearly an age gap and Richard himself had stated that they had three other brothers, and that their parents were still around, so why did I get the feeling that when it came to the Princes, Richard and Collin made up their own familial unit?

Richard was going to say no. He'd already bought Collin his ticket and the popcorn. There was no way he was going to give in again. Even his eyebrows said no. But then he surprised me and I watched as his lips twitched and he released a put-upon sigh.

"Fine. I'll buy you both dinner," Richard lamented. I blinked in surprise, not having seen that coming at all. God. *Richard was a softie.* He was worse than *I* was, and I'd always thought I was a sentimental fool. The fact that Richard had made a point to include me in the food discussion to soothe my anxiety, was just…mind boggling. I'd never had a friend like him before—or at all really.

He was thoughtful and firm. Responsible. Kind.

God, was it fucked up that I wanted him to spoil me more? I wanted him to watch me, to give me all his attention. I wanted to hear more of those startled little huffs he made when he was surprised by a joke, like the joke had snuck up on him and shocked the laugh right out of him. I wanted to be the center of his universe. I wanted him to want me just as badly as I was beginning to want him. And…fuck. Fuck. Fuck. Fuck. This was bad…*so very bad.*

Crushing on a straight boy only ever led to heartbreak.

Besides, he's homophobic. Remember, Blair? I reminded myself, except the words felt hollow now and didn't seem at all right. How could this generous, sweet, soft-hearted man possibly be homophobic? It didn't make sense.

Maybe there was more to Richard than I had thought there was.

We went to a Mexican restaurant despite Collin complaining the whole time about us missing the opportunity to go to the pretzel shop. He'd Googled it though, and discovered it had closed at 8, right before our movie had let out, so really he was just complaining for the fun of it.

I didn't mind though, and neither did Richard. It was nice to listen to his scratchy little voice fill up the silence. Collin never seemed to stop talking. He had an opinion about everything and a rant to back up each statement. His footsteps were loud and enthusiastic as we made our way down the moonlit sidewalk and towards the Mexican restaurant a few blocks down from the theater and where we'd parked.

The building was at the entrance of the shopping complex. From our seats on the outdoor patio, I could see the mall peeking out from behind it like a hallway full of consumer delights. String lights decorated the walkway and its cobbled pavement, the night sky shining above despite the spring chill. Each shop was lit up, decorating the walkway with its own personal lightshow as my gaze dragged down clothing stores, to dessert stores, to skateboard shops.

It didn't escape my notice that Richard had specifically chosen a restaurant he knew I could eat at, and...once again I was overwhelmed by the rush of gratitude that choked up my throat at the thought.

We ate outside. Richard sipped at water while Collin and I sprawled in our seats and the chill night air tickled the tips of our noses. The smell of greasy-delights and fried cheese wafted in on the breeze. I inhaled greedily, taking a tentative bite of my bean burrito as I observed Richard people watching. For once his gaze wasn't on me, but I didn't mind because it meant that I could stare at him instead.

He looked like a god like that, all tall and built with his chiseled jawline and his dark brows. There was something about him that screamed 'do not approach' in the same way something about me always seemed to scream 'I'm easy to hurt.' We were opposing images. Yin and yang. But somehow that was what made it feel so right to sit beside him.

If I had been with anyone else I would've been thinking about my impending doom, my fear, my doubt— But instead I couldn't help but think about how lucky I was to still be here, to be sitting beside these two adorable men, watching the stars where they peeked between buildings.

It was like I was in a different world entirely. A world full of possibility, of understanding, of opposites that attracted instead of repelled.

Richard gave me hope, and hope was a dangerous, dangerous thing for a person like me to have.

By the time we finished eating, I was too exhausted to argue with Richard when he insisted on buying me a few things before heading back to Elmwood. I'd told him earlier about my duffel bag going up in smoke and he'd made a few concerned glances at my ripped-up Dracula hoodie as he'd tossed it in the wash for me before we'd gone to bed that morning.

There were so many things I wanted to say, but all that came out of my mouth when he commanded me ahead of him and toward a clothing store was a sarcastic, "Yes, sir."

Which…I could tell he liked more than he cared to admit, because his cheeks got all pink and he got this pleased little flicker to his lips that made me want to both smack him and smack him with my lips.

Stupid little shithead.

Fuck.

I liked him so goddamn much and I barely knew him. I knew it was wrong. I knew I needed to run, that I didn't have time to have feelings like this, that they couldn't ever be reciprocated. That didn't stop me from soaking up his attention like a sponge though as he wandered off to shop on his own when it became clear that I was too far gone and way too full to be any help.

The clothing store had a pleasant ambiance, though it wouldn't have been my usual choice. There was a section in the back that sported a wide variety of punk-esque clothing items, and I could see Richard's blond head poking up over one of the racks. I found a wall near the entrance to lean against, sighing as I shoved my hands in my pockets and stared at my too-large shoes.

"Food baby?" Collin commiserated, leaning against the wall beside me, both his hands on his distended belly with a proud little smile on his lips.

"Twins actually," I responded, before I snorted out a laugh.

"Congratulations." He grinned back at me, clearly pleased, his big brown eyes so familiar and yet so… New. New possibilities, new friendships, new family. "When are you due?"

"Probably as soon as we get home," I countered, only to realize that Richard had walked up and was eyeing us both with thinly veiled disgust. Maybe he'd had a question—but…clearly his disgust held more importance than his question. I could practically see the thoughts in his head as he shook it and walked away.

Humans.

God. I should probably stop speculating about the presence of vampires and just fucking ask him. What was the worst-case scenario?

He'd kill me.

Maybe. Probably. I mean *I'd* kill me if the situation was reversed. There was probably a reason everyone in town was so fucking suspicious of me all the time. They probably didn't want newcomers knowing their secret. Actually, this whole thing made a weird amount of sense. No wonder everyone had been treating me weird. I figured it might be best for me to just let things…play out as they needed to.

Collin was still cackling from my joke when Richard returned with his arms full of bags and he nodded his head towards the door. That was quick.

"Wait. I thought you said a *few* things, Rich. Not the whole fucking store?" I panicked a little as I hurried after him, having to practically run to match each of his long strides.

"Your definition of a few and mine are different," he snarked back casually like a little shithead, though he had the amused look on and not the pissed off one as we paused in front of a shoe store and he pursed his lips in thought, clearly debating with himself. "What shoe size are you?"

"Richard, I swear to god."

"If you don't tell me I'm just going to guess," he threatened, arching an eyebrow at me. "And then you wouldn't be able to wear them, and it would be a complete waste of my money."

Motherfucker. How did he know me so well? There was only one thing that would get me to acquiesce.

"Besides. There's a sale," Richard added, only sweetening the deal. I gave in. Because of course I did. And it had nothing to do with his boyish grin afterwards, or the way my stomach flipped when I saw it, and everything to do with the buy-one get-one fifty percent off deal advertised in red and white on the front window.

Maybe if I told myself that enough I'd start to believe it.

Maybe if I gave myself more time I could convince myself that I didn't like him.

Maybe.

Chapter Twenty-Two

Blair

AFTER CALLING CHASTITY to ask if she'd keep an eye on Boots, Richard made me stay the night at his place. It wasn't really a hardship though. His whole fridge was stocked with fruits and veggies he told me to have free rein over, and he had Cartoon Network on his TV. Which I'd never been allowed to watch growing up so it felt almost naughty to partake in now.

I liked it. *The naughtiness.*

He offered me the spare bedroom but I told him I was more comfortable sleeping on the couch, so Collin got the bedroom, and I got the TV.

Some of the cartoons that played were genuinely a bit freaky and I watched them with morbid fascination, my eyes glued to the screen as each baby carrot in the bag on my lap made the journey to my mouth.

Richard got up close to three in the morning. I only noticed him because I was becoming accustomed to the feeling of his eyes on me. I turned to look at him, my skin a myriad of colors from the flashing lights on the TV screen as I caught his gaze.

There was something…*different* about him. An edge to him that hadn't been there earlier that day. His eyes were luminous in the dark, reflecting the light almost like a cat's. Or maybe…maybe that was just because if I squinted it looked like they might be glowing.

He probably thought I would be asleep.

Fuck. Was it time for him to feed?

What did that even entail? Should I leave? Did he need privacy? If I acted weird he'd know I knew, or, alternately, I'd look like a crazy person because he was just a normal dude who had trouble sleeping.

It was a Russian roulette of fuckery.

"Can't sleep?" he asked quietly, for once sticking to his side of the room. His voice filled the space between us like syrup, thick and honey-sweet. I shuddered, sitting up, pulling my cocoon tighter around me, suddenly very aware of my bedhead.

God. He looked like sex on legs standing there, his eyes bleeding red, lips bitten pink and kissable. Richard was…he was…he was *something*.

Richard is straight, I supplied myself helpfully, or *unhelpfully*.

"Got a lot going on in my mind," I replied, watching him a little warily as my toes curled in the carpet. If he was a vampire, and this was his normal feeding time, what was going to stop him from crossing the distance between us and taking a bite of what I so obviously had on offer?

What I lacked in courage I made up for in blood.

"I can imagine." He blinked at me, slow and sleepy, almost like he was hypnotized as he took an unsteady step closer. "You've had quite the day."

I nodded, plucking at my borrowed hoodie underneath the blanket nervously. Richard hadn't let me see inside the bags he'd bought, claiming it could wait for morning. At first I'd wanted to complain but I'd held back, especially when I realized that it was going to be suspiciously like Christmas getting to open all those gifts. Despite feeling immensely guilty I also felt…excited. I'd never had anything like that. Christmas had always been a religious affair and what little excitement had accompanied it had been swallowed up by Jeffrey's guilt when he received gifts that I didn't.

I didn't care about the gifts. It was the inequality. The feeling of being an outsider in my own home, unwanted in a way my 'brother' never was. Why my aunt had even taken me in I'd never know. She had despised me from the moment I'd met her, her eyes cold, lips twisted.

You're just like your mother.

I figured it was because I reminded her of her dead sister. But I refused to ever ask outright. In fact, I was hoping soon enough I could get out of Elmwood and hide away somewhere she could never look at me with those cruel, emotionless eyes again.

Jeffrey would join me wherever I went. I'd make sure of it. We'd live happily ever after, our own little family, like Richard and Collin.

Except…

Why did that thought make me feel sad all of a sudden? Empty. It seemed wrong to want a future that existed outside of Elmwood. A future without Collin's chatter in my ear and Richard's gaze trailing over my neck. This strange town with its nosy people and penchant for odd hours had become like a home to me in such a short time. The fact I'd nearly died didn't change that.

I'd stared at the burning husk of my childhood home just that morning, wondering who would mourn me when I was gone. I'd wondered who would even *notice*. The feeling of displacement, of being invisible, had followed me all day until the answer finally came to me while scarfing down carbs and watching the stars dance overhead. With my ass freezing on an iron chair and Richard's heavy gaze caressing the slope of my collarbones I realized suddenly—

Richard would notice.

He may not be interested in me romantically but he *would* notice I was gone. Collin would too. Maybe Vanity? Definitely Chastity. She'd miss my mad cashiering skills. Despite my predilections, I was accidentally building a family in Elmwood, and for once in my goddamn life I wanted to stand up for something.

But then…then I remembered nails. The *click* of acrylic, the brush of pain down my spine, the burn of tears in the back of my throat.

I remembered darkness.

I remembered the way it felt when my lungs ceased to work and they filled with terror instead of air.

I remembered being held down by invisible hands as I was forced to accept my punishment, frozen and quaking.

I remembered sitting with my knees cramped against my chest, the air in my lungs stale, the walls closing in—and—

No.

Running was the only option. I couldn't do that again. I couldn't face her. She would find me here, just like she'd found my mother.

"Where did you go?" Richard spoke again, shocking me out of my own dark thoughts. Only this time his voice was much, much closer. His body too. I jumped, my back hitting the couch cushion behind me as I realized that he was kneeling in between my parted thighs, his legs spread, dark eyes full of want.

He looked hungry…

God. Just watching his throat bob made me ache.

"Sorry. What?"

"When you get lost like that, there's somewhere you go, isn't there?" Richard said softly, holding very still. I wasn't fooled though. "In the back of your mind, a memory, a place. You're thinking about something that makes you sad." Despite the fact that he was positioned lower than me, submissive in the way he knelt, I knew there was heat and power coiled tight in that massive body. It was a trick, the play of a predator just waiting to strike.

I shook my head no but my mouth answered for me anyway. "My family."

Richard nodded, accepting my answer for the moment, his gaze heavy as fine silk as it trickled across the swell of my knees underneath the *Scooby Doo* blanket I'd slung across it.

"Um." I shuddered as his eyes dragged up the shape of my thighs, tracing over the crease in the fabric at my hips, dangerously close to my dick. Jesus god, this man was going to murder me and he didn't even have to kill me to do it.

Death by sexual frustration.

What a way to go.

"I think about my family." I wasn't sure why I was still speaking, or repeating myself for that matter, only that with Richard's attention on me I felt more seen than I'd felt my entire life.

I wasn't a shadow of my cousin, a replacement, a freak, a tattle-tale. I was Blair, a living breathing man with feelings, with memories, and thoughts and emotions. Permanent. Immovable. I was *alive.*

I'd often wondered if I would ever stop feeling like broken pieces of boy stitched together with threaded lies. And here was my answer. I wasn't Pinocchio when Richard looked at me. His attention made me real, like a spell it wove its fingers through my soul.

I trembled in the face of my own wonder.

"Somehow I don't think they're pleasant memories." He spoke softly, eyes nearly black in the dark as the light from the TV caressed the back of his bleach-blond head. "You get this look on your face, like you've gone so deep inside that you're struggling to find your way out again."

"Reliving my horrors like a picture show on replay."

"Is your family horrible?"

"Only sometimes. Only some of them." I spoke softly, my words sitting in the silence between us, heavy and full of meaning. "I've never…talked about it before."

"You can talk to me." His voice was sweet as honey, his big hands tense where they gripped his thighs. They were thick enough the seams of his pants threatened to spill him out onto the living room carpet. *God.* The idea of seeing him in the flesh was almost too much to bear. It helped distract me enough from our conversation that I was able to speak.

"I don't know why but I believe you," I said, my voice brittle and broken like the boy I used to be. "It's not…it's not easy."

"Hard things never are."

The way he said it was so stupidly simple it almost made me laugh. And then I did laugh, because there was nothing else I could do when those big hands were tensing where they clenched his own thighs and Richard's tongue was bright pink where it flickered out to wet his lower lip. I couldn't help but drag my gaze down his body again, my lashes fluttering as desire flooded my body so viscerally it nearly choked me. Richard was sitting between my spread thighs like a worshiper before his altar. Begging. But I felt like he was the god and I was at his mercy.

Speak.

Speak, Blair.

Speak.

I couldn't get the words to come out. As much as I tried, as much as I wanted to, my mouth remained empty and my throat remained dry. Richard waited for what felt like a century as the next episode of the cartoon I was watching began to play behind him on the TV. And then, when it was clear I wasn't ready, he slowly rose to his feet, towering above me, his shadow casting darkness across my blanket-covered lap.

"I'm going to grab a snack," he finally said. His words were short and to the point, but his voice was gentle.

It said, 'take your time.'

It said, 'there's no rush.'

It said, 'your demons are yours.'

It said, 'I'm here when you need me to be.'

I watched his back as he headed into the kitchen, moving without turning any lights on. Night vision maybe? My thoughts were in shambles. My heart beat an uneven staccato in my chest as Richard padded around for several minutes, heating something up in the microwave inside a massive black mug. I couldn't see what he had filled it with but my imagination filled in the gaps as he headed off toward his bedroom, mug in hand. If I sniffed hard enough I could almost catch the scent of copper.

Memories I didn't want to remember threatened to resurface.

Rain. Lights. Blood.

Richard walked towards me again, his movements stiff, his nostrils flaring. He set a second mug down on the table and I stared at it in confusion before my gaze shifted back to him. He was across the room in seconds and a weird feeling washed over me like something bad was about to happen and I was just waiting for the other shoe to drop.

"I'll drop you home tomorrow," Richard said, halfway to his bedroom. It was clear his words were a dismissal. The warmth in his voice was gone, instead replaced with a robotic quality I'd never heard before. A soldier, devoid of emotion.

My pulse raced again, except this time it was with anxiety. My hands began to sweat as I bunched up the fabric in my lap and tried to recover from the emotional whiplash. *Had I done something wrong? Was he punishing me for not answering him earlier?*

Why did it hurt so damn much that he might not want to keep me? I wasn't a stray. I was a full grown man with independence I had fought tooth and nail to earn.

Pathetic.

I was so distressed by his words it took me a minute to realize he was still speaking.

"I had your car towed so it should already be there. Chastity's been taking care of Boots."

Richard had taken care of everything. Me included. Was that all this had been? A mission? Something for him to accomplish to feel better about himself? I felt sick. Was this because I'd flirted with him? He'd finally run out of patience with the gay boy and his delusions.

I blinked away the ache in my chest and nodded in his direction, remaining silent as he waited for what felt like an eon, dark eyes trained on the rise and fall of my chest. Or maybe he was watching the bare swoop of my neck where my borrowed hoodie had slipped to reveal my collar. Wishful thinking.

"It's better this way," he said gently, his eyes warm but distant. "You'll be more comfortable."

I wanted to scream at him but I didn't.

Instead I just watched as he turned his back toward me and walked the rest of the way into his room. The door slipped shut with a quiet *snick* and I collapsed against the cushions, the throbbing in my chest only aching more as I curled into the blankets that still smelled of Richard, and tried to figure out what I'd done wrong.

The scent of hot cocoa filled my nose and I reached for the mug in front of me almost blindly. It was warm and I held it tight until the heat leached from its surface and my fingers turned to ice.

Chapter Twenty-Three

Blair

THAT MORNING, RICHARD was colder to me than he'd ever been before. It was like night and day. Yesterday he'd been all sunshine, his words sweetly spoken, his gaze a heavy caress that gave me goosebumps. Today he was a spring pre-dawn, brisk and too cold for even the flowers to open up to.

He still made me breakfast though.

Even Collin noticed how weird he was acting, which made me feel at least a little better as the teen flounced around the kitchen declaring everything inside the fridge inedible.

"Ew. Since when do you buy vegetables?" he complained unhappily, his bony rump in the air as he dug around inside the produce drawers. "Kale? Really?"

Richard flipped him off, which made me do a double take. Because *Richard*. Flipping someone off. I didn't even know he knew how to do that.

"Just eat your eggs." Richard pointed to the table where I sat and Collin's eggs sat untouched. Real eggs. Not tofu, like mine.

"Ugh, you're no fun." Collin flopped down into his seat, shaking his shaggy auburn mane like a disgusted Justin Bieber as he poked at his plate. "At least at Mom and Dad's they have Pop-Tarts."

"Then spend the night there," Richard responded, ignoring both me and Collin as he brusquely walked down the hallway and into his room presumably to get ready for the day.

"What's his problem?" Collin muttered, shoveling food into his mouth. Without Richard there to complain to, he had zero qualms devouring his entire plate. "Bitch-ard."

"How should I know?" I grunted, shoving a bite of food into my mouth and swallowing painfully around the lump in my throat. Richard was a good cook, that much was clear. I had a hard time forcing my way through my own food despite this. Things just…weren't adding up.

Why would he rescue me, make me breakfast, take me out to a movie and a shopping spree and then dump me off to the next available buyer?

God, I felt like a two-bit whore. Except typically people wanted to fuck *them*, and Richard clearly didn't even want that.

Maybe I'd misjudged him?

Maybe he really *was* the prick I'd originally assumed he was. Or maybe, this was just a 'vampire problem' that I couldn't possibly hope to understand.

Fucking fuck. My head hurt. My heart too.

Traitor.

"You should be careful," Collin said after a moment of silence, his fork clinking on his plate.

"Pretty sure Richard's bad attitude isn't going to hurt me," I hummed, arching an eyebrow at him.

"No. I mean. At Vanity's."

I blinked at him in confusion, watching his face for clues but he didn't give me any, just chewed another mouthful and watched me with an expression that was both shifty and wise.

"Why?"

"No reason." He shrugged. "Just…yeah. Be careful." He quickly shoved the rest of his food into his mouth, scraping the crumbs from his plate before he scurried over to the sink and deposited the dishes, no doubt, for Richard to deal with later. He flounced away and I stared at the sink in contemplation.

I would've helped out, but Richard was on my shit-list currently. His cold shoulder had really fucking thrown me off all night and this morning.

I'd miss him, and his TV, despite how grateful I was to have a home to go back to. I missed Boots and my plants fiercely even though I knew my place with the sisters was only a temporary home. Now that I had no extra money about to roll in I'd need to find a second job—maybe even a third— if I wanted to get the fuck outta Dodge. Maybe the house had been insured? Whatever the fuck that meant. I'd have to Google it.

The mystery of the fire's cause would haunt me until I disappeared like smoke on the horizon. Now that there was a day between me and the tragedy, it was easy enough to explain away why it had happened. Old wires. Electric…*malfunctions*? Something like that. It was an abandoned house after all.

All I knew was that the brain could play tricks on you when you were high on adrenaline. I'd gotten lucky in my escape, but that didn't mean that someone had deliberately set my house on fire. And even if they *had*, that didn't necessarily mean they'd been trying to kill me.

There was only one person I knew that would want me gone—and she was across the country.

Feeling better, I rose from my seat and padded to the kitchen sink, plate in hand. The countertops were made of granite and they glistened, not a crumb in sight aside from the little bits of egg from Collin's plate that had splattered across the counter when he'd dumped his dish.

Maybe it was petty of me, but I decided not to wash mine too, glaring at the two dirty dishes sitting inside the basin as revenge filled my soul.

I got about a foot away from the sink before I regretted acting like an asshole.

Maybe Richard had regretted taking in the resident gay-goth. That was his own prerogative. I was better than that. I wouldn't let his little hissy fit affect who I was.

And what I was was one *polite* motherfucker.

I made my way back to the sink and blasted the hot water. It burned my already sore fingertips but I reveled in the pain as I very painstakingly cleaned both dishes. It was my personal *fuck you* to Richard and his assholery. When they were dried and put away I stared at Collin's crumbs on the counter, trying to decide if it was evil of me to leave them or not.

I cleaned them up.

Collin returned to the room wearing a new outfit that consisted of the same style of items he always wore. Ripped skinny jeans, a long T-shirt with different colored sleeves, and beat-up red Converse. It didn't escape my notice that Collin didn't take his shoes off when he was inside the house, his dirty sneakers prowling the floor without reprimand. Maybe it wasn't normal to be yelled at for that sort of thing?

Fuck. I didn't know. That would be a whole new level of fucked up if that were the case. I couldn't count how many times I'd been punished for dragging dirt across my aunt's carpets, despite the fact that most of the occurrences had happened between the ages of eight and nine.

It was like every day I got surprised with more and more reasons my childhood had been completely and utterly fucked up. *Yay for me! Bing, bing, bing, and the prize for most fucked-up childhood goes to Blair Evans! Your award is a lifetime of flashbacks and existential crises. Congratulations. Enjoy.*

"You look like you've seen a ghost," Collin commented curiously, breaking me from my reverie. "You got beef with Converse?" He waggled his eyebrows at me and did a jaunty little heel click.

"Nah, Dorothy. Just judging you because your socks are no-shows."

Collin gasped, his hand slapping to his chest in mock outrage as a high falsetto voice left him. "Well, I do declare! These are all the rage in Kansas." He did another heel click with even more enthusiasm and I was filled with a surge of warmth as it became clear that the kid totally vibed with my sense of humor. "Besides, some of us wouldn't be caught dead wearing knock off keds and socks with Dracula's asshole on them."

"I do not have socks with Dracula's asshole." I gasped, surprised and impressed by how quickly he'd roasted me right back.

"But if it was an option you would." He grinned, wide and Cheshire-like and I snorted, shaking my head. He wasn't wrong.

"You're not wrong."

"See?"

Our banter was interrupted as Richard opened his bedroom door. "Collin, come help me carry this stuff," he urged, holding the door open, his ice-prince eyebrows lowered to their full-freezing degree.

"Coming!" Collin wiggled his scrawny ass at me and heel-clicked his way down the hallway as I laughed and shook my head.

It wasn't until we were inside the car, Collin in the front this time—I insisted—and Richard was driving me to Vanity's house, that I realized the teen had been trying to cheer me up. He'd clearly sensed my foul mood and was as miffed with Richard as I was. I couldn't help but be grateful and confused.

As Richard had packed the trunk with the bags he'd bought for me, he'd been more heavy-handed than usual, slamming the trunk shut with a little too much force as he moved around to the driver's side.

And *that* was how I ended up arriving at Vanity's apartment with an entire entourage bearing gifts.

Collin insisted on petting Boots before they left so we all filed into my bedroom. Vanity was watching us from the couch, her head tilted curiously as I gave her a jaunty wave and the quiet sound of Boots's mew filled my ears.

Proving he was the best cat in the world, he came to me first.

And then he *betrayed* me because before I could sink my fingers into his dense black fur he was abandoning me to climb up the leg of Richard's pants.

Traitor.

As I watched Richard stroke his fur and cradle him to his chest, my heart began to hurt again. I wanted to be that fucking cat. Collin was complaining where he'd flopped onto my bed, his long legs sprawled, his red hair a splash of color on the plain bedspread and I couldn't help but glare at Richard and try to figure him out.

The man was an enigma.

Why had he banished me from his house so quickly? Hadn't we been having a moment? A whole bunch of them actually. We'd become... friends. Or something close to it. Friend-adjacent at least. Or maybe...Maybe it was all in my head? Maybe these were pity gifts. 'Sorry your house burned down' gifts. 'Sorry your family sucks' and 'Sorry I'm an asshole who isn't emotionally available' gifts.

God, that's rich coming from me. Hypocritical. It wasn't like I'd ever really been real with someone before either. I'd given them bits and pieces of me, small enough it wouldn't hurt if they never gave them back, but never the whole...picture. Maybe that was *my* problem.

I was so out of tune with reality I would rather believe Richard was a vampire than that he was just a normal dude with normal dude problems and zero interest in spending time with a loser like me.

When the brothers left, I headed back into the front room with Boots draped over my shoulders like a scarf. He was purring and I sighed, flopping down onto the couch, making sure to keep a careful distance between me and Vanity because I was too raw for touch—but lonely enough I still craved the company. "You look like shit," she said indelicately for the second time in our friendship.

I shrugged. "I feel like shit."

"Touché." She was quiet for a moment, pursing her red lips in thought. Her outfit today was an all black catsuit, the name tag on her chest glittering in the light where it read 'Trisha.' She'd told me early on in our friendship that she had seven different name tags for work. A new name for each day of the week. She got a lot of joy from fucking with people and I respected that. "You wanna get high with me and watch *Drag Race?*"

"Fuck yes."

It was kinda weird sitting alone with Vanity. I'd never really had the opportunity to do it before and to be honest she intimidated the fuck outta me. There was something about how put together she was, how pretty she was, how confident, that really made me feel small in comparison.

As we shared a joint however, those illusions began to fall away.

Vanity was quiet as she blew smoke towards the ceiling, her long legs slung casually to take up as much room as possible, ankles crossed.

"You know, I fucking hate this place," she hummed as she glared at one of the silver crosses that was hung up on the wall between a portrait of her family and one of Prudence by himself. I couldn't shake the feeling that I'd seen him before.

There was something about his dark hair and his pale eyes that struck a chord of familiarity inside me.

"The apartment's not so bad." I shrugged, shifting a little as I grabbed one of the throw pillows. Boots leapt to the floor to glare at me as I took the joint from her dainty fingers, startled when our skin brushed and hers was almost feverishly warm.

"Not the apartment." She shook her head. "This town."

"Oh." I didn't know what to say to that so I smoked instead.

"Everyone knows shit about you before you even know it," She said softly, folding her arms and leaning forward, a lost sort of expression on her face I'd never seen before. Vanity high was... wild.

Wild.

Like her guard had lowered completely.

"That shit with my brother?" She chewed on her painted lip and I marveled at the fact the lipstick didn't transfer. *How? Was she a witch?* "Everyone's treated me weird because of it my whole fucking life. They either judge me for it or they pity me."

"That sucks." I didn't know what to say. I couldn't even imagine what that was like. I was sincere though I didn't know how to help.

"I just want him back, you know?" She sighed again, reaching for the TV remote before she paused and turned to me. "You ever feel this need to rebel growing up?"

"Yes." Now *that* I could relate to.

"My parents are strict," she continued to explain. "Like super fucking strict. After Pru died, they basically locked us away."

Sounded familiar.

Also… kinda strange that Richard and Vanity basically shared a tragic brother-losing back story. Was one of them lying? No. *No.* There was no way. That was the paranoid part of me talking again.

"My aunt was strict too." I was surprised as the words left my lips and Vanity turned to me, clearly just as surprised. I realized then that I hadn't really gone out of my way to get to know her. To listen to her. To relate.

I'd given her the surface of me without letting her look beneath the reflection of what I had decided I would show her.

Shit.

I was a bad friend. I resolved myself to be better, braver, because she deserved it.

It wasn't her fault she intimidated me.

"What was she like?" Vanity asked, clearly ready to move on.

"Commanding." I flinched at the thought, my nails digging into my knees as I listened to the beginnings of rainfall patter against the windowpane behind me. I swallowed the lump in my throat, surprised when the words continued to flow. Words I'd wanted to say to Richard the night before but hadn't been able to. "Controlling. Unforgiving."

"I can relate." Vanity sighed, grabbing the joint back from me and inhaling smoke until the room smelled of weed and camaraderie. I'd smoked once before in the back of Jeffrey's car with him. He'd gotten the joint from some kid at school he'd told me he'd paid for it.

And we'd giggled and giggled as we'd plowed through an entire bag of McDonald's fries and two large orange sodas. I'd spilled on the seat, and he'd just laughed and shoved a handful of napkins towards me. Later my aunt had commented on the stain and Jeffrey taken the heat for it. He'd squeezed the back of my neck as he'd walked by, smooth talking his way out of the situation with skills he'd been forced to master.

My coping mechanism of choice was forgetting, and Jeffrey's…well. His was smiling.

I swallowed around the lump in my throat and turned my attention back to Vanity with a sigh. "Makes it hard to trust people when they don't trust you," she said softly, almost to herself.

I just nodded and watched as she sprung into motion and flipped the TV on.

Later, when Chastity appeared, she looked startled to see us together.

"Rude," she huffed playfully before flopping down on the couch between us smelling like stale fries and spring air. She grumbled unhappily and changed the episode we were on, grouching under her breath about us watching her favorite show without her.

Today her hair was LaffyTaffy lime and I stared at her beautiful fluffy head with fascination.

"You guys are high." She glared at us both. "Did you at least save some for me?"

Vanity shook her head and giggled and I joined in, my limbs buzzing with a floaty sort of feeling as I clutched at the pillow I had in my lap.

"Assholes."

The world was foggy around the edges, soft and forgiving as I shifted off the couch and slid down to lay on my back on the plush carpet with my pilfered pillow clutched tight to my chest. Vanity disappeared for a few minutes and returned with a new joint which she lit with an arched eyebrow and a smile and passed over to her sister.

Chastity smoked like a chimney, her little lungs huffing and puffing as she complained and complained about one of the customers that had come in right at the end of her shift and demanded a refund on his meal after he'd eaten the entire thing.

"I get the whole refund thing, I do," Chastity continued, "but only when the restaurant has actually messed up the order. But like—to freaking have the gall to tell me you were dissatisfied after you tongued your plate clean?" She fumed and I watched her in fascination. "Fuck you."

I couldn't stop staring at her hair. When she moved, she looked like a lime-colored dragon, with scales painted on her cheeks and everything. Between the two of them, she was definitely the more colorful one, like a chameleon changing patterns every day.

"Seems to me an empty plate means satisfaction," I replied when Vanity didn't.

"Thank you!" Chastity threw her hands up in frustration. "That's exactly what I said." There was a lull in conversation and the audio from the TV echoed through the mostly empty room.

"So did you give the guy a refund?" Vanity asked from where she lay sprawled across the couch with her feet in Chastity's lap. Chastity's jaw dropped open and she paused, an almost guilty look crossing her face before she slumped over and sighed, her answer muffled in the cushions.

"Yes."

I laughed. I couldn't help it. The giggles started and they wouldn't stop, bubbling up like poison in my chest as they echoed through the room. Eventually Vanity joined in and then Chastity, the sound of laughter ricocheting around in my head. It didn't even feel real. This moment. This town, these people, *anything*.

It was all one big fucking dream that I would wake up from and find myself alone in my bed in Oregon, with two black eyes and no future.

My heartbeat was insanely loud in my own head as I tried to remember what it felt like to breathe normally.

"What happened to my car?" I asked after a couple minutes, confused by my own question for a moment before I remembered why I'd asked it. "Richard said something about it getting towed."

Vanity made a face but quickly smoothed it over, staring at her sister and waiting for her to respond. When she didn't, Vanity spoke. "Looks like someone broke in. They tore up the seats a bit and fiddled with some of the shit with the ignition." She shrugged. "They must've seen the fire and thought 'sweet, free shit.'"

Yeah, because that's what everyone thinks when they see a fire, I thought, but didn't say out loud. I figured Vanity was just trying to make me feel better.

Alarm buzzed in my chest as I realized that meant it likely wasn't drivable. Who the fuck saw a fire and decide to break into the fucking car in the driveway? *Assholes.*

Feeling paranoid just made everything worse so I was learning to avoid it as much as I could.

"I don't have the money to pay for repairs," I said honestly, surprised as the words popped from my mouth freely instead of feeling like pulling teeth. Vanity snorted and Chastity laughed.

"Yeah. We kinda figured." Vanity glanced at her sister and shrugged, her red ponytail swishing. Either she was a natural blonde or she was just really really good at bleaching her roots because everything about her hair was perfect down to the slick way it was coiffed and the swoop of her bangs where they were pinned back from her face. "We didn't know your insurance situation, figured you had it, but…" She shrugged. "Our family has more money than we know what to do with—and I was feeling guilty, so I just paid for it all."

"I don't want pity money."

"It's not 'pity' money." Vanity rolled her eyes skyward. "I told you. I feel guilty. I was talking about you last night while I was at the bar and when Chastity called me to tell me what was going on I might've accidentally announced to the room that your car was sitting there abandoned."

"What? You just told everyone 'hey, Blair's in town and he's got a piece of shit car to loot?'" I joked with a snort, figuring she was just trying to make me feel better.

"No, you shithead. Well, *kinda*. I mean, I was in shock and I wasn't really thinking. So yeah."

That seemed kinda weird, but I figured in small-town-speech this was just her way of making room for me in Elmwood beside its weird politics and its hive population. Could I still call them hive people if they were all vampires? Vamp-hive? Vamp-hive-mind? Fuck.

"Okay…well…" I exhaled, catching her gaze and throwing her a soft smile. "Thank you. Seriously." My fingers curled tighter around my pillow, bunching up the fabric till the ivory roses deformed within my grip. "My car is kinda the only thing I have and it really…It really means a lot. So thank you."

She flushed, a weird almost constipated expression crossing her face. "You're welcome." She bent over Chastity's lap, fumbling for the remote so she could turn up the TV, signifying the end of our feelings discussion. *Thank god.* Feelings weren't my favorite topic of conversation even on a good day. And besides, I was having more fun listening to my own heartbeat than opening my mouth.

Chapter Twenty-Four

Richard

EITHER SOMETHING WAS seriously wrong with me, or I was in love with Blair Evans.

How that was even possible I didn't know. Not when being in love with him meant knowing enough about him to even love him in the first place. Maybe it was just infatuation? Obsession?

No. That was *worse*.

That was *way* fucking worse.

"What the fuck is your deal?" Collin shoved the front door open and I glared at him from where I was nursing a mug of blood in the kitchen. Warming it up in the microwave always made it taste chemically but it was leagues better than dealing with the flavor of it cold.

"What?" I huffed, setting the mug down, honestly a little glad that

Collin had come in fists swinging because it meant I'd get to fight him and stop thinking about apple-green eyes and that freckle at the tip of Blair's nose.

"You were a total asshole to Blair yesterday." Collin stomped towards me, probably attempting to be intimidating but the illusion wasn't even close. He'd given me the silent treatment when I'd driven him home the day before, and I'd been too distracted by my inner turmoil to call him out on it. I figured he'd come to me when he was ready to talk. Apparently, I'd been right. I crossed my arms to mirror him and cocked my head.

"I don't know what you're talking about."

"You were all. 'You're so cute,' 'Lemme stare at you for five fucking hours,' 'Omg I'm gonna buy you a zillion gifts just cuz I'm a nice guy.'" Collin threw up some air quotes for good measure. "Then the next morning it's just 'FUCK YOU, you little black haired twink,' 'how dare you stumble into my evil lair even though I'm the one who invited you.'"

Wow.

He'd really thought this through. Also, should I be alarmed that he knew the word 'twink?' Why would he know that?

"First of all—"

"And don't try to tell me you don't think he hung the sun with his asshole because I know what sorts of faces you usually make and 'heart eyes' was not in your repertoire until Blair moved into town and you got your lil mission thingy from SAC."

"I don't think you know what you're saying."

Collin glared at me. "Fuck off. Okay?" He shoved my chest, pushing up into my space, his eyes burning with anger. "I fucking *know* you dude." The counter dug into my lower back as I glared at him, surprised to realize we were nearly eye level.

He was growing so quick and it was honestly terrifying.

"Get out of my face, *dude*." I glared down my nose at him until he huffed and stalked away, flopping down at the table with a dramatic scrape of his seat on the tile. "You don't know what you're talking about," I repeated.

"I think I do," he countered, deflating a little, the fight leaving him. "I think you're just… I think you feel stuff—or whatever—that you're not used to and since you're such a *tight ass* about everything you just freaked."

Wow. He knew me better than I thought he did. I was momentarily floored as he continued.

"But you gotta understand that it's not okay to just…treat people bad because you're scared."

Shit.

Was that really what I'd done?

A voice in the back of my mind whispered yes, that's exactly what I'd done. I'd realized how close I was getting to Blair, how quickly I was dropping my guard, letting him in and I just…I freaked. I didn't know what to do with the secrets I was keeping from him. I didn't know what to do with the feelings either.

"Shit." I scraped a hand down my face, blocking out the overhead light as I sighed beneath my palm and processed his words.

"You owe him an apology," Collin pointed out. "And me. Because I now have emotional trauma from babysitting you and your shitty emotions."

"How about I forget about the fifty bucks you owe me instead? And the fact you've sworn at least three times since coming in here." I dropped my hand as I exhaled through my nose and made my way over to the table, falling into the seat across from him as I waited for his response. He mulled this over, clearly deciding whether or not fifty dollars was enough collateral. Neither of us really cared about the swearing. It was habit to chide him at this point.

"Deal." Collin grinned, his pissed expression melting away as he spat in his palm and held it out to me.

I sighed and mimicked the motion, slapping our palms together and ignoring the sticky heat between them because even though it was a tradition I'd started with him, passed down from my summers with Markus, it still was gross as fuck.

I wiped my hand on my jeans and breathed for a moment, trying to figure out what to say.

"I talked to The Council," I started, because talking business was and always would be easier than discussing my feelings.

"And?" He waved a hand at me impatiently to continue. "Are they gonna drop the case?"

"I think so." I folded my arms and Collin glared at me, clearly waiting for more. He was drenched like he'd biked all the way from our parents' place to my apartment in the rain. And I suddenly felt bad because the fact that he'd been too angry with me to ask for a ride meant more than his words had.

We were close.

We always had been. He was my kid as much as he was my brother and I'd never let something like this come between us before. Collin was probably freaking out just as much as I was about the whole thing.

"You think, or you know?" Collin pushed again and I sighed, pinching the bridge of my nose as I forced myself to speak.

"I've explained that I believe he's innocent," I said softly. "And that there haven't been any signs of him continuing the pattern his mother started." Collin nodded. It was an unspoken rule that we never spoke about Markus, but he knew. *Of course* he did. Markus was the reason my parents had fallen off the deep end in the first place, the reason they'd abandoned all of us despite the fact that they'd discovered only a few months after his death that they were pregnant again.

Collin was a surprise baby that no one else in my family had been willing to raise. So I had. Nine years old with a kid to care for while my mother drowned her sorrows in bottles of expensive wine and my dad disappeared for weeks at a time.

That was before they'd taken the change, anyway. I couldn't say whether or not they were better or worse for it.

One by one, my brothers had followed afterwards. Christopher was the oldest, and he'd been the loudest about his decision.

"We can't lose anyone else," he'd said, his eyes flashing with self-righteousness. I'd been young enough to believe him too. Benny came after, though he'd had to wait until he reached twenty-five, and then Charlie. By the time it was my turn, it felt like tradition.

I hadn't realized until I'd seen the look on Collin's face that maybe it hadn't been the best decision.

Collin had always gotten the shit end of the stick, and I'd made it my life's mission to not continue the cycle. I wanted to be good for him. Stable. Dependable. Loving.

That started with honesty. "I can't control what they do," I said softly. "I've told them my suspicions about why Blair came to town in the first place, but they still won't clear his name until I go in front of the town council at the next meeting. It has to be a unanimous decision."

"Or what?" Collin swallowed, his big eyes wide and just a little wet with fear. "They're just gonna execute him? Because they think he might maybe one day end up crazy like his mom?"

"I won't let that happen." I was surprised by how firm my words were. They fell on the table between us, heavy with the weight of honesty. "If it comes to that, I'll take you both and we'll leave."

A weight that had been sitting on both our shoulders melted away as I realized that was true. I'd rather leave this town behind, leave everything I'd built, my family, my career, than see Blair killed for something he would never do.

"Okay." Collin smiled at me and his forgiveness melted the twenty-ton weight that had settled atop my shoulders. "*Okay.*" He bobbed his head. "Cool. Cool, cool, cool." He rose from his seat and walked over to the cupboards, scrounging around until he found his usual box of hot cocoa and a box of Pop-Tarts I'd picked up from the store for him just that morning since he refused to eat anything I'd stocked the fridge with.

"You still owe Blair an apology though," he reminded me and I sighed, letting my head hit the table in front of me because I realized he was right.

I was a coward.

An absolute fucking coward.

I hadn't spoken to Blair in four days. I'd seen him in passing sure, ducking out of sight as I watched him sit on the curb outside his apartment with Boots on his lap and a parade of nearly dead plants beside him. They were sunbathing and it was adorable and sweet and—

Fuck.

Stop it.

I couldn't face him. I just. *Couldn't.* So I did the only thing I could and headed to the diner to turn in my notice. I'd gathered the information I needed to clear his name so there was no need for me to pretend to work there anymore. An added benefit being the fact that I wouldn't be around to see the results of my manipulations. It wasn't that I didn't want to see Blair, it was the opposite.

But I didn't know what to do with these new feelings rising up inside me. The stronger my feelings for Blair, the guiltier I felt about lying to him. I wanted him, but there was so much standing in our way. Even if I forgot for a moment that I'd been essentially spying on him since he'd come to town, there was still the fact that he didn't remember the supernatural existing.

Chastity was surprised when she saw me enter the diner. She cocked her head while she waited for me to sit on my usual stool, her arms folded. Ty was rustling around in the background. I could see a hickey peeping above the white collar of his usual outfit. He hummed under his breath quietly enough I only caught it because the diner was empty. The sun was setting and soon the night rush would return and Blair would receive a ride from Vanity to work.

Jesus fuck, was I a stalker?

"I need to quit," I told her without preamble, realizing too late I'd forgotten to even greet her. Her head swiveled like a parrot as she narrowed her eyes at me.

"You don't work here, Richard." Her lips twitched. "Not officially anyway. You could've texted."

Somehow texting seemed disingenuous when she'd been generous enough to help me out in the first place. It wasn't her fault I was a hot mess and I was in love with her employee—stop. *No.*

No, *I wasn't.*

"Either way." I cleared my throat. "I'm done. I'm out."

Chastity continued to stare at me, her hands on her hips as she inspected me from head to toe. I felt about an inch tall, surprised by the feeling. Maybe she could see the truth written on my face? God I hoped not.

"You got all you needed? Blair's good then?" It was no surprise that both the sisters had discovered what I had about Blair. That he was innocent. That he was hurting. That all he wanted was a clean break.

We'd all seen the bruises. We'd seen the way he flinched away from touch and the way he seemed to second guess himself at every moment like he was just waiting to be told he was doing something wrong. That he wasn't allowed to be here.

It didn't take a genius to connect the dots.

"As good as he can be until I get a chance to plead his case," I said, grateful I wasn't the only one that was ready to champion for Blair. He was slowly but surely building a fan club in town and it made my heart warm to think about it. I was so weak for him it terrified me.

There was so much between us.

The truth.

The town's secrets.

My own family's history.

So much of that I could work with, but the fact that he didn't even remember that Elmwood was a supernatural sanctuary was an obstacle that was unsurpassable. It was against the rules to tell a human about the sanctuary. Punishment was death.

I knew this.

I fucking *knew* this and yet I was *so close* to just spilling the secret that my heart hurt just thinking about it. The only thing that stopped me was the thought of what would happen to Collin if they found out.

The only way out of this was if he figured it out. And then subsequently if The Council cleared his name. And then if Blair forgave me for the lies I'd lived just to get close to him. The idea that I'd deceived him into liking me made me sick to my stomach. Everything between us had been genuine on my end but there was still a cavern of deceit between us that was so deep I could never climb my way out.

"What do you want me to tell Blair?" Chastity asked, watching me with an expression that was knowing enough it made my skin crawl.

"Just say I quit." I didn't know what else to say and my nerves were rubbed too raw as I rose from my seat and waved goodbye without listening to her response. Maybe it was cowardly of me, in fact I knew it was, but I had no choice but to hightail it out of there as quick as I fucking could. Collin was waiting in the car and he arched an eyebrow at me.

"So…how'd it go?" he hummed, his feet up on the dash despite the fact I'd told him a million and a half times to knock it off. I climbed in and ignored him, trying to get my breathing under control even though I hadn't needed to breathe for over six months and the tightness I felt in my chest was all in my head.

I pulled out onto the road, my head down, eyes straight ahead. Silence burned between us but Collin remained charitably quiet. He could sense that I was struggling, probably like a shark with blood in the water, so he just hummed under his breath and leaned his head against the window to watch the rain.

He didn't even comment when I took him out of town, the 'You're leaving Elmwood' sign disappearing behind us as the dark forest bled like ink blots across our windows.

I needed to breathe.

I needed to fucking breathe.

And I couldn't do it here. Not in town. Not knowing what I'd done. What I'd have to do. And that was the sickest part of the whole thing. The fact that after everything, after the lying, the spying, the soft moments spoken privately in the shelter of the night—I was going to have to go in front of the entire fucking town and betray Blair's secret.

I would have to broadcast the deepest parts of him. Dissect his trauma like a surgeon, clinical, and emotionless. Because if I showed any weakness at all my decision to spare him wouldn't be seen as unbiased. The secrets he hadn't even admitted to me yet would bleed like an open wound for all to poke at, so I could save him from a monster he didn't even know existed.

I turned on the radio, blasting the music loud enough to cover the tirade of guilt that banged around inside my skull until I felt bloody and bruised from the inside out. I white-knuckled the steering wheel and pressed my boot hard into the gas pedal. Collin stared at me, his eyes alarmed, his brow furrowed in concern, but for once I didn't have the energy to soothe him.

I wished there was someone there to take care of me. To pick up my pieces. To let me heal.

But there was just me and the road and Collin's dark brown eyes.

And I was just a monster with no choice but to betray the person I loved.

Chapter Twenty-Five

Blair

I FOUND RICHARD after I'd had to awkwardly beg Chastity to let me borrow her car for a few hours. The fact that I'd had the courage to ask her had given me a burst of pride that had rocketed me into my next set of decisions. Richard hadn't shown up to work for several days before Chastity casually informed me that he no longer worked at Benji's, like that wasn't a fucking nightmare-fueled revelation.

Did he quit?

Was it because of me?

Was he avoiding me?

What had I done wrong?

These questions plagued me through the rest of my shift before I finally gave into temptation and asked if I could leave early. Chastity gave me a knowing look, tossed me her keys, and while flicking her dish towel at my ass, sent me on my way out the back door. That was another thing I'd recently found the courage to do—use the employee door.

I'd been forced into opening the bags Richard had bought for me when I'd run out of clean underwear. I hadn't wanted to do it because it reminded me of how awkwardly we'd left things. There were two sides of Richard. The quiet side, the one that was always on guard, the man that had lost his brother and his family in one fell swoop. Then there was the Richard that was soft, kind, *gentle*. He never did things by halves and the six plastic bags that had lived in the back of my closet for days before I'd had the strength to open them had just been a reminder of the side of him I'd lost.

The worst part was that I didn't even know what I'd done wrong.

I wanted to believe it was for a reason that wasn't 'You're gay and you make me uncomfortable,' but that was the first place my mind went because of the way I'd been raised. It would probably take me years, maybe even my whole life, to undo the damage my aunt had done to the way I perceived the world around me and myself.

Looking at the plastic bags had reminded me of the loss of my duffel bag. It wouldn't have mattered so much if the clothes inside were just clothes. But they weren't. They were memories. Pieces of Jeffrey I'd held close to my heart hidden in the back of my dresser so they wouldn't be found by prying eyes.

I'd mourned the loss of my other clothes keenly and hadn't wanted to think about the fact that I'd needed them replaced at all. And despite how I'd avoided thoughts of both Richard and the gifts he'd bought me, I was still forced to wear the shoes he'd helped me put on at the mall every day. Every time I looked at them I was reminded of what I'd lost. Shining new and scented like plastic. Clinical. But soft nonetheless.

This time however, when I opened the other bags, Richard's scent hit my nose. A sense of longing so visceral it made my knees weak overwhelmed me. Palms slick with sweat, heart racing, I realized all I wanted was to *see* him. To hear him. To figure out why the fuck he'd pushed me away at all when all *I* wanted was for him to pull me closer. I separated each bag with care, inhaling his scent greedily because it was the closest I'd gotten to him in days.

I laid each item of clothing out on my bed and stared at them. Four vampire themed hoodies. Three sets of spooky-campy socks with an assortment of bats and candy corns on them. Frowny-face boxers. Black skinny jeans with more rips than denim.

How was it possible that Richard knew me so fucking well?

Was he just freakily observant?

It was like he'd taken note of every outfit I'd ever worn in front of him and gone out of his way to replicate what I'd lost in the fire. Sometimes it felt like Richard had made it his mission to make me as comfortable as possible. But then I reminded myself that he'd gone and left me in the dust.

What an asshole.

I'd stood up right then, trembling with fury and ready to fucking fight, though I deflated rather quickly when I realized I had no reason to be angry. Boots had soothed the ache in my chest with cuddles and I'd watched him weaving through the terra-cotta pots on my windowsill while I tried to figure out what the fuck to do about Richard. I had no idea how to approach him, to speak to him, to confront him. I had no reason to. Not really.

Except now I did.

Because Chastity had just informed me that Richard had officially quit three days ago and I was going to fucking blow a gasket if the reason he left was because I'd given him heart eyes at three in the morning and mentally projected 'fuck me' all over his living room wall.

Richard was surprisingly easy to find after I narrowed down his three typical hangouts. He wasn't at the diner, or his parents' house, which clearly meant he was at home. When I arrived, I realized I'd been correct because parked in stall number three was his silver Audi, with a new half empty bottle of Pepsi in the cup holder on Collin's side.

I parked in visitor parking, losing some of my steam when I tried to storm out of the car and forgot to unbuckle my seatbelt in the process. Anger made my fingers clumsy so it took me a second too long to fix my mistake before I was shoving the car door open and slamming it directly into something solid. Paranoia made me jolt back, terrified I'd scratched Chastity's car.

And then I realized the immovable object I'd hit was actually Richard's solid body. And the mortification began to set in.

Fuck.

When had he gotten there?

He made a quiet little *oof* and stepped out of the way, looking surprised but unharmed despite the fact that I'd quite literally body checked him with a metal door.

"Blair?" His voice was scratchy and low and I hated the way just listening to it fill the space between us made my knees weak. *You're angry, remember? Furious? C'mon Blair. Don't fold just because you've got a bit of a crush on the guy.* I fumbled my way out of the car, shutting it without casualties this time as I shielded my eyes from the setting sun so I could squint up at Richard and his stupid perfect face. I braced myself for the rollercoaster of emotion it took to prepare myself to look at him.

Except, to my surprise, when I glanced upward and saw Richard's face I realized he looked...*bad*.

Still sexy as sin of course, but in a sickly I've-been-unable-to-sleep-for-days kinda way instead of his usual small-town-bad-boy-with-a-hard-on-for-flannel kinda way.

There was something off about him.

Something was wrong.

Richard's usually artfully styled hair was poking up haphazardly, one side flat from where he'd probably slept on it. His eyes were nearly black, pupils dilated, eclipsing the red-brown of his irises where they were surrounded by dark circles that looked so fragile I worried the skin might break.

Exhausted, confused, distressed.

I'd never seen him like this before and it—*infuriated* me.

How dare he toss me aside like yesterday's underwear and yet when he looked worse for wear the only thing I could think about was making sure that he was going to be alright?! It wasn't fair. I barely knew him. How could I care so much for a man that I knew so little about?

"Are you okay?" I questioned, my words clipped and to the point, because at least I still had my dignity to maintain. "Seriously."

"What?"

"You look super...like—" I flapped my hands around, searching for the word I needed to describe what I meant. "You don't look like *you*. Where's your hair gel?" I looked down, gasping in horror, "Are you wearing *sandals*?" His boots were gone. His *glorious,* designer, shiny black boots with their custom laces and rubber soles—*gone.* Disappeared. Replaced instead by the worst pair of sandals I had ever seen in my entire life. His feet looked bare and naked without the boots to hide them. Foreign. Alien. "*What is* wrong *with you?*"

Richard blinked at me. One. Long. Slow. Blink. "Are you upset with me because I'm wearing sandals?" he asked. His lips were twitching again, the stern set to them melting as he struggled not to smile. God, he was so handsome I wanted to strangle him.

My warring emotions would've been funny if they weren't confusing. "Fuck you, Dick-chard. I'm serious." He stopped smiling, staring at me again as his eyes began to warm and I watched him reach for me only to abort the movement after barely a flicker of fingers.

Maybe he hadn't been reaching for me at all.

"I'm okay. Just…been a rough few days, that's all." Richard glanced to the side, clearly guilty about something. Then he turned back to look at me, his eyes wide and infuriatingly sweet as they stared imploringly into mine. Blood-red. Sweet lil vampire motherfucker. I wanted to stab him with his own fucking fangs.

But then I realized he'd been telling the truth and I was suddenly blindsided by his honesty. The fact that he'd admitted vulnerability so easily made my heart flutter and my toes curl inside my still too stiff new shoes. I shook my head to clear it. "So you're not…hurt? Emotionally distressed? Constipated?"

Richard laughed, that same squawking noise I'd come to associate with his normally stoic figure filling the evening air with magic. My heart did a happy cartwheel in my chest, my stomach flip-flopped, and I tried my hardest not to smile in return. Playing dirty, the fucking scoundrel.

"Nah, baby. I'm okay." Richard was smiling now, though the echo of laughter still danced like dust motes in the air between us. His lips split in that same boyish grin I'd only seen once before but had burned inside the back of my mind as a core memory. He had dimples like Collin did, his eyes creasing at the corners as the smile on his face shaved off nearly five years. It was clear to me now that Richard was younger than I'd thought he was. Originally I'd guessed closer to thirty but now…now I realized just how much worrying about others had aged him. Luckily he aged like fine wine but still. No twenty-ish-year-old should have worry lines quite so dominant.

I ignored the term of endearment that had escaped so naturally from his lips even though my knees were weak from possibility and my pulse throbbed hard in response.

Baby, baby, baby, baby.

Am I his baby?

Does he want me to be?

Do I even want that?

"Alright. Then, fair warning: I'm going to yell at you, and you're going to listen and not say a fucking word until I say you can." My voice left me in a rush and I was surprised and elated to find that I hadn't wobbled. Not even once. I was ready to be brave. Ready to stick up for myself. Pride overwhelmed me as I rose to my full height and took a steadying breath.

The tide of anxiety ebbed away and I held my shoulders high as I stared into Richard's stupidly handsome face and something inside my chest slotted into place.

Richard blinked his ridiculously long lashes, his expressive eyebrows raising in surprise though he remained obediently silent as I soldiered onwards. The sun was low on the horizon, dipping behind the mountains, its last rays creeping across the parking lot unable to reach us where we stood in the shade. I could hear crickets in the distance, peaceful and unaware of the fire that was boiling under the surface of my skin.

"Look. I don't know what your problem is with me but it fucking stops now," I said, my voice ripe with righteous fury. I crossed my arms and puffed myself up as large as I could. It wasn't impressive, but it was something. I felt like one of those fat mice on the Discovery Channel as they climbed to the top of their little hobbit holes to call to the wild for a mate. Except, instead of a mate, I was calling for blood.

Richard was watching me, his expression neutral, though I could see the way his eyebrows were rising in confusion as I spoke.

"I get that you were being nice the other day but you're fucking confusing, man. You're so hot and cold. One day you're all 'Blair this, Blair that,' 'let's feed Blair,' 'lets call him baby,' 'let's buy him a whole new wardrobe and—and—cute themed boxers—'" I waved my hands around. "And then suddenly you're all 'I quit my job because I can't handle being around a gay guy!'" Breathing was becoming difficult but I forced myself forward, too far in to go back now as I stepped into Richard's space and felt his breath fan my cheeks. "So, which is it?"

Richard blinked at me in confusion. "Which is what?"

I threw my hands in the air in frustration, my hair a cloud of inky black tendrils as it wafted around my face, whipped wild by the wind. My nose was cold so I sniffed, aware of how pathetic I looked dressed in clothing he'd bought for me, gesticulating like a hamster on crack, with a pink nose and my shirt hanging off my bare shoulder. "Which are you?"

But maybe the ridiculousness of what I was doing was what made me brave.

Richard somehow looked even more confused than before, so I rephrased more or less patiently than before.

"Look. Collin told me what you are."

That got his attention. His whole face grew slack, the color draining as his eyes widened and panic seemed to squeeze the life from his lips. I hadn't thought it was possible for him to look *more* tired but I'd been wrong. There was a haunted look to his face that I couldn't stand being there. "What I am?" His voice was nothing but a croak.

What the fuck.

I blinked at him for a few seconds before it occurred to me what it sounded like I was about to say. *Vampire.* Jesus*, please tell me that my life has not become Twilight.* "No. Fuck." I shook my head, crossing my fingers in front of my chest to ward off whatever it was he was thinking. "I'm not talking about…whatever the fuck you think I'm talking about. Jesus." I inhaled, building up steam once again. "I mean. Yes. He told me—but I'm not intimidated by you, Richard Prince."

Fucking fuck. This was getting so confusing. Everything was coming out all wrong.

"You're not?"

"No!" I hissed with fury, stalking away from him on the pavement then back towards him in an angry mating dance, until we were chest to chest again and I could poke a finger directly between the luscious swell of his pecs.

Richard was staring at me, a weird confused-amused expression on his face as he moved to interject, "I'm honestly just surprised he told you."

And why wouldn't he? Because I couldn't protect him? Because I was small and inexperienced and no match for his big bad big brother and his prehistoric way of thinking? Fuck that.

"Of course he did. People like us…we stick together."

"People like…you?" He was hedging at something, though it was clear he had about as much idea about what was going on as I did. God, this had all gotten so confusing with the double meaning and the fucking supernatural espionage. I wasn't cut out for this level of verbal double entendre.

"Gay people. Clearly." I waved a hand down my body with a little wiggle to encompass myself within the realm of 'gayness' I was proclaiming. "Me and him. We're gay."

Richard stared at me.

God, now he was just being purposefully obtuse.

"Wait, what?" He blinked, clearly confused. "Why would I have a problem with you both being gay?" His lips were twitching and it was seriously pissing me off. If he fucking smiled I swear to god I was going to scream. I jabbed him in the chest again and his nostrils flared, pupils flooding his eyes black with something I wasn't brave enough to call lust.

"What I'm talking about," I growled, "is the fact that you're a huge fucking homophobe and there's no point hiding it because Collin told me the first time I met him and—"

Richard put a hand over my mouth.

I stopped talking.

It wasn't that I couldn't make noise, because I could if I wanted to. I grew silent because the touch of his broad scratchy palm on my lips made me so weak-kneed all my focus moved to not collapsing and away from my angry tirade. Richard stared at me, meeting my gaze with his own, his brow lowered and fraught with tension.

He waited a long deliberate moment before removing his hand. I pushed it away from me belatedly, my heart thumping erratically in my chest. My lips were tingling. *Tingling*!

"You done?" Richard asked softly, his voice gentle, dark eyes hard.

"Not even fucking close." My hands picked up their flapping again with vengeful fury. "You don't get to just do that! You don't get to just voodoo me with your stupid pretty eyes and your gravelly voice and—and—*shut me up*. You're so *infuriating*!"

"And you're not?"

"No!" If he grabbed me again I couldn't be held responsible for my reaction. "Yes! *I don't know*. Irrelevant. We're not talking about me. We're talking about you. You and your hateful ways."

"Can you just…listen to me for a second?" Richard spoke softly, holding his hands out in front of him placatingly. I stared at them. I stared at his broad palms, the lines etching their way between his fingers, the thickness of them, the strength.

I exhaled and tipped my head up to the rising stars looking for patience. Miraculously, I found some.

I nodded.

"What made you think I was homophobic?" Richard asked again, his voice gentle. It was that gentleness that made me look at him again. His gaze was searching my face, his eyes heavy with remorse, confusion, and amusement. A cocktail of complex emotion I knew I could get drunk on.

"I told you. Collin said so."

"Collin…said I was homophobic?"

"Well," I hedged. "*No*. But he didn't have to. It was clear. You know, in the context clues."

"In the clues…I see." He started nodding, though it felt suspiciously mocking. "Sorry. I'm just—" He shook his head. "I'm wrapping my head around the fact that the guy I've been hitting on since he moved to town somehow not only didn't catch onto the fact I was hitting on him but also somehow decided before he'd even met me that I'm homophobic."

Wait. What?

"Wait, what?"

"God, this is not at all what I thought was happening." Richard shook his head, looking confused and amused and infuriatingly handsome.

"What did you think was happening?" I asked, because apparently my brain had left the station and my mouth had decided to stay behind.

"I don't know, a *Twilight* remake? Fuck, Blair." Richard reached a hand up to run it through the back of his shorn short hair in frustration. "I can't be homophobic."

I was so fucking confused. My head was full of bees as I watched Richard's face through the fog that filled my thoughts. "What—"

"I can't be homophobic because *I'm* gay."

"What?"

"I'm gay. One hundred percent, completely, irrefutably gay." Richard was staring at me, his dark circles only more pronounced as the sun completely sank behind the horizon and I was filled with a million swarms of butterflies. If I got any more full of wings I was sure I'd float away.

"You can still be homophobic if you're gay, Rich." *Ding, ding, ding, and the award for stupidest statement of the year goes to Blair Evans.*

"God, I know." Richard pinched the bridge of his nose. "But I'm *not* okay? I'm…just… realizing I must be *exceptionally* horrible at flirting." I blinked at him, and blinked at him, and blinked at him.

And then I couldn't help but laugh, because he *was* horrible. He was fucking horrible, or maybe I was? Maybe we both were. One of the first things he'd ever told me was that he was bad with people, and here I was misunderstanding him…*because he was bad with people*. What a joke. A cosmic fucking joke.

"Oh my god." I felt like my brain was breaking. It looped back to all the conversations I'd had with Collin and I realized with sickening clarity that he must've been referring to…something more…*supernatural*. It was clear to me now that I'd totally misunderstood.

God, I felt like an idiot.

But I couldn't help but laugh anyway, the tension bleeding from my shoulders as my head thunked against the barrel of Richard's chest and laughter bled from all my pores. I could feel my anxiety, my anger, my grief leaking down like fresh rain into the soil, disappearing like smoke between molecules. "I feel so stupid."

Richard snorted. The noise was so unrefined it took me by surprise and I only laughed harder as he joined me, his squawking guffaw filling the world with its music. His amusement was a symphony, trickling like music to my ears.

"You're not *stupid*," Richard managed between giggles. He snorted again, and I tipped my head up to look at him because I needed desperately in that moment to see him happy, to know what it looked like, to taste his laughter on my tongue.

God, Richard was glorious like that, his chin tipped towards the sky, his cheekbones painted porcelain with evening sunbeams. There was a freckle on the corner of his jaw that I wanted to sink my teeth into but I refrained, instead basking in the majesty that was Richard fucking Prince.

Gay vampire extraordinaire.

There were a lot of things that still didn't make sense to me but I was learning that with time came clarity, and I was strangely okay with that. When our laughter died Richard looked down at me again, his lips pulled into a wide grin, his dimples flashing.

"See, and here I thought you quit Benji's because you didn't like my nail polish," I joked, chewing on my lip as I saw his brow scrunch up as he valiantly tried to keep himself from laughing again. My stomach hurt from all the use it had just gotten and I was suddenly ravenously hungry.

"Your nail polish was the first thing I noticed about you." He shook his head, eyes crinkled at the corners. "I'd never seen anything like it, except on the internet. You were...*are*...larger than life. Small—"

"Hey!" I protested.

"Small, but larger than anyone I'd ever met."

I flushed, embarrassed now as I edged away from him. I'd had so few genuine compliments in my life it was almost painful to hear them. My heart thudded unsteadily and I crossed my arms to protect myself, kicking at the gravel with the toe of my new shoe as I waited for my ears to stop burning.

"For the record, the first thing I thought when I saw you was that you were hot," I admitted, kicking at another pebble. "But then I told myself that I couldn't date you."

Richard made a noise, a quiet sad little sound in the back of his throat, and I lifted my head to look at him, meeting his dark imploring gaze and trying not to melt in the heat of it. "Why?"

"Because of Collin. Because I'm leaving," I told him honestly. "I can't stay here. I honestly should've left the second my house burned down."

Richard cocked his head to the side, watching me with a look so heavy it made my feet sink into the earth below me, anchoring me with his attention like a tether on a bungee jumper. I was leaping into the unknown but I was strangely okay with that.

"Why didn't you?" Richard asked.

I wanted to lie. I wanted to say it was because I needed money, or because my car had broken down, or because I needed time to figure out where I was going next. But instead—

Instead, I answered his honesty with my own, the words bright as citrus on my tongue.

"Because…" I swallowed. "You called me *baby*." My voice was small, too embarrassed to look at him. I stared at his shoulder instead, admiring the swell of it where it filled out his dark red flannel button-down. "You called me *baby*, and you came when I needed you—and for the first time I thought…"

"You thought?"

"I thought maybe there might be something out there that could be… good." I swallowed around the lump in my throat. "And maybe I could have it."

"*Oh*, baby." Richard made a soft noise, growly and honey-sweet. It echoed inside my bones, making my knees weak and my head spin. "I wish I could be yours."

Fuck. I wanted so badly to take him up on his offer, but…Jeffrey's face flashed in my mind and I was reminded of my goals. Get money, get away, get safe. Could I really do that here? Where *she* could find me? It was only a matter of time after all.

There was nothing tying me here but my parents' ghosts.

"Could you be mine if you know there's an end date?" I said softly, staring at the muscle in his jaw as it jumped. He swallowed and I caressed his Adam's apple with my eyes, wishing more than anything I could follow its wobble with my tongue.

Richard didn't speak for a long time.

I waited, and I *waited*, listening to the crickets chirp and the nighttime noises that filled the world with their orchestra of sound. A car passed by on the street going fast enough the *woosh* of the wind slid down the side of my neck.

One of Richard's neighbors turned on the TV and a sports announcer's tinny voice filled the silence, and still I waited.

My palms were sweaty, my breath shallow, as I stared at him and watched the helpless twist to his expression as he caught my gaze and then looked away. He'd never looked more beautiful or more cruel as I realized Richard's silence *was* his answer.

I nodded my head.

Fine.

Okay.

Fine. This was fine. *This was all fucking fine.* I hadn't thought we'd have a future together anyway. So why...why did it hurt that he didn't want it?

And why did it hurt even more when I turned my back to him, climbed into my car, and drove away?

He didn't stop me.

He didn't call, or text, or trail my car out onto the street.

Instead, I got to watch his figure become a speck on the horizon and my tears were fat and hot as they slipped down my night-chilled cheeks. Rejection tasted like hot cocoa, pine trees, and spring rain. For the first time in my life, the night's familiarity was a prison and not a comfort. And I trembled with the realization that the loneliness I'd felt before coming to Elmwood would be nothing compared to the loneliness I felt when I left it.

I called Jeffrey.

Because of course I did.

Near death experiences, alienation, and the supernatural weren't enough to get me to call him for help. But getting my heart broken was.

He picked up on the second ring and my heart was in my throat as I spoke. "Jeffrey?"

"Blair." His voice was quiet, awed, angry. He inhaled raggedly in that same familiar way he always had when he was overwhelmed and a feeling of desperation welled up in my chest.

I'd left him without a word. No call. No text. Nothing. I'd left with my hope as a companion along with the dream that I could finally become the kind of person he would be proud to call his brother.

But that didn't mean it hadn't been shitty, and unfortunately that realization hit me pretty late as I listened to Jeffrey's breath catch and I curled into a little ball on top of my bed covers and tears threatened to spill down my cheeks.

I willed them away as I spoke again. "I'm so sorry."

"Fuck you." Jeffrey's voice wobbled.

"I fucking suck."

"You do." He inhaled again. "Jesus, Blair. You couldn't have fucking texted me?"

"I'm sorry—"

"I came home and there was blood all over the fucking kitchen, man."

"I know—shit." I scrubbed a hand down my face. "I'm sorry. I don't know what I was thinking."

"No shit, Sherlock."

"I just. I wanted—"

"What?" He sounded angry but that was a good sign. Anger usually came before forgiveness where Jeffrey was involved. "What did you want? To fucking,—to leave me? What the fuck man? What about *the plan*?"

"Jeffrey—" I breathed raggedly, a tight feeling in my chest expanding until each breath felt like pulling teeth. "I just." Fuck. Fuck fuck. "She caught me, okay? At the bar."

"Why the fuck was she at the gay bar?"

"No," I hurried to correct. "I guess. I guess one of her church friends saw me exiting and called her to…to give her a heads up."

"Fuck."

"I know." I inhaled again, so incredibly relieved to hear Jeffrey's voice, I realized how fucking stupid I'd been to avoid him. What had I been thinking? There was no universe that me not communicating with him would end in him being amazed by me, impressed. Jesus. He was my fucking brother.

"I just. I had to go," I said softly. "I know it was early. I know I didn't say goodbye. And that was shitty of me man, I'm so fucking sorry, but I was—I was—" The tightness only grew tighter as the words I'd kept close to my heart forced themselves out with each ragged breath. "I was drowning." Jeffrey made a ragged noise and I scrambled a hand to the back of my neck, squeezing until I felt blood well beneath my fingernails as I tried to anchor myself. "I was fucking drowning. And she—she—"

"I know," Jeffrey exhaled raggedly. "Hey." His voice was a soothing buzz inside my head as I struggled to breathe. Distantly I registered that there were tears burning lines down my cheeks but I couldn't feel them. I couldn't breathe. I couldn't breathe. *I couldn't breathe.* "Hey. Blair, buddy," Jeffrey soothed, voice sweet as holiday caramels. "It's okay man. I get it. I forgive you."

"S-sorry," I gasped out. "I'm sorry."

"I know, bud. I know." I could hear rustling on the other end of the line while Jeffrey arranged himself. I could so easily picture him back in our shared apartment, his back to the wall, his guitar case leaning up against the desk he used to store his plethora of books more than he used it for the college courses he was taking. "It's okay."

It's okay.

It's okay, it's okay, it's okay.

"You don't…you don't think I'm a coward?" I managed to force out. "For not staying?" I wasn't sure when these feelings had surfaced, but I realized then they'd been burning inside my chest since the day I'd left and I wanted—no, *needed*— to hear him tell me it was okay. That I'd done what I had to do.

"You're not a coward, Blair," Jeffrey said softly and then his scratchy voice was followed by a short, awkward laugh. "A horrible texter, sure. But a coward? No."

A weight that had been crushing me finally lifted. Inch by blessed inch.

"I really am sorry," I choked out again, squeezing my neck until I felt the sting of my nails severing flesh for a second time.

"Do me a favor?"

"Anything."

"Just. Don't cut me out again," Jeffrey said softly. "You scared the shit outta me. If you can do that then we're cool."

"I won't," I promised. "I won't, I promise."

"Good." Jeffrey laughed, clearly amused by me as he often was. "Now why did you call? Somehow I get the feeling it wasn't because you felt bad about ghosting me. Shithead."

I told him about the house, the plan going up in smoke—*literally*—the fire—

I told him about Richard.

To his credit, he didn't interrupt. He let me ramble on, my words fumbling and stilted as they often were. It was hard to tell him how I felt because I didn't even *know* how I felt. Everything was so fucking confusing. All I knew was that whatever had been happening between Richard and I was no longer a possibility.

He'd chosen not to take a chance on it, and I didn't blame him.

I didn't.

God knew how long I'd be in town. It wasn't this fault, but still, the loss of what could've been wrecked me.

When I finally hung up, I had blood beneath my fingernails but I'd finally managed to calm down enough I could breathe again. There was a scratching sound at the window and I rose on wobbly legs to open it, letting Boots back inside. He mewed at me, clearly concerned, as I reached an arm out and let him climb his way up until he perched in his normal spot wrapped around my shoulders like a scarf.

I loved that fucking cat.

"You're the best cat ever," I told him, letting myself be cheesy and bland because he had no idea what I was saying. "Fuck all other cats."

Boots mewed in agreement and I laughed, burying my face in his damp fur as he purred around my throat and the tip of his tail flicked the shell of my ear.

"Fuck 'em." I reached down to stroke the petal-like leaves of one of the succulents I kept on my windowsill. It was getting brown and squishy and I had no idea how to fix it. Google said to stop watering so much but when I tried that the leaves just fucking fell off anyway.

I was cursed.

"Who needs boys when I have you guys?" I told all of them, taking turns patting each terra-cotta pot in solidarity.

My shift at the diner started much the same as all the others. Except I had a day of overthinking behind me and my conversation with Jeffrey on my mind. There was just...so much going on. I didn't know what to do with myself. My talk with Richard yesterday had somehow created more questions in my mind than it had resolved.

Maybe he wasn't homophobic like I'd originally thought, but he *was* apparently not interested, at least, not enough to take a chance on me when we both knew we had a timer on our relationship. It was fair, it really was. In fact, I wasn't even sure if I was interested in anything right now either. I certainly hadn't been before I'd met him.

Would it be nice to officially lose my virginity? Yes. Was I dying for it to happen right this second? No. (*Yes*)

Sometimes it felt like the universe had its own plan for me. No matter how much I plotted and schemed, something always seemed to happen to throw a wrench in my plans. The fire was the most recent relevant example.

I still had no explanation for what had happened, or why it had occurred. Chastity told me she'd help me figure out who my house was insured under since I refused to talk to Sandra unless forced. Later, the police had called me to declare the damage accidental. I had been promised that it was being investigated to rule out arson, but I had yet to hear anything different. No one seemed overly concerned so I was trying not to freak myself out.

Which was a tall order, you know, considering the fact that I was quite literally the most anxious person I had ever had the misfortune to meet. Unfortunately I was stuck with me though, so I'd have to deal.

I washed my hands, staring at my reflection in the diner's bathroom mirror as I tried to reconcile the person in front of me with the man I'd been when I moved to Elmwood. It had only been a few months, and yet in that short time it felt like I'd been reconstructed from the ground up. There were so many parts of myself I had yet to discover and each passing day made the journey to finding myself closer and closer to its end.

Was I the kind of person that stood by what I believed in?

Who protected those who mattered to me?

Who sacrificed for my future? My hopes? My dreams?

I didn't know yet, but I was getting closer and closer to my conclusion and it didn't look like it was in my favor. Maybe I needed to work on my self-esteem.

Should I stay in town, where I knew I'd be found but I had a potential future? Or was I willing to give up the only family I'd ever known, aside from Jeffrey? Was I willing to give up a future with Richard because I refused to take the chance that I could be found?

What was the worst that could happen?

But maybe, for once in my life, things would look up for me.

I thought about my aunt and uncle, my head whirring as I tried to come up with the probability that they would just leave me be. They'd never wanted me. That much had been clear from my first day in Oregon. No matter how much I'd groveled, sucked up, and rolled over, it hadn't done a thing. When I looked to my uncle for support against my aunt, he'd always responded with blank-faced sympathy. Like he felt bad for me in the sense that he didn't know what the fuck to do with me.

My aunt's apparent desire for children was not shared by him.

He was a mannequin with no face and no opinions of his own, a blank canvas for her to paint and repaint as many times as she wanted. An accessory. I'd learned early on that looking for sympathy and protection from him was futile.

I remembered a particular instance when I was nine. I'd spilled my juice on the counter and thought nothing of it, figuring I'd wipe it up as soon as I was done eating. At that point I didn't understand that the quartz counters stained under colorful liquids. It wasn't like my brain had room for information like that, not when it was full of survival and adventures. As I'd lived with my aunt and uncle, they'd begun to upgrade the house. I'd only realized how strange it was how much money they'd fallen into looking back with hindsight. There was always another project. New carpet. New counters. Repainting the front hall six different shades of ivory till it was 'just right.'

But at nine, my imagination took up all the spare real estate inside my head. There was no room for some of the rules that were imposed at my new home but never explained. Besides, it hadn't gotten bad yet and I'd had no idea that it could be worse than it already was. Even then, I'd understood upon seeing the stained counter that something bad was about to happen.

The fear was almost worse than the punishment. I hid the spill with the cutting board that sat on the counter, hoping, because my aunt very rarely cooked herself, that she wouldn't notice.

I had been naive, and she had been on the hunt, looking for any fault that would justify the need she felt to punish me.

That night I wet the bed for the first time, shaking and terrified because every creak in the hallway sounded like the devil was on her way to show me my punishment. Jeffrey was in the next room over but I hadn't gone for help. Instead I'd just lay in my own mess, staring at the ceiling and trying to figure out if I was still asleep and this was a bad dream, or if the nightmare was real.

I'd gone to my uncle the next day, shaking and sick with nerves. Like a fool I'd told him what happened and he'd nodded along, promised me everything would be fine, lied right to my fucking face.

She came for me then, hours later in the dark of night just as I'd feared she would. Her talons were sharp, her perfectly glossed lips pulled into a derisive sneer. She looked just like my mother despite their opposing hair colors, but the faces she made at me were not ones I'd ever seen on Mom. They were identical twins but nothing about them was the same. And I was filled with fear as my mother's face morphed into my aunt's and I realized with sickening clarity that he'd told her. *He'd told her* and in response she'd locked me away in darkness for retribution.

You ruin everything you touch.

Taking advantage of my kindness.

I take you in, and this is how you repay me?

There were other punishments too, but the closet was the worst of them.

The isolation.

The hunger.

The darkness.

I didn't like thinking back on it, though it served as a reminder for what I couldn't do.

I never relied on my uncle again. I knew what he was after that and I pitied him even as I hated him.

Looking in the mirror was always a surreal experience. Sometimes if I blinked I would still see the small dark-haired boy staring back at me that I'd been for so long. Haunted and hunted, my eyes ringed with the discoloration that only followed nightly terror. How no one had noticed what was going on with me was a question I was sure I would take to my grave. Maybe they had noticed? Maybe they just hadn't cared.

I was my aunt's problem. Maybe I deserved it. Maybe there was something wrong with me all along.

Now at twenty-three, at least I looked a little more well-rested. Vanity had taken it upon herself to get me the nicest mattress possible only a few days after my move to their place. I had no idea why she felt the need to replace the one she already had in my room. In fact, after our smoke session on the couch, she'd done everything in her power to make sure I was comfortable. It was weird, and attentive in a way I'd never expected. *Was this friendship?* It felt above and beyond it.

Even though she was kind, I didn't know how to talk to her. There was a barrier between us that wasn't there between me and Richard. With him honesty was effortless, he expected nothing and therefore I didn't feel like I was giving up parts of myself when I gave him everything. Vanity was different, there was something behind her gaze that was just as haunted, just as hunted as my own. Except there was something else there too... and I didn't know if I was just paranoid because of my upbringing or not but it seemed...it seemed like she might be hiding something.

Everyone's hiding something, I reminded myself. *Especially you.*

I splashed water on my face, shaking the drips from my bangs as I watched the droplets dance down my sallow skin like tears. I smiled at myself, just to see if I would still recognize my reflection.

Instead I saw my mother. Her eyes, her mouth, her nose. She crept into my crevices, filling up my empty spaces like sand. I stopped smiling, an ache in my chest I hadn't felt for a long time resurfacing. I rubbed the spot where my chest hurt before I reached to check that my apron was re-tied. I headed back out into the diner with my heart on my sleeve and a ketchup stain on the front of my apron.

The fluorescent lights from above were as friendly as ever, though for some reason tonight they felt cold. There was something crackling in the air, anticipation, nerves, paranoia. I shook it off, heading back behind the swinging door bisecting the counter and headed to the sink to relieve Chastity from dish duty.

There were only a few more hours in our shift and it was getting late. She'd been covering nights ever since Richard had quit and I realized now why she'd been so desperate to hire me in the first place. It was clear Benji's needed the help, and no one seemed willing to work through the night shifts. Probably because they were all vampires, I added privately. They wanted their 'days' free.

Vanity's original excuse that the town worked from home seemed flimsy now. I had only barely believed it at the time, which was laughable thinking back on it.

Hindsight and all that.

"You cool if I head out an hour early?" Chastity asked when we'd worked our way through the busiest stretch of night. "Vanity just texted me that she's stranded at the club."

The nearest club was in Ridgefield, and I'd only learned about it after a week living with Vanity and Chastity. They both seemed to frequent it. Which didn't surprise me considering the fact that it was the only place near Elmwood that served drinks other than your typical beer on tap. Elmwood imported basically everything from the surrounding towns and had hardly any farms or businesses of its own that were able to sustain their own inventory as far as I could tell.

Most of the time Vanity could be found drinking and chain-smoking at the club, a lost sort of expression on her face. My car was still in the shop so I'd been getting rides with either Chastity or Vanity. Though every time I'd ridden with Chastity we'd made a habit of picking Vanity up. She smiled at us every time we pulled up, but her gaze always lingered on me, a twist to her lips that I didn't have the people skills to decipher.

"Yeah, that's cool." I shrugged and continued to scrub down the dried mustard stain on the counter that I'd been whittling at for a minute already. "I don't mind locking up. It's only a few blocks home."

"Sweet, thanks, Blair." Chastity grinned at me, her pigtails swishing. She looked like Sailor Moon today, little twin buns with curly ponytails waving from their rounded tips adorning her now pink head. "She's been drinking more lately."

Chastity grimaced, glancing around to make sure the last two remaining customers were far enough away they couldn't hear. If they were werewolves or something that wouldn't do either of us any good. I was still figuring out the logistics of how the town worked, but the longer I observed our customers and the comings and goings of the townspeople, the more it became clear to me that there was likely more than one kind of supernatural creature living in the population.

The sheer number of customers that came in requesting practically raw meat was just a testament to that fact. Or the couples! God, the couples. I'd noticed them my first week in town, but now I had an explanation for the weird age gaps and the food-waste. They were a mishmash of human/vampire relationships more than likely—or vampires who had taken the change at different points in life.

I still didn't understand how Richard was able to be out in the daylight. He did avoid it somewhat though, I was observant enough that I'd noticed *that*.

Chastity continued to speak and I zoned back in, my brow furrowing in concern as her words registered. "She's been sleeping badly too," she added softly. "I think…I think it's because the anniversary of Prudence's death is approaching. She always gets like this, it's just never been this bad before." My brow furrowed even lower, tensing as I waited for her to continue. She did without prompting, a fretting sort of twist to her soft lips. "His death hit her hard, you know?"

"I'm sorry," I said softly, even though I felt stupid the moment the words left my lips. Sorry wouldn't bring him back. It was generic.

Unfeeling. Clinical.

"It's okay, really, it's been a long time." She shrugged and offered me a gentle smile. "He and Vanity were always super close. Closer than I was with either of them. Especially right before he died. It was this…*huge* tragedy. Still is."

"Accidental?"

"Something like that." She closed up after a moment, reaching out to gently squeeze my arm in apology for not being able to explain more. "She was really messed up for a long time over it. Claimed it wasn't fair, you know?"

"Death never is."

"Exactly!" Chastity slapped my arm in agreement. "It isn't. But once someone's gone…there's only so much you can do." She glanced to the side again, clearly hiding something, but I didn't press.

There was a beeping noise that signified Chastity had gotten another text and she sighed, pulling her phone out and glancing guiltily at me. "Sorry. I know I told you not to text while the customers can see but… there are always exceptions that need to be made."

"Hey, man. Don't stop on my account." I shrugged and turned back to my mustard stain, scrubbing the counter clean as I listened to the little clicking noises that signified Chastity was texting. "You could probably just head out now. Ty and I can handle clean up."

"Really?" She perked up, her big brown eyes glittering. "Fuck, you're the best."

"Aye, aye, captain." I saluted her and she rolled her eyes though she quickly sent out another text before reaching for the ties on her apron and pulling them open. She always hung up her apron neatly in the staff room and I'd come to copy the behavior.

"Drive safe." I waved at her as she headed out, glancing over her shoulder to check on me and Ty one last time before the back door dinged and she stepped out into the night.

Ty nodded to me with a shy little smile, remaining as quiet as ever while we worked our way through the last ticket of the night. Soon enough it was closing time and I waved Ty out the door when it was clear the cleanup was minimal.

I flipped the sign to closed and turned off half the overhead lights, heading over to the sink to begin rinsing and scrubbing the remaining dishes. It was nice to be here alone, peaceful even. The best part however was the trust. I'd never had something like this back in Oregon. A place that was all mine to work in, to have responsibility, to be trusted like a real adult.

At the thrift store I'd worked at, I'd known I was being watched. More than half my shifts had been under the cover of darkness because my manager had taken pity on me. Her mother was friends with my aunt and we'd spent our late shifts shooting the shit and talking about what we'd do the second we left town.

She'd given me as many shifts as she could despite it being against my aunt's orders. Honestly, aside from Jeffrey, she'd been the only person to remark on how weird my aunt's behavior was. "You're an adult," she'd said. "Why the hell does she get to decide how much you work?"

I hadn't known what to say. Her incredulousness was refreshing but isolating all the same. I never told her about the cameras. The closet. The origin of my scars.

It was easier that way. Simpler. And she'd still given me shifts so at the end of the day I figured I'd made the right decision despite feeling like I was lying to her by omission.

Sometimes I still felt like an impostor but every day it got easier and easier. Moving here truly had been the best choice for me and my personal growth, even if I ended up leaving. Elmwood was inside my soul now, curled up like roots beside my insecurities, giving me something to anchor myself to when the existential thoughts became dark waters blanketed by rain clouds and my world was full of thunder.

"Ty left?" a voice rumbled from behind me and I jumped about forty feet in the air, my back slamming into the counter as I whipped around, brandishing a dirty spatula in my defense.

Richard.

Because of course it was fucking Richard. I should've recognized his voice right away, and his creepy-not-creepy way of moving completely silently. I realized belatedly that he must still have keys—either that or I'd forgotten to lock the door, which was equally as possible.

He looked better than he had the last time I'd seen him, though the dark circles underneath his eyes remained and there was a tension to his jaw that I wished with every fiber of my being that I could smooth away.

His eyes were dark, hooded by the feeble fluorescents as he made his way to the counter and traced his fingertips along the laminate. I wasn't sure if I was grateful or resentful of the distance between us. Confused. I was confused.

"I'm sorry about what happened yesterday," Richard said, breaking the silence between us.

He sounded so…blank. Like a statue come to life. I was reminded once again of one of our first conversations and the fact that he'd so clearly told me how hard this sort of thing was for him. *I don't people well.* That's what he'd said, or something like that. I watched his fingers play with the edge of the counter, the only part of him that made it clear how vulnerable he felt.

"You don't need to be sorry," I told him softly. "Honestly I feel like you handled it really well. I mean, I showed up at your house and basically verbally karate-chopped you."

Richard snorted, his lips twitching like he was trying not to smile. He wouldn't look at me though, and that made my heart hurt.

"You know, it's the first time someone has cared enough about me that they even wanted to 'verbally karate-chop' me."

"Well." I blinked, unsure what to say. "You're welcome, I guess."

That got a *real* smile out of him, the sight of it blinding for the split second that it broke like sunrise across his face. God, he looked good. His shoulders were encased in his leather jacket which I knew firsthand was softer than butter, his chest pressing obscenely at the buttons on his black flannel button-down.

"I liked it," he added.

"You liked me chewing you out?" I raised an eyebrow.

"No. I liked that you stood up to me." He shrugged, continuing to pick at the counter as he stared rather pointedly at the napkin dispenser. He was staring presumably at his own reflection, and I couldn't help but ache for him because he didn't know what I knew.

He still carried the burden of the secret.

He didn't know that to me it didn't matter whether he was human or not. *It didn't matter.* The only thing that mattered was the soul he carried, harbored like a fugitive inside his own body, so scared of being vulnerable he'd imprisoned himself in his own solitude. A fortress between him and the rest of the world.

I knew what that was like.

I knew what it felt like to be a shadow of yourself, to be terrified of being tangible because being tangible meant being vulnerable.

"I'll stand up to you anytime you want," I told him, trying to be cute but coming off just slightly too awkward. Talking to him was difficult now because I cared too much about what he thought about me.

"You know, I've been thinking a lot about what you said," Richard murmured. "About leaving town and us…whatever we could be…having a timer?" I nodded, urging him on.

I didn't know where he was going with this, so I didn't speak, my heart in my throat as I mirrored his movement, gripping the edge of the counter tight enough my fingers turned white.

"If that was the only thing in my way I wouldn't hesitate, but there are things in place here that you don't understand," he said softly, finally—*finally* looking at me. Richard's eyes were blood-red. How had I never truly noticed? They glowed in the dark, ringed with lashes darker than sin. The tense muscle in his jaw jumped again.

I wanted to scream at him.

I wanted to scream that I knew. I fucking *knew* and he didn't need to hide. In fact, I was probably the most equipped human on the entire fucking planet to date a vampire. I'd basically been prepping for it since the day I learned how my dick worked.

I remained quiet though, because with all my cards on the table the game would be over far too soon. I didn't know if I had a winning hand or not and I wasn't willing for this all to be over so soon if I didn't.

You're a coward, Blair.

Nothing but a fucking coward.

"I understand," I said softly, my words like satin in the darkness. Richard was watching me, his brows twisted, his eyes bright with vulnerability. I didn't know what he wanted from me but I was loath to deny him anything. I didn't know how it was possible to feel so strongly for someone in such a short period of time. It wasn't love, but it was close enough.

"Blair, I—" Richard bit off, forcing his hands to loosen their grip. He twisted around the edge of the counter and pushed his way through the swinging door that separated the kitchen from the dining area. "I want you—" He exhaled raggedly, his footsteps heavy on the tiled floor.

With each centimeter that closed between us my heart beat faster. I could hardly breathe through my own anticipation as he drew closer and closer. He bowed his head so he could speak in the space between us, a whisper, a promise, *a prayer.*

"I want you so fucking bad I can't think about anything else. It's *infuriating.*"

His breath curled like spun sugar around the shell of my ear and I melted, holding very still as the scent of leather and pine filled my nose. The cocoa that usually tinged his scent was gone, replaced instead with the saltiness of sweat and the promise of sin. I couldn't help but see the mirror between Richard's words and the ones I'd spoken to him out of frustration.

"You make me remember what it means to be young."

I couldn't look at him, couldn't, or I'd shatter into a million tiny pieces and there would be no way for me to put myself together again.

"But I can't have you." His breath caressed the slope of my neck, tickling my skin until gooseflesh rose and the weakness in my knees I always felt around him only got worse. "*I can't have you*," he repeated, voice breaking.

Richard raised his hand, his fingers tentative and gentle as they dragged along the fragile skin on my inner wrist. I tingled from the touch, my dick twitching to attention as my breath caught in my throat and I waited with anticipation for more. He didn't stop there, tracing across the fabric of the hoodie he'd bought for me, up my forearm, the sensitive crease on the inside of my elbow, my bicep.

His thumb slid along the seam across my shoulder, dragging over fabric inch by blessed inch until suddenly the fabric barrier disappeared and Richard's bare skin was against my own. He felt like ice, his caress cool where my skin felt overheated and flushed.

"Why can't you?" I asked him, even though I already knew the answer.

"Don't ask me that." Richard's voice broke, his words overwrought with desperation as his thumb pressed hard against where my pulse throbbed in my neck. He was close now, his body in front of me, blocking my line of sight to the window as he filled my vision, my senses, my heart. I liked to imagine that he could see the blood dancing under the surface of the fragile skin at my throat, singing to him like a siren call. *Taste me, lick me, devour me. Give me everything and in turn I will give you all I have to give.*

Richard's nose bumped against the shell of my ear, the pressure of it barely there and gentle as he dragged it along the velvety flesh and his hand closed carefully around the barrel of my throat. When he spoke again, it was against the vulnerable hollow at the top of my neck. "All my life I've never struggled for control," he breathed. "Until I met you."

"*God—*"

"You make me want to forget everything I've built so I can feel alive again." Somehow his words sounded like a prayer, and I was helpless in the face of his worship.

Chapter Twenty-Six

Blair

EVERYTHING WAS PERFECT until suddenly it wasn't.

Richard's scent was in my nose, his body brushing mine in a tease that shook me all the way to the bone. I orbited him the same way he orbited me. A gravitational loop that shifted for infinity. When Richard was in front of me it was like the rest of the world ceased to exist. So much so that I'd forgotten for a moment that we were in front of a window in full view of the street outside.

Headlights blinded me for a moment and I blinked in confusion, sucked out of my own head as I watched a car approach the front of the diner. My head was so foggy with possibility it almost felt like being drugged. There was customer parking out front as well as out back so I wasn't that alarmed by the approach, other than the fact that we were closed.

The car stopped, its lights overwhelmingly bright as I held up a hand to shield my gaze from their flare. Richard made a noise in front of me, an alarmed sort of gasp, before a snapping sound ricocheted through the air and suddenly I was flying.

Pain erupted along my side as I slammed into the counter along the back wall, crumpling like a marionette to the floor as I stared at Richard's silhouette. His body was ringed in a halo of white light, his figure turned black by the glare of headlights as my pulse throbbed in my throat and I stared at his outstretched hands realizing, too late, that he'd just fucking pushed me.

"What the—"

"*Stay down,*" Richard commanded, voice nothing but gravel as another snapping sound filtered through the roaring in my ears.

It took me a second too long to realize that what I was hearing was gunfire.

Gunfire.

In Elmwood?

What the actual fuck?

There was a cracking sound, the shattering of glass, as the second bullet ricocheted into the room, the front window spreading in a spiderweb of destruction. I could only see half of the damage from where I lay huddled on the ground, my body cold and shaking.

My fingers were numb, my mouth copper bright with my own blood. I must've bitten my tongue when I'd fallen, but my pain was the last thing on my mind as I watched Richard stand in front of me and I tried to figure out why the fuck he wasn't ducking down to safety. There was a moment between us, suspended like dust motes in space, before what he was doing hit me.

Maybe this was his way of showing me the truth without ever having to say the words. Or maybe he was just protecting me. Maybe he was just a scared little boy who didn't know what to do.

Either way his body jolted as a bullet connected with his chest. He fell to the ground in front of me, his body shaking, his red eyes wild.

Three shots.

Three shots, that's all it took for my world to crumple as the car sped off into the night with a screech of tires and the flare of light. Clearly they'd gotten what they came for, though what that was, I still didn't know.

We were left scrambled in the aftermath, the darkness all-encompassing as Richard slowly turned to look at me with a desperate, lost expression on his handsome face.

Somehow I knew there was no going back from this.

He knew that too.

My pulse raced.

Two things were abundantly clear in that moment. First and foremost: Someone was trying to kill me.

Fool me once, shame on you. Fool me twice, shame on me.

Second, Richard Prince *wanted* me to know his secret. He'd taken a bullet for the truth to come to light. Brave fucking shithead. Or maybe… maybe he was just stupidly noble, and not a vampire at all.

I had so many questions and no answers and I reached for him with everything but my hands as I stared at his chest, looking for damage.

"Holy fucking shit, Rich." I moved to scramble to my feet, my hands shaking as I breathed through the pain echoing inside my body from the fall.

"They might come back," Richard said, shoving me back down, probably harder than he intended. His gaze was wild, the whites of his eyes glistening as he crawled on his knees to close the remaining distance between us and his big cool palms cupped the sides of my face. He held me there, firm and still, searching my eyes for something almost desperately.

He must've found it because eventually he relaxed. It could have been seconds or hours that passed, my perception of time skewed by the adrenaline that had replaced the blood in my veins.

"Are you okay?" Richard finally asked, voice cracking.

"Dude, what the fuck." I hadn't realized until that moment that I was laughing. I stopped abruptly, the shaking in my body refusing to stop even though I willed it with all my might to.

"Blair," he grunted, shaking me just a little. "Blair, please—"

"Yes. I'm okay. *Fuck.*" Richard's whole body was still as stone, eyes darker than I'd ever seen them before. He trembled, his hands unsteady where his fingers dug into my hair and his palms squeezed my jaw in a possessive grip. With his hands covering my ears the world grew blissfully quiet and I inhaled raggedly as I stared into his eyes and tried not to be completely fucking broken by the expression I saw on his face. *Fear.* Strength. Determination. "Are *you* okay?" I countered, reaching up to tangle my fingers in the lapels of his jacket. "You don't look okay."

"I'm fine," he grunted. *Fucker.*

"You just got fucking shot, didn't you?" Distantly I knew that we were at the precipice of something. Either he was hurt or he wasn't, and whatever I discovered would change our course for the rest of the time we knew each other. My hands became frantic as I fumbled over his chest, searching with a crazed sort of desperation for a bullet wound I knew deep down didn't exist. Shot or not, there was nothing to find. I knew this. But Richard didn't know I knew.

There was panic in his gaze, like he didn't know what to do. He'd orchestrated this whole reveal of the truth out of bravery but his courage had run out. I could see on his face that he wanted to shove me away, to protect himself and his secret. But there was something deeper inside his core, something closer to his heart, his soul, the foundation of his very person that wouldn't let him push me away.

The part that wanted to be young with me. At least one more time.

I'd never seen him so distressed.

"I'm fine," he said again, trying to stop my search in a futile attempt though we both knew nothing he said or did could dissuade me. He didn't let go of his hold on me. I didn't want him to.

I had to know.

I had to fucking know.

Was I crazy?

Was he going to bleed out on the floor in front of me? Would he become just another number in a long line of deaths that seemed to follow behind me? If Richard was Charon then I was the river Styx.

I found the hole in his shirt.

It was barely the size of my pinky, unassuming where it had ripped through fabric and my heart in one fell swoop. I fingered over it, tucking inside the fabric until I touched cool, unblemished flesh. No blood. No wound. Nothing. I looked up into Richard's eyes and saw the panic there had evolved into a quiet sort of resignation.

He was silent. So was I. Our stuttered breaths were the only sound aside from the rapid *thump, thump* of my heartbeat.

"Rich?" I said softly, my heart in my throat.

It took him a long time to answer but when he finally did his voice was made of smoke. "Yes?"

"Rich…" I inhaled raggedly, trying to figure out how best to ask him what I needed to ask. This couldn't go on. *We* couldn't go on. Not like this. Not with all the lies. "Rich, why aren't you bleeding?"

That seemed like the best way to explain it.

"Don't say the bullet didn't hit you or I swear to god." I exhaled, suddenly incredibly aware of the heat of tears burning down my cheeks. "Don't tell me I'm crazy because I fucking *know* I'm not, okay?" My fingers bunched in the fabric of his shirt and I trembled, the familiar fuzz of the flannel making my knees weak. "Please don't bullshit me. Please. Rich—I can't—"

He shushed me, his hands slipping to my shoulders, his head dropping down until his forehead pressed against the spongy skin along my cheek. He was cool to the touch, his breath hitting the base of my throat in quiet puffs. He held very still, the sound of my breath echoing between us as one of his hands slid to smooth over the delicate skin on my neck. He held me there, hand to throat, chin to forehead, the silence between us louder than anything I'd ever heard.

I waited.

I waited and waited and waited, and for the first time my patience was rewarded because after an eternity he spoke.

"I'm not who you think I am, Blair," he said quietly. "I'm not…*what* you think I am."

"Then what are you?" My voice was nothing but a croak and Richard shuddered, like every word out of my mouth wounded him.

"I'm not human, for starters."

I tipped my head back enough that I could stare at the ceiling, soaking up his words like a sponge as every theory, every stray thought, every assumption I had made became real. Solid. True.

"God, fucking *finally*," I said, laughing softly as a weight that had been wearing me down bled from my trembling thighs into the tile beneath me. It felt like being reconstructed again, remade, reborn.

"What?"

"God—" I laughed, I fucking *laughed*, my shoulders shaking as I curled my fingers in the fabric on his unharmed chest and I pulled him tighter against me. "I've been waiting for you to tell me for ages."

"You...*knew?*" He sounded confused, *hurt*, but I couldn't stop laughing.

"I figured it out, yeah." I pulled him closer, our bodies aligning like parallel puzzle pieces as his scent filled my nose again and something slotted itself inside my chest, squeezing my heart so tight for a moment I thought it had grown in size.

"You don't...care?" His voice was tentative, hopeful.

"Fuck no." I laughed again, unable to help myself as the adrenaline in my system fueled my amusement. "Richard. I literally told you the first time we were alone how much of a boner I have for vampires. You think the fact you *are one* is a problem for me?"

"I didn't say I was a—"

"Yeah, some things don't need to be said, dude." I pushed him away far enough that I could look him in the eyes again. "You think you're so sneaky, but you're really fucking not."

"What gave it away?" The hope was back in his eyes and his lips twitched as he watched me, seemingly fascinated. Sometimes he looked at me like

I was an art exhibit, too precious to touch but too beautiful to look away from. I'd never been looked at like that before and it frightened me, but not in the way I was normally frightened.

It was potential. It was a future. It was connection.

Terrifying and brilliant and world ending.

"Well, I mean. The whole 'everyone going out at night' thing was pretty fucking weird." I shrugged, explaining myself for a couple tense minutes as we both calmed down enough to be able to think about what to do next. He listened to me patiently, nodding along with my story though I noticed his eyes stray to my mouth at least ten different times during our discussion.

At first, I thought he wanted to kiss me until I realized the fact that my mouth was still actively bleeding. I'd almost forgotten the pain in my tongue, too absorbed with our conversation to think of anything but connecting with him.

Richard looked starved—a rabid sort of attention to him as his gaze snapped from my eyes to my lips, to my eyes again.

"I have about a million questions for you," I said softly after a moment of silence, the copper taste in my mouth carrying more meaning now that I knew what he needed.

"Can they wait?" he asked softly, the tense muscle in his jaw flickering as he seemed to retreat inside himself. It was like he wanted to run again, to get as far away from me as possible and forget about how much he *wanted*.

If there was one thing I'd learned about Richard, it was that the man had a hard time taking what he wanted.

Maybe I should've been more freaked out that he clearly wanted to suck my blood.

But hey.

I was actually pretty fucking flattered.

"I guess," I hedged. "Some of them can anyway." I pursed my lips as I looked at him, debating how to phrase what I needed to say. "Are you hungry?"

"Like... Now?" His lips twisted in confusion.

"Yes, Richard. Now."

He was about to lie to me, I could see it on his face. But he stopped himself, holding statue-still for a moment before a sigh left his lips and he moved to pull away. "Yes."

"Fuck yeah." I grinned. He looked confused for about two seconds before realization dawned on his face about the same time that I reached for the back of his head and pulled him in tight.

Our lips bumped against each other, tentative at first, soft and careful. The first kiss was made of hummingbird wings, flickering and chaste. The second kiss was longer, steady, sweet as nectar. My fingers tangled in the back of his hair, my nails scratching at his scalp as he remained immovable, lips firmly shut.

We kissed for another minute before I grew fed up with his self-restraint. "Open sesame," I hummed, watching his brow flicker in surprise and then amusement. He didn't open though so I took matters into my own hands, biting at his lips with purpose until he couldn't help but laugh. "C'mon motherfucker. I know you want to," I urged, the blood on my tongue smearing along his full lower lip. The hand he had on my throat gave a gentle squeeze and my lashes fluttered.

Watching Richard's pupils dilate up close was a sight to behold. His nose betrayed his desire as his nostrils flared and he inhaled the fresh scent of blood almost ravenously.

"Please—" I'd never begged a day in my life and liked it. But with him… God, I did. I wanted to plead with him every day for the rest of my goddamn pitiful existence. "Please, Rich. Lemme in— I wanna—"

"Fuck," he sighed between us, using his grip on my throat to push me hard against the counter. "Can you hold still?"

I squirmed in his hold, testing it before nodding, eager for anything he was willing to give me.

"Are you sure?" Richard questioned, a concerned but desperate twist to his lips. "Because I don't know how well I can control myself around you."

"God, Rich. You could kill me and I'd say 'Thank you.'"

Richard groaned, rolling his eyes heavenward like he was looking to god for strength before he leaned forward, his fingers tensing around the column of my throat. His hands were huge, his palms pleasantly scratchy, and I melted in his grasp, my Adam's apple bobbing as I swallowed. "Just…" He was trembling and I couldn't help the way I spread my thighs wide, urging him to crawl between them till our bodies were flush. "Just a taste?"

"Fuck yeah, big guy." I groaned, biting into my tongue in the hopes of aggravating the wound. It hurt. *So good.* "C'mere and taste me."

Richard made a broken little noise in the back of his throat, clearly still fighting an internal battle. "Just once," he rationalized, and I held a celebration in the back of my head.

"Just once. That's it," I urged, watching his eyes begin to glow softly, the flicker of red around his pupil causing a shiver of pleasure to surge up my spine. I couldn't believe this was real. I couldn't believe it was happening. And to me of all people. If there was a god out there he sure fucking loved me.

"Okay," Richard murmured after an intense internal debate.

Oh, thank god.

Richard leaned forward, giving in to his instincts as our lips met again. I was good this time, holding obediently still as his fingers squeezed my neck along with the beat of my pulse and he fluttered barely there kisses against my lips. They felt like butterfly wings and I was about to complain that this isn't what we'd agreed to before he was diving in for longer, broader strokes.

I melted, trembling beneath the onslaught of his attention. My lips parted and he groaned, a growly sort of desperate noise that rumbled in the back of his throat and vibrated between our lips. My toes curled, my cock throbbing where it pressed against the confines of my skinny jeans.

"Stick out your tongue," he urged, voice nothing but a hoarse whisper, commanding all the same.

I stuck out my tongue.

"Fuuuck." Richard didn't waste time, he sucked me down in a matter of seconds, the cool wet suction making my eyes roll back as he held me tight enough I couldn't move. I couldn't do anything but take it, the muscle in my tongue trembling as I attempted to hold it obediently still. "You taste like sex—" he gasped, before his kisses grew nearly violent.

He chased me back inside my mouth when I got too tired to remain tensed, the broad strokes of his tongue made me weak-kneed and breathless. I'd never been kissed like this before, *devoured* really.

I was an all-you-can-eat buffet and Richard was a man who had dieted his entire life. He sucked and licked and plundered, rubbing the tip of his tongue along mine, tasting the back of my mouth like a man on a mission. He chased every last drop of blood I had with an almost animal-like intensity.

Which—maybe that's what he was. He wasn't human after all. I was playing with fire and I had never been more ready to be burned. Maybe he'd get too violent. Maybe he'd kill me. I found I didn't care as long as he kept doing that thing with his tongue along the back of mine.

My cock was so hard I could barely breathe but I didn't dare try to touch it. I didn't want to break the spell between us. Richard's abandon had been hard-won and I was loath to let him fall back into his human shell.

Minutes passed, maybe hours, but I didn't care. I didn't even care that I'd been fucking shot at either, because Richard was kissing me—and god... I'd never known what living felt like until that moment, with his big hand on my throat and these honest, hungry little growls escaping him almost like they were leaving without permission. Like he just couldn't help himself.

We were interrupted by the sound of the sirens growing closer. Richard didn't let me go but he did pull back. His lips were kiss swollen, his eyes blood-bright and glowing softly. "Someone must've called the cops," he croaked.

I just nodded, because apparently I became stupid when my dick was hard.

He looked at me for a moment longer, examining me with hungry determination before his jaw clenched tight and he debated with himself over something. Clearly the animal part of him won because instead of gathering himself and rising to greet the approach of law enforcement he just kissed me again.

And again.

And again.

And god…I blessed everything in my life that had led me up to this moment. Richard's kisses were intoxicating. They were smoke and cherries, chocolate-dipped temptation wrapped in butter-soft leather. I wanted him to crawl inside me and make a home for himself, cracking open my ribs and burrowing beside my heart where it lay vulnerable and fragile inside my breast.

The police took us both in for questioning but my head was in the clouds. I answered everything, met their suspicious gazes with emotional detachment. I figured now that I knew the town secret, the population would become more welcoming. But that would take time—and a lot of gossiping—before everyone realized I was in on their big secret now.

I was, however, annoyed when they released me to go home and it was clear that Richard had finished up much more quickly than I had. I wasn't sure what I'd been expecting. Maybe some more jolly-old make outs on our way out the police steps? Maybe a goodbye hug? I don't know.

What I didn't expect however was just…nothing.

Nothing.

He was gone and I was forced to sit on the front steps and phone Chastity for a ride. I really could've walked home, but now that I had my suspicions about the fire and the gunman I wasn't eager to be out on my own with no witnesses.

"Hello?" Chastity's voice rang over the phone and I sighed.

"Hey." She was quiet as I explained the situation, her voice full of concern when I got to the whole 'shooting' bit and she asked if I was okay.

"Yeah. I mean. Nothing hit me. I'm a little bruised but it was the counter that injured me and not the shooter."

"Did they figure out who did it?" she asked quietly, the sound of rustling in the background. I figured she was pulling her coat on so she could come get me. I was still wearing my work apron and I smelled like French fries, but hey. At least there was someone there to pick me up, even if it wasn't the person I necessarily wanted it to be.

"No. They're claiming it was a coincidence."

"Bullshit." Chastity's voice was bitter and sharp as something clattered and then there was the sound of a car door shutting. "They're claiming coincidence when only a week ago your house was fucking set on fire with you *inside it*?"

"I dunno man." Honestly the fight had left me the second I'd stepped out on the cement steps in front of the police station and realized that Richard wasn't waiting for me. "Maybe someone just really fucking hates Benji's."

Chastity was quiet for a second. We both knew I was lying. There was something…very wrong about this whole thing.

"And at the party," she said after a tense few seconds. "At the party it was almost like someone…drugged you."

"I was fine. Just not used to alcohol." She was right, though. Thinking back on it, that had been the first time I'd experienced something that hadn't sat quite…right. *Man, did this date all the way back to my first week in town?*

What the fuck was happening? Was I really in danger here? *Why?* Was it because someone didn't want me to know about the supernatural? And if so—now that I knew, what was going to happen?

"I'll be there in five minutes," Chastity said after a moment. "You stay put and stay within sight of the police station, okay? We shouldn't take any chances. Not when we're not sure what's going on."

"Yes, mom," I responded, though my joke fell flat as I waited as long as I could before hanging up the phone. Jesus fuck.

I was in trouble.

Chapter Twenty-Seven

Richard

I KISSED HIM.

I kissed him, I kissed him, *I kissed him.*

My lips tingled and my cock ached as I slammed my way into my apartment and down the hall toward my bedroom. I wasn't sure what I needed. Escape. Silence. Time to process.

I'd never kissed someone before. Unless you counted that time I'd kissed Chastity in the first grade when we'd had a pretend wedding, and then subsequently a pretend divorce.

What was I doing?

I was hiding so much from Blair it seemed silly to think that one of my secrets coming to light could make up for the deceit I'd been participating in from the moment he'd come to town. He deserved better. He really did.

So why was I thinking about kissing him again?

"Oh my god." Collin pushed his way into my bedroom after me, dressed in his Christmas pajamas, his red hair wild. "What is your deal? It's like three in the morning."

"You're usually up this late anyway." I yanked my shirt off my head following my jacket, and then my pants, and Collin made an angry squawking noise.

"What are you doing?!"

"Showering."

"Why?"

"Because." I needed some sort of control back after I'd relinquished it all. God. What was wrong with me? I was terrified of what I'd done, yet I'd never felt more alive. More fulfilled. Happy.

My lips tingled and I realized with a jolt that I was grinning. Collin stared at me, nearly naked in the dark of my bedroom, my expression manic and a slow grin began to travel across his cherubic features.

"Something happened," he sing-songed and I flipped him off.

"Nothing happened."

"Something *totally* happened." He followed after me as I made my way into the bathroom, slamming the door on him so he wouldn't follow me inside because I knew he would.

"Tell me, tell me, tell me," Collin chanted through the door and I ignored him, though my smile remained. When I caught a glimpse of myself in the foggy mirror I hardly recognized my reflection. I looked…

Young.

Happy.

Carefree.

I couldn't remember the last time I'd done something just because I wanted to.

Took something just because I wanted *it.*

And I *wanted* Blair Evans.

I wanted him more than I had wanted anything in my entire life.

Even the meeting I'd been summoned to by The Council hadn't put a damper on my mood. I'd had to report on the shooting at Benji's before they learned about it from someone else. And the whole time I'd been there I couldn't help thinking about big green eyes, lush pink lips, and a tongue that was both sharp and slippery.

Collin was waiting in my room when I reappeared and I smiled at him again, ignoring the weird look he gave me as I crawled onto my bed and shoved a pillow over my head. It was far too early to sleep but that didn't mean I was emotionally equipped to do anything other than relive what I had privately dubbed 'the kiss of the century' at least a thousand times in my head.

My dick throbbed and I shoved my comforter over it in the hopes that Collin hadn't noticed. God. I wanted to touch Blair. I wanted to suck on his throat. I wanted to bite his collarbones, his shoulders, his fingers. I wanted to pull his sweet little wiry hips open and slick my tongue inside his tight little hole.

"You're acting super weird so I'm going back to bed," Collin called like he was punishing me from where he stood inside the doorway. Good. Let him leave. I had stuff to do anyway. "Goodniiiiight." He made no move to leave despite his words and I sighed, shoving my pillow off my head to glare at him.

"Go to bed."

"Jee-sus," Collin huffed, flicking a knowing look at me. "Fine." He made his way out the door but peeped back in at the last minute. "Please remember these walls are thin and I am a growing boy who needs his beauty sleep." He batted his lashes and I threw my pillow at him just to hear him cackle his way down the hallway and to his bedroom. He'd be going home to our parents' place tomorrow and I didn't want to put a damper on his fun.

I had a week and a half until The Council meeting. There was plenty of time to spend with Blair. To get to know him. To show him that no matter what he heard, what I was about to do was to protect him.

The idea of The Council hurting him now was unforgivable.

I'd rather run than let them touch him.

There were so many questions running through my head surrounding our fate and the mystery of Blair's attacker but somehow the only thing I could truly focus on was how pretty he'd looked with his tongue out and his pale eyes crossed.

I wanted to stick my cock down his throat and watch him choke.

Shit.

Shit shit shit.

I made quick work of my erection, my recent experiences fresh on my mind as liquid pleasure heated down my spine and my hips snapped to meet the grip of my fist.

One thing was for certain. I wasn't giving Blair up.

I wouldn't.

And despite it being medieval, I fell asleep knowing deep down that he was mine.

Chapter Twenty-Eight

Blair

CHASTITY DROVE A vintage Volkswagen bug. It was painted a pale shade of blue and had fat pink clouds all over it. I wasn't sure if it was a hand painted decal or if it was some sort of vinyl wrapping, but either way it was very…her.

She pulled up to the curb and honked her little horn, ignoring the fact that we were in front of the police station and it was late even for Elmwood's standards.

God, what was wrong with this town? Aside from the obvious.

I suppose I probably couldn't ask myself that question anymore, not now that Richard had told me the truth.

God…Richard.

Fucking Richard. With his stupid perfect hair, and his soft lips, and the dimple on the left side of his cheeks that was just slightly deeper than the one on the right. I shouldn't like him this much. I couldn't *afford* to like him this much.

I was like an ogre, layers on layers on layers of trauma no man should ever have to unfold.

"Get in!" Chastity called, waving at me with more exuberance than a woman with little to no sleep should have. I followed her urging, tripping a little on the bottom step leading down to the street before I righted myself and pulled the passenger-side door open. Boots leapt at me the second I slipped inside, and I buried my face in his fur searching for comfort before he escaped my embrace and wriggled across my thighs to get comfortable. I buckled up out of habit more than anything as I turned my attention to Chastity.

My little furry friend curled up on my lap, his tail flicking as I stroked his fur.

"You look like you need food," Chastity said with a little frown. "Something greasy."

"Yeah. That's hard to accomplish when usually the grease comes from pig fat," I joked softly, even though she was right.

"What if I told you that I know this fucking awesome twenty-four hour diner in Ridgefield that sells a mean veggie burger and salad."

I blinked at her, then my stomach gurgled. "Didn't you literally just get back from picking Vanity up from Ridgefield?" I pointed out.

"Nah. She ended up calling me when I was halfway there. She booked a room for the night, said it wasn't fair to ask me to drive her all the way back home and then drive her out in the morning to pick up her car."

I nodded, brow furrowed as the stars blurred along the skyline and the pine trees that trailed along the side of the road reached towards them with a familiar desperation. "That was nice of her."

"Just wish she would've told me that before I drove halfway there. God, sisters can be such assholes sometimes."

"Amen," I agreed, even though I genuinely had no idea what she meant, I had no sisters. She seemed to mean it though and I liked Chastity and her forthright opinions about everything. Usually she was correct.

"I figure she owes me. So we drive out to Ridgefield, we snag some delicious fucking food, and then we crash her hotel room." Chastity was grinning, though even *I* could see the almost manic look on her face.

It made me wonder if maybe she was going to have just as hard of a time sleeping tonight as I was.

"Sounds like a plan."

"Great." Chastity grinned at me, her little pigtails swinging as she pulled out onto Main and headed north towards the interstate. Ridgefield was nearly an hour away and was the most commonly traveled to town in the area. It was where Richard, Collin, and I had gone to the movies and where most of the night life—aside from Elmwood's weird ecosystem—thrived.

It was also the home of the nearest Walmart.

Fuck Walmart.

We had an hour to kill so I figured it was as good a time as any to come clean. Boots began to purr and the rumbling gave me courage to speak.

"So, I found out something interesting today," I hedged, leaving Richard out of it because I had no idea if he would be punished for breaking the town rules by talking about fight club or something. God. This wasn't Rocky, what the fuck was I doing?

"What?" Chastity blinked at me, flicking the radio on only to turn it down low enough all it did was fill the car with a pop ambiance.

"Vampires are real, who woulda thunk?" I grinned, twisting to watch her expression. Her face did a whole ballet before she finally settled on an expression that clearly meant relief.

"Oh thank fucking god. You have no idea how hard it was not to accidentally slip up!" Chastity slammed her hands on the wheel in excitement, making the car swerve a little. "Seriously. I am *so* relieved."

"Really?" I perked up, some of the tension bleeding from my shoulders.

"Oh my god yes. I have a chatting problem, okay? I'm a real gossip whore. And half of the good shit involved some sort of supernatural bullshit and you're probably the only person who ever actually listens to me when I talk. Besides Ty of course."

Because Ty never spoke, he was an excellent listener.

I blinked at her, surprised. I had always figured everyone listened to Chastity like I did. She was made of sunshine and cotton candy and rainbows, and also apparently fury. "Really?"

"Yes! I'm like…the dumb one, you know? Between me and Vanity, she's prettier, smarter, has the better job." Chastity shrugged and I stared at her, honestly floored. "Everyone knows she's better than me, *even me*. So when you came to town it was…nice. Because for once I got to be the one that helped out, you know?"

"You giving me somewhere to stay and a job at Benji's was the nicest thing anyone's ever done for me," I told her honestly, still feeling pretty blindsided. She smiled, a sweet private little thing and nodded.

"I was happy to do it. Vanity protested later, because she always does. She was all worried about me hanging out with a stranger. Which is just…*hilarious* now, because she's the one that won't shut up about you."

I blinked again, brow furrowing. "She's cool now about it though, right?"

"Yeah, but she's weird like that. She's all 'this is the best thing ever' one second and then 'doom and gloom' the next." She shrugged, pulling left onto the interstate. The trees were sparser here, farther out where they blurred like spikes along the skyline. "She's been weird for a while now, but it got weirder when you came to town."

"Your brother?"

"Yeah. I think so, anyway." Chastity grinned. "Either that or she has a cruuuush on you."

"Oh god no." I grimaced at the thought. "Not that your sister isn't hot shit. But I'm like, gayer than a pride parade, you know?"

"Yeah, I figured. It was pretty easy to tell after you looked at Richard and got all cow-eyed." She blinked toward me, exaggerating the flutter of her lashes.

"Oh, fuck you," I huffed, crossing my arms and turning away, though I couldn't help but smile a little.

"She's always been weird about the Princes too," Chastity continued to chatter. "Ever since their family started turning, our family has been having a fit about it."

"Why?"

"Well, I mean—it's kinda hard to explain." Chastity frowned out at the road, the dashboard lighting her face up with a pale blue glow. I stretched out my legs, the leather seat squeaking underneath me as I adjusted myself for the long ride. "It's a long story."

"We've got time."

She glanced at me again, as if checking to make sure I wasn't lying before she nodded along and smiled.

"Okay, so—" She inhaled, her chest puffing up and filling out the curves of her pink frilled dress. It came to mid-thigh and hugged all of the right places. While Chastity and her sister were different, they were both undeniably gorgeous. It made me honestly sad that she couldn't see that. "The Princes and the Rains have lived in Elmwood for ages. A lot of people like to say that they founded the town, though there's not really anything that backs that up. It's just…a nice story."

"Old money," I realized after a moment, connecting the dots.

"Yes! Exactly. Most of the buildings on Main were funded by one or both our families. It was like…this *thing*. Build a utopia for the supernatural— protect them—and in return we'd be protected." Chastity smiled at me a little as she settled back into her seat. "We were all supposed to stay human, you know? It was an unspoken pact. Protect but don't join."

"So what changed?" I asked, because clearly something had if Richard was a vampire, and I suspected much of his family was as well.

"This is where it gets a bit…*tricky*." Chastity bit her lip, seemingly weighing her words before she spoke. "It involves your family. You sure you wanna hear?"

"Is it bad?" It sounded bad. The way she said that sounded…really bad, actually.

"Um." She paused. "Yes? Pretty fucking bad."

I weighed my options. Did I want to know? *Not really*. But at the same time, it wasn't like there was anyone in my family left to mourn. They were all gone now and I had hardly any memory of them anyway. There was no reason to protect my memories if they cost me my future.

"Tell me," I decided, my voice even.

"So…fifteen years ago? Sixteen? Something like that. There was this…"

Chastity seemed to weigh her words. "*Tragedy.*"

I thought back on one of my first conversations with Richard, my head spinning as I connected the dots. "Richard's brother? The one between him and Collin?"

"Yeah. Him and…others, your parents included." She nodded at me gratefully. "His name was Markus." A sadness filled the air as she spoke, a weight settling in the car. "He was nine. The Princes used to have this treehouse out in the woods behind their house that he and Richard would go play in all the time." She perked up a little. "Hey! Actually it's not that far from your house."

I nodded along, waiting for her to continue, though my mind immediately shifted to one of my first memories in town. The treehouse. Its burnt husk. The haunted feeling that had followed me all the way home.

"Anyway. So during the summer there was a string of fires. No one knew who was starting them. For a long time everyone just thought they were accidental, you know? But one of them… One of them burned the treehouse down and like half an acre of the woods surrounding it before they got the fire under control. No one had realized that it hadn't been empty and Markus was… Well. He was just gone." She swallowed, clearly recalling the memory. "We were all…so fucking sad, especially Richard. Vanity and I were still in elementary school and our classes all made up cards for us to give to their family."

The trees along the road danced in my vision as I processed her words, the sadness of child loss heavy in my heart. I couldn't imagine going through that, losing someone like that. I'd lost my parents, but it wasn't the same.

"Richard's parents pulled him out of school and started homeschooling all their other kids too. They got reclusive, secretive. Our families stopped meeting up like we always had and it seemed like nothing was ever going to heal the loss of what had happened. They blamed my family for his death, even though it wasn't our fault."

"Did they ever find out what went wrong?" I asked, dread sitting tight in my belly. Chastity had told me this involved my family and god… I couldn't imagine how, not after what she'd just said. She grimaced and my pulse began to thrum with anxiety.

"They did, yeah." She seemed to gather herself for a moment before she was able to respond. "There were all these clues, you know? I don't…I don't really know the exact details. All I know is that everything led back to your mom and her accomplice. When they figured it out they went to investigate and…that was when they found your dad."

"Wait, what?" My ears were ringing.

"He'd been…yeah. Murdered?" Chastity swallowed, clearly struggling to tell me the next part. I wasn't sure I wanted to know anymore. God. I wanted to tell her to stop but… But something inside me knew I needed to know. "And when they went to find your mom to investigate she'd set herself on fire at the bottom of where the treehouse used to be."

"Why?" My voice came out choked, my head swimming. I could feel Boots as he crawled up my chest, slinging himself around my neck, holding me as I did my best not to crumble. He really was the best fucking cat.

"Well…" Chastity trailed off. "There's this thing in town…where we kinda deal with our own problems. The Council has rules in place to protect everyone, to protect the secret, the population. And some of those rules are a little medieval."

"So they think she… She what? Killed Markus and instead of letting The Council deal with it she…"

"Yeah. Took it into her own hands." Chastity looked grim and she reached across the space between us to gently pat my thigh. "Everyone thought she was crazy. Still do. When stuff like that happens, the city takes it to The Council that runs the Supernatural Alliance Committee, SAC for short, and they decide on a suitable punishment. Hunters who can't follow the code of conduct are…killed. It's barbaric but it keeps bloodshed to a minimum."

I was quiet for a long time and Chastity didn't push. The quiet murmur of the radio rattled around inside my skull as I processed all of this. "Is that why everyone in town has been so…scared of me?"

"Pretty much, yeah," Chastity admitted. "Not all of us are stupid enough to believe that kids turn out exactly like their parents. I mean. Look at me for example. Do you think my parents are proud that I earn my money ringing up customers and cleaning ketchup off countertops? No." She laughed. "But I like it. I like that I earned it on my own. I like that I'm good at it, and that it's mine and mine alone."

"Fuck. I just thought everyone didn't trust me because I was an outsider."

"I mean, that too, but mostly it's the whole…cursed lineage thing." Cursed lineage. Fuck. That was one way to put it. I had a hard time reconciling my memories of my parents with the images that had just been painted for me.

But, god. Who was I to tell Chastity she was wrong? Especially when I didn't remember.

I'd distantly wondered when I first moved here if my life was about to become a horror movie and god, I'd been right. Just not the kind that I'd thought it would be.

"What about your brother? Prudence?" I asked, because I had a feeling all of this was connected somehow.

Chastity grew sad again, her lips flicking down in a little frown as she struggled to speak. "Pru was an adult when all this happened. He'd just turned twenty. So when the evidence pointed in his direction as an accomplice he was convicted as an adult. He'd always been close to your mom. He took art lessons from her, learned how to paint and shit. He'd show us all the time. I don't think I ever saw him happier than when he'd come home from your house all paint-covered and wild. It wasn't that far of a leap to make, apparently, to assume he'd help her get the gasoline." She shrugged, picking at her pink steering wheel as she kept her eyes on the road. "The shitty people said he was in love with her. But I know he wasn't. He wanted a mom...and yours, *well*—she was the closest he'd ever get. Ours isn't exactly the loving type." I could tell how hard this was for her so I didn't push. "Your parents, and you, were already gone—but The Council sought justice as they always do."

I kinda wanted to tell her to stop, that it was enough, that she didn't need to explain anymore.

"They claimed that it was Pru's fault, you know?" She struggled to speak, starting again. "A lot of people said that he was just as crazy as your mom. They said that he knew about the whole thing. That maybe he was the one that set the fires in the first place. With your mom gone they wanted someone to blame." So much was beginning to make sense. The fact that I'd recognized Prudence right away—the looks everyone in town had been giving me like they thought I was only a second away from attacking them at any given moment. The reason just standing in the presence of the treehouse had felt so soul sucking.

Markus had died there.

My mother too.

In a way, maybe part of her spirit had remained. Caught between blades of resilient wild grass and blossoming with the flowers that burst through the charred remnants of her insanity.

"So when they found the evidence—" I spoke softly as Boots purred.

"Pru was killed." Chastity sighed, slowing down as we approached our exit. "So instead of one death, we ended up with four. It was this whole… *fucking thing*, you know? All of us were affected. You included."

"My aunt took me with her," I said softly, feeling rattled. "To live with her, my uncle, and my cousin."

"Yeah, I heard something about that." She shrugged, chewing on her lip. "You were homeschooled so the most anyone really knew about you was because of what your mom did. The Evans's have always been well-off, honestly almost as well-off as both the Rains and the Princes are."

"Do you…do you really think they did it?" I asked, searching for answers even though I knew she didn't have them.

"I dunno, Blair. It's been a long time since I spared a thought wondering why or how it happened." Chastity smiled apologetically. "Honestly most of us have just tried to move on from it all. But…man. The whole thing tore the town apart."

Chapter Twenty-Nine

Blair

BY THE TIME we reached Ridgefield, we were both exhausted and starving. Chastity offered to pay for my food and I didn't even bother refusing. She claimed it was her apology for the fact I'd been shot at while on the clock and I laughed, even though my head was full of bees and I was still trying to wrap my mind around what had happened. I'd get paid that week, but it was still nice that she cared enough about me to treat me.

I couldn't help but think about the Evans fortune she'd mentioned. Was it still there? Waiting? How would I even go about figuring that out? Just thinking about taking the money they'd left behind made me feel both an immense amount of relief and guilt. Was it shitty of me? Probably. But, fuck. *They were dead*. Maybe I'd need to talk to Sandra myself and see if she knew the person who was in charge of my parents' accounts.

I shuddered at the thought.

Chastity hadn't been lying when she'd claimed the diner made a fucking delicious veggie burger. I inhaled it greedily, along with a plate of fries all to myself, and Chastity matched my pace with a plate of eggs and sausage of her own. I'd hidden Boots underneath my hoodie and he sat warm and sweet, curled up asleep against my belly. Maybe I looked a bit pregnant? But no one had said anything so I wasn't going to.

The restaurant smelled like grease and therapy, and I couldn't think of a better way to end a shitty day.

By the time we finished eating, we were both exhausted. Vanity had apparently texted Chastity the address to the hotel for 'safety reasons' and neither of us bothered to text her that we were coming as we pulled into the parking lot.

Vanity's sleek black Tesla sat in the hotel's charging dock near the back and we passed by it as we pulled into one of the visitor parking spaces and climbed out of the vehicle. Both Chastity and I were blessed with short legs so neither of us had to speed walk to keep up with each other as we made our way through the front doors and into the hotel lobby. It wasn't as nice as something I would've assumed Vanity would rent.

But hey, she'd been drunk when she booked it, and it wasn't like it was horrible either. Plus, it was pet friendly. Chastity had checked before she'd decided to bring Boots along for the ride. The ceilings in the lobby were tall and covered in yellowed lights, and there was a long winding hallway to the left that led to rooms marked 100-135.

We ended up climbing into an aged elevator and hitting the button for the third floor. We rode up in silence, too full and too tired to speak as we made our way down the hall and towards room 323. Boots rumbled where I held him cradled inside my hoodie and I waddled beside my pink-haired comrade as we searched for our destination. The whole place smelled like shampoo and cigarettes and I sniffed at the air as Chastity found Vanity's room and began knocking rapidly at the door.

It only took around twenty knocks for the lock to rattle and a soft sigh to sound behind it.

"Oh my god. It's five in the morning. What are you doing here?" Vanity swung the door open, looking impeccable as always, except this time she was wearing a put-upon expression that I'd only ever seen aimed at her sister.

When I looked closer, however, I *did* notice what Chastity had been talking about. Behind her concealer (*why the fuck was she wearing makeup to bed?*) there were dark circles ringing her eyes, and her lips trembled in exhaustion.

"We needed food, you have a hotel, is there any other explanation you need?" Chastity pushed her way into the room, all five foot-nothing of her. I was grateful she hadn't brought up the shooting, I didn't want to relive it again. Vanity stepped to the side and rolled her eyes before her gaze fell on me. I must've looked even more like shit than normal because she winced, frowning down at my outfit with thinly veiled disgust.

"You're gonna make the whole place smell like French fries," she complained, but she let me in anyway, moving towards one of the queen size beds and collapsing face-first on top of it. "You can stay, but you both get the other bed, and no one disturbs me until at least eleven a.m."

"Okay," I agreed readily, honestly just ready for the day to be fucking over already.

Chastity claimed Boots from me and I headed into the bathroom to shower off the sweat and grease that had made its home on my skin.

I thought about Richard again.

All night, whenever there was a lull in my thoughts, he'd popped into my head.

Richard, Richard, Richard.

Pop, pop, pop.

I couldn't get our kiss out of my mind. It was playing on repeat with symphonies composing themselves in the background. Fuck. Richard was…

He was…

Something.

And I was going to fucking find out what that was.

I laid in bed beside Chastity and stared up at the yellowing ceiling for a long time before I was finally able to fall asleep. She snored softly beside me, her body star-fished in a way only the truly relaxed could be.

Thoughts rattled around inside my head, ricocheting off the walls of my subconscious as exhaustion finally pulled me down into a restful slumber.

I was seven again.

There were pages and pages in front of me, splashed with a wide variety of colors that had no rhyme or reason to them. I scribbled hurriedly, the crayon in my hand squeezed so tight my knuckles were white as I worked.

Page after page, picture after picture. There were trees and animals, houses and flowers, insects and umbrellas. For a long time I continued to draw, the hours ticking by like seconds before the pictures on my pages began to turn into something more sinister.

A treehouse, a gas tank, a lighter, a window. I scribbled what looked like a little boy, his eyes wide and dark, his auburn hair carrot-bright where he peeked back at me and waved. He was inside the treehouse, a big sunny grin on his face.

With a sickening lurch I realized the little boy looked suspiciously like Jeffrey. This dream was different than the others. Despite being a child again there was something inside me that remained of my adult self. I watched on in horror as my small chubby hands began to draw the beginnings of flames.

There were voices in the background now, wrought with tension. "I told you I don't appreciate you using that kind of language." My mother's voice echoed down the hallway behind me. The kitchen remained blissfully empty as I pulled out a new piece of paper and began to scribble on it as well.

Fancy shoes, a witch's cape, long pointed nails.

"And I don't appreciate being treated like a thief in my own sister's house." My aunt's voice was cool and collected despite the anger behind her words. I scribbled harder.

Green eyes, bleached hair, painted lips.

"I told you I'd be happy to help you should you and Greg need it," my mother answered, her usually calm voice breaking with thinly veiled anger. "But I'm not going to just…give you whatever you want all the time. I understand that you're wanting to adopt and I'd love to help you, but we have boundaries

for a reason, Ly—" I scratched my crayons on the paper loud enough that I wouldn't have to hear her name.

"You're selfish, that's what you are." My aunt's voice was full of ice. "Lazing about up here all alone in your fancy little mansion, sitting on piles of cash with no one to use it on except your useless little boy."

Bleached hair, pointed nails, gasoline.

"Get out." My mother's voice shook.

"What?"

"I said, get the **fuck** out of my house." There were footsteps approaching and I snagged my drawings, running from the kitchen and down the long winding hallway towards my bedroom. When I was tucked safely inside I cracked the door open, drawings clutched to my chest. The voices echoed down the hallway followed by the click of heels.

"You'll regret this," my aunt said coolly when it was clear my mother had opened the front door. Wind whistled through the air like it always did and I trembled in fear as the wicked witch said her last goodbyes. "You'll wish you'd been more generous."

The front door shut with a bang and I sighed, relaxing a little when it was clear that she was gone. I didn't like her, or her bright hair, her fancy words, and the cruel twist to her lips when she smiled. I didn't understand why my mom had invited her over in the first place. She looked like a caricature of my mother but without the light she always seemed to carry.

When I glanced over at the window I saw a flash of black hair disappearing around the corner of the house and I frowned. Prudence. He'd probably come for another lesson only to escape the moment he saw my aunt's car in the driveway.

He didn't like her. He'd told me that the other day as I'd shoved a cookie at him and asked him to draw his motorcycle with my new set of crayons while

376

he waited for my mom to finish up her phone call. I told him I didn't like her either. He'd laughed.

There were footsteps down the hallway and then the door to my bedroom pushed open and my mother stepped inside.

"Oh baby, I'm sorry you had to hear that." Mom dropped down to her knees, holding her arms out and crowding me in against her chest. There was a smudge of paint on her cheekbone that rubbed off on mine as she squeezed. I could feel the wet smear of it but I didn't wipe it away.

She smelled like cinnamon sugar cookies.

I inhaled her scent greedily, allowing myself to be bundled up like I was still a little kid. I was seven now, big. Too big for cuddles, and way too big to be coddled. I never said no though.

"S'okay."

"It's not okay," My mom shook her head, kissing my cheek and smudging away the paint streak as well as the dirt I was sure was still across the bridge of my nose leftover from my earlier adventure in the woods. "No one gets to insult my baby, especially not in my house."

"I'm glad the witch is gone," I told her matter of factly. Her face twisted like she was trying not to laugh, but then she failed and her whole face lit up with sunshine.

"Witch, huh?"

"Yeah," I agreed, grimacing. "Too bad we don't have a house to squash her with."

My mom snorted and shook her head. "No more Wizard of Oz for you my little friend, you get dark real quick."

I shrugged but smiled, wiggling my eyebrows at her in a way I knew looked funny enough she laughed.

She always laughed.

"What do you have there?" she asked as she noticed my pile of drawings. I let her flip through them and I watched her face grow a little pale.

"Just stuff I've seen," I told her, then flipped through the pile until I found the one Prudence had done for me.

"Pru did this one. I'm not that good yet," I told her as I shoved it towards her. She was still staring at my other drawings but she shook her head, focusing instead on the portrait of Prudence's motorcycle that was artfully crafted, despite the rendition being created entirely with my broken crayons.

"He's a good boy, don't you think?" Mom hummed softly, frowning down at the drawing as she waited for my response.

"He's okay."

"You love him," she accused, laughing as she gently pinched my cheek, "you just like to play it cool. My tiny little macho man." My cheek stung and I flushed.

I kinda did love Prudence.

He had a motorcycle. And tattoos.

He was nice to me, even though I could tell he was a bit different on the inside than other people. He didn't smile much, or at all, unless he was painting or talking to me and my mom. He looked…sad. I thought maybe he needed a little brother. I figured I could adopt him.

I'd always wanted a big brother.

I didn't know what to do about Richard. As I sat on my bed with the door shut and Boots staring at me from the top of his cat tree I debated with myself. The kiss we'd shared had been frankly earth shattering. I had no other way of describing it. Did I want to kiss him again? *Yes.* Did I want to suck his dick? *Also* yes. Not that I had all that much experience doing it. And I'd never had the favor returned.

I'd already jerked off *twice* to the memory of Richard holding my throat and telling me—no—*ordering* me to stick out my tongue. *God fucking damn.* It was like living a real life porno, except one of the main characters was a vampire with commitment issues, and the other was an emotionally constipated runaway with a penchant for swearing at inanimate objects.

I'd stubbed my toe just that morning on my bed frame, and had a few choice words to say to it.

Was it weird for me to text him? Considering the fact that we'd survived a shooting together I was pretty sure he wouldn't mind. But…*man.* It wasn't like anyone had taught me the proper protocol for hitting up your crush after you shared an adrenaline fueled make out session and he *kinda* sucked your blood.

The only person I felt like I could talk to about this was Jeffrey.

Contemplating calling him over Richard again seemed like a stupid thing to do. I hadn't even called him when my house burned down for god's sake.

But then I remembered how frightened and alone I'd felt these past few weeks, my anchor cut, moored by uncertainty. And I figured maybe the most courageous thing I could do in that moment was actually trust Jeffrey for once, and let him take some of the burden I'd been carrying as he always told me he wanted to do.

I'd had his number memorized since I was eleven and spent two hours writing it down over and over on a piece of notebook paper. I'd thought one day I might need it, though back then I was thinking it would be because I was stuck on a cruise ship in a storm, or stranded during the zombie apocalypse—not that there would be cell service during an apocalypse but still. I was eleven.

"Hello?" Jeffrey's voice echoed in my ear and I melted, tension bleeding out of my body as I flopped onto the mattress and clutched my phone tight in a misguided attempt to hear him better.

"Hey Jeffrey. It's me again. I'm like. Freaking out."

"Blair?" His voice got quiet as he whispered my name, no doubt checking to make sure no one was listening in. "Are you okay?"

"I'm okay," I said, then realized the entire reason I'd called him in the first place was because I *wasn't* okay. "Well. Kinda. Not really."

Jeffrey snorted, a familiar sort of noise. "So which is it? Kinda okay, or not really?"

"Both?"

"So is that why you're calling? More boy problems?"

"Yeah," I admitted, sounding like a pouty little kid, embarrassed by myself. "I just—I wanted your advice about something."

"Okay." Jeffrey made a few noises like he was shuffling shit around and I could so perfectly picture him back in our shared apartment, his back to his poster-cluttered wall, legs sprawled out to take up as much space as possible on his bed. Fuck, just picturing him back home made me homesick, and also…want to get him the fuck out of there.

Just like when we were little, as soon as the words started, they didn't seem to want to stop. So I told him everything. I told him my suspicions about the party, the house fire, the shooting. I told him about Richard and the clothes he'd bought me. I told him about Vanity and Chastity and the way they'd taken me in without question. And the entire time I spoke he listened quietly, patiently, 'hmm-ing' and 'haa-ing' in all the right spots in the way he always did to make sure I knew he was listening.

When I finally finished speaking, my mouth was dry and my throat hurt.

"Sounds like a wild ride," he hummed thoughtfully in that same wise way he'd always had. I'd grown up thinking he was the poster child for 'bad boy' only to discover that Jeffrey was just… Jeffrey. No label ever really seemed to stick. He'd been larger than life back then, even though there was only a year in age between us.

"Yeah, it's definitely been weird." I waited for him to talk again. Admitting how badly I'd messed up our plans had been harder than telling him about the existence of vampires. But I figured he had to know if he was going to eventually move up here with me. Which…I hadn't really asked him about yet.

"You sure you're okay though? That the whole…*fire thing* or whatever was a coincidence?" His voice was full of worry, deeper than my own and just scratchy enough it sounded like he'd taken up smoking cigarettes.

"I honestly don't know. I don't know anything," I admitted quietly. "I'm fucking scared, man."

"Why don't you just run?" He said it like it was so simple.

Just run, Blair.

It's fine.

"I'm tired of running," I finally answered after I picked apart my own response. "I'm always fucking running." I inhaled raggedly. "I like it here… I…I want to stay."

"So you're not gonna leave? Even though someone might be out to get you?"

I paused again, really thinking my answer through. I had two options here, which was more than I'd had for most of my life. I could stick around and see what happened, maybe get a few more kisses in with Elmwood's sexiest asshole. Or…I could run. I could start over somewhere else. Alone. *Again.*

"I'm staying," I decided after a moment. "At least for now."

I could practically see him nodding even though he was silent for a minute. "You know, Lydia's been talking about you lately," Jeffrey hedged softly. I flinched, just hearing *her* name tearing at the lining of my stomach.

"She has?"

"She's been asking me questions."

I swallowed, that same sick feeling in my gut only growing. "Did you tell her?"

"Did I tell her where you went?"

"Yeah," I exhaled raggedly.

"No, bud. I didn't fucking tell her where you went." Jeffrey sounded pissed off and I didn't blame him. It wasn't his fault I had trust issues, even though it kinda was. "She doesn't know shit man. I wouldn't rat you out like that. We're not kids anymore."

I made a soft noise in assent though it took me a second to be able to speak again. "You'll let me know if she does? You know…um. Find out?'

"Blair, you'll be the first to fucking know."

"Okay."

"Okay," Jeffrey exhaled raggedly, trying to calm himself down. He didn't usually get worked up like this but both of us were easily affected when it came to our aunt. Our approaches to coping were different. I was all avoidance where Jeffrey was all fight.

"So…" I hedged, wanting to talk about something else. "What should I do about Richard?"

"Did you text him?" he asked and I blinked. I blinked again.

"What?"

"Did. You. Text. Him?" Jeffrey asked again, amusement coloring his tone as he let out a snorting huff of a laugh.

"No…"

He laughed again, the sound louder as he shuffled around. "Well, that's your answer. Text him—feel him out— and then move forward. If he's all 'Yeah let's make out again' then boom! Success. If he's all 'I'm busy' then you have your answer. It's a win-win situation."

"So your advice is to just ask him what's going on?"

"Yup. People tend to love honesty, I'm sure your guy will too."

God, sometimes he was so stupid and so brilliant all at once.

"Okay…" My brow furrowed and I chewed on my lip. "So what do I—"

"Just say, 'Hey man, how are you?' Start there," Jeffrey interrupted me. "It'll be pretty clear how he feels by how he responds."

"Should I mention the shooting thing?"

"*God*, no. Jesus. Do you wanna make out with the guy or not?" Jeffrey huffed in exasperation. "No mention of any sort of guns, murder, or… vampire shit or whatever." I could literally hear him shaking his head now, his hair rubbing on the posters behind him. "Play it cool."

"Play it cool…" I repeated.

"Yeah," he agreed, like it was the simplest thing in the world. "Cool as a cucumber." What a lame-o. *I loved him.*

When I finally hung up with him I felt both better and worse. Jeffrey's advice made sense though, and it had been nice to get to talk to him again. I'd missed him more than I cared to admit. His easy acceptance of everything I told him only solidified what I'd already known. Jeffrey was *the fucking best.*

I pulled out my phone and stared at Richard's contact page for ten long minutes before I began to painstakingly type out a text.

Blair: Hello, Richard.

Ugh no. That was too formal. I deleted it and tried again.

Blair: Sup, Richard.

God no, that didn't even sound like me. I was pretty sure I'd never said 'sup' to anybody un-ironically in my life. *Delete.*

Blair: Hey, man. How are you?

That was better, more fluid. Chill. And also exactly what Jeffrey had told me to say, *motherfucker.* Before I even had a chance to hit send I looked down at my phone and realized during the time I'd been waffling back and forth trying not to sound like an asshole—Richard had texted me.

Richard: You okay?

Ah, fuck him. How dare he be so effortlessly cool.

Blair: Yes, why?

Richard: You've been typing on your phone for like ten minutes and a text hasn't come through. Wanted to make sure you weren't having a panic about texting me or something.

Blair: Fuck you

Richard: Actually, I'd like to fuck you, if that's on the table.

I stared at my phone, jaw dropped for a solid thirty seconds before Richard's words actually registered and I threw my arms in the air in celebration. *FUCK YEAH*. Fuck me? Any day of the week, motherfucker! I pumped my fist in delight and wiggled around to get comfortable before replying.

Blair: You wish.

Richard: I do.

Blair: Stop flirting with me or I'll kick your ass

Richard: Bold of you to think I wouldn't like that.

I stared at my phone, struggling to figure out how to respond. Holy shit, the man was holding nothing back. *Was this the moment that I got all honest with him? Or did I flirt back? Fuck. I didn't know how to flirt.* What a mess. *Maybe I should call Jeffrey again.*

Blair: What are you doing tonight?

Richard: Dropping Collin off at my parents' place then hopefully sticking around home for the rest of the night.

Blair: You down for visitors?

Richard: Yes.

Chapter Thirty

Blair

I DON'T KNOW what I expected when I showed up at Richard's house after dark. But it certainly wasn't what ended up happening. I'd convinced Chastity to drop me off on her way to the grocery store and she'd given me a knowing look, though she'd mercifully remained silent.

I knocked on Richard's apartment door only once before it opened and he grabbed onto my wrist and hauled me inside. His hands were greedy and cold, like he'd just been outside and absorbed the spring air. Dark eyes met mine, full of something almost like wonder as he crowded me up against the now closed front door with his fingers still twisted tight around my wrists. My skin buzzed where we touched.

"You came." He looked surprised, like he hadn't actually expected me to show up. Which was honestly just ridiculous. For a runaway I was being surprisingly stubborn about the whole thing.

I wanted to snark at him, but apparently I'd left all my snark behind in the passenger seat of Chastity's car. I was all attitude out. Instead what was left behind was a fluttery, excited sort of feeling. It tingled in my chest, dancing down my arms—and my legs—until it settled at the tips of fingers and toes.

I'd never had sex before. Not…penetrative sex, not any kind of sex—*reciprocated, anyway.* Fumbled bathroom blowjobs didn't count. I didn't really know what was about to happen now—but god—*I was ready,* whatever Richard and I ended up doing.

"I wanted to," I said, honest and earnest for probably the first time in my life. "Fuck, it's all I could think about since the last time I saw you."

The muscle on the left side of Richard's jaw—my favorite one—jumped as he clenched it and then released, his head thunking against mine until the soft skin on his forehead met my own.

"I told myself I wasn't going to call you," he whispered, like a secret.

"You didn't," I reminded him. "You texted me." Well, apparently I hadn't left *all* my snark behind in the car.

Richard laughed, the sound vibrating between our bodies as my fingers bunched up the front of his shirt. For the first time *ever* he was wearing an actual normal T-shirt. Go figure. It was soft and entirely too thin because when I looked down I could see his nipples—and god—*Richard had nipples.*

I must've done something to make the universe love me. There was no other way to explain how I had managed to get the sexiest man on Earth to crowd between my thighs, his lips pulled into a self-deprecating little smile.

"God. *That's* why," he said after a moment, his voice scratching its way through his throat. "*That's* why I couldn't help myself."

"Why? Because I have no brain to mouth filter?" Thank god I hadn't accidentally said 'Richard has nipples,' out loud.

"No, because you…" He inhaled sharply, his nose bumping imploringly against mine as his eyes crinkled at the corners. It was his way of forcing me to catch his gaze and I was too weak to deny him. When our eyes met it was like an electric current ran through my body. My toes curled, my belly flipped inside out, and I watched in real time as Richard's sunny grin broke through the clouds of his stoic expression. "You make me laugh. All the fucking time."

"I also make you swear," I pointed out.

"That too." Richard was smiling at me, rubbing the tips of our noses together with a boyish, excited sort of innocence that made something ache inside me for the boy he could've been. The boy who had been robbed of his childhood by misfortune and neglect. Too much responsibility too young.

"Elmwood was supposed to just be a stop for me," I blurted, totally honest for once. "But I guess that's because I didn't know about you yet. I mean—I should be running for the hills."

He cocked his head to the side, an infinitesimal movement that knocked our noses together once again.

"Why? You never really said." His breath caressed my lips and I wondered distantly if he only had to breathe when he talked, or if it was something he had to do all the time. *Was he even dead?* Or was this a living-dead sorta situation?

Either way, his question didn't alarm me the way it would've months ago when I'd first arrived to town.

I blinked. Surprised as something occurred to me. I don't know how or when—but apparently at some point—I'd started acting like Richard already knew why I'd run away from home in the first place. I'd stopped suspecting him, stopped hating him, stopped distrusting him. It was behavior that was so abnormal for me it took me a second to wrap my head around it.

Did I trust, Richard?

No. Of course not.

That was a fat fucking lie.

The only conclusion had to be—

Yes?

Holy shit. *I trusted Richard.*

"This is a conversation that I'd rather have after we have some mind-blowing sex," I told him rather pointedly. He snorted, shaking his head in disbelief.

"Sex and then trauma?"

"Wouldn't have it any other way." I shrugged.

Richard grinned at me again and then shuffled back a little. Our knees bumped, our toes brushing but I felt his loss keenly as he released my wrists and placed both of his hands on the wall behind my head, bracketing me in. Our height difference was even more apparent like this. He had to bend down to touch me, and my neck ached as I tipped my chin up to meet his gaze. "I have to be honest with you," he spoke softly, voice scratching through his parched throat. I wanted to bite his chapped lips and soothe the ache of my teeth with my tongue. "I've never done this before."

"Me neither."

"No." He shook his head, the light catching on strands of his fuzzy head before he repeated himself with tension creeping into his tone. "Blair. I haven't done *it* before."

"Yeah, I know." I blinked at him. "Me neither. Not really."

"Collin said—but I wasn't sure—" Richard stared at me, a confused almost hopeful expression on his face. "You're…"

"A virgin, yes." I blinked. "*Mostly*." He arched an eyebrow but didn't comment. I didn't have the brainpower to deal with the fact that apparently *Collin* knew whether or not I'd been fucked and was *telling* people. I blamed Chastity and her big mouth.

"Me too."

"Yeah, I think we just established that," I teased him, gently bumping his shin with my toe to soothe any of the ache my words might have caused. "I've kissed before, dry humped—that sorta thing. Oh! And performed oral like twice. But it didn't count because no one reciprocated and it was like…over in two seconds."

Richard blinked at me, his lips wobbling as he tried not to smile. Amused by my pain, the shithead. The sunny grin had fled about the time he proclaimed his inexperience.

"I haven't done any of that," he admitted quietly, almost shy. There was an ashamed sort of twist to his eyebrows and I wanted to smooth over it with my fingers until his smile came back. I barely managed to refrain, my fingers twitching where they stayed obediently still pressed to the cool wood of the door.

"Not even kissing?"

"Not like what we did the other day," he admitted—casually blowing my fucking mind because *holy shit*. *That* had been Richard's first time making out with someone? The dude was a fucking natural. Call the kissing police because someone had clearly robbed the fucking bank. It gave new meaning to the little sighs and grunts he'd made. They'd clearly been authentic and god, the thought of hearing him again...*Fuuuuck.*

"Holy shit, Rich."

"I know." He fidgeted, clearly uncomfortable.

"No, no." I flailed a little, accidentally smacking him in the chest with my wandering hands. "Shit. Sorry, I'm not judging you. I'm just... impressed?" I floundered to find the words. "Man, you had me about to come in my pants like a fucking teenager."

Richard blinked. His big, dark eyes flooded with heat and he cocked his head curiously to the side. "Really?"

"Yes, really!" I continued to flap, suddenly finding it incredibly important he recognize just how phenomenal of a kisser he was. "Dude. I was pretty sure my brain was going to leak out of my ears. You were all bossy—and hot—and *growly.* Like a fucking tiger." I nodded enthusiastically. "A sexy, blond, leather-clad tiger."

"Is that...good?"

I spluttered, "Is that good, he says?" My hands accidentally whacked him again but I couldn't seem to stop. "You know what, Rich? Fuck you." I bunched my hands in the front of his too-soft T-shirt and dragged him up against me again. Damn. All that muscle was bound to be distracting. His pecs flexed against my hands and I died and went to heaven. "I'm pretty sure I have to kill you now, you know, because you just...*existing* as this perfect specimen of a man is like—totally universally unfair."

"You think I'm perfect?" Richard's voice was soft, sweet, humbled. It was obvious he was letting me drag him closer, we both knew if he didn't want to move there was nowhere on this Earth I could take him without his permission. All six-foot-four of him pressed tight to my body and I shuddered, pressing into the hard line of him with a twitch of my hips. I was so distracted by how much I wanted to climb him like a tree it took me a moment too long to realize what I'd said. I froze, blinking dazedly as I forced my eyes from his pecs and caught his gaze again shocked by what I'd just admitted.

"Well, I mean…" I flushed. "I *have* eyes."

"No." He shook his head. "Did you mean, physically? Or…" His expression was tentative, hopeful. And I realized for the first time that maybe Richard had insecurities too. It almost felt ridiculous that a man so fucking…*perfect*, could not realize just how awesome he was—but then again—I thought about all of our previous conversations. The way he held himself, eyes guarded, a hunted sort of twist to his expression, like he was just waiting for something bad to sneak up on him. The way he searched for praise and approval. The way despite his large body sometimes he took up as little space as possible.

Maybe growing up he'd missed out on the same praise I had. His childhood had been full of days pieced together by grief and loss. And the more I learned about him, the more I realized how little room in his life he must've had for things that made him happy, for things that made him like himself. He'd had to grow up far too soon and as a result he'd never gotten to figure out who he was without his big brother persona on.

Maybe Richard was just figuring things out the same way I was?

Man. What a fucking thought.

Mind blown.

I was officially mind blown. And…I'd waited too long to reply.

"Sorry, I just. Had an aneurysm thinking about the fact that you might not know how absolutely fucking awesome you are," I told him honestly. "Because you are. Awesome, I mean. And hot. But the two things are not mutually exclusive." I blinked again, brow scrunching up. "You're both hot and awesome. Hot-Awesome. Fuck. This is coming out all wrong."

"Hot-awesome, huh?" Richard's lips were wobbling like he was trying not to laugh, which was just fucking *rude* because here I was trying to freaking fix his shitty self-esteem and the motherfucker was *laughing at me*.

"You're an asshole," I told him, jabbing him in the chest. He nodded, lips continuing to wobble, his eyes crinkling at the corners. He tried to scowl again, probably to make me stop freaking out like an offended maiden, but it didn't work so he gave up the battle, and smiled all over again, rudely forcing my heart to do this crazy somersault in my chest. My heart was out of shape, it couldn't handle doing that level of acrobatics.

"I may be an asshole, but I also have it on good authority that I'm hot-awesome, so really how bad can I be?"

"Oh, fuck you." There was something dancing in Richard's gaze that grew heavy and hot as he leaned in close, his breath tickling along my cheekbone.

"You have no idea how badly I want that," he said, his voice sweet as honey where it dripped down my spine and settled molten hot between my thighs. I was once again reminded of how close we were, of the width of his shoulders, of the way he was caging me in against the door. My cock twitched.

"Yeah?"

"Oh, fuck yeah." He sighed, crowding me up against the door again, his nose burying itself in the sweaty hair at my temple. My back rubbed up against the wood and I wanted to whine. I wanted his hands back on me—my wrists felt weirdly bare without him. God, the front door was getting more action than I was. "You have no idea."

"Then tell me." I was breathless, my earlier offense having disappeared the moment my dick got on board once again.

"That first day, at the diner…" Richard breathed, his lips bumping up against my cheekbone. He was teasing. He was fucking teasing and I loved every single second of it. "I couldn't stop staring at your legs, the way your hoodie got caught in the back of your pants and lifted up just high enough I could see your sweet little ass twitch every time you had to lean across the counter to clean it."

Ho-ly shit. My cock twitched, my toes curling as I listened with rapt attention.

"God, I wanted to shove you against it," Richard groaned, like the *thought* alone was getting him off. "I wasn't supposed to want you, but—" He was practically trembling, his big hands slipping down the wood behind me, following the silhouette of my body in a steady glide. One massive hand settled heavy and demanding around my hip. He squeezed me there, tighter than he probably meant to because it hurt so good my eyes threatened to roll back inside my head. "Every time you leaned over I couldn't think about anything else—it was confusing, and amazing, and fucking…*God, Blair*. I've never thought about another person like that before."

"Rich—"

"You have no idea how many nights I've laid awake, picturing sinking into your tight ass. I bet you'd squeeze me so good—" He was trembling with fervor now, his nose rubbing and tickling at my hairline, causing tingles to cascade across my body as his lips trailed to the sensitive shell of my ear and his tongue flickered out to wet it.

I gasped.

"You're so little, baby." The way he said *little* made me begin to shake with need. I'd never liked being small, always figured there was nothing I could do about it though. I just…was.

But when Richard talked about it… God, I was so fucking turned on I could hardly think straight. "I can practically wrap my entire fucking hand around your throat," he breathed, voice scratchy and low. "Makes me wanna climb on top of you and make you just…" He trailed off, his whole body quaking. His hand gave my hip another squeeze.

"Make me what?" My voice was nothing but a quiet croak. The sweet scent of arousal was thick in our little cocoon and Richard was shaking where he held me tight, his fingernails digging into my skin hard enough to bruise.

"Makes me wanna make you fucking *take* it," he grunted, clearly embarrassed but soldiering onwards, too turned on to stop. "I could hold you down, speak to you all sweet, and you'd spread those sexy thighs wide open like a pretty little flower."

"Richard," I gasped softly, slipping my hands upward till my fingers could scratch along the skin of his throat on my hunt to get my hands in his hair.

"I've never wanted someone like this before. It's confusing—and overwhelming—and *amazing*—and—" His voice broke.

I shut him up with a kiss. I could feel the prickle of the stubble across his jawline as I tangled my hands in white-blond locks and listened to the way he groaned in response. Richard bent down to devour me with so much enthusiasm it made up for any clumsiness he might've had. He tasted like pine trees and spring air and I inhaled him greedily, too far gone to acknowledge the fact that at some point his fangs had dropped and they were digging hard enough into my bottom lip to break skin.

The burst of blood between us made him whine, a low animal-like sound that echoed in the quiet apartment so loudly I was sure it might rearrange the earth around us. It all seemed so surreal.

I had my tongue down Richard Prince's throat and he was just… He was *letting* me, giving back as good as he got, his hands possessive and far too tight as he squeezed around my hips. He migrated, fingernails scratching gently along my lower back leaving fire in their wake. I tingled all over as I arched into the touch, pushing into where his belt buckle dug into my sternum, ignoring the uncomfortable ache as my own fingers dug into the meat between his shoulders and neck, and I tugged him closer.

The moment was suspended in time. Richard tasted like freedom, like choice, like being young.

When I finally broke away it was because I needed to breathe. *Stupid fucking air.* I gasped, my head thunking back against the door—or it would've, if Richard hadn't raised a hand quick enough to catch me before I made impact.

"I…" He breathed raggedly, cradling the back of my head as he tipped his chin back and sighed, a low broken noise. "I didn't realize it would feel this good. God, it is so hard to control myself with you."

"No one asked you to," I pointed out, breathless and quaking. I refused to be held up against a door any longer because my legs were just about ready to give out and the last thing I wanted was to end our little… activity…early because I'd managed to lock my knees and pass out. "But before you like—eat me or whatever—can we at least sit down on your couch or something?"

I watched Richard's throat bob as he swallowed and then his head dipped down and he caught my gaze again. His eyes were black with lust, though his words were carefully controlled. "Yeah, baby. We can sit down," he said softly, gently leading me away from the entryway and into the living room.

I was so far gone on him that I forgot to take off my fucking shoes.

I shook away the automatic chastisement that had been programmed inside my head. There was no room for that here, not now. Not when Richard was looking at me with eyes so full of lust just glancing inside them made me want to fall to my knees.

"Water?" I said as soon as I'd fallen to the now familiar cushions of his couch. I knew if he touched me again I was going to come in about five seconds, and I needed a breather so that I could at least maintain some of my dignity.

"Of course." Richard ducked away, padding off into the kitchen as I caught my breath and glared down at my lap.

"Motherfucker, promise me you'll last at least three minutes or I'm cutting you off." I threatened my dick angrily where it very clearly pressed against the zipper on my jeans.

The clattering in the kitchen stopped.

I blinked, glancing over the back of the couch suspiciously. Did vampires have super-hearing? No, right?

"Did you just threaten your own dick?" Richard called from the kitchen, the laugh in his voice not even a little concealed.

Motherfucker.

"No," I denied, even though we both knew I was lying.

He started laughing, the sound different than before, a low melodic little chuckle that echoed through the open kitchen across the counter to where I sat rigid on his couch. I squirmed while I waited, way too pleased that I'd made him laugh even though I was still pretty fucking embarrassed. Richard returned a minute later with a tall glass full of ice water. "You okay?" he asked, because he was just polite like that.

"I'm fucking awesome," I grunted, reaching for the glass with grabby hands. He handed it over, shaking his head with amusement as he sat down on the cushion beside mine, his body turned to face mine. "What about you?" I asked, the cold glass slippery in my grip. The condensation tickled the pads of my fingers and I squeezed tighter for fear of dropping the glass on the couch and spilling it all over Richard's living room. I'd already spilled in his house once, I wasn't ready for a repeat. Unless it wasn't water I was spilling—then I'd be completely on board.

"I'm doing pretty 'fucking awesome' myself," Richard teased, his eyes twinkling with mirth. They were blood-red again, glowing softly like he truly couldn't help himself. I had about a million and a half questions, but like I'd told him earlier, they could wait until after the sex.

Sex, trauma, then questions.

"Can I suck your dick?" Richard said at the same time I was about to open my mouth and ask if I could suck his. I blinked, processing this. My body was apparently on board before my brain though because I was already nodding enthusiastically as my eyes bulged and I took an icy sip of water.

It burned down my throat, making me cough a little. "Um, yeah." I nodded again. "Whatever you want, man."

"Is that something you want?" Richard asked, tipping his head to the side. Sometimes he reminded me of a loyal hound, all curious and head-tippy.

"Um. Do I want my dick sucked?" I rolled my eyes. "Why yes, Richard. I suppose that would be permissible."

He snorted, biting at his lips and shaking his head as he slowly lowered himself down to the carpet, kneeling between my knees. My cock twitched at the sight of him and I had to spread myself uncomfortably wide to accommodate his shoulders. We'd been in this exact position before, but it felt different now. For obvious reasons.

"You said you've never done this before, right?" he asked softly, blinking up at me through his impossibly long lashes. They cast spiderwebbed shadows across the hollows of his cheeks and, in the dark like that, the glowing of his blood-red gaze was only more mesmerizing. He looked hungry. I swallowed, taking another sip of my water before he gently arched a brow at me, waiting for my answer.

"Uh, no." I shook my head, handing him the glass, which he took and placed on the coffee table behind his back.

"So you won't know if I'm horrible or not," he joked, with a boyish twist to his lips.

"Rich, I'm pretty sure you could quite literally bite my dick off and it would still be the best blowjob I've ever had."

He rolled his eyes heavenward though they twinkled in amusement. The nervous tension in his shoulders melted away as he exhaled and brought his big hands up to lay on my inner thighs right above my knees. I trembled. Every touch made sensations burn through my body like wildfire.

"It would be the only blowjob you've ever had," he reminded me cheekily. I shut him up by grabbing the back of his head and pushing him towards my dick.

"Less talking, more sucking please," I hummed, wiggling down to get comfy even though my heart was in my throat. I was probably more nervous than I should be, but hey. First blowjob? First time being touched by someone other than myself?

It was kinda a monumental thing.

What if I smelled bad? Oh god. *What if I tasted bad?* What if he hated it—and he didn't tell me—and then he finished out of a twisted sense of obligation and not because he actually wanted to and forever and always he would think of me as smelly Blair the inconsiderate prick with the inconsiderate prick.

"Hey," Richard squeezed my thighs, tight enough to bring me back to the present as I ducked my head to meet his gaze. "What's wrong?"

I blinked, trying to force the panic out of my head, and chest, and fingers. "What if you hate it?" I said, voice trembling. "Or my dick stinks?"

Richard's nose crinkled up in surprise and a startled laugh left his throat.

"Hey—" I protested, wiggling uncomfortably. His hands rubbed along my thighs, thumbs tracing circles through my jeans along sensitive flesh. "Don't laugh. It's a legitimate concern."

"I guarantee the last thing on my mind right now is what your dick smells like."

"I showered, like twenty minutes before I came here," I continued to ramble. "But I mean, it took me ten minutes to get here, and then there was the whole make out sesh at the door... What if in that time—" Richard's hand came up and covered my mouth, effectively silencing me.

"Do you trust me?" He blinked, dark eyes full of warmth and heat—

and understanding. I thought about it. I nodded. "Good," he whispered softly. "Then trust me when I say I promise I will stop if I am at any point uncomfortable in any way."

I nodded again, grateful that he'd taken my words away from me. His palm smelled good, like cedar and smoke. I wondered if he had lotion that smelled that way or if he was just so fucking lucky that his pores absorbed the scent of the woods every time he stepped out the front door.

"I'm going to take my hand away now, okay?" Richard said, voice soft and honey-sweet. "But only if you can be good for me. Can you do that?"

I didn't know if I could do that. Could I be good? Maybe? Probably. *Fuck.* That sentence was the single hottest thing I'd ever heard in my life. I squirmed a little, my cock waking up where it pressed against my zipper.

"I'm gonna need you to verbally confirm that. Okay, baby?" Richard urged. "Can you be obedient for me? Nice and quiet?"

I nodded. "Yes."

"Good." He nodded back at me, his thumb rubbing gentle circles under the swell of my cheekbone. I was hyper-aware of where his other hand was still squeezing my thigh, stunned by the fact he was officially the closest anyone had ever gotten to my dick before. "When I let you go, you're going to relax. You're not going to think about whether or not I'm enjoying myself. You're going to lay back and let me take care of you." Richard's voice was gentle but firm as he spoke. "Nod if you agree."

I nodded again.

"And if at any point you need me to stop, or you get uncomfortable, or you have a question for me, I want you to tell me. Can you do that? Nod if you agree." I nodded again. "Good boy."

The praise went straight to my dick and it twitched helplessly. I was sure at this point I had to be leaking all over my frowny-face boxers. I didn't even care. They were frowning anyway, what did they care if they got a little precum on them?

I melted back against the soft leather cushions, my lashes fluttering. God. There was something about being given permission to let go that made the feeling all the more powerful. I was a puddle of relaxation, my nerves having disappeared somewhere far down inside the earth beneath my feet.

"Can I take your pants off?" Richard asked, always the gentleman. I nodded, blinking dopily down at him, smiling when he smiled. It was like the second he'd given me permission to relax that was all my body wanted to do. I'd never felt so…present before. Centered in my body. Happy. "That's real good, sweetheart. Just like that," he urged, reaching for my belt and unbuckling it with practiced precision.

It was a good thing he was the one in charge of undressing because even though I'd been putting on and taking off belts for ninety percent of my life, I was sure if I tried at that moment I was going to accidentally brain him with my belt buckle. Think happy thoughts. Happy…thoughts.

I exhaled, letting the newly built-up tension fade away as I relaxed again and felt Richard's fingers slip the belt from its loops. Inch by inch it slid free, the sound of leather on denim echoing through the quiet room.

My breathing felt impossibly loud but, for once, I didn't mind.

"You're doing so good," Richard murmured, obviously unable to help himself as he leaned forward and his teeth nipped at the soft skin right below my belly button and above my waistband. It stung and I jumped a little, my cock twitching. He nibbled on me there, nostrils flaring like he was trying to inhale my scent. "Just relax."

My abs trembled and a soft little whimper left my lips as he pulled back. I felt the loss of his mouth keenly as he made quick work of my button and zipper, the *ziiip* sound too loud in the quiet room. Getting my skinny jeans off posed a challenge but Richard accomplished it with grace, tugging them down inch by inch until they tangled around my ankles and he gingerly peeled each foot free.

When I was bare aside from my hoodie and boxers he sat back, eyes dark, lips pink. Richard's gaze as it dragged down my body was so heavy it felt almost like a physical touch. His tongue flickered out to wet his lips and he groaned, a helpless little noise, like he was so turned on just looking at me his normally stoic facade melted away.

"Look at you," Richard breathed, leaning forward to bury his nose in the spongy skin on the inside of my right knee. I trembled. "So fucking beautiful."

He scrubbed his cheek along my leg hair, lips catching on sensitive skin as he dragged his mouth inch by blissful inch upwards. My cock throbbed, leaking eagerly against the inside of my boxers until a wet spot began to form.

I didn't know what to say so I remained silent, my eyes half lidded as Richard's fingers circled my ankles, bunching around them and giving them a gentle squeeze. His nose was buried in the meat of my thigh, the top of his blond head blinking at me in the overhead light as his hips twitched, humping the air, looking for friction. The idea that just touching me turned him on enough that his hindbrain had been activated was flattering to say the least.

I couldn't believe that I was the cause of it.

Watching his thick thighs flex and tremble as his cock pressed up against his zipper was the single most erotic experience of my life. His shoulders were tensed, the sheen of sweat glistening on his brow as he stared up at me from where his face was buried in the meat of my inner thigh. His nose ducked under the edge of my boxers, plucking at them imploringly as my mouth grew dry.

"Can I take your boxers off?" Richard asked, voice nothing but gravel. "Please?"

I nodded helplessly, a frantic sort of jerking motion to my head, my words for once abandoning me as he made quick work of my boxers, shucking them off and down onto the neat little pile of clothes he was making. He folded both items of clothing, as well as my socks, piling them all atop each other and pushing them to the side before he finally turned to look at me.

My hoodie had rucked up to my ribs, my cock flushed and eager where it tapped against the dark nest of curls that led like a treasure trail down my lower abs. I was just as wet as I'd suspected, my balls drawn tight, the tip of my cock glistening. Just looking down at Richard made my dick twitch and my lashes grow heavy.

I'd never been bare before someone else like this before. It made me feel both powerful and vulnerable, all at once. Like a god come down to Earth, trapped in human skin but finally able to feel for the first time in his long, lonely existence.

"Fuck," I breathed, unable to help myself as Richard stared at me, his lips parted, tongue wet. God. I wanted inside his mouth so fucking bad it hurt. My hips twitched.

His eyes were rivers of wine, intoxicating, beautiful, dangerous.

They said, 'trust me.'

They said, 'let me have this.'

They said, 'let me worship you.'

And who was I to deny him? I was just a little boy stuck in a grown man's body. Pinocchio learning how to be real while I picked up pieces of my broken childhood and tried to pin them back together again.

"You're beautiful," Richard said softly, reverently.

All my life I'd sat in churches' hallowed halls but I had never felt as spiritual as I did in that moment with his attention on me.

"Open up for me, sweetheart. It's okay."

I hadn't even realized that I'd begun to shut my legs. I jolted obediently to attention, following his command with eager anticipation. My legs spread open, the dark hair decorating my thighs and calves catching the light as Richard smoothed his hands slowly, gingerly, up my shins to rest on the meat of my thighs again. Just looking at the difference in our sizes was enough to get my cock to leak.

"Wider," he urged, his voice low and thick with lust. I did as I was told, my quads beginning to shake and ache as I held them as widely spread as I could. Richard hummed his growly approval as he directed my body till my calves caught on his shoulders and my ass slipped to the edge of the cushions. "That's it, baby. Now hold them open for me—"

I reached down, my fingers sweaty and numb with anticipation as I bunched them up behind my knees to keep myself in place. It was easier like this, some of the strain taken from the muscles as my cock leaked a steady drip against my lower belly, decorating the curl of my dark treasure trail with jewels of pleasure. I wanted to be touched so badly it hurt–my dick pink with anticipation, my lips parted as I whined.

"So fucking good for me, aren't you sweetheart?" Richard's voice had dropped another octave. It was so deep now I hardly recognized it. "Stay

406

still," he demanded with such natural authority I could do nothing but obey.

It was like the moon calling for the tide. Richard commanded and I obeyed. There was no other option. It was inevitable, irrevocable, irresponsible, and irresistible. A siren call to the parts of me that begged to be seen, had always begged to be seen.

Richard leaned forward, his breath tickling my thigh as he pressed a chaste kiss to the side of my left knee right over a scar I'd had since I was six and had tripped up the front steps walking home from another adventure in the woods. It was old enough now it was nothing but a glimmer of silver, but still he noticed.

All my life I'd been nothing but a shadow and yet when Richard shined his light upon me, I became tangible. His attention was a magic spell I hoped I'd never break.

My thighs jumped as he placed a kiss just a few inches higher on my leg. The higher he went the more sensitive the skin was. He was exploring, his brow lowered in concentration like he was truly enjoying what he was doing to me as much as I was. Kiss after kiss, touch after touch, he traveled his way up my thighs till I trembled and quaked and my cock was wet with desire.

"You're so hard," Richard breathed in wonder when he neared my dick. I tried not to hump his face, I really did, but I couldn't help the fractional little twitch of my hips. He didn't seem to mind when the tip of my cock dragged its sticky pleasure across his cheekbone. Instead, he just groaned, a helpless sort of grunting noise. "God, you're so wet."

Richard reached up with one tentative hand, stroking his fingers through the trail of precum that decorated my belly. My abs jumped, my hips twitching as I inhaled raggedly. His fingers were warm now, like he'd been soaking up the heat from my body. And then—he did something I knew I'd play on repeat in the back of my mind when I was bringing myself off for the rest of my life.

He brought the sticky pads of his fingers to his lips and sucked them inside.

I whined, loud and helplessly, my head tossing back against the couch cushions because Jesus fuck. I didn't know how he expected me not to come when he did shit like that.

When I looked down again he was making a thoughtful face, his brow quirked as he lapped at the pad of his index finger with his too pink tongue. There was no hint of fangs anymore but it suddenly occurred to me that I hadn't even thought to ask about the state of his teeth before I agreed to him sucking me down.

"Your fangs?" I questioned, surprised when I hardly recognized my own voice. It was scratchy and broken already, and he'd hardly even touched me.

"What about them?" Richard blinked up at me, brow furrowed in confusion. A few seconds later what I was asking seemed to dawn on him and he laughed, a low throaty sort of noise that made my toes curl and my nipples harden. "*Oh.*" He grinned, glancing down at my cock, then back up at me. "They're retractable."

They're retractable, he says. *Motherfucker.*

My head thunked back against the couch again and I groaned, my abs twitching with each aborted breath. I had never been so hard in all of my life and I didn't know if I should beg or demand for him to touch me.

"Patience, baby," Richard urged from between my legs. I refused to look at him, trying to calm myself down enough that I wouldn't come the instant his lips wrapped around me. God. The idea of sinking into all that wet-hot pink heat made my head spin.

"I'm patient," I retorted, though it really came out as more of a plea than anything.

"You're right," Richard hummed. There was the sound of clinking as I assumed he undid his own belt. Then a zipper. Then silence. "You're so patient, aren't you sweetheart? You've been waiting so sweetly for me, all wet and ready." My dick jumped.

I nodded, unable to help myself. It was like his words cast a spell over my mind.

I had been patient. I'd been so patient. I was being *good*. Frustrated tears pricked at the corner of my eyes and I blinked them away.

"Fuck," Richard swore in wonder, the slick sounds of his fingers wrapping around his own cock filling the silence. "You look like porn."

My legs trembled and I glanced down at him, noting the way the tip of his tongue peeked out of his mouth in concentration as his brow furrowed and his fist moved hot and heavy over the tip of his flushed red dick, twisting, twisting, *twisting*. His hips snapped up into his own grip, eyes dark with heat. "Tip your hips back for me," he urged, shifting on his thick thighs, his pants open around his cock and a thatch of pretty blond hair. I could see sweat gathering there and I wanted to lick it up, too mesmerized by the thick crown of his needy cock to do anything but obey.

He was big. So fucking big.

I shuffled, the leather squeaking beneath me as I somehow managed to tuck myself close enough to the edge of the couch that my ass fell entirely off it and my heels dug into the cushions on either side of me. It was only vaguely precarious because Richard reached up with his free hand and dug it into the meaty flesh on the back of my thigh holding me securely in place.

That didn't last long because he moved, his nails scraping gently across my skin, tracing whorls of hair, moles, and sweat until he reached one of my ass cheeks and gripped it tight in his broad palm. "Fuck," Richard breathed again, his other hand speeding up like he just couldn't help himself. The slick sound of him fucking himself got louder as I watched his hips snap inside his fist. He was wild with lust, his eyes black, his mouth open as he shoved his mouth against the sensitive skin on the inside of my knee and panted his pleasure. I squirmed to get a better view of his dick and he growled.

"Hold still," he urged, leaning back again so that he could see what he was doing as he tugged my ass open until the cool air from the overhead fan hit my hole and he could admire as I clenched up automatically. "Oh, fuck." Richard's hips snapped into his grip, the sound wet and eager as he stared at me—all of me—his mouth open in awe as he dragged in broken breaths. "Can I?"

I nodded frantically, unsure what he was even asking for, but ready to give him whatever he wanted. I was completely at a loss for words as my ass clenched around nothing and I watched his eyes grow red with lust. "I'll take care of you, baby. Promise," Richard urged, voice nothing but a wet growl as he slid his hand away from his cock, sticky fingertips trailing up my inner thigh slowly-slowly-slowly toward where I wanted him most.

I gasped, my head tossing back as I finally—*finally*—felt the pad of his thumb pressing into my crease. I'd played with my ass enough times to know I liked it. Loved it, even. My cock leaked and I trembled, forcing myself to hold still even though what I wanted to do was push back into his touch. Richard's fingers were sticky with his own precum, the salty-sweet scent of arousal filling the air as he rubbed soothing circles around the sensitive skin that framed my hole. I clenched as he played with me, and my toes curled as I tried to hold very, very still. I felt so empty—I just wanted him deeper—

I knew if I disobeyed him he'd stop. And god... I'd never wanted something more in all my life.

"Open up for me," Richard groaned softly, shifting until his cheek was pressed against the sweat-spongy skin of my inner thigh so he could watch from up close. He leaned forward, his eyes dark as he spat onto my hole before rubbing at it again while retreating to his spot against my thigh to watch. "Just the tip, baby. I promise."

I nodded frantically again, my breath leaving me in short broken gusts as I forced myself to relax enough that he could get the very tip of his thumb inside me. Any more than that and I knew we'd need lube but fuuuck. It felt so good to have a part of him inside me I didn't mind the slight sting. He whined. Or I whined. We both whined, the sound of our pleasure echoing in the otherwise quiet room as he hooked his thumb down and gently tugged me open.

"You're so pink inside," he commented curiously, his voice full of wonder. The fact that he was looking that closely at the most intimate part of me made my head spin. I felt both vulnerable and powerful all at once, my hole clenching around his finger as he tenderly pulled his way out. I wondered if this was something he'd always wanted to do, a fantasy that I'd made come true. "Can I come on you, sweetheart?" Richard asked, so politely I nearly wanted to laugh.

I didn't. Instead I just sobbed, a dry broken little noise as my head thrashed up and down.

He rose up onto his knees, thick thighs tensing as the spongy head of his slick cock pressed against my crack.

"Fuck," Richard swore again, holding my cheeks open with one greedy hand while his other dove down to fist his cock. He started slow at first, gingerly teasing. I watched his hand move with reverence, my gaze never leaving the thick tip of his cock. My mouth watered.

The slick glide of his fist on his cock filled the silence as panting, helpless grunts left his lips. My head was full of cotton, my cock so hard I could hardly feel it anymore. It drooled against my belly, decorating my pale skin with sticky wet pleasure as I felt the head of Richard's cock slip up against my hole. His crown was hot and big enough when I fluttered against it my eyes rolled back. I wanted it inside me. Fuck—

"I won't go inside—" Richard promised, his voice broken and barely there. "I just—I just wanna know what it feels like." He snapped his hips up into his grip and I whined, my ass clenching and unclenching against him just to hear the broken whine he released every time I did it. "Just a little?" he questioned, brow knit together, his eyes searching, begging as he caught mine. "Just a bit? I promise."

I nodded, eager and desperate as he pushed up against me, stripping himself faster and faster, the slick noises filling my mind with memories I'd play on repeat for possibly the rest of all time. I'd be on my deathbed and still replaying the almost innocent way Richard couldn't help but whine as he leaked his pleasure against my most empty hole.

His hand moved faster, twisting around the tip, pulling back his foreskin, eager and wet and *hard* as he began to fuck his fist in earnest. Watching his arm flex as he fucked himself was a sight of its own. His veins danced, his muscles flickering with strength and desire. Richard kept releasing these fucked out little 'uh, uh, uh' noises that went straight to my dick and I couldn't help the way I shoved back against him, eager for more.

When he came his release hit my hole, my thighs, the front of his couch. I listened to the way he whined—low, helpless, and animalistic—as his hips continued to flex like he just couldn't stop himself. He was an animal, searching for friction.

I had never felt more desired in all my fucking life. I'd never felt more masculine. More wanted. More free.

I stared down at him, at the disheveled state of his normally perfect hair, the bitten red swell of his lips. "You're fucking amazing," Richard groaned, apparently somehow capable of words as he rubbed his face against my thigh like an overgrown cat and blinked up at me.

My cock dripped and I stared at him, jaw open. I'd never been so close to coming untouched in all my life. Part of me figured Richard would need a minute to recover before he returned the favor. In fact, I honestly wasn't sure I even *needed* him to touch me at this point. All I had to do was close my eyes and remember the face he'd made when he'd come all over me, brow furrowed, his lips parted and pink.

He took me by surprise, a wicked grin—boyish and free breaking across his face as he leaned forward, opened wide, and sucked my entire cock down in one go.

For a man that had never given someone a blowjob before, he was a fucking pro. My hips snapped up against his face, because of course they did, the liquid hot suction making my eyes roll back as my balls drew up tight.

Richard groaned around me, grabbing my hips and hauling me in tight as he sucked and choked, and *sucked* and *choked.* He learned his way around my cock like it was his mission to do so, his brow lowered in concentration as he quite literally sucked my brain out of my dick.

I couldn't help the way I whined, loud and with abandon, my toes curling as I released my sweaty thighs and squeezed his head between them. He didn't seem to mind, sucking me down deeper as his free hand came up to gently roll his palm against my balls. It was a teasing caress, but it was enough.

A few more minutes of him sucking on me, and I was done for. Richard pinched and rolled my balls, saliva dripping down my cock and gathering at the sweaty, sensitive skin at the base of my dick as I swore and thrashed. I was pretty sure I was scratching the shit out of his couch, my shirt having rucked up to my neck as he pulled me in deeper and deeper and deeper.

The man was fucking ravenous.

The fact that formal, serious, put-together Richard was apparently a fucking lion in the sack was news to me. He sucked and licked, pulling off to bite at the fragile skin on either side of my cock just to watch me squirm.

I could feel tears burning trails down my cheeks but I couldn't stop. I couldn't fucking stop, my thighs clenching tight around his head as he sucked me down again, the hand on my balls squeezing, rubbing, rolling, as his free hand slipped down my sweaty crack to where his come still teased the skin of my hole.

The moment his thumb tucked up inside of me, I came.

I came and I came and I came and I came.

It seemed to go on forever, my eyes rolling back into my head as I snapped my hips up against his mouth and my thighs squeezed so tight I was sure I'd have the pink imprints of his ears left behind.

Richard swallowed everything, lapping at my belly to clean me when it was clear the stimulation was too much and there was no way I could take any more. His tongue traveled my skin, lapped at my abs, my thighs, down between my cheeks as he sucked his come from my still needy hole.

When I was clean he pulled back.

"You okay?" Richard asked, gently rubbing circles into my trembling thighs as he helped me back onto the couch. He soothed the tense muscles in my thighs, his lips kiss swollen, a stray streak of cum decorating his chin.

"Fucking, great," I told him, slurring my words as I reached down for his big stupid head and pulled him up towards me. "Fuckin' kiss me," I urged, licking away the streak of cum on his skin, enjoying the scratch of stubble as I did so. He grinned, the masks he kept in place completely absent as his eyes twinkled and he eagerly followed my command. His massive body was heavy as he crowded against me and I squeezed him between my thighs, enjoying the scrape of denim against my sensitive skin and the way his cock rubbed up against my belly button.

Richard's tongue was hot and salty as it slid inside my mouth and I sucked eagerly around him, trembling with my fingers tangled tight in his sweaty golden locks. Jesus god. If I died today I would die with no regrets.

Richard tongue fucked me for long enough that I was panting again, my eyes unfocused, my lashes wet with tears.

When he pulled back he was still smiling, though it was softer than before. His pupils were large enough they flooded his entire iris making his eyes appear black. I didn't know for sure, but I was starting to realize that Richard's eyes seemed to have a direct correlation with food.

"You hungry, big guy?" I asked, my lips tipping up into a grin that mirrored his.

"You offering?" he teased back, though there was a serious note to his voice that I couldn't overlook. It was clear we still had a lot we needed to talk about. But now wasn't the time for blood fueled revelations or panic attacks, so instead I just offered.

"Fuck yes, Rich. Anytime."

He nodded, seeming to debate with himself, his brow lowering as the crease between his eyebrows appeared again. And then I did something I'd been wanting to do since I'd fucking met the guy. I reached up and gently smoothed the wrinkle with the pad of my thumb. He blinked at me, confused and soft, hopeful. His forehead relaxed.

"Let's talk first," I said gently, watching his dark gaze flicker with relief. "That way you'll be more comfortable."

He nodded again, silent for the moment, though he reached for my hand and tucked it against his lips, his palm swallowing mine entirely as he kissed my pulse point with a drag of tender lips.

"Later," he promised, tongue lapping at the thickest of my blue veins as he peeked at me through his lashes. He sucked at the vein and I nearly came again as I felt the brush of fangs against the sensitive skin.

"Later," I agreed.

Chapter Thirty-One

Blair

WE WERE TOLD it would take two weeks for Benji's to get fixed up. The owner had to call in to a custom glass company to replace the front windows and luckily they had some in stock but there was a whole installation process involved that meant no shifts for any of us.

While the money part hurt, because of course it did. The freedom did not.

I'd also gotten paid recently so my padded bank account added to my charitable mood.

Honestly it was easier to ignore my impending doom when I had money in the bank and an almost-boyfriend to spend time with. I'd have to deal with my future soon but…for now I was content to let what happened happen. It was a weird feeling—the banishment of fear. We'd always been close companions and yet somehow when I was with Richard it almost felt like I got to become the Blair I would've been if I'd had the chance to grow up without it.

I spent every waking moment I could at Richard's house, lurking inside his refrigerator and watching reruns of SpongeBob on his TV. Collin had been unfortunately stuck at their parents' place for the time being and I missed seeing his sunny face every day. The sex though selfishly made up for it.

Richard didn't seem to mind that I was there so much, in fact he liked the company, or so he told me on the second night he'd picked me up and I'd fretted over it.

"But like, what if you get annoyed with me?" I asked as I shoved a peanut butter covered piece of celery in my mouth. "I mean, we should have distance, right? I was here yesterday. Google says that it's—"

"Do you need distance?" he'd asked, arching an eyebrow at me as he waited for my response.

"No, fuck no." I shook my head. "What I need is another blowjob." I waggled my eyebrows in his direction and he laughed, shaking his head.

"Well, there you go." He chewed on his lip. "Besides…I like having you around."

The shy way he added that made my belly fill with butterflies and I smiled at him, ducking my head to avoid his gaze because sometimes looking at him was too much for me to bear. I wasn't used to the compliments or the affection. Each time he brushed up against me, or kissed the back of my neck while I was scrounging around his cupboards for sustenance, a new shiver of both want and anticipation curled down my spine.

Somehow, though, I couldn't shake the thought that something was going on that I didn't know about. It all seemed…too good to be true.

Maybe I was just paranoid though. Like always.

On my seventh night in a row hanging out at Richard's place we finally had…*the talk*. I'd been amping myself up all week to tell him about my past, and in turn ask him about his. I knew I'd learned about it from Chastity but…it was different now.

It felt like a disservice to him to trust a strangers' recollection of his childhood trauma when I spent every waking moment I could making a home, squeezed between his sweat-sticky arms.

Richard and I had just dropped off Collin at their parents' house after he'd called for an escape. We'd bought him ice cream, and listened to him complain about Christopher, his older brother, for the millionth time. Then sadly, it had been time to deliver him back to his mansion-prison. At least I figured it was a mansion, based on the wrought iron gate.

He'd waved at us before climbing up the long winding driveway, his solitary little figure disappearing off in the distance. Dropping him off was bittersweet, it meant sex for both of us, but watching him shrink into himself the farther away from the car he got made me feel about two inches tall.

I wished there was a way to just adopt him. The fact that he was required to go home and sit alone in that big empty house made my stomach flip with remorse. It wasn't like his parents would even be there. Even when they were back in town they never seemed to interact with him aside from their disapproving comments about his future.

He was apparently the only member of their family that refused to take the change. Which gave light to all the conversations I'd had with him in the past. Maybe my assumptions about him had been incorrect—or maybe they were? But…either way it didn't matter. I hated to see him disappear up that driveway almost as much as I hated the thought of seeing my aunt again.

I didn't know how to help though and Richard reassured me that he was doing his best to change what was happening.

I was wearing one of the hoodies Richard had bought me, the sleeves tucked around my knuckles as I wrapped my arms around one of my legs where my foot rested on the passenger seat. Richard always gave me this annoyed-amused look when I did that and I liked it more than I was willing to admit.

"I was thinking we could do something different," he offered, staring out at the dark road in front of us, his headlights painting it orange with their touch.

"Scooby Doo instead of SpongeBob?" I offered, even though I knew what he was hedging at.

He snorted, arching an eyebrow at me in a frankly judgmental manner. I grinned at him and he rolled his eyes, turning his gaze back to the street. It was only six p.m. so most 'normal people' places were still full of people outside of Elmwood. The mall in Ridgefield would be open at this time and I knew what he was about to suggest before he even said it.

"I want to take you somewhere," Richard told me, voice soft.

"Like where?" I questioned, cocking my head to the side, lips pursed. Maybe we'd go to that Mexican place again? The Guacamole had been fucking awesome.

"I'll tell you when we get there."

"Oookay." I grinned at him. "Because that's not murdery at all." Okay. So no mall then. I watched him out of the corner of my eye, inspecting his face for clues though I found none. It was kinda nice just spending time with him, even if all we did was sit in silence. I settled down for the ride, plucking at my seatbelt and shifting until the seat squeaked and I had both feet on the dashboard.

Richard glanced over at my feet, his brows twitching but he didn't say anything, just turned back to the road.

"This okay?" I asked, because now I felt fucking weird about it. If I'd been with Jeffrey he would've thrown a French fry at me or something to reprimand me.

"I don't mind," he said quietly, staring out at the road in front of us as it trailed off into the distance. I watched him with a soft expression, my heart beating an uneven staccato in my chest.

"Would you mind if Collin did it?" I asked out of curiosity, staring at my own bony ankles where they stuck out of my checkered vans.

"Absolutely." Richard laughed, his lips quirking upwards, the dimple in his cheek jumping. "But you're not Collin."

"I'm not," I agreed, my heartbeat thudding more quickly. Richard's fingers twisted around the steering wheel, his knuckles turning white with tension as he pulled out onto the main stretch of road that would lead us to the interstate.

"You never told me why you couldn't stay in town," Richard said softly, after a few minutes of comfortable silence. I was jolted out of my reverie, my gaze snapping from the morphing tree-filled skyline as I turned my attention back to him. He wasn't watching me, but I could tell he was nervous, shoulders tight.

He expected something bad, and I wished I could give him something else but... Fuck. His instincts were right.

"I've never really…" I grimaced. "Talked about it before."

"You said that," he reminded me softly, his words unassuming but gentle. I nodded, inhaling raggedly. Sometimes my memories were so foggy searching through them was like swimming through syrup. Maybe that was because of the trauma? I'd never really let myself think too hard about it before.

"Just…" I inhaled again, trying to get air in my lungs because the car suddenly felt stuffy and my throat was tight. "Just give me a second, okay?"

"Okay," he agreed readily, patience echoing in every syllable as we pulled onto the interstate and his car picked up speed. I could feel the quiet purr of the engine beneath us, and it was soothing where it vibrated away some of my frayed nerves. My feet tapped a nervous staccato where they dangled above the dash, my fingers picking at the rips in my jeans. It took a long time before I felt capable of speech, and even then I wasn't ready.

"So, you know my aunt took me in right?" I confirmed softly, my heartbeat echoing inside my head. Richard nodded. He didn't look at me and I was grateful. It was hard enough talking about this without feeling his eyes on me.

I swallowed.

You're a coward, Blair.

You're just like your mother.

Soft.

No. No. No I wasn't. Not anymore.

I swallowed again, reaching for the switch that would roll down the window so I could let some of the forest air in. With pine filling my lungs I inhaled greedily, my fingertips numb with nerves as I forced myself to speak again. "Well. She…um. Sucked." *Nice. Real eloquent.*

Richard nodded again, waiting for me to continue. His jaw was flickering with tension as his knuckles turned white where they wrapped around the leather steering wheel. He looked gorgeous like that, pissed off and patient, his thick chest filling out his flannel enough that the buttons threatened to pop.

"She…" I struggled to find the words, I'd never even had the guts to admit them to myself, let alone to another person. "She used to, um…" I swallowed.

"It's okay," Richard said softly, glancing over at me, his brow furrowed with concern. "I can kinda guess. You don't have to say anymore." He so easily gave me back all the pieces of myself I'd grudgingly given him. I didn't know what it was. Maybe it was because of the selfless way he let me protect myself, but I was finally able to find the courage to continue.

"She'd lock me in the closet sometimes," I said softly. "For…a while. I don't know if it was days or hours or—" I shook my head. "But—my whole childhood was like that. Stuck in the fucking closet, literally and figuratively."

Richard nodded along, his jaw clenched so tight now I could literally see the vein on his forehead about to pop. "She did worse things too," I said softly. "She'd hurt me…just because…she needed to. It wasn't about me. I know that now— But I always thought it was because she didn't like me—not at all—" Richard was silent so I continued speaking. "She liked to use me against Jeffrey like a weapon. If he misbehaved it would mean punishment for me, whether that was physical, mental, or both." I swallowed, suddenly finding my rhythm, my heart stuttering in my chest. "She had cameras that would watch us. At Sunday dinner there'd be a weekly report for our water usage—or electricity—and whether or not we'd broken the rules— and after she'd evaluated us she would...punish accordingly." I could feel my heartbeat in my fingertips and my throat was dry as I spoke. "But the worst thing she ever did was convince me that I'm not...worth fighting for?" It was hard to find the words to properly explain what I meant. "I gave up on myself for so long, I figured, she had to be right, you know? I mean. She saw something that other people didn't. I was just...a bad egg. Like my mom. It was as simple as that."

"Blair, no—"

"No." I waved him off. "I know that now." I shook my head, my bangs falling in front of my face. I let them stay there, hiding behind them because for some reason it made me feel like I could be braver when I was half concealed. "At least, I think I know." I swallowed. "I'm trying to know."

Richard glanced over at me, warmth in his gaze. His eyes spoke of affection. They spoke of friendship, of companionship, of understanding. When he looked at me like that I couldn't help but feel like I was every inch the man I had tried so hard to become. I had potential. Maybe I wasn't a flower yet, but I was budding, stretching my petals to the sun, searching for what would give me life.

"When I found the papers that said I owned the house up here my first thought was, god finally...*finally* I have a catalyst big enough that I can get myself to leave." I was embarrassed really, of how long I'd stayed, of how long it had taken me to realize something wasn't right with her and not me. "It was like...on my own I couldn't leave, you know? I was stuck." My brow furrowed. "Repeating the same cycle over and over, going crazy because I kept expecting something would change... And when it didn't—when nothing ever got better I just... I decided that it must be what I deserved."

Richard didn't speak again but he did reach out, his big palm covered in fine lines that spoke of a life I didn't know about. He placed it palm up on my leg and I tangled my fingers inside his, staring at the size difference as I squeezed between his thick fingers and dug my nails into the squishy bits on the back of his palm.

I wasn't able to pierce skin but it still felt good. It felt good to…To feel something, other than the aching, overwhelming sickness brewing in my gut.

"So when I saw the papers I figured, maybe it was a sign? If I couldn't leave for me, then maybe I could leave for Jeffrey."

"Jeffrey?"

"My brother—cousin. Ugh. I don't know what to call him." I shook my head. "Yeah. Anyway. I ran for him, because he'd been trying to protect me our whole lives but he was just as stuck as I was. I figured it was my turn to be brave, you know?" It was hard to admit how much of a coward I'd been. "But as soon as I'd left I realized I'd been kidding myself. That all along I knew deep down that I had to leave for me," I amended. "That I *was*, leaving for me."

The night sky was calming where it surrounded us, casting starlight on the boughs of trees as they reached towards the moon and we sped down rain-slicked streets. Droplets decorated the windshield and the wipers cleared them away. A clean slate, only to fill again moments later.

"I figured I could sell the house, you know? Make enough cash that I could go somewhere truly anonymous, call up Jeffrey and be like 'hey, man, you know how we always talked about getting out? Well now we can' and it was going to be because of me, you know? Because I made it happen. Because I'd been brave. It all kinda went to shit though. I mean…I left before I was supposed to without talking to him—because she found me at the club—and there was this whole…yeah. Horrible thing. I didn't call him." I bit my lip. "I should've called him." I shook my head. "I realize that now."

There was an exit that looked like it led to the middle of nowhere and Richard took it. I was nervous for about two seconds before I reminded myself that he could've killed me at any point since we'd started spending time alone together. Despite the fact that he kept constantly telling me that he couldn't 'control himself around me' he seemed to always be in perfect control.

We slowed down, the slick crunch of tires on wet leaves sounding through the crack in the window as I was silent for a while, mulling over my past. The rain evolved into nothing but a drizzle, then a sprinkle, then nothing at all.

"So you're leaving because she can find you here?" he asked after several long, cricket-filled minutes. I nodded.

"I know it seems cowardly to let her dictate my life still… But…" I shuddered. "I just… I want to be free."

"To have somewhere that hasn't been tainted," Richard agreed quietly. He was silent for a moment, clearly processing my words. "What if you weren't alone here?"

"What do you mean?"

"What if when she came, you…didn't have to face her alone?"

I shook my head. "That wouldn't change anything, Rich. The whole point is that I'm too much of a coward to face her by myself."

"But—"

"The problem isn't everyone else, Richard. The problem *is me*. It always has been. Just not in the way she made me think it was." We turned down a winding road, the asphalt turning to gravel the farther we traveled. The car rattled along and the slower we got, the more pronounced the tree trunks around us became, despite the fact it was dark enough it was nearly impossible to see more than ten feet in front of us.

It felt like we'd been driving for ages before we took another turn and headed towards what looked like a break in the trees.

"If you're about to take me to a field to play baseball I'm going to throw myself out of this car," I told him, clearly referencing *Twilight*. It was a test of sorts, to see if he would get the reference.

"Whatever you say, spider-monkey," Richard responded with a twitch to his lips. He looked stupidly proud of himself for knowing what I was talking about and I couldn't help but hide my smile against my shoulder. *Did Richard watch vampire movies in his spare time?* We approached what looked like a clearing ahead and I gripped the edge of my seat as the car went over a few pretty spectacular bumps.

It was dark enough out that at first I didn't realize where he'd taken me. It was only when he'd parked the car and he'd gotten out that I tasted the salt in the air and the swoosh of waves echoed loud enough to quiet the orchestra of self-loathing in my mind.

I pushed open my door, whacking it into Richard for the second time in our short relationship. I hadn't realized he'd come around to open it for me, and so I just spluttered an awkward apology and side stepped around him like a gay-penguin.

The waves were louder now, echoing through the world around me in a sound so familiar it made my soul ache.

I'd forgotten how much I missed the ocean. I'd spent so much of my life listening to the waves crash, searching for answers inside the foam as it painted the sand white.

I distantly recalled mentioning how much I missed it to Richard one of the times I'd been over at his house over the past couple days. There'd been a commercial for sunscreen playing between episodes on the TV and I'd sighed wistfully, telling him about my balcony at home and how I used to just sit out there and listen to the ocean.

The water in front of me now was a million miles away from my lonely balcony and yet listening to it still had the same effect.

My heart beat thudded unevenly in my chest as I grabbed onto Richard's arm, squeezing bone and muscle though his bicep didn't give beneath my grip.

"You took me to the fucking ocean," I said, not even glancing at the aforementioned ocean and instead tipping my head back so I could look Richard in the eye. He ducked his head down, meeting my gaze as our breath mingled with the salt in the air and the feeling that had been fluttering like a fledgling between us solidified into something… new.

"I took you to the 'fucking ocean,'" he agreed, a twist to his lips that I knew now meant he was amused.

Richard chased after me as I bounded across the beach toward the water. We'd abandoned our shoes and pants by the car and I dug my toes into sand, side stepping the rock outcroppings dotted along the beach as I plowed my way toward the crashing waves.

The water was shockingly cold as it burned along my calves and I cackled, my head tossed back to the stars as I let the tide drag away the weight on my shoulders left over from our conversation in the car. Richard was behind me and I listened to the way he laughed, a happy, joyful little sound full of boyish wonder.

"What are you doing?" he asked, confused but clearly a bit delighted.

"I'm freezing my ass off," I told him, turning around to give him a sunny grin before I latched onto his wrist and began tugging him deeper into the wet sand. A rush of water fled forward, drowning our bare feet and shins as Richard chuckled and I allowed myself to finally breathe. My lungs expanded with the promise of a future and I grinned at him so hard my cheeks hurt with the force of it. He was beautiful. *Young* in a way I got the feeling he never allowed himself to be.

"You're going to make yourself sick." Richard laughed though he didn't stop me as I bent over and shucked my boxers, tossing them towards the relative safety of dry sand.

"I wanna swim."

"This is the coldest time of year," Richard reminded me but I just shrugged, reaching for the hem of my shirt and tugging it up over my head. I handed it to him with reverence because he'd bought it for me. I couldn't help but feel free as I stood naked in the surf and the moon painted my skin blue.

"You can join me…or not." I shrugged, waggling my finger at him as I shuffled backwards just to feel the waves meet the back of my knees. I had gooseflesh all over but I didn't mind. The shaking was from excitement not the cold.

There was no one around for miles so I didn't bother hiding myself even though everything inside me screamed that I should. Being naked in front of him now was different than when we had sex. This was intimate in a different way. In the way where his heart reached for mine, bound together with laughter and life.

I didn't want to hide anymore.

I didn't want to run.

I just wanted to live.

"Fuck it." Richard made a quiet noise behind me and I watched with fascination as he made his way back to our shoe pile and began whipping off the rest of his own clothes. He returned with a grin brighter than the morning sun, his hair glowing in the moonlight, his cock long and thick where it listed just slightly to the left, its root nestled in a patch of gorgeous golden curls. I wanted to suck him down, explore the sweat salty skin with my tongue till his cock grew full and he couldn't help but want to fuck.

I didn't though, instead I just took a step back into deeper water, the tide tugging at my legs.

"C'mon slow-poke." I grinned, splashing backwards as the waves crept in. His laughter was infectious and I giggled as ice enveloped me and Richard chased me the deeper I went. He wrapped his arms around me when he finally caught up, the swell of muscle in his chest brushing up against my chin before he bent down and buried his nose against my fluffy temple. He was solid and sweet, as I reached up to the back of his neck so I could yank him down with me to meet the next wave head on.

Icy wet laughter exploded as we burst out of the water. Richard's smile was brighter than the reflection of the moon in the water as he grabbed my hand, tugging me toward the next wave now that he knew what to do.

Enveloped in the icy, inky darkness with his fingers squeezed tight round mine I realized how much I was growing to care for him.

When we surfaced again and I kissed him like my life was on the line. I slipped my tongue inside his mouth and he grabbed my hips, hauling me against the naked line of his body, his nails biting into my flesh hard enough to remind me that this was real. That I was here.

"You know, I Googled the average temperature of water along the Oregon coastline," Richard told me as we dripped our way naked along the rocky shoreline. It was dark enough out that the trees behind us were just shapes in the distance, the rocky outcrops that peeked out of the water along the shoreline lost behind moonlit shadows. "It's supposed to be warmer here," Richard said. I shivered and laughed again, shaking water droplets from my fingertips as I pressed up along his side and we continued our trek down the beach.

It was…beautiful, peaceful. The stars above glowed brighter somehow, like the city lights—even in a town as small as Elmwood—affected how brightly they were able to shine. "Really?"

"Well…" He looked sheepish, kicking at a stray rock as he headed down the hill in front of me, making sure I had solid footing, his back to the ocean so he could watch my descent. "In the summer, at least."

"It's April, Rich," I reminded him, teasing, because there was no one I trusted more in the world than him to know exactly what date it was.

"April 17th." He smiled. "Which means you might get hypothermia.

Or something worse."

I shook my head at him, finding it incredibly adorable he'd taken the time to Google it. God, he was such a nerd. A sexy nerd. Fuck. Just looking at his shoulders made me want to climb him like a spider-monkey for real. I could still feel his fingers on my hips, the bruises stinging deliciously when I reached down to press against them.

"But if you stick around for the summer we could come back. It'll be more comfortable then. Less…ball shriveling." He offered with a laugh, chewing on his lip in an almost shy way. It sounded suspiciously like he was offering me a future here, and I didn't know what to say to that so I just hummed noncommittally and let him pull me further down the beach before looping us back towards our pile of clothing.

I shivered again and dug my feet deep into the sand just to feel it sink between my toes.

"Wait." I blinked, realizing something. "But don't you have like…an 'aversion to sunlight' or whatever?"

"I do," he agreed, watching me as I shivered but stubbornly refused to call it quits and head back to the car.

I was at the ocean for god's sake. I wasn't going to let a little wind chill thwart my romantic not-date.

"It's different for everyone though," Richard explained. "Some of us can't be in it at all, some of us can be in weak sunlight, and some of us are only mildly irritated by it. Human genetics play into it so no one can really predict the outcome."

"So which type of vampire are you?" I asked, tucking my hands inside my armpits to try and conserve warmth. I missed my hoodie desperately, eyeing where it sat atop our clothing pile only a few hundred feet away from us. It had a fat black vampire cat on it with huge yellow eyes and a caption that said 'You're mine, meow.' It was probably my favorite clothing item Richard had given me. Aside from the frowny-face boxers, which were my number one favorite for obvious sex-related reasons.

I still missed the clothing that had burned up in the fire, but I tried not to think about it too much. Thinking about it wouldn't bring it back.

"I'm the third one."

"The mildly irritated one," I confirmed. He nodded. The ocean waves crashed along the shoreline and I sighed, soaking up the wind and salt as I tipped my head back towards the stars.

"Seems unfair, you know, that you can go out in the sun and not everyone can," I commented conversationally. "Seems convenient."

He shrugged. "There are perks to it, yes. I get to have more of a presence in Collin's life despite turning." Richard stared out at the dancing waves, a constipated look on his face as he clearly debated how to answer. "I didn't get the perks some others got though."

"So explain to me how it works." I brought my hands up to my face, breathing onto my fingers to warm them. "Is it genetic? Were you born this way?"

"No." Richard shook his head. "I only recently turned. Most of us refer to it as 'taking the change.'" He looked at me. "In Elmwood, there are laws in place that allow for legal turnings. The application process is complicated and tedious however, and applying doesn't mean you'll be approved. However, anyone that knows the secret and is considered an 'acceptable age' can submit an application to the Supernatural Alliance Committee. Those that are approved will then be asked to attend what the town calls a 'mass turning.'"

"Wow." I blinked. "So those just…happen all the time then?"

"No." Richard shook his head, clearly trying to find the words to explain himself. "It's quarterly. Four times a year. But you have to put your application in well ahead of time because there's a long waiting list."

"So potentially now that I know the secret I could also become a vampire." I blinked at him. "If I wanted."

"Potentially…" Richard was clearly uncomfortable with that train of conversation so I moved on, cycling back to my first line of questioning.

"So, the sun aversion thing is genetic then? Some people turn and get it, and some don't."

He sagged in relief and nodded. "Yes, exactly. There's no planning it."

"You said that there are other perks though? That the others get?" I tried to clarify.

"Yes." He bobbed his head like a cute lil bobble head and I tried not to find him incredibly adorable, and failed. A gust of wind whipped my bangs in front of my face and I was forced to abandon my hand blowing if I wanted to get my hair out of my eyes. I was surprised it had dried so quickly, but figured it had something to do with the amount of time we'd been walking.

"Some people have a more dominant…" Richard's brow furrowed as he tried to come up with a word to describe what he was trying to say. "Vampire gene. *Yes.* Vampire gene." His lips thinned and he frowned. "Forgive me if I don't make sense. I've never had to explain this to anyone before."

"You're doing fine, man. Continue." I waved him onwards though he got distracted by my hair, his eyes continuously flickering to where my bangs hung in my face as he continued to speak.

"Those with a more dominant vampire gene also get…for lack of a better word, 'perks.'" He stared at my bangs again, then huffed, frustrated with himself, or me—who knows, as he reached out and began methodically tucking my hair behind my ears. His fingers were gentle and softer than they looked and I melted a little, my breath still puffing away along my frozen fingers.

Jesus. Maybe skinny dipping hadn't been my best idea.

"There are positives and negatives, just like with everything else. Some of us have superior hearing, superior strength, those that are especially weak to the sun can oftentimes have more perks. Some can even influence those around them."

"Like vampire magic," I hummed and he shook his head with a laugh.

"I suppose that's one way to put it."

Man. This was fascinating shit. For real. His reality was so far removed from anything I'd ever heard before it was hard to believe him even though I knew there was no reason not to.

"Vampires…aren't the only creatures out there, are they?" I asked curiously, thinking a mile a minute. Richard nodded.

"There are infinite species, yes. Sanctuaries like ours house them, though different places tend to attract different creatures. Elmwood is primarily populated by humans and vampires."

"We've gotta have werewolves." I could feel my heart racing. "I've served so many raw steaks over the past few months there's no other explanation." I blinked. "I know humans eat them too. Don't gaslight me. It's different."

Richard laughed. "Yes, there are werewolves. Ghosts too. Though they aren't what you think."

"I've never seen a ghost."

"I hope you never do." Richard frowned and I hurried to change the subject again. "They're cursed beings. Stronger than any of us."

"What about blood drinking? How do you eat?" I asked, because it had been killing me trying to figure it out.

"SAC sends out rations to the residents who have decided to take the turn," Richard explained. "The human residents can donate as much as they want, and they get a subsidized paycheck from the committee in return."

"And who pays the committee?"

"The citizens." Richard cocked his head at me. "It's really more of a second government than anything else. There are taxes, rules, regulations. There are even prisons, though far from Elmwood, thank god."

"Sorry, this is just—" I blinked. "Super fucking fascinating."

We stopped walking, close to the edge of the water again. I wanted to dip my toes inside it again but I knew this time I would get too cold and the night would be over far too soon.

"So why did you take the change?" I asked, more than a little curious. It was something I'd wondered, especially after hearing Collin talk about how averse he was to it.

Richard pursed his lips, turning to face me fully, his lower lip caught between his teeth. He debated with himself, then...spoke, his words a quiet, vulnerable rumble.

"After Markus died our family was desperate to stay together. Desperate to never have to feel that pain again. They all turned, one by one, until it was my turn."

"So why did you?" I asked, more than curious, but also aware I was treading on dangerous ground.

"I…" Richard trailed off for a moment, a soft sigh escaping his lips. "I suppose I just…didn't want to put up a fight about it. I never—meant for Collin to feel alienated by my choice."

"That's not your fault."

"If I'd known…what my life could be—" Richard's gaze met mine as his lips twitched upwards. "I don't know if I would've done it. Taken the change, I mean." I knew what he meant. If he'd known he could have… this. Things might've been different. But he hadn't known. Suddenly it became imperative he understand that he hadn't messed up, that I accepted him just as he was. Fanged or not.

"I don't know if you've realized this about me but I'm kinda a slut for vampires," I told him.

Richard's eyes darkened with lust immediately, nearly black in the hollows of his face as his lips tipped into a feral little grin and he dragged his gaze from the top of my head down, down, down to my toes. My cock twitched.

"Oh, I've noticed," he purred.

Oh, good. I'd successfully cheered him up!

I cleared my throat, embarrassed and more than a little turned on. But no. No. *Focus*, Blair. I had more questions.

"Are you allowed to…" I waved a hand between us. "You know—drink from humans—people—me?"

Richard cocked his head to the side, clearly amused. "All at once?" He teased.

"Ugh." I whacked his arm, even though I'm sure it hurt me more than it hurt him. "You know what I mean."

"I can do whatever I want as long as the donor is willing," Richard told me. Ew. Donor. What a completely unsexy name for it. "I could even turn you, if I got the correct paperwork."

"Can we call it something else? Donor sounds like you're about to steal my kidney and Hannibal Lecter it into sausage to feed your friends."

Richard snorted, his nose scrunching up in disgust as he shook his head at me. "Fine, what would you call it then?" The moonlight was bright enough it made his hair shine nearly white. He was gorgeous like this, free of inhibitions, his walls down, carefully cultivated facade left behind the tree line.

"I dunno," I shrugged. "But definitely not 'donor' Jesus, I don't think I could've come up with a more unsexy name for it."

"Fine, well." Richard laughed again, dimples flickering in the shadows cast by a passing cloud. "When you come up with something better, you let me know."

"Fine. I will." I smiled at him, my cheeks hurting from the force of it as I reached up to gently shove at his chest. "And it's gonna be so sexy you're gonna be mind blown."

"Sure." He nodded along, reaching up to snatch my wrists, holding them captive so the flat of my palms remained anchored against the solid swell of his pecs. I could feel his nipples and I resisted the urge to rub up against them. My own hardened in response *(or maybe that was the cold.)*

"Is that something you want?" I asked after a moment, my voice softening as my touch did, fingers scratching imploringly against the soft swell of one of his glorious pecs. "To drink from me?"

"God, yes." Richard's pupils dilated and I was blessed enough to watch it happen, my throat suddenly dry as I watched him lick his lips. "I…"

He blinked. "I shouldn't want to as badly as I do."

"Maybe it's not such a bad thing to want things," I pointed out. "Maybe that's what keeps you alive."

He seemed to think this over for a long moment, his thumbs massaging circles into the sensitive skin on my inner wrists as he contemplated how to respond. "You're right." He agreed after what felt like eons. The tide crept towards our toes and still we remained.

"Is there something I have to do before or…" I trailed off, wanting to know everything before I was willing to move onwards. "You know, like…prepping myself?"

"It isn't sex, Blair." Richard laughed, his face lighting up in disbelief.

"Why not?" I offered, my heart beating an unsteady dance along my breastbone. I swallowed the lump in my throat as the waves finally caught up to us and ice-cold water bathed the tips of my toes. I could've moved. I didn't. "Could it be? Sex, I mean?"

"You want me to drink from you…during sex," Richard clarified, a look of raw disbelief on his face.

"Would that be something we could do?" I still wasn't sure what the rules were for this sort of thing, but I wanted to find out. God it still felt so fantastical—like I'd stepped into a world that didn't actually exist. It was too…amazing to even comprehend that all my life I'd been searching for something that had been in front of my face all along.

Richard swallowed, his eyes growing dark, hooded, heated. *Oh god*. My toes curled in the wet sand and I shuddered, my eyes trained on the scarlet wetness of his parted lips. "It would be my pleasure," he murmured, leaning down until only centimeters remained between our lips. I could feel his breath on my skin and I melted, clinging to the damp wet of his skin as he crowded me closer, closer, and closer still. He only stopped when we were sandwiched together, his hips against mine, our cocks bumping, as his nose buried inside the hair at my temple like he couldn't get enough of my scent.

"When?" he asked, voice eager and thick with lust. I could feel his dick perking up against my thigh and mine rose to match it.

"Today?" I offered. "Right now?"

"No." Richard shook his head, laughing as his nose rubbed up against me. He released one of my wrists to grab my chin. His grip was bruisingly tight but I didn't mind. I was used to pain following touch, but never had it hurt so good. "When we get home."

Home.

I liked the sound of that.

Chapter Thirty-Two

Blair

"I'VE GOT IT!" I declared when we pulled into the parking spot at Richard's place.

"What?" he asked, curious.

"Blood sharing," I decided, grinning over at him. "Like…blood partners in crime." I bobbed my head. "Isn't that way sexier than a 'donor'?"

Richard blinked. He blinked again, a kaleidoscope of emotions flickering in his eyes. Then he just nodded, lips wobbling as he tried not to laugh, and failed. Fucking asshole. "Sure," Richard agreed, clearly humoring me.

I rolled my eyes at him, prepared to wait patiently inside the car. I'd learned if I didn't I was likely to smack him again with my car door. Despite my earlier protests I found I kinda *liked* the attention anyway. We parked, and he stepped out, the headlights flicking off halfway through him rounding the front of the car. God, I felt like a dog he was training, sitting there obediently until he opened the door for me and his face lit up in this surprised, pleased little smile. Whipped. I was whipped.

Was that cute? Or gross?

Maybe both.

We headed up the steps to his apartment, the scent of salt still heavy in the air despite the ocean being miles behind us. I honestly hadn't realized Elmwood was so close to the beach. An hour drive wasn't the most horrible thing in the world. I could see myself making the journey on my own when I needed time to think, especially now that I knew where it was.

It was a soothing thought really. I could be thousands of miles from where I grew up but still have the ocean close enough to touch.

We climbed the steps to the third floor, the wind echoing through the hallways, the leftover scent of spaghetti trickling in our noses from one of the apartments we passed by.

When we reached the door, Richard unlocked it and I bumped up against his back in impatience. He snorted, shaking his head in amusement as he shoved open the door and I ducked under his arm to get inside. I'd never felt so free to be myself around another person. It was a heady feeling. Boots mewed at us as soon as we entered, glaring from his position atop the couch where he held domination over the parade of my plants that I'd liberally decorated the living room with. Over the past few days I'd begun infiltrating Richard's lair. Boots was the first part of my entourage to come with me, we'd figured it was easier that way. Plus I missed him, and Richard liked him.

After that I'd brought my plants. When Richard had seen them he'd clearly tried not to laugh. Half of them were dead but I refused to abandon them in case they might miraculously burst to life again. Even though I knew they were…sad looking I was still mildly offended so I'd flipped him off.

He'd kissed me every time I told him one of their names. I hadn't known how to deal with how much that meant to me. Richard's kisses were drops of sunshine.

We hadn't known each other long and yet it felt like I'd been waiting my whole life for someone like Richard to come along.

"So…" I trailed off as I headed backwards into the living room, my eyes trained on his face and the slash of shadow that painted his cheekbones. God, the man had *cheekbones*. Better than half the cast of *America's Next Top Model* I'd grown up binge watching with Jeffrey hidden in his blankets in the middle of the night.

Except Richard wasn't just gorgeous, he was…real. As much as I called him perfect in my head—and to his face, apparently—the 'flaws' I saw on his body were more attractive than anything I'd ever seen before. They made him real, tangible. I found myself falling in love with the freckles across the bridge of his nose, with the slightly pointed tips to his ears, with the thin almost silver scar that bisected his lower lip, only visible when he smiled.

I loved the way his laugh was anything but attractive. I loved the awkward constipated face he made when I did something he didn't have a reaction for programmed in his head. His constant wonder when I made him laugh made me feel like I was a gift he was slowly unwrapping, day by day, inch by inch.

All my life I'd been a nuisance. A punching bag. A pest. Someone to look after. A burden. But when Richard looked at me I was made of nothing but possibility. I found myself wanting to please him, to make him smile, to make his life better.

My mom had told me that she knew my dad was the one from the moment she'd met him. I always thought it was a silly notion, that you could just look at someone and know deep down that they were your person. There were so many things to factor in, whether or not either of you were morning people, how you dealt with grief, anger, how compatible your sex drives were—whether or not either of you cleaned.

I'd explained away her logic more times than I could count, telling myself that what she'd spoken of was nothing but wishful thinking, a fairytale.

But I was realizing a little more every day that maybe all along I'd been the one in the wrong. My mother had been gone for years, for so long that her words should've faded away into nothingness, and yet still they remained. Tucked like treasure, held precious beside my heart. If vampires were real, couldn't fairy tales be real too?

Maybe there was a place in the world for finding love without the millions of questions.

Maybe when you found someone that just…fit into all your empty places, it was okay to figure it out as you went along.

Maybe not everything had to be set in stone.

Maybe uncertainty was worth being…uncertain for.

"Where did you go?" Richard asked softly, startling me out of my reverie. He stood before me, his broad shoulders filling out leather and flannel, eyes dark and red with blood lust. Broad palms scraped along my jawline as he tucked his fingers around my ears, burying them in the soft black strands that always tickled my ears.

"What do you mean?"

"Your eyes." He nodded his head, glancing down at me. "They were a million miles away."

I didn't know how long I'd stood there, just staring at him as I thought. It could've been seconds or minutes, but in the end it didn't matter because like always, Richard noticed. It was like he always hunted for the little pieces of me, looking to understand, to know me in a way no one had ever taken the effort to do before.

He did it in such a shy, almost tentative way though, like he was frightened I would reprimand him. Like he was worried that his attention was unwanted.

He couldn't have been further from the truth.

"I was thinking about you," I told him, letting him squeeze me in close, his nose bumping up along mine in a way I was quickly coming to associate with both Richard and his personal brand of affection. He had to bend to touch me and my heart fluttered as I nuzzled him back. Richard was sweet and awkward, like he didn't know how to express himself and let instinct take over where his mind lacked.

"Good things?" he asked hopefully, the velvet tip of his nose freezing from the outside chill. It was spring but the world hadn't seemed to realize that yet. The constant rain, the night chills, all of those things should've turned me off, but I found myself loving them because they belonged to this silly little town with its rules and its particular brand of darkness. Tucked between mountains like a secret just waiting to be discovered.

"Of course." I blinked, realizing I was taking too long to reply again.

"Sorry. I'm in my head a lot tonight," I explained.

"We don't have to…" he trailed off, clearly struggling to say the words 'have sex.'

"I want to, Rich," I told him, as firmly as I could. "I want that. I'm just—" I inhaled, my nostrils flaring. "I'm just realizing a lot of things about myself today and it's a little overwhelming."

"Things that have to do with me?"

"Yes." I shrugged helplessly.

"Like what?"

"Like—" I swallowed. "That you're stupidly noble, and sweet, and you take good care of your little brother— And every time I'm with you it's like the pieces of me that have always been hard for me to see are suddenly right in front of my face." He opened his mouth to interrupt me but I soldiered onwards. "You're attentive. You're smart. You're honest." He grimaced, glancing to the side in a shy way that made my pulse throb. He was so unused to compliments it was clear I was making him uncomfortable. "I'm realizing just how much I like that."

"Thank you—" He tried to interrupt me again but I shook my head, shushing him softly with a chaste kiss that made my lips tingle as I pulled back incrementally so I could speak again.

"You spend so much time worrying about others that you never worry about yourself. All your free time is spent on Collin or me—" I shook my head. "You never do things to take care of yourself. I… I want to help you." God it sounded stupid when I said it like that. "I want to be the person you come to when things are too much. I want to be the quiet place you go to when everywhere else is too loud and all you have the energy to be is just…you."

"Blair—" Richard's brows were lowered, his eyes shining enough that if I didn't know any better I'd think there were tears inside them. The muscle in his jaw jumped and I melted in the firm grip he had on my face as he leaned down, inch by inch to kiss me again.

His upper lip brushed mine first, gentle, shy. A tease. This was different than what I'd done to him. It was...sinful, more intimate. I inhaled sharply, my lashes fluttering as his tongue slid out, sweet and wet, to trace over my lower lip.

I parted my lips immediately, unable to do anything but obey his silent command to open up. Richard had no prior experience but it didn't matter because when we were being intimate, a different side of him came out and he was suddenly lost to instinct. The perfectly pressed man disappeared, replaced by a lonely boy who wanted nothing more than to connect, all sharp teeth and hard cocks, and desire older than time itself.

My hoodie was the first article to make its way to the floor. This time Richard didn't stop to fold it, instead he let his own jacket join it, his eyes dark and hooded with lust as they dragged over the bare expanse of my naked chest.

Despite sharing several hand jobs and another—very memorable—blowjob earlier that week, we had never gotten to this part during sex, bare in more ways than one, vulnerable. I trembled, my nipples hardening under his gaze as he reached out, entranced by the sight, his fingers tentative and almost shy. It was clear he wasn't thinking about what he was doing as he acted on his own desire like it had him under its spell. His thumb brushed one of my pebbled, pink nipples and he groaned helplessly in response. I stared at his lips as he panted out a horny little breath, enjoying the way I squirmed beneath his touch. Richard seemed to realize, too late, he'd touched without permission. He grew still, glancing up at me through his expressive eyebrows, a look of guilt on his face like a kid who had gotten caught with his hand in the cookie jar.

It was such an honest, innocent expression I couldn't help but be charmed. This was my first time too, but it felt natural for me to search for his pleasure, like letting him experience this was more important than experiencing it myself.

"Sorry," Richard spoke, his voice nothing but a quiet growl. I shivered and shook my head.

"Do it again," I commanded.

He did it again.

I gasped.

Something broke between us then, his movements turning ravenous and eager, eyes filled with a dangerous glint that had my knees shaking and my fingers tingling.

Soon Richard's mouth joined his fingers, his face buried between the soft dip in my chest, biting along my sternum like he couldn't get enough of it. I was distantly glad his fangs were retractable because it was clear now that if they weren't he would've sliced my chest to ribbons in his hunt for more skin, more touch, more taste.

Why was that so hot? It shouldn't be so hot.

His mouth warmed up the longer he laved it over my skin, like the warmth of my body was heating him up from the inside out. Broad strokes tickled the sensitive nubs of my nipples as Richard herded me down the hallway, one of his hands dragging slowly, possessively, down my back till he could grab at one of my ass cheeks while the other remained firmly planted on my hip.

His hands were large enough it almost felt like if he tried he could wrap them entirely around my waist. I couldn't help the helpless little noises that escaped my throat as Richard bit his way to the other side of my chest and my back hit the door to his bedroom. His fingers dipped between the globes of my ass and he gave my hole a few desperate little strokes before his hand slid up to grip my hip again. The wood chilled my skin where it dug in almost painfully and I shuddered, my head thunking back against it, a stray swathe of my bangs catching on my kiss swollen lips.

I tingled all over, my skin alight, my cock twitching.

"Fuck," Richard hissed, clearly annoyed that he had to release me to get the door open. One of his hands left my hip and slid to the handle. He fumbled with it—more clumsy than I'd ever seen him— like he was so absorbed in getting to touch me, to taste me, to feel me, that even his motor functions were struggling to work.

It was flattering in the best way possible and I stared at him in fascination as he finally got the door open and we fell back into even blacker darkness. It was too dark for his bed to be anything other than a vague shape and I stumbled back towards it, my dick throbbing against my zipper.

Richard's eyes flashed, reflecting back at me almost like a cat's in the night. Distantly I wondered if he could see in the dark better than a human could. It wasn't the first time I'd had the thought, but this time I shelved it for later, figuring I could ask him when my brain wasn't located inside my dick.

"On the bed," Richard said, his voice a low command that I shuddered in response to. He seemed to realize how bossy he'd just been and he grimaced, smiling in apology. "Sorry." He shook his head. "On the bed, *please*."

I laughed, unable to help myself, shivering from his attention and not the cold for once. "Hey, don't hold back on my account," I told him with a little grin. I didn't get on the bed.

"But this is your first time too," he responded, voice low and sweet. "I want you to like it."

"Well then, let me tell you that being bossed around by you is the single hottest thing that has ever happened to me." My grin softened and I reached out to poke him in his still clothed chest. "It would be even hotter if you would get naked, though. Just saying." I shrugged.

Richard snorted, shaking his head in disbelief at me though his boyish grin was back, dimples jumping as he moved over-eagerly to unbutton his flannel shirt. He had an undershirt beneath it—because of course he did—and I groaned at the sight of him with the black fabric parted, his thick chest pushing obscenely at the thin fabric of a painted-on white tank top.

I'd never seen him in anything but dark colors before and the sight of him as he stripped off his shirt and stood before me dressed only in paper-thin white fabric made my head spin. He looked vulnerable like this. Human, even though he was far from it. That much was clear as I watched his eyes glow, red as a blood-moon, scarlet and sinful in their lust.

Richard's brow was lowered, his eyes beseeching as he waited like a dog for a treat for me to give him permission to move.

"I'm pretty sure I said naked," I reminded him. He snorted in disbelief, his nostrils flaring as he shook his head, smiling, his fingers dipping into the hem of his shirt so he could tug it up and over his head.

God. *Richard.*

Richard's chest was a work of art. He was sculpted and thick in all the right bits but with skin so thin I could see the bumps of his ribs when he stretched his arms over his head like that. His shirt fluttered to the floor and my cock throbbed. *Jesus fuck. How the hell did I get so lucky?* He was a porn star and GQ model rolled all into one. *That* body with *that* face—so hopeful, dark with desire... Sure, we'd been naked on the beach just an hour or so ago, but this was different. I'd touched him then but it had been friendly. Staring at him now there were no illusions. He was going to fuck me. And I was going to *love* it.

"Holy shit," I breathed out, unable to help myself as I fanned my fingers along the leagues and leagues of pale flesh. He had a generous trail of golden hair leading from the middle of his belly, down his tight lower abs, and disappearing in the hem of his jeans. My hand traced it absentmindedly, catching on the soft curls, tugging at it, tugging harder when I noticed the motion made Richard gasp and his cock twitch.

I realized then that I hadn't gotten to touch him yet. Sure we'd had sex. Plenty of times actually. But he'd been so exuberant about touching me, bossing me around, forcing me to do as he said that I hadn't gotten a proper chance to touch him back. And that was *such* a fucking shame.

"You're beautiful, Rich," I told him softly, playing with the golden curls that led their way to the hard swell of where his cock bulged inside his jeans. This time it was my turn for my eyes to be wide with wonder as I tipped my head up to get a good look at his face. He looked wrecked. I'd never seen that face on him before, so broken apart by my casual words spoken in a setting so intimate he had no walls up to protect himself against them. So I repeated myself, because he needed to know it was true, he needed to know I meant it. "You're beautiful."

I hoped my words would penetrate, would travel back in time, would comfort the scared little boy I saw hidden behind his eyes, the boy who had grown up too fast. The boy whose foundation was death and loss but still managed to wake up every day like it was okay for the world to keep spinning.

"Blair—" Richard's head dropped down, his forehead resting against mine as his breath puffed against my lips. "You can't say shit like that to me."

"Why?" I expected him to complain, to tell me he couldn't handle it, not like this. Not now. I waited for him to tell me it was too much, that *I* was too much, as I'd been told hundreds of times before. But he didn't.

Instead he said, "Because it makes it really hard for me not to throw you down on the bed and just fucking—" He inhaled my scent greedily, one of his hands slipping down my spine, catching on sweaty salt-damp skin to wrap squeeze me close to him in a grip so possessive there was no room for god or air between us. "Fuck the hell out of you."

Oh.

Oh.

That was not what I had been expecting at all.

"Well, what are you waiting for?" I responded, the words escaping my lips without much thought other than an eager desire to get fucking railed by the gorgeous god in front of me.

Richard chuckled, a low incredulous noise. "I can't," he said softly. "You don't realize how much I have to hold back around you. You're so—" He inhaled, hand sliding down to grip one of my asscheeks. I arched into the touch, desperate for the tease he'd subjected me to earlier. Thick fingers pulled my cheeks apart, rubbing up against my hole through dry denim for a second time, only this time he didn't pull away. I suddenly wished I wasn't wearing pants at all, the jeans I was wearing were too tight for him to do much more than grab and pull. "You're so fragile."

Fragile? Motherfucker.

"Fuck you, Edward Cullen," I grunted, bumping our noses together as he let out a startled little laugh. "I've told you this before and I'll tell you again: If you break my fucking legs but I get to have your cock inside me it will be well worth the rehabilitation."

"You don't mean that."

"Rich." I pulled at his pubic hair in reprimand, he inhaled sharply, his fingers pressed more insistently against my needy hole. "I want it. I want everything you can give me. I want your excitement, your pleasure, and most of all your surrender. I want you to lose control for once in your goddamn life and take what you want from me."

"Pretty sure you're going to be the one surrendering," he joked after a tense moment where he processed my words. I shrugged.

"There's power in surrender too, and besides, you have no idea how long I've wanted you to fuck me," I told him honestly. "This is by no means the first time I've had something dick adjacent up my ass this week. I'm prepared."

He looked confused for a moment and then his expression cleared as he realized what I was implying. "Oh."

"Yeah, 'oh.'" I laughed. "Pretty sure half the town has been talking about the fact that I bought lube and condoms down at Moonies. Chastity wouldn't stop laughing."

Richard flushed, something he'd never done in front of me before. I was surprised he even still could. "They're nosy."

"Yeah, they are," I agreed. "And you're stalling."

He laughed again, shaking his head in disbelief, his nose bumping back and forth against mine as his free hand moved to stroke over the hollow of my throat. I was hyper aware of his touch, my ass pressing back against his fingers in a clear invitation. "You want me to…"

"Fuck me?" I blinked. "Yes."

"And…"

"Drink from me?" He nodded. "Yes. Oh my god, yes. I've been waiting for you to taste me since the second I figured out it was an option."

"And you're not afraid," he confirmed.

"I probably should be," I admitted. "But it's… It's *you*, Rich. *It's you.*" I swallowed, giving up the biggest piece of myself I ever had before as I trembled in his arms. My cock still ached against my zipper, my lips tingling as I pushed up onto my tippy toes so I could press a gentle, soothing, kiss against his lips. My voice was raw when I spoke again. "I've never trusted someone like I trust you."

I expected him to reply and say something like 'maybe you shouldn't.' I expected to be crushed, for my feelings to be shoved aside because in the grand scheme of things they were inconsequential. It wasn't a declaration of love, of marriage, or even a future.

But…for me…it was the bravest thing I'd ever done. Trusting him was one thing, *admitting* I trusted him was something else entirely.

"Thank you," he said instead, those two simple words breaking me apart and rebuilding me as my heart thumped against my breastbone hard enough I knew he could hear it, super-hearing or not.

We didn't speak again for a few minutes. Instead Richard made quick work of both of our buckles, our buttons, and our pants. They joined the trail of clothing we'd left on our way to the bed before he finally, blissfully lowered me to the mattress.

Maybe I wasn't the best at following orders, since I'd ignored his command to get on the bed before he'd forced me there. But he didn't mind.

My boxers were still on, my cock tenting them obscenely. I wasn't sure I was ready to let them go just yet, too vulnerable in my own skin as I watched his muscles tense as he shifted and I wondered—not for the first time— what it was about me that he could possibly want.

I was prickly and unsociable. I had no skills great enough to write home about. I swore too much—*way* too much. And my body was in no way, shape, or form built like his was. The only thing even vaguely similar about us was our cock length. Which, admittedly, made me pretty happy.

Richard urged me up the bed, my back dragging on the soft scratch of the comforter as I found my head buried atop his pillows and his hips forced my legs wide enough to accommodate him between them.

"How do you want to do this?" Richard asked me, his voice a quiet rumble I felt echoing through our abs where they pressed tight together. Our treasure trails caught and the shift of his obliques pressed into mine in a tantalizing tease that had my lashes fluttering and my balls drawing up tight.

Don't come, I ordered myself, exhaling softly as I refocused on what he was trying to ask me.

"The sex or the blood part?" I clarified.

"Both?"

"Oh." I blinked. I hadn't really thought this through. My brow furrowed as my fingers found the soft curls at the back of his neck, scratching through the fuzzy strands to feel the way they tickled my fingertips. "Missionary? That's supposed to be more..." Romantic. *Ew.*

Was I really suggesting missionary because it was…romantic? *What was wrong with me?* "Wait."

He waited.

"From behind," I decided after a moment. "It'll be easier for you to get inside me, and then you can like—" I mimed a chomping motion with my teeth, waiting for his response. "Besides, I figure it would be pretty hot, you know?"

"Everything about you is hot," Richard spoke softly, lips twitching in amusement. I wasn't sure if he was humoring me or if, god forbid, he was being sincere.

"That is probably the least sexy way you could've said that," I complained. "Your sincerity is killing my boner." He laughed, his nose scrunching up as he wiggled his hips, readjusting himself until—

Ah. Oh. *Oh fuck.* His cock lined up with mine and—

Fuuuuck yes.

"You like that, huh?" he hummed, voice filled with wonder. "You like me on top of you."

"Oh, fuck." I bucked my hips up against him, unable to help myself as the pressure against my leaking dick made pleasure course down my spine. I was pretty sure I wasn't going to last more than a minute with him inside me, but somehow I found I didn't care. It was almost like I craved the connection more than I craved the sex.

"I'm not going to last long," he warned. I just shook my head, stating nonverbally how little that was a problem for me.

"Me neither."

Richard grinned at me, that same boyish smile I loved more than air itself, his dimples dancing as his eyes twinkled. "You're sure this is what you want?'

"God, how many times do I have to tell you?" I huffed in mock frustration. I respected the fact that he wanted to make sure. I didn't blame him. What we were about to do…was earth shattering for both of us.

For the rest of our lives we would remember this moment. His life, admittedly, would be much longer than mine, and that was why this was even more important than words could explain. No matter what happened in the future, no matter where I went, no matter who I was with, Richard would always be my first.

I wouldn't have it any other way.

Richard ground down slow and deliberate against me one last time, making us both gasp before he pulled back. I could feel how hard he was, both of our boxers sticky from the foreplay. I was too worked up to enjoy any more though, my body aching for the final event, the finish line.

When Richard moved I tried to gather some semblance of control again, aware that I was seconds away from release at any given moment. He shifted around to reach better and I watched his back muscles flex as he leaned over me and pulled open the top drawer in his night stand. He rustled around for a minute and distantly I wondered if he alphabetized the contents of his nightstand too, or if that was a privilege only afforded to the medicine cabinet.

When Richard popped back up it was with a triumphant grin. He shuffled back into place between my legs, looking eager and ridiculous and so incredibly hot. His hard cock was pressing up against the slit on his boxer briefs, thick and juicy, and way too fucking delicious. My mouth watered as I stared. Somehow I wasn't surprised he was a boxer-brief kinda guy.

They were made of dark clingy fabric and left absolutely nothing to the imagination. Mentally I compared our cocks, figuring we were close to the same length though his was clearly thicker. I'd seen glances of it as we'd experienced each other but watching him fuck his fist wasn't the same as touching it or tasting it myself.

I couldn't wait for the day that would be an option.

The idea of laving my tongue, wet, hot, and sloppy over the head of his thick, uncut cock was enough to make me lightheaded. To taste the salt on my tongue, to feel the crown as it rubbed along the back of my throat and my eyes rolled back as I let him fuck deep, deep inside me.

My dick bobbed and I watched in fascination as Richard's gaze slid to it with a desperate sort of desire. His hips snapped up in response, humping the air like he couldn't help himself, searching for friction he was so turned on just looking at me. God. He was so horny his body was reacting without him even needing stimulation. I could relate.

He was gorgeous. Sweat glittered at his temple, the sweet salty scent of arousal filling the space between us as he his heavy gaze met my own, a condom and a bottle of lube in hand. He set them to the side of my hip and the cold bottle bumped up against my feverish skin, causing me to jump a little.

"Sorry," he murmured, quickly fixing the problem, his forearm hair brushing along the sensitive skin by my ribs. My hands had at some point tangled up in the pillows by my head and I lowered them now, one hand catching in his thick blond locks, tugging the short strands through my fingers as I watched him with hooded eyes.

"Did you want—"

"Can I finger you?" Richard asked, interrupting me before I could finish. He blinked sheepishly, clearly embarrassed. I doubted he'd meant to cut me off, but I didn't mind because I had literally just been about to ask him that.

"Fuck, yes," I breathed, spreading wider to encourage him. He grinned, wicked and bright, a flash of pearly teeth that sent shivers down my spine.

"Your boxers…?"

"Burn them for all I care." I wiggled my hips in impatience. He laughed, shaking his head in amusement as he reached for the hem of them and paused one last time before he pulled them off. He glanced up at me, inspecting my expression, watching the way my flush traveled from my neck all the way down to my chest. He licked his lips, a hungry look on his face as his gaze caught on my throat.

I swallowed, and he watched.

A pause, and then Richard moved, so quickly I had a hard time catching the movement. It seemed like I blinked and then suddenly I was naked. My boxers were abandoned across the room, just a dark smear on the floor as Richard's hands grabbed my hips and hauled me down until I was practically half in his lap.

The skin on his thighs was cool to the touch but rock hard with flexed muscle. I knew from experience it would get squishy when he relaxed, but for now it was deliciously rigid. Richard's eyes were dark with lust as he dug his fingers into the squishy parts of my inner thighs and held me deliberately still so he could stare at where my cock drooled on my belly with rapt fascination.

"You're so hot," he breathed, repeating his earlier statement but with much more awe this time. I shuddered. I hadn't realized I had any sort of praise kink— But I supposed all things considered it made sense. I'd received so little praise in my life that receiving it during such an intimate situation broke me apart in ways nothing else ever would have the capability of doing.

I wanted to tell him he was hot too, but I was distracted, watching his abs flex as he exhaled raggedly and he rearranged my body till my knees practically hit my chest, and he had full access to my ass. For a man that had never done this before, he was surprisingly gifted.

He reached for the lube, the bottle clicking open with a soft *snick* as I waited with bated breath for him to touch me again.

It was cute that he tried to heat it up but I already knew the lube would be cold despite the way he rubbed it between his palms. Most of the time it seemed like Richard didn't really have much of a temperature of his own, not like me. It was yet another thing that reminded me that he wasn't human. Not anymore, anyway.

I wondered if he regretted turning. If he regretted choosing to give up the human parts of himself so early in his life. Now wasn't the time for that line of questioning, however, so I didn't ask, allowing him to psych himself up for a moment, his lip caught between his teeth.

"We don't have to," I told him, mirroring his earlier statement. He shook his head, smiling down at me, though he couldn't seem to look away from where my hole winked pink and inviting between my cheeks. It was a private feeling, to be looked at there.

Of course I'd showered and cleaned myself liberally before coming over to his house in preparation for something like this. I'd taste like ocean water but underneath that I was ready. But mentally preparing and actually executing the plan were two entirely different things. I was nervous, but somehow less nervous than I had been the first time he'd touched me. My hole fluttered and an empty ache buzzed inside me.

"I want to," Richard reassured me. He wasn't placating me. He'd really thought about it, his lips pulling into a wicked grin as he unceremoniously pressed the pad of his thumb against my hole and gave it a soft, circular rub.

I couldn't help myself, a gasp leaving my lips as I held very, very still. I didn't want him to stop, not for anything.

I'd waited so long for this to happen it almost didn't seem real.

He applied more pressure, his thumb teasing, the wet squelch of lube loud in the room as he liberally began rubbing it into my skin. I didn't know what he was doing, only that it felt really fucking good for my ass to be played with, so I relaxed back and melted into sensation. I was glad he hadn't decided to just fucking plow me, because despite my own *personal* experience I didn't think I was ready to be fucked rough.

In the future, yes, but for now... For now I was grateful for his gentle attention as he toyed with me, tugging, rubbing, soothing each brush of his thumb against my fluttering hole with another circular press. By the time he applied more lube, my hole was clenching and fluttering against his finger eagerly. It felt *so* good. Better than anything I'd ever felt before. The more he played with me the floatier I felt, until I was nothing but a lax puddle of pleasure, my head spinning, my breathing shallow.

When my hole felt relaxed enough Richard reapplied lube. He must have sensed I was ready because this time he pressed his middle finger against my eager hole and somehow I knew—*I knew*— he was about to push inside.

I held myself very still, trying not to hump back against his finger for fear of scaring him off as he pulled gently at my rim, a fucked out expression on his face. God, if I didn't know any better I would've thought *he* was the one about to be fucked. He looked wild with it, his eyes glowing in the dark, his lips bitten red and wet from where he had no doubt licked them. I'd been too out of it to watch before, but I watched now.

"I'm going to push inside you now, okay?" Richard said, gentler than he'd been the other times we'd been together. He was focused and tentative, almost reverent.

I supposed this was different for both of us. I nodded. He exhaled, tension bleeding from his shoulders. "If I hurt you, tell me," Richard urged, voice soft.

I nodded again, more enthusiastically this time.

"I'm gonna need a verbal response sweetheart," Richard reminded me gently. "Can you be good for me? Can you tell me if you need me to slow down? Or if it hurts?"

"Yeah," I croaked sweetly, even though just getting that one simple word out ached deep down inside the floatiest parts of me. "Promise, Rich."

"Good boy."

Good boy. I was a good boy.

Good boy, good boy, good boy.

The praise made my head spin and the last of the tension in my body bled away as a broken sort of whine escaped my lips. Richard pressed a little harder against me, his other hand holding the back of my thigh to keep me open. I could feel the scratch of his leg hair on the back of my ass and I wanted to wiggle to feel more of it but I managed not to, my head spinning, mouth dry.

"That's it," Richard urged, pressing more insistently. "Breathe, baby."

I breathed.

His finger slipped inside, easy as butter. It felt weird at first as it always did. A foreign sensation that felt more bad than good for the thirty seconds it took my body to catch up with my brain. By the time he had sunk in to the second knuckle the strange feeling had passed and I was grinding down against him, eager. Maybe it was slutty of me but I didn't care. I just wanted him to fuck me.

"More," I urged, my gaze slipping down to where I could see his forearm disappearing between my legs. His brow was lowered in concentration, his short hair glistening with sweat. I could hardly see him in the dark but somehow I didn't mind. It felt private this way. *Special.*

So much of our time together had happened without sunlight, it seemed fitting that something so intimate would too.

Richard did as I urged, his finger slipping all the way inside with a quiet gasp from me. I wiggled down on him, squeezing to test the feel of him inside me. If I hadn't been watching his face I probably would've missed his reaction, but god. *He was trembling*—his lips parted— jaw dropped in amazement as he stared at where his finger was disappearing inside my body.

"You're so hot inside," he spoke softly, reverently. God, I could so easily picture what he was thinking about. He probably couldn't help but imagine what it would feel like to sink his cock deep inside, replacing his finger with himself, where he burned hot and bright and desperate.

"You feel so good," I spoke—slurred, really—my voice breathless and croaky.

"More?" he urged, not waiting for my response before he eagerly poured more lube over his fingers and slipped a second inside me. I jolted, the cold of the lube shocking me for a moment before it passed and the thickness of his knuckles made me whimper.

It was like the more he put inside me, the more I wanted of him. I was insatiable. My hips fucked back against his fingers, taking him inside myself, listening to his quiet gasp of amazement as the lube squelched obscenely in the quiet of the room.

"That's enough—" I urged, impatient now to feel him. Richard shook his head no and I whined, low and unhappy.

"I don't wanna hurt you," he refused, voice gentle. "Just a bit more, baby, I promise."

I nodded because really I had no choice, even though I was aching and hard and my cock fucking hurt. I was glad he hadn't tried to touch it yet because I was sure the moment he did this would be over far too soon.

Two fingers turned to three, then four, his pinky tucking up inside me like I was a human shaped glove. I was sloppy and loose and my head was spinning. At some point I'd started crying, tears of overwhelming pleasure slipping down my cheeks as my hips chased his fingers with desperation. Squeezing around him made him groan so I did it over, and over, and over. "Please, please, please," I urged, grinding down against his knuckles. I was close, I was so fucking close, I—

Richard was a cruel bastard.

He was a cruel bastard because he fucking *stopped*.

I sobbed, a broken noise echoing through my chest as he gently began to pull his fingers out. My hands clawed at him desperately, hunting for his wrist so I could hold him inside. I wasn't ready to be empty yet, an animal-like need inside me that called for connection.

"No, no, no," I begged, shaking my head. "Don't go."

"I know, sweetheart," Richard urged, letting me hold him still, the pads of his fingers rubbing soothing circles deep inside me, glancing along my prostate with each gentle press. "I know, but I have to get my hand out if I'm going to put my cock in you." My prostate was swollen with heat and arousal, each brush of his fingers caused little flickers of pleasure to jolt more precum from the tip of my dick. And then I realized what he'd just said and I—

Oh fuck.

Richard's cock.

For a minute there I'd almost forgotten that was even an option. I pushed his hand away immediately, wincing as his fingers tugged at my rim on the way out.

He laughed, an incredulous sort of noise. "Baby—" he admonished. "Fuck. You gotta be gentle. I don't wanna hurt you."

"Sorry," I slurred, sniffing a little because apparently at some point my nose had started running.

"S'okay, baby. Just be sweet to yourself, okay?" he urged, gently helping me lay my thighs down on the bed again. *Be sweet to yourself.* The way he said it was so… Kind, so gentle. My head hurt. My heart hurt. I started trembling and he smoothed over my sore thighs with big swipes of his sticky hands.

"I'm going to turn you over now, okay?" Richard urged, shifting back enough that he could more easily manhandle me. I just nodded, twitching as my head bobbed against the pillows. One of his hands was warmer than the other (probably the one that had been inside me) and he grabbed my hips, gently, effortlessly, flipping me over onto my belly. The switch in position caused my head to spin and I breathed through my nose, allowing my body to settle as Richard arranged me onto my knees, my face still squashed in the comforter.

It was a surprisingly comfortable position, though it took him a minute to figure out what to do with the difference in our size. Since I was so much shorter he ended up having to anchor my legs on top of his own so he could reach.

By the time my breathing had evened out, I was in this zen sort of calm space I had never felt before. I'd never been so docile or relaxed in all my life. My body was trembling and shaking, sweat gathering at the back of my neck and behind my knees but I didn't even care. My hole clenched around nothing, achingly empty now that it knew what it felt like to be full. I whimpered, arching my back in an attempt to entice Richard to fill me up.

"Fuck," he swore, one big hand slipping up my sweaty lower back, his fingers catching along the knobs in my spine as he urged me to arch my ass up for him. "I forgot about your tattoo."

Oh.

I'd forgotten too, apparently. Reverent fingers traced over my tree boughs, worshiping the lines etched so deliberately in my pale flesh.

"It's beautiful," Richard said after a moment of silence, our breaths the only sound in the quiet room. "*You're* beautiful."

They were the same words I'd told him but the repetition didn't lessen their impact.

I swallowed the lump in my throat, another sob threatening to escape from my lungs as I arched my back and pushed up against him. The movement forced his cock to settle against the crease of my ass. Greedy hands squeezed my waist, then slipped down to part my cheeks so he could push the fat head of his cock against my rim.

"Oh fuck," Richard swore again, his voice a low throaty groan. His hips jerked against mine, fucking forward on instinct. I groaned in response, pressing back against him so I could feel the way his cock dragged sticky-sweet against my rim, begging to push inside. "*Fuck.*"

Fuck, indeed.

"I'm not going to be able to last," Richard warned, his voice broken, heated with desperation. I shook my head, fumbling around beside me to find the small foil packet he'd placed there earlier. My movements were uncoordinated but eager as I handed it back to him, though part of me wanted to just offer for him to push inside without it.

I figured that was a discussion for another time though, some of my sanity returning to me as I realized just how far-gone Richard was. His hips kept making these aborted little thrusting motions, his cock tucking up against my hole, catching then dipping just inside, enough that my whole body quaked with the pressure.

I'd never been hungrier for cock in my entire life.

He took the foil packet, making a soft whining noise as he pulled back enough that he could awkwardly fumble it on. Sex-drunk Richard was a sight to behold. He was clumsier than normal, his movements less coordinated, fuzzy with pleasure. It took him a long time to figure out how to get the condom on, and when he finally did, he let out this adorable little triumphant "*Yes!*"

I laughed, unable to help myself, ridiculously charmed by him as he lay the sheathed head of his cock against me. "I'm gonna go slow, okay?" he promised me, his voice low and earnest.

My head bobbed eagerly as I waited with bated breath for him to follow through.

The first inch hurt. It was like the sensation I'd felt with his fingers but worse because his dick was so much thicker. I breathed through the uncomfortable feeling, like a cock-taking champion, forcing myself to relax as he slid inside inch by blessed inch.

Richard was endlessly patient even though I knew he was struggling to hold back. The eager almost hurt-sounding noises he made every time he sunk in a little further went straight to my dick.

My cock had wilted a little during the initial penetration but it perked up again the second he slid all the way home. His cock was just the perfect length to bump up against my prostate on his way in and I whined, unable to help myself as I clenched around him and got used to the sensation.

It still hurt a little, but the pain went away quickly as I got used to the sensation of being full. Richard's grip was insistent where he squeezed my hips, his fingers tucking into the crease where my torso met my thighs. He didn't seem to mind how slippery I was, or how much I was trembling. Instead he just murmured reassurances against the back of my neck as he sunk down to lave wet, eager kisses along delicate skin.

I'd been so enthralled with the feeling of being fucked I'd honestly forgotten that he was going to bite me for a moment.

I remembered now though, now that his fangs dug into the top of my tattoo, not breaking skin, just reminding—his tongue eager as he soothed the sting of the abused flesh. Just thinking about taking his bite only made me harder where it leaked eagerly against the dark bedspread.

"That's it," Richard growled, lips dragging across my sensitive skin before he dug his teeth gently into the back of my neck in warning. "Relax, baby. Let me in."

I did as he said, relaxing until I felt his thighs press against mine, his pelvis flush with my ass. By the time I was ready for him to move, his hips were making these aborted little thrusts, like he just couldn't help himself. I wondered what it felt like for him, to be enveloped in liquid heat, his big cock snug inside my tiny little hole. It was the single hottest thing I'd ever experienced in all my twenty-three years of life.

"You're so tight," Richard breathed against the back of my neck. I pressed back against him, listening to him gasp as I squeezed around his girth. My cock jumped at the sound and a fresh drop of precum slipped from the tip and down onto the mattress. "So fucking—hot inside."

His hips twitched inside me. Somehow the fact he was unable to wait for permission made the pleasure all the better.

"Can I?" Richard breathed, almost begging. "Please. I wanna—" His hips made another little thrust. "I wanna get deep—" Another thrust. "Please, baby. I need to feel you."

I couldn't bring myself to torture him anymore so I just nodded, pressing back into his pelvis in a clear signal for him to continue. I remembered after a moment how important it had been to him that I be verbal so I forced myself to speak, even though it was the hardest thing I'd ever done.

"*Fuck me.*"

Those two words were all he needed to start moving in earnest. It was like he truly couldn't help himself, his hips slapping hard enough to make my ass bounce—the sound loud enough it rivaled the *thump* of the bed frame hitting the wall. He grunted every time he pulled out, sinking back in, his teeth catching on my spine, my shoulders, the back of my neck.

"Oh fuck, oh fuck," Richard whimpered, fucking me harder.

I was being loud and I couldn't help myself. Little 'ah, ah, ah' noises filled the room every time he sunk inside me on a particularly enthusiastic thrust. He was thick and hard—velvety soft as his crown caught on my rim every time he pulled back, before popping back inside and filling me full again. It felt so good my eyes rolled back, my tongue lolling as my hole sucked him greedily inside with a wet *squelch*. I had never been so full in all my life. This wasn't like the times I'd fucked myself—or when I'd fantasized about this very thing. It was better, so much better.

Richard was sweat, and sex, and passion. Every noise that escaped his lips sounded like it was being punched out of him. I doubted he ever let himself go like this outside of the bedroom, and that only made it sweeter that he felt safe enough with me to do so.

Several long minutes passed and I whined even louder. I knew all I had to do was brush a hand up against my cock and I was going to spill all over his mattress, but I didn't want to come first, not when I knew Richard still had more of himself to give.

"I'm close," he urged, voice breathless and sweet where it trailed over the shell of my ear. I could feel my hair in my mouth but I didn't care, allowing myself to get fucked harder and harder, hard enough I began to sob into the pillows as his pelvis slapped against my ass.

I'd never felt this close to another person before. I wasn't sure if that was the thought that eventually ended up sending me over, or maybe it was the fact that Richard made this angry little grunting noise right into the shell of my ear. Either way, it was an instant explosion of bliss and I came, my cock spurting against my fingers where I'd reached down to grab it.

I fucked my fist through my orgasm, lights flickering behind my lids as pleasure coursed like blood through my veins and my cum slipped between my sticky fingers.

Richard whined, a low animalistic sound as his hips fucked up once, twice, three times before stilling. I knew it wasn't over though. His orgasm was just the beginning. The seconds stretched on for what seemed like hours as we both caught our breath.

I don't know what I'd expected, but this was better. Richard's lips trailed down over my neck, making love to it with his tongue as he reached around me with both massive arms and hauled me up into his lap. He was still inside me and I whimpered, trembling as his hips jerked up on instinct, never mind the fact we both had already come.

I dangled, gasping for breath as he pressed me tight against his sweaty chest, his thick thighs spreading me open, his cock twitching where it remained buried deep inside me. I knew what was coming and still I felt surprised when his teeth dragged over my neck, slow, deliberate.

There was no warning, no more words exchanged between us as Richard's fangs trailed a tantalizing dance down my sensitive flesh and his tongue laved, wet and eager over the skin between my neck and shoulder. I tipped my head to the side, giving him more room to work, wordless permission that I wanted what he was about to do.

"Please," I croaked.

He broke.

The first thing I felt was pain. It seared through my veins, making my head spin and my mouth go dry. A broken noise escaped my lips, my fingers turning to claws where they dug into Richard's thick forearms, where he held me prisoner against the rippling muscle of his chest.

Then the pain melted away, morphing, changing, evolving into a pleasure so all-encompassing that for a long, frightening moment I forgot what it felt like to breathe. I wasn't Blair anymore, I was pleasure and sin. I was hunger. I was lust. I trembled with the force of feeling, my head spinning as I heard Richard inhale greedily and I felt him begin to suck.

The pulling sensation of blood leaving my body was unlike anything I'd ever felt before. It felt like we were connected, our very molecules blending together into one as Richard's body became my own and he eagerly absorbed the very essence of me.

My eyelids were purple when I shut them, the pleasure making me limp as Richard held me firmly while he drank, and drank, and drank.

When he finished, he helped me gingerly down onto the bed with big, gentle hands. The comforter was soft against my belly and I must've dozed for a moment because when I opened my eyes, all I had to do was glance over my shoulder to see him again. My hole clenched, sloppy and wet, and I whimpered. I was dazed, my head foggy, as I tried to make sense of Richard's expression.

Minutes or hours could've passed, though the room remained dark.

"You good, sweetheart?" he hummed, crowding up behind me, his unclothed cock resting against my right ass cheek. I didn't feel sticky so I figured he must have cleaned us off at some point but I'd missed it. Though I missed his cock inside me the most. It felt like time was skipping frames but I didn't mind, because for once in my life I could finally be blissfully, wonderfully, *amazingly* still.

"M'good," I slurred, blinking up at him sleepily as he cupped my cheek in his large, broad palm and gently pushed my hair behind my ears.

"You did so good, baby," Richard urged, his thumb tracing circles along my temple. It was hard to look at him—to look at anything really—but I managed. His gaze was heavy, his eyes a brighter red than I'd ever seen them before. There was a little streak of blood leaking out of the corner of his mouth and I wanted to smooth it away with my thumb but I didn't know how my hands worked anymore.

"Did I taste good?" I asked, because apparently being fucked made me stupid.

"You tasted delicious," Richard laughed, his brow scrunching up with amusement as he continued to pet me.

"I'm all sweaty," I complained, embarrassed that he could probably feel how wet the hair at my temples was.

"It's okay, I am too," Richard reassured me. I realized he was right, because our thighs were practically sticking together and I laughed, wiggling to get comfortable. He gave me a gentle little squeeze.

"Sleep it off, sweetheart," Richard urged softly, leaning down to kiss one of my disgustingly sweaty temples. "I'll make you something to eat when you wake up."

"Really?" I asked, surprised and pleased, my words still slurring on the tip of my tongue.

"Whatever you want," Richard agreed. Then he paused, quiet for a second as he seemed to mull over his next words. "Was it… I mean…" He trailed off, looking more insecure than I'd ever seen him look before.

His face said, 'Did I do okay?'

It said, 'I've never done this before.'

It said, 'Please, tell me I didn't hurt you.'

"It was the most fucking awesome experience I've ever had," I told him, somehow magically finding the words to reassure him. He melted, sagging in relief, his head dropping down so he could bury his face in my neck while his arms squeezed me close. "Ten out of ten, would recommend. Would do again. Repeatedly."

"Thank god," Richard whispered against my neck, and then he laughed.

That was the last thing I remembered before I fell asleep, my eyelids too heavy to hold themselves up anymore.

Safe, content, loved.

Chapter Thirty-Three

Blair

I SPENT THE night at Richard's for the first time. Well, the first time since we'd become...whatever it was we'd become. It was different now. When the morning sunlight began creeping in through the sun blockers over the windows, I blinked my eyes open and stared at the ceiling. The sunlight was so muted it hardly did a thing at all other than allow my eyes enough light that I could finally make out the details of the room.

Richard's room was just as orderly as the rest of his house. Aside from the trail of clothing he'd opted to leave on the floor. I snorted softly, realizing he'd probably felt pretty proud of our debauchery and wanted to remember it. I examined the rest of the room, noting the sparse walls and the single nightstand made of beige wood beside his king-sized bed. I was actually surprised he had a king bed at all, he seemed more like the type to have a queen or a twin, never expecting guests.

Maybe even Richard liked to have luxurious things.

I realized that train of thought was kinda ridiculous actually considering the fact that the man wore fucking designer boots. Of course he liked nice things.

Now that I knew him better I knew he'd probably spent three weeks picking the perfect pair. He'd probably researched it too—compared prices, quality, design.

What a giant fucking nerd.

I kinda loved him.

Richard wasn't in the room so I took my time rising. Surprisingly, my neck didn't hurt, and when I reached up to test the injured skin there was nothing left behind for me to inspect. The skin was clean, not a scab or bruise, nothing that caused pain at all even with all my poking and prodding.

When I was done I rose from the bed, grimacing as I picked through Richard's dresser for something to wear, and trudged all the way to the bathroom. I showered off the sweat and other things from the night before, feeling refreshed as I stepped into the stolen clothes and stared at my reflection in the foggy mirror.

It was hard to see so I raised a hand and smudged away the condensation.

I looked…the same.

I wasn't sure why that surprised me. I didn't know what I'd expected. That no longer being a virgin meant I'd somehow look older? More refined? It seemed funny just thinking about it. I shook my head to clear it and leaned close enough I could inspect the side of my neck properly. Just as I'd suspected: Nothing.

Richard probably had some sort of venom or something to speed up the healing. I added that to my growing list of questions I needed to ask him. I shrugged and sighed, pulling away and trying not to feel self-conscious as my too-big eyes, and too-big ears stared back at me.

I'd never liked my face. I couldn't really see what Richard saw in me. But then again, I wasn't sure if my personal criticisms had come from my own lips or from my aunt's, so there was that too.

When I made my way into the kitchen I found Richard there. He was scrambling something on the stove with Boots wrapped around his neck in a mirror of what I always did. They both perked up the moment they saw me. "I heard you get up," he said, because that wasn't creepy at all.

"Like…normal people heard me? Or 'you were listening to my breathing pattern' heard me?" I tried to verify, poking fun at him as I wandered closer, walking gingerly because my hips ached a bit. It wasn't bad. We'd been careful, but I could still feel the phantom pleasure of his cock pushing up inside me with every step I took.

"The…first one?"

"Liar." I grinned, leaning over to inspect what he was making. Tofu stir-fry. *Fuck yes.* A weird breakfast meal—but hey—the man was cooking for me, I wasn't going to complain. "I have to go back to Chastity's place soon," I hummed, hooking my chin around his bicep to spy as his other hand gently stirred the veggies. I could smell them browning up, the scent of pepper and spice filling my nose as I sighed happily and melted against his side. Boots stared at me with his big yellow-green eyes and I smiled right back at him, reaching up to stroke along the white patch between his eyes. He blinked me away, clearly annoyed.

"I thought you didn't have work till the diner was repaired?" Richard asked thoughtfully, shifting us around until he had me sandwiched in the crease of his elbow, his body half shielding me from the heat of the pan.

"Yeah," I hummed. "That's true. I just...don't wanna be a dick, you know? They're letting me stay there and I've barely been there at all this week. I'm sure they're both wondering where I am."

"That's sweet of you," Richard commented softly, glancing down at me, his lips ticking upwards. "You know they don't expect you to be there all the time though, right?"

"I know." I shrugged. "I just... I don't want to be rude."

"Okay," Richard hummed, leaning down and placing a frankly adorable kiss to my forehead that had me tingling all the way down to my toes. "Eat first. Then we'll head out. You can leave Boots here if it's easier." Richard grinned. "I may or may not need a reason to trick you into coming back sooner rather than later."

"Yeah, yeah. You sneaky motherfucker. *I see you.*" I grinned. Richard laughed.

"I should get some rest anyway, I'm not usually up this late—I've got something going on tonight too—but I didn't want you to have to wake up alone."

Technically I *had* woken up alone, but I didn't point that out.

I was mildly curious what his plans for the night were if they didn't entail fucking me—but I figured I'd ask him later.

Breakfast was a quiet affair, but not because we didn't want to speak. There was a warmth between us now that hadn't been there before, an understanding. Richard watched me eat like a total creep though he tried not to be obvious about it, and I groaned around every particularly delicious bite of food.

By the time we settled into the car, my belly was full and my heart was fuller. I didn't know what the future held for Richard and I but for now I was content with what we had. He made me smile more than anyone I'd ever met before, and just talking to him made the world around me slow down, and made the present more tolerable.

It was barely ten when we pulled up to Vanity and Chastity's apartment. I felt a little weird living there still, but I figured it was only a matter of time before I found my own place and moved on. I spotted Vanity's car as I waved goodbye to Richard and headed towards the entrance.

I stared up at the building in front of me, finding it more intimidating now that I'd spent the past twenty-four hours in Richard's cozy home. It looked...too big. Too *fancy*. I sighed, shaking my head at myself.

I was being ridiculous. Fucking ridiculous.

I regretted leaving Boots with Richard as I crossed the sterile front lobby, tossing a wave at the employee that manned the front desk. I'd been attempting to befriend him since my first night here, despite the fact that he'd given me that same suspicious gaze everyone else did when they met me. At least now I understood why. Before, I'd just figured he'd never seen a boy with ten plants in his arms and a cat around his neck.

So, yeah. I didn't blame him.

Just thinking about what my mom had done made me sick to my stomach. And to be associated with that...wherever I went...god, maybe it really was best I move on from this town. No. *No.* They'd just have to deal with it. Fuckers. I was staying. Fuck them all.

I hit the number for our floor on the elevator and listened to the music playing on the speakers in silence. Before I could get my key out the door to the apartment clicked open.

"Hey," I grinned, feeling more chipper than normal as Vanity opened the door the rest of the way and her dark, assessing gaze met mine. There was something…different about her. Her eyes were ringed with dark circles, her normally perfectly coiffed hair disheveled like she'd just woken up. For most people it wouldn't have been that alarming, but this was Vanity—the girl that wouldn't be caught dead without her Louboutins and red lipstick.

She let me into the apartment, shutting the door behind me with a *snick*. I stared at her back, brow furrowed in concern. "You okay?" I asked after a moment, confused and worried.

She shook her head, clearly debating with herself as she very slowly turned to face me. "Where were you?" She asked.

I blinked in confusion. "What?"

"Where were you?" Vanity repeated. "Last night. Yesterday. The day before that too. You keep disappearing and no one knows where you're going."

A weird suspicious feeling began to bubble up in my chest and I narrowed my eyes at her, debating how to respond. My fight-or-flight response kicked in, years of this exact line of questioning burning bright in my chest.

Where were you, Blair?

Who were you with?

What were you doing?

"I don't like your tone of voice," I pointed out, surprised by how quickly the bravery overtook me as I took an awkward shuffling step away from her. I suddenly wished I hadn't left Richard's house at all. This seemed like it was leading nowhere good.

"I'm sorry," Vanity sighed, reaching up to pinch the bridge of her nose. "I just…" She grimaced, emotions performing gymnastics across her face before she spoke again. "I was worried."

Oh.

Oh.

That was kinda nice right? She didn't need to worry but it was sweet that she had.

"It's cool."

"It's just—" She chewed on her lip, eyes darkening as she stared down at my shoes. "With the whole fire and shooting thing…we're all pretty on edge."

I nodded, shuffling awkwardly from side to side. Should I hug her? Was that what I was supposed to do? I really liked Vanity but interacting with her was nowhere near as effortless as interacting with Richard was.

"So where were you?" Vanity asked again, her tone softer this time. For some reason I felt apprehensive answering her, but I figured in the grand scheme of things it wasn't a bad idea to have both sisters know where I was.

"Um. Richard Prince's place," I hedged, feeling weirdly protective of this little truth. I didn't want to share it, not with her, not with anyone. But that was silly right? It wasn't like I was ashamed of being with Richard. It was the opposite, in fact. I coveted it. Our time together was ours alone, precious as spun gold.

Vanity's eyes bulged out of her head for a second and she paused, arms crossed in front of her, one of her long painted fingers tapping along her forearm as she seemed to mull over how to respond.

Man, I didn't think my sex life mattered this much. Why was she freaking out like that?

"Richard?" she clarified. I nodded, not sure how much clearer I could've been.

"Tall, blond, hunky." I shrugged, and mentally apologized to Richard for objectifying him. He was so much more than his appearance. I knew that better than anyone.

"Wow." She blinked. "I did not see that coming."

"Me neither." I shrugged, sure we were going to move on now that the big reveal was over. I was about to turn to head through the living room to my bedroom but she stopped me, her nails digging into the soft flesh on my upper arm in a way that made my blood curdle.

"Blair, wait." Her voice was full of urgency, her dark eyes full of fear. I paused, even though my heart was beating wildly in my chest and I couldn't help but want to get away as quickly as possible. The feeling of acrylic meeting my flesh reminded me too much of things I had sworn, for my own sanity, I would never think of again. "I don't think you hanging around Richard is the best idea."

Her words cut through my panic and I blinked in confusion. "What? Why?"

It seemed ridiculous to me that anyone in town could possibly dislike Richard. He was so serious and sweet, there wasn't a single bone in his body that could cause a look as dark as the one on Vanity's face.

"There's stuff you don't know about him," Vanity hedged.

"Yeah, if you're talking about the vampire thing, that's old news," I shrugged. Once again she blinked at me, eyebrows raising as she inspected me. She was probably looking for signs of an existential crisis but lucky for her, and me, there were none.

"That…wasn't the only thing I was talking about," she added softly, her lips thinning. They were painted red as per usual but somehow they lacked her usual luster.

Man, she was really torn up about all of this, wasn't she?

"Then what were you talking about?" I questioned, confused and more than a little alarmed. *More secrets? Jesus Christ, did it ever end?* And I'd thought the supernatural reveal thing had been the biggest secret being kept from me.

"Look." Vanity sighed, releasing me for long enough that she could fold her arms again. She looked tiny in her red silk pajamas despite the fact that she was easily a head taller than me even without her heels on. "It's probably easier if I just…show you."

"Okay, so show me." I waited and she sighed, glancing to the left and staring almost angrily at the sofa like it was its fault I was being difficult. Prudence's face stared back from the portrait behind it and I shuddered, looking back to Vanity, confused and annoyed.

"I can't…until tonight."

I blinked at her, confused. But…she really did look freaked out, and I didn't know what else to say, so I just agreed. Besides, Richard had told me he was busy tonight so I figured there was no harm in humoring her.

What was the worst that could happen, right?

Famous last words.

It was dark out. So dark I couldn't see more than a few feet in front of me. Vanity had insisted that we walk to the Town Hall as it wasn't that far from their apartment and she didn't want either of our cars to be spotted. I thought it was kinda weird she was being so secretive but I didn't want to judge.

So we walked, working our way behind houses and businesses that should have been bursting with life in typical Elmwood fashion. But... just like the night I'd stumbled upon the secret, everything remained completely empty. We were careful not to be seen, even though there was hardly anyone about. I continuously glanced Vanity's way, both curious and apprehensive. I wondered why Chastity hadn't been invited to this—I hardly ever saw the two sisters apart. Maybe that should have been an omen. Vanity and I had barely ever spent time alone together, there'd usually been a buffer of people between us, and I worried I was being overly awkward as we moved silently through the night.

I wished she would break the silence but she didn't.

For once she wasn't wearing heels, instead clad in a tight pair of black jeans and sneakers that looked like they'd seen better days. It was an outfit unlike any other I'd seen her in, and I couldn't help but stare every time she stepped in front of me and I got a good look at her in her T-shirt.

When we finally reached the edge of the Town Hall property she signaled at me to be quiet. I had no idea why we were here—confusion buzzing inside my chest as I watched her walk carefully through the trees' shadows where they cast slashes of darkness across the cultivated grass. When we stepped onto the sidewalk that cut through the cultivated lawn surrounding the building her feet skipped across the cracks and I followed behind her obediently, my heart in my throat.

She led me to the side of the massive stone building, ducking underneath a long reaching tree limb before gesturing for me to go in front of her. Having her at my back felt weird, but I brushed the feeling off. I reasoned it away because I knew I'd always distrusted women, because of obvious reasons.

My anxiety felt claustrophobic.

I didn't know why, but I knew I didn't want to be there.

It didn't take long to I realize Vanity had been leading me to a window. It was cracked open, the noise from inside bleeding out onto the grass along with a patch of fragmented light. A hush fell over the crowd and I leaned in, more than curious.

"Before we continue I'd like to address a few things," a calm voice echoed out into the silence. I couldn't see inside without alerting the people to my presence, so I ducked down, shuffling close enough to the window I could hear better.

The man began to discuss a bunch of details about construction starting out on Spruce and Vine, and the fact that school was letting out early for the full moon. Apparently there were werewolf packs that were migrating through the area, and they wanted everyone to stay vigilant and keep an eye on their pups so there wasn't any conflict.

I arched an eyebrow at Vanity and she shook her head, ponytail swooping back and forth as she gestured at me to be quiet and wait. I hated waiting, but I did it anyway, cool stone brushing against my side as I huddled below the window pane. Eventually, what felt like eons later, the man talking said something more interesting.

"As for more pertinent SAC business," he spoke and I blinked in surprise, though really I shouldn't have been. *Wasn't SAC the name for the supernatural whatchamacallit that both Chastity and Richard had mentioned? The second government?*

I perked up, listening curiously, my skin prickling. My anxiety only doubled as I felt Vanity's eyes trained on me, but I ignored both her and the feeling in favor of paying attention to what the man was about to say. Somehow it seemed important. I didn't know why. Maybe it was the hush of the crowd? Or maybe it was just instinct that had me holding still.

My hands were clammy and cold as I swallowed.

"Richard Prince, the active Youth Liaison, would you please come forward?"

Wait what?

Richard?

Was this his big plan for tonight?

My brow furrowed in confusion and my gaze snapped to Vanity again to see if she knew what was going on. She just pointed at the window, forcing me to turn back to it. I knew if I stretched onto my tippy toes I'd be able to see inside but somehow deep down I knew I didn't want to know what Richard's face looked like right now.

Something wasn't right.

I could feel it in my bones.

The same way I had with the treehouse—the same way I had when I sensed Boots in peril underneath my house, or even the fire. It was a sick sort of feeling. One that left me weak-kneed and reeling.

"Richard here has been an excellent asset for our town, especially recently. As you all know, SAC and the City Council work hand in hand as often as we can to resolve issues that affect the townspeople and our livelihood." The deep voice continued, "As most of you are aware, a few months ago the Evans's heir stepped foot back inside our town. It was brought to The Council's attention immediately and action was sought to soothe any of the fears you all might have."

"Many years ago our town was rocked with the tragedy revolving around the Evans family and their deaths. We had reason to believe that their son's return could be influenced by an act of insanity or even revenge. No one was more concerned than us that there would be a repeat of his mother's crimes." There was murmuring then, voices echoing through the room as the crowd seemed to process this. It was loud enough I figured there had to be at least a hundred people gathered, maybe even the whole town.

The mention of my mother made my already sweat-clammy skin turn to ice.

What was Richard's part in this?

Why would I seek revenge? It wasn't like it was the town's fault my mother had started killing people.

Now that I knew the secret I understood why they held the meetings at night, but that was the last thing on my mind as the councilman's words ricocheted like pinballs inside my head. *Insane? Me?* Maybe I'd worried I was once upon a time, but I knew now I wasn't. It wasn't like that could be genetic, could it? God, the thought hadn't even occurred to me— not even when I'd moved here and rediscovered their deaths—or when Chastity had mentioned it.

I was average. Normal. Maybe with an extra sprinkle of trauma, but I was dealing with that in the healthiest way I could.

But they didn't know that. I supposed in a fucked-up way it made sense that they'd wanted to make sure I wasn't up to no good.

What my mom had done colored everyone's perception of me. That had been obvious from the moment I'd stepped into town.

"Richard stepped forward and volunteered to monitor our new guest, looking for signs of deceit. His task was to make sure the town wouldn't be rocked with another tragedy as it had been in the past."

My ears were ringing, my hands shaky and cold, but I couldn't turn away.

Richard had…

Richard had been *watching* me?

What the fuck.

"We believe there's been sufficient time for Richard to have gathered a feel for why Evans would be back in town," the man continued, eviscerating me with his words as memories from my first interactions with Richard popped into my head. He'd been suspicious, watching me with those dark eyes, asking me millions of questions. God. Fuck. *Fucking fuck.* I was so stupid.

Had all of it been a lie?

No. *No.* Maybe they just meant at the diner? But we'd gone past that. We were…we were *more* than that.

Please, god, let it be just at the diner.

Don't take this from me.

Please.

"He's been observing him in and outside of work," the man said.

All my hopes crumpled to the ground as those words truly hit.

I thought of kisses that tasted like seawater, homemade stir-fry, the way Richard had painted my nails and arched his eyebrows at me when I'd told him he looked like Fred from Scooby Doo. I thought of his greedy hands, his bright pink tongue, the way his lips danced when he found me funny, his dimples, his *laugh*—the—the—*romancing?* The way he'd held me tight the night before. The way he'd cradled my face in his massive palms and his scarlet eyes had promised me forever.

Maybe that had been a lie too.

Had it all been a ploy to get me to let my guard down so he could find out why I'd come to town in the first place?

So he could pry my secrets from my fragile chest, only to parade them in front of strangers that only saw me as a shadow of my mother.

God, I felt so stupid.

That couldn't be all this was right?

It couldn't.

Because I'd *told* him. I'd fucking told him everything he'd needed last night and still we'd…we'd…

There were noises and words that I didn't catch as Richard was brought up to what I assumed was the microphone. The sickness that rolled inside me only grew blacker and blacker the longer I stood their listening. I wanted to leave. I didn't want to hear this. I didn't want to hear what he'd say about me. I didn't want to hear my darkest secret displayed like it was nothing more than a cheap parlor trick.

Like the years of torture, of pain, of abuse were nothing but a mission for him to accomplish.

Was that all I was?

A mission?

I turned to go, my head spinning, but Vanity reached out and held me tightly in place, her nails digging into the sensitive flesh on my upper arms. It should've hurt but I was too—

Numb, numb, numb.

She shook her head, dark eyes full of pity.

Wait, she mouthed. *Listen.*

I waited.

I listened.

"I've had the opportunity to observe Mr. Evans for the past few weeks," Richard started, his voice cool and collected but I couldn't focus on anything but what he'd called me. *Mr. Evans.* Not Blair, not *baby,* not *sweetheart.* My name in his mouth was as boring as if he'd been talking about the weather. "After careful consideration I've decided that it is impossible that he came to town to start trouble. He was running away from trouble, not towards it."

Voices murmured again but my head was spinning too much to catch the words. It didn't matter that he was clearing my name, it didn't matter that what he said was the truth. What mattered was the fact that I had trusted him. *Trusted,* Richard. Something I hadn't done for as long as I could remember. And all along…*All along he'd been using me.* Was he going to get promoted? A pay raise? Was I just a paycheck for him? A way to gain clout?

When it was clear Richard wasn't elaborating the councilman did for him. "Richard has brought it to our attention that Blair was running from an abusive home."

And there it was.

My secret. My past. The thing that had torn me to shreds, laid out in the open for all to see. Like it didn't matter. Like *I* didn't matter.

My knees practically buckled and Vanity held me up. Her lips were wobbling, a look of remorse on her face so visceral that it tore me to shreds. I wasn't imagining any of this. If I had been she wouldn't be looking at me like…that.

She took pity and released me. I immediately bent over the bushes and retched. My heart was in my throat as I threw up the poison that had built up inside me. If I'd thought I was drowning before, it was nothing compared to the sinking sensation I felt now.

My throat burned, bile rising all over again.

Blair was running from an abusive home.

"There's someone outside," a voice murmured, right up against the window.

"Hush," someone else admonished in return. Both Vanity and I jumped into action and she grabbed for me again, not pausing to even let me wipe my mouth as she began to quickly tug me away from the window and back towards the path that would lead us toward the apartment.

As I reeled and I ran, Vanity ran alongside me.

My stomach roiled and I barely managed to keep myself together, bitter sickness making my tongue burn with its acidic bite. By the time we reached her apartment again I was lightheaded and my body was numb.

I waved to the front desk guy again in a daze on our way towards the elevator, even though I felt like I'd had my heart torn out and stomped on right in front of me. He frowned in concern but waved anyway, and Vanity shuffled me into the elevator with a vicious grip.

It took the entire ride up for me to realize the reason I was hurting so badly was because somewhere, somehow I had fallen in love with Richard.

Vanity's nails squeezed hard enough to distract me. In a way the familiar pain was soothing. Comforting. It reminded me of…*her*, and while most of the time those memories accompanied panic attacks and terror, there was also the feeling of loss I felt, of comfort. Because for the longest time she had been my mother, even though she wasn't.

In a way I missed her.

I wished for a moment she was here. To hurt me. To remind me that there were things worse than the gaping wound that weeped inside my chest.

But I didn't have that.

All I had were memories.

Chapter Thirty-Four

Blair

VANITY DIDN'T BOTHER me for a while. She let me lick my wounds in private, which I was grateful for. I missed Boots. I missed my plants. I tried not to think too hard about the fact that they were tucked safe inside Richard's home and I wasn't. When I finally emerged like a droopy hermit from the darkness of my room Vanity was laying on the beige couch in the living room, a joint in hand. She waved me over, blowing smoke into the air.

I inhaled it into my lungs, collapsing opposite her, our feet bumping up against each other.

"You wanna talk about it?" she asked softly after a long, quiet pause. She handed the joint over and I stared at it, watching the tip burn bright red. I didn't feel like smoking. I didn't feel like anything.

"No." I handed it back to her, figuring it was my own right to wallow. I'd earned the pain I felt now, with every stolen kiss, every brush of fingers. It was the last part of Richard I had, because I was sure as hell never letting him touch me again.

The pain hurt, but at least I felt *something*. The crippling numbness from earlier was gone. In a way I was proud of myself, that I'd lived my life fully enough since leaving home to even experience heartache at all.

God, wasn't that sad?

I'd been so sheltered I was fucking *proud* of myself for getting my heart broken.

"When I took you there I wasn't expecting him to…" She bit her lip, shaking her head. Somehow she looked worse than I did, her hair a mess of red-tipped curls spilling across her shoulders. "I knew he was the Youth Liaison… Not that he'd just tell everyone like that…"

"Detached about it like a fucking robot?"

"Yeah," she grunted, taking another slow pull from the joint. I figured her landlord must not care about the smell, either that or her fucking wealthy family owned the building. That would make sense. She'd admitted owning the apartments that surrounded theirs, after all.

"You're a good friend," I said softly, curling my knees up to my chest. I was still wearing the clothes that Richard had bought me. The black polish on my nails was freshly painted and I stared down at them, blinking away memories as I contemplated what I was supposed to do next. Chew them off probably so I didn't have to look anymore. Then what?

When I looked up again there were tears in Vanity's eyes. She swallowed, her lips wobbling as she shifted until she was hunching over her knees, blonde curls falling forward in a curtain in front of her face.

"I'm really not," she disagreed softly, mostly to herself.

"Do you think that…" I swallowed, my throat tight, hands shaking. "Do you think it was all a lie?"

"Everything…between you and Richard?" she clarified, turning to look at me, her lashes wet. "I…don't know, Blair. I'm not really the best person to ask about that stuff, Chas has always been better at the feelings shit than me."

"But you…you grew up with him, right?" I asked. "Do you think that… Knowing him, that this is something he would do? That he would manipulate me like that? Just to…to get a promotion or…*I don't know.*" I wanted desperately to believe that I was wrong, that it was impossible. But I knew demons, and Richard had the potential to be the worst one yet.

"I don't know." She shrugged, chewing on her lip hard enough it looked like it might bleed. I probably should've realized there was something going on with her, but I was too blinded by my own heartbreak to see it. "Maybe? He…he's always been serious, you know? He follows the rules to a T. I don't think he would've done it to hurt you but…"

"But to accomplish a job he was given, maybe," I finished for her, a sick feeling twisting like a serpent in my gut. She nodded, clearly at war with herself.

"I'm going to go to bed," I said softly, my internal clock broken beyond repair by this fucked-up town.

"Get some rest," she urged, watching me with dark soulful eyes. "You'll feel better in the morning."

I nodded.

"Tomorrow will be better," she added softly. "We'll make it a good day, okay?" Her lips tipped up into a smile that was supposed to cheer me

495

up but really just looked twisted and sad on her face. "I'll take you out. There's a vegan buffet like two hours away and I'll drive you out there. We'll smoke and binge eat and you'll forget all about Richard."

"Okay," I agreed, because I knew getting out of town was probably the only thing that would stop me from confronting him. Or seeing him. Or breathing in the pine needles and remembering his scent.

I'd have to pick up Boots soon, but I figured I could ask Chastity, or even Vanity for help.

That was a problem for future Blair, and not present Blair. My head was too foggy to come up with solutions right now.

"It'll be the best last day ever," Vanity said softly. "I promise."

I didn't know what she meant by 'last day,' but I shrugged to myself, heading into the kitchen to get a glass of water before I went off to bed. That night I dreamed again, but for once it was a pleasant dream, full of sunshine and not violence.

It was summer. The sun was blinding, the world full of wonder as I laughed and laughed, chasing my mother's shadow through the woods. Her voice echoed between tree trunks, wrapping around their branches and pulling me towards where I could see the flap of her long, pale blue skirt.

"You snooze, you lose!" she called with an evil little chortle that made me pick up speed and plow clumsily onwards. She'd promised me earlier if I could catch her she'd bake me my favorite cookies, and I was still young enough that the promise of a treat was the highest reward she could've given me.

Tree limbs whipped my skin, but I ignored the pain, plowing forward with my breath puffing and my throat burning.

I stumbled a little when I had finally almost caught up to her. She stood still up ahead. I knew it wasn't winning if she stopped before me— but maybe I could convince her to make me cookies anyway. I plowed into her back, smooshing up against the soft fabric of her skirt as I inhaled the scent of brown sugar and home.

I peeked around her to see what had made her stop—and I saw the forest before me open up into a massive clearing. It was full of wildflowers and bugs, fluttering from bud to bud as the sunlight painted the tall grass gold. In the center of the clearing was a tree, so thick around the base my little mind could not comprehend it. It was larger than life, a giant in a world full of ants.

Most amazing of all, however, was the treehouse I saw perched atop its branches. There were real windows and everything, and a roof with shingles that protected it from the near constant rain. Behind the glass I could make out movement but I didn't look too closely. Instead my attention quickly snapped to the rope ladder that hung down the tree trunk from the bottom of the house all the way to the meadow floor.

"What do you think lives in there?" I asked her, surprised and delighted. "Elves?"

Mom laughed, twisting around to look at me. The sunlight blocked her face and I squinted up at her to try and make out her features. I couldn't. She was nothing but a blur, her warm, soft fingers reaching down to ruffle my unruly hair.

"A whole bunch of little boys do," she teased softly.

"Like Peter Pan?" I clarified and she laughed again, shaking her head.

"Something like that." She shrugged, turning back to stare at the treehouse.

A butterfly flitted in front of us and my attention caught on it immediately. "The boys inside aren't lost though."

"They're not?"

"No." *She shook her head.* "But…" *Something in her expression wavered.* "You can never really tell if someone's lost just by looking at them anyway."

"Oh." *I didn't really understand but I pretended to; I didn't like looking stupid. She scrubbed a hand through my hair again, and I tipped my head to look up at her. Her long dark hair tickled my cheeks as she bent down, kneeling so she could look me in the eye.*

Despite being eye level, she was still blurry and I wished more than anything that I could see the details of her face one last time.

"There will be times in your life when you're lost, Blair. You won't know where to go to move forward." *I listened, because I didn't know what else to do. I wanted to go home and eat cookies and I knew if I interrupted that might not happen for a long time. I could be patient, at least when cookies were at stake.* "When that happens, I want you to think of this moment," *my mom continued, and I nodded solemnly.* "Use your heart as a compass. When something feels wrong, listen."

I nodded again, attention caught on another butterfly. She laughed and sighed, pinching my cheeks in retaliation for not listening before she rose and took my hand.

"You caught me, didn't you?" *I didn't, but I wasn't about to tell her that.*

She hummed to herself, her chipper spark back as she squeezed my hand and began leading me through the woods towards home.

I glanced one last time over my shoulder at the treehouse, before I turned my back on it and the little not-lost boys inside.

"Cookies?" *I implored and my mother laughed.*

"Cookies."

Vanity was acting weird. When Chastity had arrived home the next day and greeted us she'd given her sister a strange look before looking back at me and mouthing 'everything okay?' I'd just shrugged and nodded, equally concerned.

Vanity was wearing sweatpants.

Sweatpants.

Her hair was somehow even more disheveled than it had been the night before, tucked into a messy bun atop her head, but most notable of all was the fact that she'd opted not to wear makeup. She kissed Chastity on the cheek, smiling at her sister and tucking a strand of her hair behind her ear before she headed off to the bathroom to brush her teeth before our excursion.

As soon as she was out of earshot, Chastity drew closer to me, her brow furrowed in concern. "What's up with her?"

"I don't know." I shrugged, chewing on my lip. I didn't really want to get into the whole Richard thing again so I didn't bring it up. I'd been trying not to think about it really. My dream was still fresh on my mind, the treehouse in my memories burned like a brand on my subconscious. It felt strange to relate it to the husk of a tree I'd seen when I'd first moved to town. Now that I knew what had happened there all the memories were tainted.

"Wait, what day is it?" Chastity fumbled her phone out of her back pocket. I didn't comment on the fact that she hadn't come home the previous night, noting the lack of change of outfit and the way her sweet little space buns looked like they had been tugged on.

Chastity had gotten laid.

"Fuck," she swore softly as she pulled up the calendar app on her phone. "It's…the nineteenth? *Really?*"

"Yes?" I hedged, even though I didn't know what day it was. April seventeenth would forever be burned in my memory though, for good or for bad, because that was the day that Richard had taken me to the beach and I'd given him a part of me I could never take back.

My heart hurt.

"It's today," Chastity fretted and I stared at her, trying to figure out what she was talking about.

And then I remembered and guilt churned in my gut because I'd forgotten.

Prudence's death.

Their brother.

No wonder Vanity was acting all weird. Chastity had warned me that this day was especially hard for her. Maybe she needed distracting and distance as much as I did? Prudence's portrait glared at me from over the couch and I shuddered.

When Vanity returned, she brought with her a new perspective. I smiled at her, watched her face bunch up in confusion because of how unnatural the expression looked on my face probably, and then turned away to give her privacy with her sister.

I'd never lost a brother. I couldn't imagine what it would feel like to wake up one day and discover that Jeffrey was gone. The loss of my parents was different. It ached deep down inside me but it had been so long since it had happened, and there had been so much trauma between now and the last time I'd seen them that they were nothing but a distant memory.

We were quiet for most of the car ride to the buffet. I tried to ease the awkwardness of the silence and Vanity did too but there was a wedge between us like neither of us really knew how to bridge the distance. I thought it was strange that Chastity hadn't been invited again, but I figured maybe she had her own way of grieving. Or maybe she just wanted to spend the day with her mystery lover and forget about the whole thing all over again.

Good for her.

The girl deserved a good railing.

The line for the buffet was surprisingly long, and made only more unbearable because the tense silence between myself and Vanity was in stark contrast with the conversation around us. She hadn't bothered to change, opting instead to remain in her black sweatpants and a thin white tank top that hugged her figure. She received more than a few appreciative looks and I surreptitiously slipped up against her side, wrapping an arm around her waist protectively to get people to back off even though the motion felt foreign at first.

She smiled at me gratefully, wrapping an arm around my shoulders, though there was a look in her eye I couldn't quite decipher. "You my boyfriend now?" she laughed softly, the dark circles under her eyes even more prominent than they'd been the day before. It looked like she hadn't been sleeping.

I puffed up my chest and shrugged. "Hey, I may be small, but I'm still a guy. I could beat someone up." I wasn't sure I was convincing even myself.

She snorted and laughed. "Sure thing, tough guy."

"I'm serious." I wasn't serious. There was no way in hell I'd last in a confrontation. But then... I really thought about it and I realized that wasn't true.

Maybe the Blair that had moved to Elmwood would've rolled over and taken a beating—or run for it at the first sign of a fight—but the person I was now... There was no way in hell I'd let anyone harass her, or anyone else I cared about.

Somehow, I didn't know when, something inside me had changed.

I wasn't the same scared little boy who had fled his childhood home and the only family he'd ever known for the possibility of freedom.

Maybe by staying... I'd found what I'd been looking for all along?

My backbone.

I was so full I felt like I needed to be rolled to the car after we left the buffet. It had been such a long time since I'd done something like that that I couldn't help but feel my spirits lift.

My phone buzzed in my back pocket but I ignored it, figuring it was Richard and I wasn't ready to confront him yet. I'd only recently turned the phone back on after self-imposed isolation. But having a backbone didn't mean I was ready to use it yet.

The ride back to town was quiet but much less awkward. The sun was high in the sky for once, though there were dark clouds on the horizon, slowly creeping in. We would get rain that night but I found myself welcoming the thought. The idea of the earth being cleansed was therapeutic.

Maybe I was just feeling zen because of all the burritos I'd eaten.

My muddy emotion from the day before seemed so far away now as I sighed, leaning back in the vegan-leather seats—I'd Googled it out of curiosity—my elbow dangling out the window as I watched the trees blur by and I listened to the quiet murmur of the radio echoing throughout the cabin of the car.

"Is there something else you want to do?" Vanity asked quietly. We still had an hour to go until we'd be back in Elmwood and I was struck with inspiration.

"The beach," I decided.

"The beach?" She arched an eyebrow in surprise but shrugged, handing over her phone to me so that I could plug in the GPS coordinates.

The drive only took fifteen minutes off the interstate. I blinked out at the sun, wondering not for the first time, whether Richard missed this. Did he still have the human desire to bask in the warmth, to feel it paint his eyelids, to let it bleed inside his pores? He'd said he'd been recently turned. I wondered if somewhere deep down he regretted it.

It wasn't the first time I'd had the thought. And now I wouldn't get the opportunity to ask.

When we pulled out onto the gravelly road I sighed, inhaling the scent of pine and missing him in a way I'd never felt before. Like there was an empty Richard-sized space beside me just waiting for him to come fill it. I hoped he'd been taking care of Boots. I knew he would be but it didn't stop me from worrying.

"You ever wish things could be different?" I found myself asking, the sun beating down on my cheeks as Vanity pulled to a stop and the crashing of the ocean echoed through the air.

"Every day," Vanity said, her voice solemn.

I could see the beach from the car despite the distance now that it wasn't dark. The waves crested white as they broke along the pale shoreline. It was just as beautiful in the daylight as it had been at night. Black and white. The same photograph but a negative of what it had been before.

The privacy and intimacy I'd felt with Richard here was gone. In its place, the sand was sun bleached and barren, my heart back home where I'd left it crumpled in the grass outside the Town Hall.

Vanity exited the car and I followed after her, shutting my door gingerly so I wouldn't accidentally slam it as we both leaned against hot metal and stared out at the water. I missed Richard again, my mind flashing back to his insistence on getting the door for me wherever we went. There were moments with him that were so inconsequential they became everything in my mind. I didn't need big declarations, I didn't need his—literal— undying love. Instead, what I craved were the little things, the things no one else would care about but meant everything to me.

I missed the crinkle at the corner of his eyes. I missed his horrible laugh. I missed the way he let me put my feet up on the dash just because he liked me. And I missed the way he filled his fridge up with food he knew I could eat, despite not eating himself, just so I wouldn't go hungry.

He did all of those things for me, never asking for praise, for recognition, but because he wanted to see the smile on my face. Because taking care of me was more important than being praised.

I swallowed the lump in my throat. "Thanks for taking me here, Vanity," I said softly, my eyes wet as a gust of wind brought salty sweetness over to rustle my bangs. I inhaled raggedly, soaking up the cleansing energy of the ocean as it righted my equilibrium and steadied me where I'd wobbled constantly since the revelation of the night before. I didn't know how to move forward, only that I needed to.

"You're welcome." Vanity was quiet again, a lost sort of sadness crossing her expression as she trembled with the cold. I wished I had a jacket to give her, like Richard had done for me. Instead I was woefully empty handed.

"Chastity told me about your brother," I said softly, watching her face shutter, like blinds being slammed over her grief.

"He loved it here," she said softly. "I haven't been back since we were kids."

I suddenly felt bad for taking her here and I moved to apologize but she held up a hand to silence me. "It's…" Vanity trailed off. "It's nice. Like visiting a part of him I thought I'd lost."

I didn't know what to say so I stayed silent. She didn't seem to mind, her eyes far away as the wind whipped strands of red-tipped hair into her face. Without makeup on she looked young, like the child inside her had never truly left. It had been hidden, a device used to cloak her own vulnerability.

"I would do anything to see him again," she told me quietly, dark eyes full of a sadness I could only imagine. She looked at me, her lips wobbling. "You get that right?" She searched my gaze for understanding, seeming to relax when she saw it.

"I do," I agreed, thinking about Jeffrey.

About Richard.

About Collin.

About Chastity.

I thought about how I'd feel if they had been taken from me, if I knew the last time I'd seen them would be the very last. So yeah, I could sympathize.

At the end of the day it didn't matter what Prudence had done, he'd still been their brother. His death was still a tragedy. That's the thing about death. It's fair that way.

Everyone gets equally punished.

The remaining hour towards Elmwood the sun began to set. My phone buzzed in my pocket again and I sighed, finally pulling it out. With salt in my hair and the ocean in my blood I felt braver than I had earlier. I opened my phone, frowning as I saw I'd missed more texts than I'd thought I had.

I opened Jeffrey's message first. He hadn't talked to me since our last phone call and anxiety bubbled up in my gut as I saw his words. The text was timestamped midnight the previous night, probably right after I'd headed out with Vanity.

Man, had it really been that long since I checked my phone?

Jeffrey: Hey, man. Call me.

That wasn't too weird on its own. Maybe he had more advice about Richard for me? I'd forgotten to tell him how well it had worked out for me before. I scrolled through my phone towards Richard's name, hovering over it as I debated whether or not I wanted to read what he'd said.

I was apparently brave now though, so I instead of waiting until later I forced myself to open the texts.

Richard: How are you feeling?

My heart hurt as I realized he'd sent that probably right before he headed to The Council meeting to testify about me. I didn't know how to feel about it, brow furrowed as I stared down at my phone.

Richard: When can I see you again?

Richard: I'm free tonight. Boots misses you. I do too.

There was a photo attached of Boots curled up on Richard's chest and my heart did a little flutter thing that made me weak-kneed.

Richard: I watered your plants. They're drooping without you.

Man. The guy knew how to lay it on thick. I couldn't help but smile as I texted back.

Blair: They're always drooping.

I froze before pressing send as the previous night caught up to me again and confusion flooded my chest as I deleted the text.

Those were timestamped this morning. Man. I wasn't stupid enough not to realize those were *not* the texts of a man who had been using me as a means to an end. It would've been easy for him to share our virginity, finish his job as Liaison, and then ghost me.

He hadn't though.

He was literally still texting me. Maybe… Maybe this hadn't been what I thought, but maybe it wasn't the worst possible option either? Maybe Richard genuinely liked me? Maybe everything between us had been authentic? Maybe he'd completed his job as quickly as he could so that he could be with me for real?

What a wild concept.

Still shitty, but hey, I'd take it.

I was learning to be positive, to be brave, to respect myself.

The possibility of a future for me in Elmwood bubbled up inside my chest. So what if my aunt found me? I had people to rally behind me. I wasn't the scared little boy who had left her condo bloodied and broken. I'd already decided I wouldn't let her hurt me again. Maybe that was naive of me, but *god*. I'd spent so long running it felt monumental for once to decide to just…stop.

I was stuck at a crossroads and it was up to me to decide which way to turn. Should I repeat the pattern, should I follow the part of me that quaked with fear, the careful part, the kid who had seen far too much, far too soon?

Or did I take the path that led me to possibility?

It was uncertain sure, but nothing I'd experienced so far that had been worth much of anything had been certain.

Did I chase the sunlight instead of running to hide in the dark?

One thing was certain, despite the fact that nothing really was.

I refused to listen to the voice in my head that called me a coward any longer. Whatever it may bring I had made my decision, and my choice was to bet on myself for once in my goddamn life.

I chose me.

I chose what would make *me* happy.

Richard made me happy. Even if he was a dick who spied on me. I could take a chance on him, confront him about it—see where it went.

Because I was brave now, I typed out a response. Before I'd come to Elmwood, the person I'd been would've cut and run at the slightest sign of rocky shores. But I wasn't him anymore. Overnight Pinocchio had become a real boy, my shattered edges mended by my own courage. The moment I realized this, the waters that had been slowly drowning me since I was a child receded.

Blair: Been out with Vanity

Blair: We need to talk. Can you pick me up from my place in thirty minutes?

Oh god. Oh god-ohgodohgodohgod. I'd said '*we need to talk.*' Like one of those cheap but good rom-coms from the '90s. I was both proud and disgusted with myself. How cliché. Another text pinged in almost immediately.

Richard: Everything okay?

It was kinda wild thinking that maybe my words caused him just as much anxiety as his words caused me. The sun was still up so this was early for him. Maybe I'd woken him up? Or maybe he'd been nervous when I hadn't texted back and hadn't been able to fall asleep. The concept that we both could affect each other so strongly gave me hope. I'd never been someone's first choice, or even their second.

Richard was... He was different.

With him I didn't feel like an honorary mention, but like I was the *only* option. Not because there was no better choice but because I was the best choice. The No-Brainer. The idea that for once in my life I could be, not just accepted, not just tolerated—but special—was enough to make my heart weak.

When I glanced up I realized I'd been zoning out for long enough that we'd passed into town limits. Vanity was speeding down Main Street and, instead of pulling away from Spruce and to her apartment complex, she continued onward. We passed the church, the police station, and the Town Hall.

I blinked, confused as I watched businesses blur into residences, and then become a spread of never-ending trees. "Where are we going?" I asked curiously, the scent of pinesap bright with possibility in my nose.

Her knuckles were white on the steering wheel as she glanced over at me, a wobbly smile on her lips. "Just one more stop, I promise." She looked both beautiful and tragic as her hair flickered in the wind.

I shrugged, watching out the window as we traveled deeper into the woods. This road was familiar to me from my trips to my parents' house, as well as the times we'd picked up Collin. As we passed by Richard's parents' place I saw Collin's solitary figure at the end of the driveway, no doubt waiting for his brother to pick him up.

He perked up when he saw me, waving with enthusiasm, though his smile turned into a confused little frown as Vanity sped up—well over the speed limit—and rushed by. Her chest was shuddering now with each ragged breath, her eyes wet, and I realized with a sickening lurch that she was *crying.*

"Hey." My attention snapped from Collin's shrinking figure to Vanity, alarm buzzing under my skin. "You okay?"

"No," she exhaled raggedly and I reached out even though the movement felt unnatural, smoothing my hand across her knuckles where they gripped the steering wheel. Though similar in size, my hands were broader than hers, my knuckles thicker. The contrast in the shape of us was beautiful in its opposition and I squeezed her white knuckles once more before I moved my hand back.

I wasn't really the best at soothing people, that was something we actually had in common. I wanted to be better though. And I was trying, no matter how awkward it made me feel.

"You wanna talk about it?" I asked, still not sure where we were going but figuring it had something to do with Prudence.

Maybe she needed the company as much as I did.

"It's okay," Vanity exhaled raggedly, lips wobbling. I tried not to stare at her, but it was hard to reconcile this young, broken little girl with the powerful woman who had first greeted me with a cool gaze armed with vague disinterest and red bottomed heels.

There was no confidence in her expression now.

We passed the burnt-up husk of my house, the road looping around the back of it as it twisted to head in the direction of town again. I couldn't take my eyes off Vanity, a weird feeling clenching my stomach as she finally began to slow down, rocks kicking up beneath the heavy weight of the vehicle.

When Vanity pulled the car to a stop, she was shaking.

"Where are we?" I asked, curious and a little alarmed. We were in the middle of nowhere, the road having come to an abrupt end. There was a trail leading off it deep into the dark spread of trees that surrounded us, and I had a bad feeling that the moment we stepped onto the path something horrible was going to happen.

I shoved the feeling aside, in favor of comforting my friend.

"There's something I need to do, and I need your help," Vanity said softly, unable to look at me as her shoulders shook.

"Yeah, sure. Anything." I nodded. "So long as you're not like, wanting some heavy lifting or something. Pretty sure that option went out the window after my third plate at the buffet."

She laughed, though the sound was brittle. "Nah. I don't need you to do anything but keep me company."

I nodded, confused but intrigued as I watched her exit the car, her body hunched over in what I assumed was sadness. I followed after her, glancing around with apprehension as she grabbed something from the trunk and then locked the car with a click of her keys. She gestured for me to head towards the path in front of us.

"Are you going to tell me where we're going?" I asked, stepping obediently in front of her, even though having her at my back felt wrong.

God. I was being so paranoid.

Stop it, I admonished myself.

She's not your aunt.

You're fine.

"You'll see." Her answer was vague enough that I didn't bother questioning her again, instead I stepped out onto the path and into the thick line of trees.

Chapter Thirty-Five

Richard

I WAITED IN the parking lot outside Blair's apartment for ten minutes before I couldn't take the tension anymore and I headed inside. Chastity opened the apartment door and eyed me critically before stepping aside to let me in.

"You look…concerned," she said, clearly concerned herself as Boots slipped from my shoulders and scampered off to corners unknown.

"Is Blair home?"

"No. He's out with Vanity." Chastity was still giving me this weird judgmental look I probably should've read into, but I couldn't because my frozen heart was threatening to leap from my chest.

We need to talk.

Did he know? Had someone told him? Jesus fuck. My head was

spinning, my breath coming out shallowly despite the fact that I didn't technically need to breathe at all.

"Okay, buddy." Chastity patted my arm and steered me towards the couch. "You look like you need to sit down."

"I don't need to sit down." I pulled out of her grasp with a jerking motion that sent her skidding back a step. To her credit she didn't look annoyed, just concerned as she crossed her arms over her chest and my gaze snapped to her face. "Sorry." My chest. Why did it hurt? Spots were swimming in front of my vision. "Sorry," I repeated again, panicked.

"What is your deal?" she asked, a mirror of Collin's words earlier that day. He'd been yelling at me. Broken promises, he'd said. Since I hadn't told him about Blair and I—he'd found out through context clues that Blair had slept over. In my bed. Naked. Context clues being the clothing I'd left scattered on the floor, entirely unlike me, because looking at it made something young and free burst through my chest.

It felt like being alive.

Blair had worn my clothing home and I'd watched him drown in my sweatpants and tried not to want to lock him away where no one could hurt him. He'd looked so…soft like that. Like everything that had happened to him hadn't managed to break the man he'd become.

There was something about the juxtaposition of his effortless masculinity that was entirely unique. He was gorgeous in every definition of the word from the top of his fluffy head all the way down to the tops of his freckled feet.

We need to talk.

My head was spinning as I stared at his shoes where they rested neatly in the alcove by the front door. They were tiny in comparison to mine and just staring at them *hurt*.

What if he knew?

What if…

What if…everything was over before it had even begun?

Forever seemed pointless without him now that I knew what his laughter tasted like.

"Richard." Chastity's voice broke through my thoughts again and I shook my head to clear it. "You can talk to me."

"I don't want to talk to you." *Shit. That sounded harsh.* "I want to talk to Blair."

Luckily she took my words at face value, forgiving me like she saw right through my cool-guy facade and to the scared little boy quaking beneath it, quaking with fear because he might've lost the man he loved. I was realizing that with happiness came the contrast of loss. What would I do if Blair knew what I'd done and didn't forgive me?

How could I blame him?

I'd betrayed him in every sense of the word.

How could he forgive that sort of dishonesty? Especially when he'd lived a life so full of turmoil already.

Was I worth the trouble?

Boots made a distressed noise somewhere inside the apartment and I leapt into action.

A man on a mission.

Save the cat. Don't think about the boy you love. Don't think about his spring-green eyes or the way he bites his lips. Don't think about his bloody cuticles or the way he scrunches his nose when he laughs. Don't think about how right it feels to tangle your fingers in the rats nest of his ebony hair.

Don't think about how he makes you feel.

Don't think about how much you love making him smile.

Don't think about it.

Don't.

Don't don' tdon'tdon't.

Boots had somehow snuck into Vanity's room. I shoved the door open, vaguely disgusted by the chaos inside. I'd been here once before on council business, asking her questions about something inconsequential. Her parties maybe? I couldn't recall. She'd been in a hurry so for the first time she'd invited me in. Though we were friends, she never let anyone into her space—not even Chastity. I'd listened to Chastity complain about that very fact at least twenty times when we'd worked together at Benji's during my last and only year in high school.

The last time I'd been inside Vanity's room, the place had been as spotless as she always was. She'd been doing her hair and deemed my presence not important enough to stop to talk to me. So I'd spoken to her reflection and the back of her shoulder while she swooped her bangs and arched perfectly manicured eyebrows in my direction.

This was *not* the same room.

It looked like a tornado had struck it.

There was clothing everywhere, tossed about like corpses on a battleground. Plates of half-eaten food lay on every available surface. The bed was unmade and piled high with what I assumed were Vanity's work clothes. There was no way I'd find the little cat lost in this mess using my eyes alone. I stepped around a pizza box and listened intently for Boots's frantic little heartbeat.

There.

He was trapped beneath the bed.

"Hey," Chastity was behind me but I ignored the steady *thump thump* of her heart as I fell to my knees, despite the mess, and shoved clothing aside to access where the bed sheets had been basically glued to the floor with a spilled bowl of Alfredo.

The scent was unlike anything I'd smelled before.

It smelled of dead things. Of rot. Of sickness.

"Boots is stuck," I explained, finally managing to rip the sheet free though it tore through some of the carpet on its way up. Fuck.

I ducked my head under the bed and big yellow eyes peered at me in the darkness. Boots blinked and I blinked back, trying to figure out where he was stuck. From what I could see he… wasn't stuck at all.

So why was he back there? And why was he howling like that?

There was a cardboard box blocking my way and I figured if I shoved it out of the way I could reach far enough back I could grab him. The box ended up outside in the relative fresh air of the room as I shifted forward to try and get a gentle hold of Blair's cat.

If I couldn't take care of Blair anymore, the least I could do for him was not lose his fucking cat in this insanity. What if he ate something? Jesus. He could get literally ill.

"Um." Chastity's voice sounded from behind me but I ignored her, struggling to fit under the bed with the way my chest caught and the swell of my shoulders. I'd never been good at slipping into small spaces. It was one of the downsides of being a large man. I managed though, my fingers brushing soft fur as Boots continued to stare into my soul.

"Richard—"

I ignored Chastity again, figuring I could only solve one problem at a time as I stroked a hand down Boots's back and gently began tugging him towards freedom. He followed me willingly enough, which only made it stranger that he'd crawled under the bed in the first place.

"Richard, seriously."

"What?" I popped out of the darkness, my hair mussed and a small cat cradled protectively against my chest. I turned around to face her, trying to figure out what had been freaking her out so much but then my eyes landed on the box I'd pulled from the darkness beneath the bed and my heart stopped for the second time.

The contents of the box had spilled out when I'd shoved it and before me lay a treasure map of deceit even worse than my own.

A bottle of pills.

A paper detailing a payment being made for Blair's car to be stored at a facility in Ridgefield indefinitely with Vanity's signature at the bottom.

Receipts for a purchase of 100 gallons of gasoline.

A gun permit.

"What the fuck." Chastity's voice was an echo in my ear but I didn't hear it. My mind whirred as I sat down hard on Vanity's bed and tried to make sense of what was before me. I didn't even think about the germs as my head spun and Boots climbed up to squeeze around my neck in his rightful place. "She's been acting weird but…*a gun*? Why would she need a gun?" Chastity reached down and began rifling through the contents of the box. She paused, unearthing something new, her expression shuttering.

I took the paper from her without thinking, horror buzzing through my veins as I read what looked like a contract to rebuild the treehouse in the woods. The same treehouse I'd spent the best years of my childhood escaping to. My and Markus's sanctuary away from the turmoil of our home. As much as his death had rocked our world, it hadn't been sunshine and rainbows before either. To rebuild the treehouse, the place that haunted my dreams, the one that had gone up in smoke and tragedy, was a mockery of his memory. He'd died there, just as Blair's mother had, strapped to the tree, determined to make amends.

But why would Vanity rebuild it?

Why would she do *any* of this?

I searched for answers, my breath stuttering as I flipped to the back of the paper and realized what her plan had been all along. She was going to frame him. For what—I didn't know. Because attached to the back of the paper was an identical document with Vanity's signature at the bottom whited out. And in its place was a name that made my blood curdle and my head spin.

Blair Evans.

I was inside my car faster than I could blink.

I'd left Boots behind in the relative safety of Chastity's arms, my head on fire as I fumbled for my keys in a movement so familiar and yet so foreign it felt like watching someone else's hands do it for me.

My phone rang and I answered immediately without checking caller ID, desperate to hear Blair's voice, to know that what I suspected to be happening couldn't be real.

"Richard I think something's wrong." Collin's voice filled my ear and

I swore softly, my fingers white where they wrapped around the steering wheel. I was quaking, a sickness welling up inside me I hadn't felt since I was nine years old and I'd stood in front of my little brother's empty casket and wondered why it couldn't have been me. "I saw Vanity drive by me and I dunno. Maybe I'm crazy but—"

"You're not crazy." I was on the road faster than I could blink. "Something is wrong."

"Fuck. You don't think she's gonna like…" Collin trailed off. "I dunno. I saw her buy a whole bunch of gasoline and cart it to her car from the parking lot at Moonies and…I dunno. You don't think she's gonna hurt Blair do you?" His voice wobbled, and suddenly it struck me again just how young he was behind the bravado. Fifteen and terrified.

"You said they were driving past you?" I confirmed, speeding toward Spruce with my heart in my throat. He gave me details and then spoke again.

"I'm sorry I yelled at you." Collin's voice shook. "I really like Blair. I want you to be happy. I want him to be happy too. I was just sad cuz you promised you'd tell me first."

My eyes burned.

"I'm sorry I didn't tell you. It's going to be okay." I didn't know that. I couldn't promise it either. But we both needed to believe that there was hope this wasn't as bad as it seemed. "I'll bring Blair home."

Empty promises.

"Tell him I wanna buy him that pretzel. You know? From the mall. Since last time it was closed."

I knew he didn't care about the damn pretzel. He just…he needed to be normal, to feel normal. I could understand that as my hands wobbled on the wheel.

"I'll tell him."

Collin sniffled. "I love you, Rich."

"Love you too, buddy."

I hung up, speeding through the burning sensation behind my eyes, my body buzzing with what felt like adrenaline.

If I was correct, I didn't have much time.

I hoped I was wrong.

Dear god, please let me be wrong.

Chapter Thirty-Six

Blair

THE WOODS SPIRALED out before us, trees climbing towards the oncoming storm like sycophants before their king. There was a hollow feeling to the woods as I followed the path deeper and deeper into their shadow, the fog swallowing up my feet and the base of tree trunks.

Vanity was quiet behind me aside from a few sniffles here and there and I respected her grief too much to question what we were doing and why. It was only when we reached the end of the trail that I realized where she'd led me.

Stepping through the break in the trees, my heart lurched and I stared in both horror and awe at the sight before me.

In the middle of the clearing was the tree that haunted my memories.

Except now instead of an empty husk, it was home to a treehouse once again.

It was a parody built with new wood, a mockery of the past. Just looking at it made me sick to my stomach. The wildflowers were still there, the tall grass dry and soft where it bit against the holes in the knees of my jeans as I stepped forward.

It hadn't been long since I'd been here last, and yet it looked entirely different.

"What...?" I turned around to ask if Vanity had known about the rebuild but when I did, I was met with a sight that chilled me to the bone.

Vanity was crying, her hair a mess around her face, eyes redder than the tips of her curls. She looked wild. Terrified. Determined.

Armed.

With a gun. And it was pointed right at me.

"Keep going." Her voice was rough with emotion and I struggled to speak. There were no words for what was happening. I'd never in all my life prepared for a moment like this. So I was speechless as I turned back to the treehouse and felt the cool press of metal bite into my lower back.

"There's a set of handcuffs at the bottom of the tree. I need you to cuff yourself and sit in the chair that's there."

Cuff myself and sit in the fucking chair.

What the fuck.

Again, my words failed me. A bird flew overhead, its chirping echoing through the clearing as I made step after step toward certain doom. Because it was certain now. I'd spotted the line of horror-red gasoline cans that circled the base of the tree.

She was going to kill me.

She was going to set me on fire in the same place both Markus and my mother had died all those years ago.

But why?

"Why?" I choked as I found the cuffs, my hands fumbling with the metal, cool to the touch but slickened with my sweat. They clicked into place, tying my wrists together, as loose as I could make them in the off chance I could escape what was about to happen.

I could feel my mother's spirit in the whisper of wind through the yellow grass. I could sense her laughter in the breeze that caressed my cheek, pushing my bangs out of my face in a mirror of the motion she'd repeated a thousand times when I'd been just a child.

I wasn't a child now but I still felt just as small.

What was the point of courage if it had brought me here?

I sat down in the chair, my legs too wobbly to hold my weight anymore as I stared at Vanity, shock and betrayal echoing across my face.

"You said you understood," Vanity said, her voice choked, wet, *repentant*. But the gun never left its position pointed at my chest. Her hands shook, but she didn't waver, staring at me through haunted brown eyes. "You said you understood that I would do *anything* to see him again."

When I'd said that, I hadn't meant literal murder, but I didn't tell her that. There was no point.

"Prudence?" God. This made no sense. Prudence was *dead*.

"Yes." She inhaled raggedly, shoving her free hand into her hair to push the bangs away, her finger still wobbling on the trigger. It would be just my luck if she accidentally shot me while planning my murder. My heart was beating an unsteady staccato in my chest and I struggled to breathe through the panic that threatened to render me immobile.

Thump, thump.

Escape.

Thump, thump.

Escape.

Thump, thump.

Maybe I could distract her?

"Prudence is dead, Vanity," I said softly, as gently as I could, terrified of invoking her wrath.

Vanity just laughed, a raw, broken noise that ended in something not unlike a sob. "Yes. I know."

"So how does killing me bring him back?" I glanced around, searching for a way to distract her enough I could get the gun out of her hands. That's all I had to do. It was simple enough. Then I could call someone for help— Maybe get her the help she needed? Clearly something wasn't quite right. There was a pile of rope beneath my feet and my toes dug beneath it, searching for stability from the earth. Was she going to tie me to the tree? Burn me? Why was she doing this? Prudence was dead.

"She said—" Vanity choked. "She said that if I killed you she'd give him back to me."

Okaaaaaay.

"Who?"

"The woman," Vanity's voice wobbled but filled with steel again the longer she stared at me. "The woman who's had him." *What the fuck.* If Prudence was dead, then how could someone 'have' him? "All this time he's been trapped by her spell. He's a prisoner, a slave, a weapon—"

"He's dead—"

"I know that!" Vanity's voice rose and I flinched back, shocked as wood dug into my back and the chair beneath me quaked. "But he's still *here.*"

She shook her head. "You don't get it. You *can't* get it. You didn't grow up with this stuff like I did. You have no idea what someone with ill intent is capable of."

"I'm pretty sure I'm finding that out right now," I said, eyeing the gun pointedly and then wincing because it probably wasn't the best idea in the world to antagonize an armed person.

"Just…" Vanity inhaled, her brow lowering in concentration. "Just know I'm sorry, okay? It's not… *It's not you*." Her lips thinned. "But I can't let him stay stuck like that. It's— It's *torture*. You said…" She swallowed. "*You said you understood*."

"I understand," I said softly, my heart aching as I watched her grief, her turmoil, her fear all coalesce. "I understand that you're fucking scared. That you feel like there's no way out—" Words boiled inside me as my head spun and pity expanded white-hot in my chest. "But that's not true, Vanity. We all get to make choices." I inhaled. "I chose to… To leave my darkness. That was *my* choice. And you chose to save your brother."

She was staring at me and I forged onwards, trying not to focus on the way the gun kept switching from pointing at my chest to my head, then back to my chest again. "But you can choose not to kill me too. There are some darknesses you can't outrun," I said softly, aching with the truth of my words. Words I'd always known but had never known how to voice. "I can help you. We can figure this out. *Together*. I know you're just doing what you think you have to do—but it's… It's not over yet, Vanity. *It's not*."

I must've said something wrong because I watched her build her walls back up again one by one, her face shuttering as her eyes grew dark. She was mourning me before she'd even had a chance to kill me.

"I'm sorry," Vanity said simply.

Then she was…quiet.

She was quiet for a long—

Long.

Long.

Time.

Chapter Thirty-Seven

Richard

THERE WAS AN unfamiliar car abandoned at the end of the road. Vanity's black vehicle was parked beside it, empty of the two people I was desperately searching for. I stumbled out of my car, for once not thinking through my actions as I crossed asphalt and headed towards a path I'd traversed thousands of times when I was a kid.

I hadn't been back here since Markus died.

There had been no point.

My childhood had ended the day his had.

My parenthood had begun a year later when Collin had first blinked his way into the world, a mirror image of the brother I'd lost. He'd felt like a second chance then and I'd taken it, despite being a child myself.

All my life, I'd fought problems left and right because if I wasn't the responsible one, the one with the plan, the solution maker, then what was left behind was just a broken boy with an even more broken family.

Blair had been broken too.

But he was also brave.

So fucking brave.

He'd never lost his will to fight, his desire to live, his need for happiness and not just survival.

He wasn't content to live in a world that mistreated him. He wasn't content to let life pass him by. He wasn't content to sit on the sidelines, to take what the world gave him, to let them steal pieces of him until there was nothing left.

For years, I'd felt like I was treading water. Holding my brother up, my family up, the town up. Struggling to keep my head above the surface when I was supporting a whole group of people that didn't even notice I was drowning.

But when I was with Blair it felt like he was swimming right beside me, holding me up. Supporting me. I could feel his legs kicking right next to mine, determination on his beautiful face, his eyes full of fire and future and fascination.

He was real.

And he was brave.

And he was in danger and I had no plan, no mission, no thought in my head other than that I couldn't let him go. I couldn't let him die.

I was so distracted by my own thoughts that I didn't notice the figure that exited the unfamiliar car in front of me until it was too late. He phased through metal like a mirage, and at first I thought I was looking at Blair himself, until the broadness of his shoulders registered and he turned his face towards me.

A ghost.

Literally and figuratively.

Pale blue eyes bore their way into my soul as Prudence Rain took a steady step towards me, his pale face flickering as the sunlight that bled through the shifting tree branches above made him half transparent.

"Richard Prince," he said softly, in that same scratchy drawl I remembered hearing when we'd been kids and our families had been friends and not the fractured acquaintances they were now. "You were just a snot-nosed kid last time I saw you." His lips quirked up in what he probably hoped was a smile, but looked more like a grimace.

I ignored the snot-nosed comment.

Prudence hadn't ever been good with people. He made me look like goddamn Mother Theresa. Being turned into a ghost clearly hadn't changed that. He'd always struggled with emotion, it was part of why everyone had so easily believed he'd helped Blair's mother set the fires.

A sociopath who wanted to see the world burn.

"You're...alive." Well. Not entirely anyway. I was in shock as he stepped towards me, not sensing the danger as I watched a flicker of tension in his jaw before the ice of his touch met the skin at my throat.

"You grew up nice. Real handsome," Prudence told me, in that same bland way as his fingers tightened and I fell to the ground with a gasp.

I'd told Blair ghosts were different than anything he would've expected.

I knew that. And yet I hadn't run the second I saw Prudence.

Stupid, stupid, stupid.

His fingers squeezed tighter around my windpipe and I reached up with desperation, scratching at his hands to get them off—though my fingernails only ever met my own flesh. I couldn't touch him. Not unless he wanted me to. His touch had the power to leach the life from my body should he choose to do so, till all that was left was an empty husk.

That was the shitty thing I hadn't told Blair. While ghosts were rare—far rarer than one might assume. They existed at the top of the paranormal food chain, weapons of mass destruction should their masters command it.

If Prudence was here then who…had been keeping him all this time? Who had *created* him in the first place?

"This isn't my idea of a good time," Prudence hummed, his grip tightening. "Wish I could say it's been a pleasure, but—I don't make a habit of choking out the kids I fucking babysat." His lips twitched upwards again and I couldn't tell if he was telling a joke or not—it didn't feel funny. Somehow I doubted he thought it was funny either. He'd always been a wise ass. Though there was nothing hilarious about the way I could feel my energy seeping from my body, sucked into him like he was nothing but a black hole as his eyes glowed in the fading sunlight.

He'd always been effortlessly cool before.

Misunderstood.

But we'd worshipped him.

Prudence was older than all of us kids, dark and intimidating in his leather jacket with his hair slicked back and tattoos painting his skin. Twenty years old and ready to burn every bridge he had. He'd been kind to us though, even though his lack of emotion had always been hard for us to understand.

Looking at him now, I realized he hadn't aged a day.

Preserved at twenty, with rain clouds behind him, framed by the crooked branches of trees that could have been a thousand years old. His body was half transparent, his thick black boots shifting in the shadows like they were only partially there.

Who had cursed him? Why wasn't he solid?

"If you close your eyes it gets easier," Prudence told me as I scrabbled to get him off me, flailing around as the ice of his touch turned blistering and the sickness of his magic began to poison my body. It wouldn't take long for him to incapacitate me. God, I was already halfway there. Fucking *ghosts. How would I help Blair now?*

"I like the leather jacket," Prudence hummed, brow arched. "You get that idea from me?"

I had, but I didn't say that.

As I scratched and struggled and the asphalt bit into my knees, a second figure exited the vehicle. She was smaller than Prudence, but only just. Her blonde hair was perfectly coiffed and I stared at her through blurry eyes as she made her way leisurely around the vehicle wearing a tight white dress—modest, expensive, uncomfortable.

"Don't kill him," the woman hummed, her words casual, fingers flickering as she played with the necklace that hung around her neck. "He'll be useful for negotiations." She cocked her head at me and Prudence's fingers loosened enough I no longer felt at risk of passing out. Beneath his touch it almost felt like being human again, but not in a good way.

I'd known about ghosts just as everyone who lived in Elmwood did.

They weren't common though, even the darkest spirits were hardly corporeal.

Prudence's presence meant something far more nefarious was at work here, but I didn't have time to figure out what as the woman stepped before me, just out of reach, her green eyes assessing.

I recognized her.

I fucking *recognized* her because I'd seen her face haunting my memories since I was nine years old and begun to keep Markus's ghost for company.

The woman in the woods.

The one I'd seen set the fire.

Except at the time, I'd been convinced the woman I'd seen was Blair's mother. I remembered the way she'd turned to look at me, her eyebrow arched, her black hair stuck to her skin with sweat and soot. Empty gasoline cans lay at her feet as she crooked her finger at me, lips twisting into an amused little smile. I'd run for help, unaware that my brother was caught inside the blaze.

Horror filled me as I watched her lips curl into a familiar smirk, green eyes glittering.

"Twins," She hummed, shrugging. "Interesting isn't it?"

"Amanda's—"

"Younger sister." Blair's aunt. The woman who'd abused him all his life. The woman who was the sole reason behind his flinches, the haunted look in his eyes, the way he second guessed every kindness I'd ever given him.

I'd never seen the devil before.

Never thought I would.

Maybe it would've made more sense to see his face in Prudence's since he was currently holding me captive, but no. Prudence was just as trapped as Blair had been his entire life. Anger burned through me and a growl trembled in my throat. I tried to lunge, but my body wouldn't move, frozen still, *trapped.*

I wanted to roar. I wanted to shake. I wanted to grab her by her throat and—

Her mouth twisted into a grimace as a bug landed on her shoulder and her nose scrunched in disgust.

"Kill it," she commanded, apathetic as Prudence reached out with a free hand to squash the bug. The grip of his other hand on my throat loosened fractionally and I tried to communicate with him using my eyes but he glanced away. In a way I couldn't blame him.

Like he'd so bluntly put it.

This wasn't his idea of a good time.

The bug guts meshed into the fabric of her dress and a blank sort of mask fell over her face as she seemed to process this. It was clear Prudence had done it on purpose. A rebellion in whatever misguided way he could.

"That wasn't your wisest choice," she murmured dispassionately, her gaze flickering away from me to Prudence. "Pull out your eye."

Pull out your…

What?

Horror washed over me and my gaze snapped to Prudence's face as a myriad of emotions flickered for a millisecond across it before he smoothed them away. He was blank as a statue as he reached up with his free hand. I watched as his fingers pressed into the socket where his eye rested, whole and unnaturally blue. His nails dug in and—

"Stop. *Stop*," I hissed, turning to the woman with desperation. "For god's sake, stop it!"

"Stop," she said, turning her attention back to me with curiosity. The longer Prudence touched me, the weaker I felt. "How interesting." She cocked her head to the side and I watched the way the sunlight glinted across the familiar shape of her button nose. I could see Blair's face echoed in hers. He was his mother's son in every essence of the word.

To see his face twisted so cruelly made me feel sick. "You realize that the only creature capable of killing a vampire without preparation has his hand around your throat and yet..." The woman's lips turned up into a wicked sort of smile. "Yet you choose to spare him," she hummed. "*Interesting.*"

"Lydia." Prudence's voice filled the silence and her eyes grew dispassionate the moment she looked at him again. He was a tool to her, nothing more. I felt sick to my stomach at the thought. Or maybe that was from his ever-present grip.

"You're right. It's getting late." She rolled her shoulders, making a flicking motion with her fingers so that Prudence would force me to my feet again. Somehow he maintained his grip on the front of my neck despite being nearly a head shorter than me. I moved, following after him as my thoughts spun and my lips grew cracked and dry. I had no choice. No matter how hard I tried to break the hold he had on me, my limbs remained just as numb, just as useless as before. When I looked down I could see his feet moving as he pulled me along. They shifted above ground like he didn't need to touch it at all.

I should've been scared for myself.

But I'd never been the kind of person who caved to my own emotions. Compartmentalize. Survive.

Clearly something more nefarious was at work and if I had any chance of saving Blair, I knew I needed to keep quiet. Somehow it felt like I'd played right into Lydia's hands, however, and as I watched her traipse ahead of us, uncaring of her own cruelty, it made me wonder what had to happen to a person for them to become so inherently evil.

Was evil inherited or was it bred through experience?

Prudence's grip burned the longer I felt it, the pain nearly unbearable as it filled my head with an incessant buzzing. I was helpless. If I'd turned into a vampire like my brother Christopher, then maybe then I could've done something useful.

Persuaded her to let me go.

Persuaded her to release Prudence from whatever spell he was under.

But I wasn't Christopher. I was just…me.

The clearing was coming up ahead and black spots swam in my vision as we broke through the tree line and I was filled with a sense of déjà vu that was so strong it made me sick to my stomach.

The treehouse.

Rebuilt.

And at its base was Blair.

I could sense his heartbeat before I saw him. Sat atop an ordinary dining chair, his hands cuffed together in his lap, surrounded by a mountain of gasoline. One spark and he'd go up in smoke just as my brother had before him, and his mother after that.

"Blair." My voice echoed through the valley, and I regretted the action immediately when Lydia stopped and turned to me.

"You know him," she said, clearly amused. "Oh good." Her lips tipped upwards as she flickered a finger toward Prudence. "Get him down," she commanded. "But make sure he can still see him."

It was clear what she meant to do the moment Prudence shoved me forward, his grip bitingly cold as it leeched the energy from my bones, my knees weak as I was forced down onto the dirt only fifteen feet away from Blair and his big green eyes.

Looking at him made my heart stutter.

He looked stricken. Terrified. Broken, in a way I'd never seen before.

I stared, starved for his attention, my head throbbing as I began to droop.

I wanted to stay strong. I didn't want to scare him. But the most I could do was watch him, desperation evident as my body began to shake.

"What are you doing to him?" Blair said softly, his voice nothing but a quiet croak.

Lydia laughed, a tinkling sort of sound. Beautiful as wind chimes. Cruel as early winter. "Well hello to you too, nephew."

"*What are you doing to him?*" Blair's voice shook. He looked like he'd seen a ghost.

Which I suppose technically he had.

"Just taking care of loose ends," Lydia hummed. I watched the shock and fear flicker across Blair's face before a mask settled there, slotting into place in a motion so practiced he'd had to have done it a thousand times before. I'd never seen him like that before.

Blank.

His eyes were vacant as he stared at his aunt with what had to be horror but was deeper somehow, visceral, vicious. There was a rumble of thunder in the distance, though the fog of storm clouds remained on the horizon. Soon enough it would meet us in the darkness. Maybe fast enough to put out the flames before the entire forest went up into smoke if we were lucky.

Blair was terrified.

As much as he tried to hide it, his blank expression only made it clearer. I knew him.

I knew his taste, I knew his smile, I knew the way he trembled when met with the smallest kindness.

He was lost again and I stared helplessly, knowing there was nothing I could do to fix this—not when I'd only made the problem worse.

I could see Vanity to Blair's right, a gun wobbling in her hand, an expression on her face that was tortured and determined. I'd known she'd be there, but it still felt wrong to see her betrayal in the flesh. We were at a standstill. And I couldn't blame Blair for being scared.

He stared at Lydia, his whole body beginning to quake.

This was the same woman who had broken him into little pieces.

The woman who had stolen his childhood.

The woman who had terrorized him.

Locked him away.

Touched him.

I couldn't blame him. What was he going to do? There was nothing but death written like poetry in the space between us. There was no time for heroics. No time for him to push through the instinct that had been beaten into him since he was eight years old and held pinched between her talons.

We would die together.

And despite his silence, with my last dying breath I would make sure Blair knew how fucking brave he was.

And then he spoke.

Chapter Thirty-Eight

Blair

"LET HIM GO." My voice was scratchy, thin with tension, but resolute all the same.

My demon stood before me and she was dressed in the white of angels, her hair perfectly coiffed, roots recently redone. She took a step forward, slow as ever, unhurried.

Just as she'd always been when she took her time with me.

"Let him go?" She cocked her head at me, clearly amused and surprised that I'd spoken at all. "You know I can't do that, love."

"Let him go," I repeated, more firmly this time, my gaze snapping to Vanity and the gun she still had trained on my chest. "He's not part of this."

"I think he is," Lydia hummed, her voice echoing through the quiet of the valley. It was like even the wildlife had fled in the wake of her horror.

"I think the second he decided he could interfere with my business he became involved."

"Just let him go." Fuck. I couldn't get my mouth to say anything else. I could see Richard clearly, his gaze foggy, his skin unnaturally blue. For an immortal he looked…surprisingly dead.

I didn't know what was happening. I was so new to all of this that my brain couldn't make sense of what I saw in front of me but I didn't need to know the details to understand that whatever Lydia was making Prudence do to him wasn't good.

That was a whole other can of worms.

Prudence.

His hand on Richard's throat, body behind him, pale blue eyes watching, watching, watching.

"You didn't say we'd have to kill him, too," Vanity spoke up beside me and a breath stuttered out of my chest as I realized she hadn't gone completely insane. Thank god.

Thunder rumbled through the valley and I shuddered, hot sweat beading along my temple despite the chill. The cuffs bit into my flesh and I tried to stop trembling but I knew I couldn't.

Looking into her pale green eyes felt like looking into hell.

Like my soul was being sucked from my body, leaving me immobile, helpless, terrified.

I still wore the scars of her nails on the side of my cheeks, reminders of being nine years old and dabbing at the five bloody streaks in the mirror as tears burned my skin salty and hot.

I had been scared then, just as I was now.

But I wasn't a little kid anymore.

"You can't get away with this," I said, my voice even, reasoning with a woman I knew had no reason. Wasn't that the definition of madness? Trying something over and over again expecting the same result. Maybe I was insane after all because I didn't stop. "If you killed just me you could. No one would notice if I'm gone." Richard made a helpless noise and I willed to whatever god there was, if there was one, that they could get him to shut the actual fuck up. "But Richard is a part of The Council. They'll know he's gone. They'll know you did it." I swallowed. "You can't get away with murder, Lydia."

I'd never said her name before.

My heart thudded. *Thump, thump. Thump, thump.*

There was a long pregnant pause and for just a moment I thought I'd succeeded.

Lydia's face was blank as it often was and I thought maybe, just maybe, she was thinking about my words. Accepting them. Agreeing.

As long as Richard left alive then I could die in peace.

"See," Lydia spoke, her voice surprisingly chipper, "but the thing is, I already have." She cocked her head at me and a sickness unlike anything I'd ever felt before rushed through me. It was thick and cloying, poison in my veins, a rush of ice bled like arsenic.

"Did you really think my dear sister's death was an accident?" She *tsked* at me and my head began to spin, my mouth dry. "I stabbed your father, and then I lured her to this very spot and set her on fire." She shrugged. "It was easy enough to get everyone to blame her once I'd laid the pieces for them to find." Lydia's lips twisted into a parody of a smile. "Poor sweet Amanda and Victor. In a way, I did my sister a favor. At least now she'll be remembered."

"You…" I swallowed. "You *what?*" There was a roaring in my ears that made it hard to hear. I couldn't have heard that right. There's no way she— "But… But *why?*"

"She had what I wanted."

She had what I wanted.

She had what I wanted.

She had what I wanted.

Lydia continued to speak as my head spun and I stared at her in horror. "You…killed them…for *money?*" I choked out, interrupting her tirade, my fingers cold and clammy. I couldn't feel my body, numb with sickness, bile rising.

"That, and killing them conveniently aligned with my other plans."

"What…other plans?" I could hardly see, my confusion was so all-encompassing. Or maybe that was the tears. My voice was choked with emotion but for once I didn't give a fuck how I sounded.

Let me be weak.

Let me be strong.

Let me be.

"Your mother always had everything I wanted," Lydia continued, the first flicker of real emotion crossing her face as she frowned. "Money. A husband that wasn't useless. Status. You."

"But you…" My fingers felt deadened, my body shaking. "But you hate me—"

"I realize now I phrased that incorrectly." Lydia took a step closer to me, and with every inch between us that disappeared, the deeper I sunk into waters made of tribulation. I was drowning in a well built with dread and premonition as water choked my legs, my thighs, my chest. "I didn't want *you* specifically. I wanted a child. And I couldn't have one."

"But—"

"It was easy enough to steal the Prince's child," Lydia hummed, cruel detachment emphasized by the way she stepped closer and closer to me. Twenty feet turned to ten, then eight, then seven— "They had four others. He was soft. Sweet. Just another lonely little boy in search of mommy's promises. He *liked* me."

"What the fuck."

What the actual fuck.

Lydia snorted, cocking her head at me. "Don't act so surprised. You're intimately familiar with all his weaknesses. He's forgiving to a fault, loyal too. Why do you think he didn't throw you away? I offered. In fact. The only reason you survived this long was because he begged me to let him keep you."

I'd wondered why she hadn't killed me earlier, that much made sense but...

Jeffrey was...

Jeffrey was *Markus?*

So much was beginning to slot into place. Collin and Jeffrey's similarities. I'd often looked at him and thought he looked just like Jeffrey had growing up. Brown eyes. Freckles. Hair like flames. Those long narrow, piano fingers and the dimple they both shared on their left cheek. Now that I knew—it was easy enough to recognize they were related.

How had I not noticed before?

Richard made a choked noise and my gaze snapped to him again. His eyes were wild, terrified, shocked. His body slumping lower and lower, big shoulders hunched. Horror flooded through me as I watched him grow weaker and weaker by the second.

How was Prudence doing this?

Why?

His blue eyes were dispassionate, though even I could see he was disassociating.

Richard's eyelids grew heavy.

My heart thundered in my chest.

"What are you doing to him?" I cried in alarm, my tears slipping like acid down my cheeks as I watched the man that meant more to me than life itself slowly slip closer and closer to death.

"Vampires have very few weaknesses," Lydia hummed thoughtfully. "I'd explain them all to you but that's terribly boring. It isn't my fault your mother didn't teach you the family secrets." She cocked her head, closing the last few feet between us until I could taste her freesia perfume and see the flecks of gold in her eyes. Our toes bumped. "And besides, you're not worth the effort."

Once upon a time, those words would have torn me to shreds.

But that boy was a different boy.

I'd shed my skin since coming here and Lydia's power, though terrifying, was weak in light of what I'd learned.

People were inherently good, no matter what my childhood had taught me. Lydia could taint as much of the world with her darkness as she could, her fingers dipping into every crevice and crack and still the world remained ultimately untouched.

She was small.

Insignificant.

Sad.

All my life I'd been scared of her. Loved her. Revered her. Dreaded her attention as much as I craved it.

I'd thought she was all powerful.

But…watching the storm clouds gather behind her head, watching the sad lifeless flicker to her all too familiar gaze, I was suddenly struck with emotion. Relief flooded my body as the fear dissipated, instead replaced with an emotion I could describe as nothing but pity.

What a sad horrible world she lived in. A prison of her own making.

Lydia's fingers brought me back to the present. They stroked through my hair, her nails just as sharp as I remembered, catching on sensitive skin as she fisted my curls and tipped my head back. "You're so pretty," she said softly. "It really is such a shame you took after my sister so much."

Her breath was warm as it fluttered across my cheek, making my sweat and tears burn as my heart gave an uneven stutter. I could see Richard clearly, my eyes flooded with the fog of unshed tears as I watched where his head hung low and his big hands limp atop his massive thighs.

To see a man so powerful brought low made me feel as though I was stuck in syrup. It didn't feel real. Richard was… He was larger than life. Strong. Noble.

He didn't deserve this.

"Kill me," I said softly, forcing myself to relax in Lydia's hold. She'd always hated when I fought back, almost as much as she hated when I didn't. I'd often wondered how she'd managed to get me to hold so obediently still. I suppose I knew the answer now as Richard grew limp and Prudence's stare bore holes in my skull. "But let him go." My breath caught. "Lydia, please."

I watched her lips twist, her expression morphing until it looked almost fond.

"I always liked when you begged," she whispered like a secret, so quietly I hoped Richard hadn't heard.

He probably had though. Because he released this ugly, wounded sound, like hearing about my pain was worse than experiencing his own. He was stupidly noble like that. A knight with shining fangs. "If you ask me nicely, I'll kill you first so you don't have to see."

"Please—" My voice broke, tears flooding as the sweat on my wrists made the cuffs slip. I could grab her. I could reach up and choke her. I could end all of this right now. But…the gun was still trained on me, Vanity's dark gaze on the side of my head.

If I killed Lydia now, I had no idea if Vanity would still be able to free Prudence from his spell.

I knew Vanity would kill me to ensure that happened.

She'd already proven her determination.

There was no choice but to fall into Lydia's web one last time.

Except this time, I knew where I was falling, and I intended to be the only one that crawled out.

"How did you get Jeffrey to believe you?" I asked her, wanting to get her talking again. Maybe if I could prove she wasn't who she said she was— maybe if I could prove she'd betray Vanity just as she'd betrayed me— then Vanity would turn on her and we could end this once and for all.

"You'd be surprised how easy it was to convince a sensitive little boy that his family didn't love him anymore. That he wasn't safe. It only took a year of cookies and whispering doubts in his head to get him to think I was saving him." Lydia stroked along the shell of my ear and I shuddered, a feeling not unlike ants crawling up my skin. "That's what I told him, anyway."

"So you lied," I pointed out, grimacing when my response made her fingers tighten in my hair. It stung. "You're a liar." I hoped Vanity listened. Dear god, please let her listen. "You told him the monsters in town were dangerous— You promised him safety, didn't you?" My head was throbbing as I pictured a little Jeffrey. Only a year older than me, stolen from his family, convinced of tragedy worse than death.

They don't want you.

She'd uttered the same thing to him she'd always whispered to me.

I don't want you.

"But it wasn't safe at all. Because all along *you* were the monster." My breath was coming in soft bursts. I knew the clock was ticking. There wasn't much time left. Richard's life was waning, his red eyes dull as he drooped lower and lower, his skin slowly turning blue. Prudence's face was impassive, a blankness there I knew was born out of necessity rather than cruelty.

His eyes were glaciers.

He was just as trapped as I was.

Just like Vanity had said.

"You think you're so smart," Lydia cooed, her voice soft as she stroked a single finger down the column of my throat. I felt her nail dig into my Adam's apple when I swallowed, and images of my childhood flashed before my eyes, memories that were nothing more than nightmares.

I had intimate knowledge of what it felt like to feel her fingernails penetrate my flesh. The feeling of blood welling up like a sickness as she cut a clear trail down my skin. Pain. Disassociation. I pushed through that now, gaze flickering to Vanity to see if what I was saying was working.

She looked torn.

That was good right?

"I'm not smart," I said softly, meeting Lydia's gaze head-on. It was like staring into the mirror and I tried not to choke on the force of emotion that ran through me.

Ticktock.

Time was running out.

"I'm not smart. I never pretended to be. I'm not even—" I inhaled raggedly. "I'm not anything really."

"That's right." Lydia grinned triumphantly, thinking she'd won, that she'd broken me.

"But I'm not your toy either," I soldiered onwards. "I'm sick of playing your games. I'm sick of being just another pawn on the Lydia chessboard."

I watched her turn to ice, the playfulness disappearing.

"Tie him to the tree." Lydia turned to Vanity, her expression cold. "Or I'll kill your brother."

Vanity startled into action, her hands shaking as she held the gun in one hand and reached for the pile of rope that lay in a mess around my feet. It looked like a serpent ready to strike and I was suddenly viscerally aware that the moment I was tied to the gasoline-soaked tree, there was no going back.

Lydia stepped away, clearly disgusted with me as she turned her gaze to watch where Prudence was zapping Richard of every last drop of life he had left. The rope burned where it bit into my flesh and Vanity stepped close, her fingers slipping along my wrists as she undid my cuffs and pulled my arms behind me. Her hands shifted, rope rubbing against my now bare wrists to loop my body through the chair.

"If you move, I'll kill him," Lydia reminded me, so I didn't move.

"She won't help you," I choked out, doing my best to convince Vanity of the truth.

The only truth.

"Shut up," Lydia snapped at me, her gaze cold. "Prudence—" She raised her voice and I choked out a sob. I knew what she was about to do and I couldn't bear it—I couldn't—

"Don't! Don't. *Please.*" Lydia's laughter tinkled through the air as she shook her head with amusement, blonde curls glittering.

Thunder echoed through the valley again, the flicker of lightning flashing white in the sky.

Purity.

A fresh start.

Rebirth.

Then it was dark again.

"Don't hurt him," I begged, even as she pursed her lips in thought. "Please."

Vanity's ponytail brushed the back of my neck and I flinched, a clammy sickness filling my belly. I felt hot and cold all over. She was ignoring me, smiling at me—toying with me. "Don't hurt him," I breathed out, desperation making my voice broken and wet. "Please—*I love him.*" Fuck. Fuck. *Fuck fuck fuck.* I knew the moment the words left my lips that I shouldn't have said them.

"You *love* him?" Lydia stared at me, a sneer curling across her lip. "I see."

Fuck.

I'd fucked up.

I'd fucked up so fucking bad.

Fuck.

Fuck.

Fuckfuckfuckfuckfuck.

"No, no, no, no." I struggled against my bonds because I *knew* that look. *I knew that look.* Lydia tossed her head back with a laugh though it was full of anything but joy. It was cold. Cruel. Calculated.

"Sometimes I forget how disgusting you are," she purred, clearly enjoying my torment. "So. I'm going to do you one last favor. Since I'm your mother and all."

"Please—" I gasped out and something cool pressed into my hands. "Please. *Please don't hurt him.*"

"Call me mommy and I won't." Lydia's gaze never left my face, calculated, cruel, a cat playing with a mouse. I knew it was just another game. I knew that. I knew she was going to take him from me regardless of what I did. But what if she didn't? What if this was my only shot to save him? I couldn't risk losing that chance.

"Mom—" I swallowed bile, my tears and snot choking me as I coughed out the word. "Mom, don't hurt him."

My fingers wrapped around cool metal.

Cool metal.

"Mommy," Lydia corrected.

"*Mommy*—" I tasted bile.

The ropes loosened.

Vanity's fingers stroked gently along the inside of my wrist, a caress that said, 'I'm sorry.'

It said, 'I believe you.'

It said, 'I was wrong.'

The rope loosened, and Vanity stepped back.

I had one chance.

I had one fucking chance.

If Lydia told Prudence to kill Richard, there was no stopping him. He'd be gone.

I'd never hear his laughter again. I'd never sit beside him and watch him laugh at stupid cartoons, or watch the way his face scrunched up when he attempted to argue with me about which character was better in SpongeBob. I'd never eat his tofu scramble. I'd never go to the beach with him in the summer, ride the Ferris wheel with him, carve pumpkins. I'd never get to watch him raise Collin to adulthood. I'd never get to comfort him. To cry with him. To seek out eternity in his arms.

Lydia walked away from me and my hopes began to sink. Two steps, three steps, four—

I had to get her to come back—

But *how*?

What could I say that would get her attention, once and for all?

"Fuck you." The words were out of my mouth before I could stop them.

She turned to face me again, her cool green eyes widening as a smile split her face. "What happened to 'mommy, please, mommy'?" she mocked, taking a step closer, the curves of her body lit with lightning as the first droplets of rain splattered across my cheekbone. "Finally find your backbone?"

Another step.

Just one more, just one—

"I've always had one," I told her, my voice shaking, my fingers slick with sweat. "I just didn't know I had a choice."

"And you're choosing *now* to use it?" Lydia laughed, shaking her head in amusement. Though I watched her smile die as I began to laugh too, and the more I laughed the more my heartbeat stuttered, because for the first time in my life I realized I was *free*. I'd always been free. I had choices. She'd built a cage with her cruelty around me but all I'd had to do all along to break free was *choose*. The only person who had trapped me was myself.

My chest expanded, fresh air flooding my lungs as my grip grew tighter, surer.

"You wanted me to believe that you were perfect. That I'm nothing but your shadow." She stared at me and I willed the distance between us to shrink. It was hilarious. All my life I'd wished for more distance and now here I was—willing it away. "I broke off pieces of myself over and over to fit into your mold, hoping you might love me." A water droplet hit my nose. "But no matter what I did it was never enough for you. But that doesn't matter anymore because—" I sucked in a breath, meeting her gaze head on, our breath mingling with the rain, her eyes boring into my own. "I see you now for what you really are."

"And what is that?" Lydia's lips curled into an amused sneer. "Please tell me, I'm dying to know what you think of me."

I could do this.

I could do this.

I only hoped it was enough.

The air smelled like pine trees, spring rain, and redemption. I was ready to face my demons. I was ready to overcome the nightmare that had haunted my every waking moment.

I am brave.

I am brave.

I am brave.

"You're jealous." I exhaled, forging forward, desperate for that one last step to close between us. "Because deep down, you know—" I took a steadying breath. "No amount of money or designer clothing could ever cover up the fact that you're just a sad *miserable* hag who is nothing but the dollar store version of my mother." The moment the words left my lips, pain exploded along the side of my face.

Her nails met my flesh as they often had before.

The copper scent of fresh blood filled my nose but instead of surrender all I smelled was triumph.

Agony erupted as Lydia's nails raked the skin from my face, my blood weeping like tears as laughter bubbled up inside me. The more I laughed, the more she hit me, but I didn't care.

This time I didn't fall beneath her fury, I didn't accept it. Instead of taking it like I always had, determination welled up inside my chest along with my laughter.

I had a choice.

I felt blood seep hot and sticky down my neck as Lydia grabbed my face, wrenching my head back so I could stare blearily at her one last time. "For the first time in my life I see that I have options," I spat out, laughing as the blood spattered across her perfect white dress. "And if I have to choose between me or you, the answer is obvious. I choose *me*."

And then I pulled the gun out from behind my back and I shot her.

She fell with a sickening lurch, a pained grunt, and an explosion of butterflies in my belly. Too late I realized I hadn't killed her.

Too late, too late, too late.

"Kill him!" Lydia's voice screeched. "Then kill the boy too." I was atop her in seconds, my wrists burning as I smashed the butt of the gun against the oozing wound in her abdomen.

Kill him, kill him, kill him.

"Make him stop!" I screeched just as I heard an unholy gurgling coming from Richard's direction. I couldn't look. If I looked, I'd lose the precious seconds I needed to get her to stop—

Vanity's voice echoed in an alarmed cry behind me. She was screaming but I ignored the words, my fists smashing against flesh. "Make him stop!" I yelled again, bloodied and dazed, the gun held tight in my grip as I brought the barrel down over and over and over again.

Lydia was laughing.

Laughing.

Laughing.

Laughing.

"Make him stop!" I screeched again as I listened to Richard's body hit the ground. The pounding in my ears was deafening, Lydia's laughter haunting me as a third voice I didn't recognize filled the air.

"The necklace!" Prudence yelled and my gaze immediately snapped to Lydia's throat.

Her cross.

Bone white.

The one she'd played with as she tortured me.

The one I'd never seen her take off—my entire fucking life.

I didn't know what the fuck Prudence meant by 'the necklace' but I could only guess. I had two seconds to decide whether or not I trusted Prudence, and my body made up my mind for me as I watched in slow motion as my fingers wrapped tight around the silver chord and I wrenched it away from Lydia's neck.

It didn't break.

I wrenched at it again and Lydia began wailing, her nails scrabbling at my face, my neck, my eyes. But still I pulled.

I pulled, and I pulled, and I pulled. The chain made a horrible noise as it cut at her flesh and I realized distantly I was screaming. Richard wasn't moving. I could see his form in my peripheral vision. Flat on his stomach, still as death.

A vampire still as death.

The chain snapped and the cross bit into my palm as I stumbled back and away, struggling to my feet to launch myself at Richard's form. I didn't know if I'd done what Prudence wanted. Maybe Lydia would follow me— maybe she'd manage to finish what she started— but fuck.

Richard.

Richard, Richard, Richard, Richard.

Was he dead?

Oh god.

Oh god, oh god, oh god. Please don't let him be dead. Please. Fuck. Fuck. Fuck. Fuck.

Prudence had moved. He was gone and Richard lay alone in the grass, his body unnaturally still as I stumbled toward him. I tripped the last few steps, stones digging into my knees and hands as I fell to the meadow floor and held tight to the gun in one hand crawling the rest of the way over.

I couldn't breathe.

He was so still.

My heart broke into two, heaving apart like walls of cement cut by nothing less than two tectonic plates catching together.

And then…

He moved.

Chapter Thirty-Nine

Blair

PRUDENCE WORE LYDIA'S body like a puppeteer. It was… satisfying and terrifying all at the same time. He held himself unnaturally still, arms crossed over Lydia's chest, her face looking back at me but nothing of her left inside it.

I figured it was easier than carting a body back, but watching him move around was morbid all the same.

"I'm sorry," Vanity said for the hundredth time and I shrugged her off. I didn't want to speak. I didn't want to do anything but sit where I was nestled in Richard's lap in clear sight of the entire line of people that I could hear rustling around in the woods as they slowly made their way into the clearing.

Richard smelled as he always did. But this time I recognized it for what it was.

Home.

He was home.

"You're bleeding," he murmured against my sweaty temple and I laughed.

"That your way of saying you're hungry?"

"Blair—" he huffed, a soft incredulous little noise that ruffled the hair at my temple.

"*Richard.*" I shoved my face into his throat, and bunched my fingers inside the back of his hair, my fingernails catching on the downy blond strands. Then in a surprising bout of honesty I murmured. "I can't do that right now. The blood—the drama—the lies—I just can't—"

"I know."

"Just let me…" I inhaled raggedly. "Just let me be normal, okay?"

"Okay," he agreed easily, his words a promise as he tucked me in close, big arms bracketing me in his embrace. I squeezed his waist with my legs, absorbing his not-heat, letting the fact that he was real—that he was *okay*, seep into my harried mind.

He was safe.

We were safe.

It was over now.

It was finally fucking over.

It didn't even feel real. My head was still reeling with the knowledge of what I'd done. I'd…killed someone. At least I thought I had. Did that make me a bad person? Did it change the fundamental parts of me? The parts that screamed for kindness, for good, for courage?

Maybe it would take me a while to find these answers for myself.

Maybe not.

Maybe I already knew the truth.

And the truth was that when it came down to it, good and evil aren't black and white. There would be people that condemned me for what I'd done. And there would be people that saw it for what it was.

A boy who'd always run learning to fight for himself.

For his love.

For his life.

For his family.

God, all I wanted was to go back to Richard's apartment and binge watch SpongeBob with him in my pajamas.

I wanted to call Jeffrey.

I wanted to eat a fucking veggie burger.

The buffet had felt like hours ago, like a lifetime had passed.

I heard a quiet noise and I looked away from my Richard cocoon. I couldn't help the empathy that ached inside me as I caught the gaze of a tear-streaked Vanity once again. Maybe I was feeling charitable, but I listened to her as she spoke this time, really listened. Despite what she'd done. Despite what had almost happened because of her.

"I called them," she said softly, her voice wobbling. "Chastity was already on the way."

The progression of people were still approaching. I'd wondered how they'd known—but it hadn't occurred to me that while I'd been hiding away for the last hour in Richard's arms, Vanity might've been taking action.

Richard held me still, though he didn't stop me when I moved so I could properly see her face.

Remorse.

Guilt.

Fear.

"I realized… I realized it wasn't worth it," Vanity said, her gaze flickering to her brother, so full of longing I had no idea how I hadn't seen it before. "I'm really…" She swallowed. "I'm really sorry."

Apologies couldn't make up for what she'd done. For what she'd tried to do.

But it was a start.

I'd been given a chance at a new life and the last thing I wanted to do with it was waste it on holding a grudge.

"S'cool, dude," I finally responded after what felt like an age. "Was kinda fun anyway."

She laughed, the noise bursting bright and surprised from her chest as she reached up to scrub at her wet eyes. "I understand if you want The Council to take care of this," she said softly.

At first I thought, hell yes. No way in hell was I disposing of a fucking body, despite the fact that apparently Prudence could wear it around like a person suit. Creepy fucker. But then I realized what she actually meant… And I was immediately shaking my head.

By take care of *this* she meant…take care of *her*.

They would kill her for what she'd done. Execute her the way her brother had been executed. It would be deserved in the eyes of supernatural law. She knew this. I knew this.

I could end her life.

I already knew what I had to do.

"No fucking way." I couldn't stop myself as I reached out to tangle my fingers around her wrist. Despite being taller than me she was so fucking frail, all brittle edges and broken glass. "No one's gonna do fucking *anything*, okay?" I shook my head at her again, bumping up against Richard's chest as he moved to squeeze me tighter. "As far as I'm concerned, this was all just a big misunderstanding." I stared at her pointedly, watching her face as it morphed through a kaleidoscope of emotion before settling on relief.

I hadn't realized so many other people had arrived yet, not until I heard a quiet sob and realized it wasn't coming from Vanity.

Chastity stepped out from the crowd, her eyes big and wet as she launched herself at me, uncaring of my gentle giant. She smashed against me, her face burying in my shoulder as her tears wet my bloody neck. "You stupid shithead," she hissed, hitting me in the chest before pulling back just as quickly as she'd come. "God." And then she was hugging her sister, her tiny head smooshed between Vanity's boobs.

I didn't even feel the pain anymore, too full of elation. Of peace.

Prudence cleared his throat, shifting in his meat suit as Vanity murmured something into Chastity's ear and she turned to face him for the first time.

"Pru?" Chastity said softly, staring at him, her voice achingly young.

How the fuck everyone just took the fact he was residing inside a corpse in stride was amazing to me. Even after he'd explained it was to make sure they could transport her properly, it was still absolutely fucking bizarre to witness. And then I watched as Chastity pulled Prudence into her embrace, uncaring of the body he inhabited, her fingers tight around his pale wrist as the sunlight shone through a break in the clouds and the three siblings were reunited at last.

It was a humbling sight.

None of them looked related but that didn't matter. I couldn't believe that I'd been a part of this, that something so…magical could even exist. And behind the magic, there were years of death and destruction, all because a single woman had decided she had the right to take what wasn't hers, that everyone else's hurt didn't matter as much as hers.

There was a lot that needed to be said between all of us, but I was in no rush to say it. My badassery earlier had me all worded out. Everything I'd felt earlier that day when going into the woods with Vanity seemed so far away now as I tucked myself into the passenger seat of Richard's car and we sped off toward the center of town.

I couldn't stop shaking.

It was embarrassing honestly, and I stared at my twitchy limbs, willing them to stop—but they never did. This was the aftermath. The calm after the storm. When the wreckage lay in pieces at our feet and the destruction was nothing but a memory.

I thought back to the clearing where the cleanup was taking place and shuddered.

Ian, who was apparently the police chief, had shown up with the head of SAC a few minutes before we'd left. Richard had stiffened as his boss greeted us with a soft smile before he'd turned to examine the damage done. When it came time for me to explain what had happened I told them, leaving out all the details of Vanity's betrayal.

Remorse had filled the tall man's face as he listened, head bowed in thought. Hearing of my mother's innocence sobered both men, their expressions somber as they murmured quietly among themselves.

According to my story, Vanity had arrived with Richard to help—only to discover that all along Lydia had been using her brother's ghost as a puppet. Maybe there were holes in my story, but they accepted it without grilling me further.

Maybe it was because I was covered in blood, and therefore smelled like a snack. But neither of them had protested when we'd turned to leave and I'd watched the way Vanity's shoulders slumped with relief like she'd been waiting for me to seek justice against her for what she'd done, despite the fact I'd told her I wouldn't.

For a dude that had about a zillion scratches, had murdered someone, and almost gotten his boyfriend killed, I was feeling pretty zen.

I figured the best thing Vanity could do to redeem herself was to move on. She didn't deserve death, just as Prudence hadn't. But that didn't mean I was in a hurry to spend time with her…like *ever* again.

What had happened to Prudence was the true tragedy.

Prudence who would never breathe again and yet he still lived, trapped among the living like a moving mannequin.

He'd explained to me the importance of the necklace right before we'd left, as he eyed where I still clutched it with desperation inside my sweaty palm. The gun had disappeared along with the evidence but the necklace remained. I hadn't let anyone touch it.

The pale ivory of the cross itself was apparently a piece of bone cut directly from his body. It was his cursed object, precious and terrible all at once. It was hard to understand, to wrap my head around. Just as

Vanity had said earlier, I hadn't grown up with all of this. So I just smiled and nodded like I understood, watching the way his shoulders—*Lydia's shoulders*—relaxed infinitesimally when I handed the necklace over to Vanity for safe keeping.

It was a gesture of good will.

She'd smiled at me, that same wobbly smile, her eyes wet and brow furrowed, as she stared at the cuts on my face. I doubted the guilt would go away any time soon. Part of me thought maybe in a fucked-up way it was good it remained. Let it teach her a lesson. Let it make her kinder. Softer. We were a mirror in that moment, linked together with shared trauma, blood on our hands.

I couldn't believe she'd given me the gun.

But then again, that said more about me than her.

Honestly, I was just glad to be rid of the whole thing. The necklace, the horror, the haunting. I'd have my memories always, but with time even those would fade. It was up to me to make new ones, better ones. To replace the horror with something fresh.

Maybe that's what this was between Richard and me.

It was too young to give it a name.

But it was real.

Tangible.

Sweet.

I was shaken from my thoughts as he pulled onto Main Street, glancing over at me, the starlight that leaked through the car window painting his cheekbones in its silver glaze.

I saw a future in his scarlet eyes.

They said, 'You're safe now.'

They said, 'I'm sorry.'

They said, 'come home with me.'

They said, 'It's time to breathe.'

And so I did.

I looked out at the starry skyline as the clouds opened up and rain began to pour its icy fingers along the leaf-strewn asphalt. The wheels churned, the wind rushed through my open window, my tears dried along with the blood on my skin until the tug of it was only a memory.

I breathed in the scent of pine, rainfall, and home. And for the first time in my life, I felt content.

It had been a long journey but I'd gotten here all the same.

Richard reached out, his big palm facing upwards as he laid his hand on my knee. I was still shaking but he didn't seem to mind. There was a promise lined through the veins on his wrist, through the swell of his palm, like a map unfurling.

I laced our fingers together, looked at the rising moon, and breathed.

I didn't talk to Richard about the Town Hall meeting until the next day. We'd both been too raw, and I hadn't been ready to crack my chest open again so soon. However, as I sat down on the toilet seat in the bathroom and Richard gently peeled off the bandages he'd painstakingly placed on my cheeks the night before, I was struck with inspiration.

"You're a dick," I told him as I tipped my head to the side and his thumb gently stroked over the pulse that throbbed with tension in my neck.

"I know."

"Seriously."

"I know."

"You couldn't have, like, warned me you were gonna freaking blast me in front of the whole town?" Richard didn't seem surprised that I was confronting him now, in fact he looked almost…relieved, like he was just waiting for me to bring it up so he could explain himself.

"It wasn't right."

"Damn straight."

"Can I…" He swallowed, leaning back until his big ass met the lip of the tub and he sat down with a loud thunk that was uncharacteristically ungraceful. "Can I explain myself?"

I chewed on my lip.

My cheeks stung, the scratches that burned across my face and throat aching as I shifted a little on the toilet seat and listened to it squeak. He wasn't asking me if he could explain. He was asking me to listen—and for a moment I searched internally to figure out whether or not I was feeling receptive to that.

Was I too angry?

Too sad?

Or…

"I'm ready," I said when I was sure, turning my gaze to his, watching the way his shoulders slumped in relief and he rubbed his big hands on his even bigger thighs, like they were sweaty with nerves.

"I'm not good with words," he whispered, and I nodded, because I knew this—he knew this—we all knew this. "But I…" I watched his Adam's apple bob as he swallowed, my cock perking up. *Down, boy.*

Trauma then sex this time.

Boo.

"When you came to town, I knew I wanted to help you."

Okaaaay.

"I just...I didn't know how. So I did the best I could." He swallowed again. "I never meant to hurt you. My intent..." Oh dear. Oh fuck. That was so fucking cute. I watched his face shift as he pulled words straight out of a Wiki-How article I'd seen pulled up on his phone that morning about how to 'healthily communicate' in a relationship. He'd left it open when he'd gone into the walk-in closet to grab me a fresh set of clothing and I'd snooped curiously at first—then gleefully. "The *intent* behind my actions was to protect you. I am more aware than anyone of both the light and the dark side of The Council. I thought...the best way I could do that was by clearing your name."

That made sense. I waved at him to go on.

"I didn't think I'd fall in love with you."

My head spun.

"I didn't...I didn't think that was an option for me. Ever. At all. Not just with you but...with anyone." Richard's cheeks tinged pink in the parody of a blush. "But you... The more I talked to you, the more I learned about you, the more I observed you, the more sure I became that I wanted you to stick around. And I didn't want them to hurt you."

"Okay."

I wasn't sure what else there was to say. Richard's expression was raw, his lip wobbling, his brow lowered in that stern-serious way that made me want to ride his dick until he went cross-eyed.

Yeah, okay. Maybe I was horny.

"I did the best I could in the situation to maintain your privacy while clearing your name." He'd clearly rehearsed that.

Fuck fuck fuck. He was so cute.

"So what we have is real then? All of it?"

He nodded, his blond head glinting in the bathroom light. My cheeks stung as my lips threatened to pull into a smile. No, no. Just one more minute of letting him stew. Like a bad dog after peeing in the house. He deserved to wallow.

"What would you have done if they didn't accept my innocence?" I asked, trying to keep my expression stoic. To be honest I wasn't sure his answer even mattered at this point. I'd forgiven him about the same time I'd seen him Google how to talk to me.

He swallowed, shuffling with embarrassment.

Good.

"I thought I could take you with me." Richard blinked. "You said you were looking to settle somewhere—and I figured if not here then… You, Collin, and I could settle somewhere else. Somewhere with maybe less SAC involvement."

I cocked my head.

"A suburb?" Richard continued, clearly worried I hadn't accepted his explanation. "I was looking at high schools in Arizona and—"

"You— a vampire—were going to relocate your family to sunny Arizona?"

Richard swallowed. "It would be uncomfortable, but I figured it would be worth it. There's a town near Phoenix I was looking at that has a—"

I kissed him to shut him up.

Gorgeous, goddamn, giant.

569

"I fucking love you," I murmured as I smashed his face between my hands and he let out a desperate, relieved little sound.

"You do?"

"Fuck yes." I kissed him again and he melted, slinging his arms around me until he pulled me snug into his lap. The ab power he had to have to hold us both on the lip of the tub was absolutely amazing. "You're such an idiot." I kissed him again. "I forgive you."

"Really?" He perked right up. His cock did too, and I ground down on him with a laugh.

"Yeah, you dork." I kissed that little furrow between his eyebrows, ignoring the way my face stung as I smiled.

"I love you, too," Richard blurted, obviously realizing he'd forgotten to tell me.

"You do?" I asked, teasing him. His brow lowered and he glared at me.

"Yes. Even when you're a brat."

"Espec—"

"Especially when you're a brat," he interrupted. He was smiling again. That same smile that made me taste sunshine, my heart in my throat. His eyes grew hooded, his pupils blown out, black and ravenous as his gaze flickered from my lips to the blood that seeped from my still healing cuts.

We were quiet for a moment aside from our breathing as I tucked my fingers around the back of his meaty neck and cocked my head to the side. "You look hungry," I teased.

Richard huffed, though he didn't deny it, his lips parted, swollen pink from our kisses, his lashes fluttering.

"You can bite me you know," I purred, leaning down to press our noses together. I rubbed up against him, enjoying the way all six-foot-four of his glorious muscle shifted beneath me. My heart thudded, *thump, thump* in my chest as I pressed one last kiss to his lips to sweeten the deal. "You know I like it."

Epilogue

Blair

A LOT CHANGED in the next few weeks. The most important change being the fact that my uncle had stepped forward with the paperwork necessary for me to access the apparent fortune my parents had left behind for me. It was ridiculous actually, how much I'd been stressing over selling my parents' house when I was sitting pretty on…god.

So many zeros.

Despite his newfound honesty, he was still punished accordingly. Though, not before it came to light all he and my aunt had done to ensure they kept as much of my parents' fortune as possible. I hadn't realized the damage a dirty lawyer could do to a contract if given enough incentive. I'd had a trust fund—still did in fact. The money of which was supposedly supposed to be going to my caregiver monthly to take care of me until I turned 21.

The forged documents showed receipts of classes I'd never taken, a bank account I didn't have, and all sorts of bits and bobs that were never given to me. For years, my aunt and uncle had been forging receipts to make it look like my monthly stipend was actually going to me when in reality it funded their mansion, my aunt's Gucci collection, and most horribly— the security system that had followed my every move since the day Jeffrey and I had moved into our condo.

I'd kept my job at the diner despite everything, but Chastity had insisted I take some time off so I could get myself feeling better. It was charitable of her. I appreciated it, especially because, to be honest, it took me a while to get back into the swing of life.

It was strange…seeing the way the town integrated itself with Prudence. He moved in with Chastity and Vanity—without the Lydia suit—the same day I'd moved out. I saw him in passing sometimes, his pale eyes trailing over me as he'd nod his head and one—or both—of his sisters herded him away.

I figured that had to be claustrophobic.

But maybe he didn't mind being attached at the hip with them. Who was I to judge?

I'd temporarily been absorbed into Richard's home. He'd given me the spare bedroom and made sure Collin organized his stuff in the closet so there was room for my clothes as well. Collin still slept over most of the time, when their parents weren't home, and as much as I tried to push him to take his bed back, he refused.

Apparently he liked having an excuse that made it easy to watch cartoons, because every time I brought it up again he shushed me with angry chipmunk hand gestures and the whites of his eyes showing. I'd kept pushing, but only because it was hilarious watching him try to shut me up.

He'd taken the news that Jeffrey—*Markus?*—was alive better than anyone else. Probably because he'd never actually met him.

His parents hadn't.

They'd fucked off again to god knows where—and when I'd asked Richard about it, he'd just shrugged. It seemed no one in their family was surprised that their parents weren't going to magically start learning how to be proper parents again.

"They'll be back," he'd murmured softly as he'd tucked me up against his side on the couch. Collin had grunted from my other side, his foot slung across my lap as he tossed another kernel of kettle corn at my mouth after plucking it from the bowl he was hogging.

"They said they need time to 'process.'" Collin rolled his eyes heavenward. "Fuck them honestly. Selfish assholes."

"Language," Richard reminded him, and Collin just laughed and threw a piece of popcorn at him, too.

The rest of the brother's had taken Jeffrey's reappearance in stride. They'd been eager to meet him, over-eager, honestly. But we'd all kinda settled on waiting until the time was right. No one knew how Jeffrey would feel when reuniting with the family he'd chosen to leave all those years ago.

There was hurt there, but mostly there was a lot of hope.

Richard and I had gone apartment hunting, but something inside me wasn't ready to be alone yet. It wasn't that I didn't like living with Richard, in fact I really, *really* did. But we weren't there yet. We'd only been on a handful of dates in our relationship's short history and both of us needed a chance to make sure this was really real before we took a step like that together.

The blood sharing between us had gotten more frequent as well, and I wasn't complaining. Richard was never happier than he was with his cock fucking me and his fangs inside my neck. I liked the euphoria that happened afterwards. But even more I liked the way he cuddled me up against his chest and let me soak up his scent like a fun-sized rage-fueled sponge.

Boots liked Richard's place better too. In fact, he was a fluffy traitor because nine times out of ten he abandoned me for either Prince brother the second they became an option. It was admittedly pretty adorable that Richard wore him around like a scarf half the time though. I did the same thing, but somehow it was cuter when Richard did it.

Maybe it was because of the juxtaposition between his frankly massive body and Boots's teeny tiny one. They made quite the set.

Life wasn't great yet, but we were learning.

I healed my physical wounds while I soaked up what it felt like to have a place in the world. But my contentment was short-lived because every time I got too happy, I thought of Jeffrey, all alone in our condo, waiting for me to call him home.

So I did.

The ride to the airport took forever. Richard was freaking out the whole time, but he wouldn't admit to freaking out. Before we'd left he kept fretting, choosing between eight identical flannel button ups like it was the end of the world.

I suppose I could sympathize. I'd spent an equal amount of time stressing over what to wear when I saw Jeffrey too, except I had done it in the privacy of my bedroom and not where he could make fun of me.

It was his own fault really.

Eventually he'd ended up deciding on a dark red flannel shirt with black accents. Go figure. I'd told him he looked handsome, *because he did*, and off we'd went.

"Do you think I look okay?" he'd asked standing in front of the closet before we'd headed out. His deep voice was uncharacteristically nervous. "Maybe I should've picked the purple—"

I held up a hand, interrupting him as I reached over and pinched his cheek, he didn't even flinch, the fucker. "You look great," I hummed, trying to be reassuring. I wasn't very good at it. Me comforting him was like a porcupine comforting a bear. 'There, there, buddy. Oh sorry. Did I stab you? My bad.'

It was honestly adorable that he trusted me enough to be vulnerable with me though. I'd never seen him show this side of himself to anyone else. He was always so…serious. So put together. Almost emotionless. It made his vulnerability even more intimate.

Richard when we were alone was incredibly expressive. He felt everything, so incredibly strongly. The more time I spent with him, the more he trusted me to open up. I still made fun of him though, which made him laugh.

Like now.

"That wasn't very convincing." Richard laughed, shaking his head. "But thank you."

And now, forty minutes later, here we were stuck in traffic and Richard was still stressing out about the color of his shirt. He didn't vocalize it, but I watched him pull at his collar six different times before I reached out to smooth my hand over his knuckles, marveling not for the first time over our size difference.

"You look great, Rich," I murmured, and he flashed me a shy little smile, relaxing—finally.

"Collin told me the purple would've been better," he explained and I sighed, rolling my eyes heavenward.

"And you trust a fifteen-year-old boy to tell you what looks good?"

He blinked.

He blinked again.

Beep, boop, beep, boop. Thoughts did not compute—I watched in real time as Richard rebooted.

"No. I really don't."

Crisis averted.

I was suddenly glad we'd left Collin at home.

We'd opted to fly Jeffrey out on an early-bird flight. He was due to arrive before the sun even rose over the horizon, which was why the traffic had been an annoying surprise. He hadn't even questioned me when I told him the time of the flight I'd booked him and once again I was stuck wondering just how much Jeffrey had known about Elmwood all along, and why our whole lives he hadn't thought to mention anything.

Maybe his easy acceptance of the early flight came from the fact he'd always been a morning person?

Or maybe it was because he knew half of his entourage was made up of the undead? Who knew?

Not me.

Richard didn't like the crowds at the airport. He said the scents were overwhelming so he stuck close to the wall, letting me lead him with my head bobbing somewhere near his chest. A tiny avenger, barking—not literally—at anyone who stood in our path. I'd never been inside an airport before, so it'd been kinda fun to watch all the people come and go.

They stared at my scars though, and that was annoying, but I brushed them off.

By the time we saw Jeffrey approaching us, my heart was in my throat.

I didn't know what I expected to happen. I didn't know what I *wanted* to happen. All I knew was that maybe, *just maybe*, it was still possible the world could right some of the wrongs done to the Prince's and all their children.

Jeffrey perked up when he saw me, waving a long-fingered hand in the air, a bright grin on his face. He'd always had a fucking awesome smile. It was the kind of smile that was contagious. Most of the time you didn't even notice you were smiling back until your cheeks started to hurt.

He was sunshine, autumn leaves, and snickerdoodles.

He was home.

I launched myself at him, skipping over the last few steps between us, my face smashing into his chest as he wrapped his arms around me and laughed, that same melodic sound I'd listened to and envied all my life.

The envy was gone now though. Something had changed between us. Something had changed within me since the last time I saw him.

I was stronger now.

Blair the coward, no more.

"You look different." Jeffrey grinned, shoving me back so he could ruffle my hair in the way he always did that pissed me the hell off. I just grinned back though, shoving at his chest playfully in response as he slung an arm over my shoulders.

"Maybe you need glasses," I retorted, even though my chest puffed up with pride. Hell yeah I looked different. I *was* different. Scars aside.

When I looked in the mirror, the man that looked back didn't cringe away from his own reflection.

Pinocchio had become a real boy.

"Who's your friend?" Jeffrey asked, turning us so we could face Richard. I watched the smile on Jeffrey's face die, inch by inch, bit by bit. He swallowed and his throat bobbed. There was a guardedness to him now, one I'd never seen aimed at me before. His walls had climbed so high, I wasn't sure I could rise above them.

"Um…" I didn't know what to say, looking to Richard helplessly as he stepped forward, his wine-red eyes full of longing so visceral I felt it in my bones.

"You may not remember me," Richard said softly, his deep voice rumbling in the space between us. Jeffrey's grip on me tightened, like he couldn't help himself, looking to me for comfort as he always had. I squeezed him back, stepping closer to Richard so that they could see eye to eye. "But my name is Richard, and I'm—"

"My brother," Jeffrey interrupted him, an apprehensive expression on his face. I'd told him everything Lydia had said and he'd had…*nothing to say about it*. I knew *he knew* the Princes missed him, but it was different… seeing one of them.

When Jeffrey and Richard had been young, they'd been what was called Irish twins. Barely a year apart. Despite their coloring and builds being different, there were still so many similarities in their features I was truly baffled that I hadn't noticed before.

They *looked* like brothers.

Richard exhaled raggedly, clearly out of his depth. Apparently our two sets of limited people skills didn't make a whole one when put together. I reached out to comfort him, laying my free hand on the juncture between his bicep and forearm and he relaxed, like my touch alone could soothe him.

Jeffrey watched the whole exchange, saying nothing for a long minute before he removed his arm from my shoulders and stepped forward. The way he and Richard looked at each other was awkward and…sweet. *Like new beginnings.*

There was an almost pissed off expression on Jeffrey's face though and part of me worried he was about to punch Richard. I didn't know why he would, only that he looked like he wanted to. He'd always looked kinda mad when he was confused though. But then the expression smoothed away and Jeffrey slung an arm around Richard's shoulders, pulling him into a half hug and slapping him awkwardly on the back.

"Nice to see you, man," he said.

And Richard broke.

He slung his arms around him, crushing him tight to his chest despite the fact they were about the same height. I watched the private exchange in awe, feeling like an outsider but honored to have been invited to such a precious moment.

It was a new beginning for all of us.

And I couldn't wait to see what happened next.

Possess Me

COMING 2023

Blair

WE WERE IN the car on our way back to town when my phone began to vibrate. It wasn't even six in the morning yet so I knew it wasn't Collin. And everyone else I talked to was sitting in the car with me.

Jeffrey had insisted on taking the back seat and I hadn't pushed because I figured he needed his space.

This was just a trial run after all. He'd come to town, meet his family, then head home to pack. There was no need to terrify him right off the bat—even though he had looked plenty concerned when I told him I wanted to buy him an apartment.

He was just as surprised by my trust fund as I was.

My phone buzzed again and I swore, wiggling around in an attempt to get the damn thing out of the back pocket of my tight skinny jeans. I still wore the clothes Richard had bought me, which made him puff up with pride and made me feel warm all over.

When my phone was finally loose I frowned down at it, cocking my head in confusion as I swiped right to answer.

"Chastity?"

"Yeah, hi, sweetie." Chastity's voice burst through the speaker, panicked, and more than a little shrill. "Um. So."

"Yes?" I waited, glancing at Richard where he was holding the steering wheel, faux casual, his red eyes trained on the road, though they kept flicking to my face. I was sure he could hear what was happening on the other end of the line so I didn't bother recounting it.

"Have you by chance seen Prudence?" she asked, her voice wobbling a bit.

"I'm not even in Elmwood."

"Really?" There was a pause, and then some rustling. "Oh fuck."

"Why?" As far as I knew, Prudence was kinda forced to stay by one—or both—of his sisters. Whichever one had the necklace at the time.

"So…I might've done a bad."

"A…"

"I lost Prudence."

What?

"How does someone lose a whole-ass ghost?" I asked.

"Very, very stupidly."

Author's Note

THANK YOU SO much to everyone who made *Bite Me* happen! This has been such an amazing journey and I couldn't have done it without your love and support. So many people have stepped up to offer their advice, expertise, and love throughout this project and it truly has become not just my baby but our baby. Thank you for allowing me to create, for loving my work, for finding adventure lost between the pages. You are amazing and I can't wait to share more magic with you in the future.

If you'd like to keep in touch with me and receive free content including a free ebook of *There's a Monster in the Woods* and exclusive chapters of my serial *Cloudy with a Chance of Dildos*, you can sign up at faelovesart.com/newsletter. Or join my Facebook group, Fae's Faves! You can also find me on Instagram @fae.loves.art.

I love you all so much! I can't wait to spook with you once again!

All shares, comments, reviews, and discussion of *Bite Me* are encouraged and appreciated!

About Fae

FAE IS OBSESSED with anything romance. From a young age she realized she had a passion for falling in love over and over again. She loves to tell stories through both her art and writing. With a passion for classical monsters, meet-cutes, and contemporary romance you can often find her with her nose stuck in a book and her pet corgi Champa on her lap.

She currently resides in Utah with her amazing husband and her collection of squishmallows. When you read one of her books you can expect to find love stories between humans, monsters, and loveable assholes that will make you laugh (and cry) as you get lost in their worlds for just a little. Every story comes with a happy ever after guarantee.

Find her online at:
WWW.FAELOVESART.COM

Lightning Source UK Ltd.
Milton Keynes UK
UKHW012046160223
416947UK00006B/204/J

9 798986 802527